SKULLRUNNER

THE GODREAPER REBELLIONS I

VYVRE ARGENT

TALON PRESS

For everyone who asks: why did they tell me that I was the monster?

FOREWORD

This is a book about pirates, and the times that made them. It is set in a world that echoes, but does not copy, the history of our own. It discusses colonialism, genocide, anti-Indigenous racism, parental abuse, abusive romantic relationships, and internalized prejudice. As the past still is with us today, readers may wish to be aware of these topics before reading.

Contents

Map   VII

Prologue: Flotsam   1

1. The Gray Lady   6

2. Death for Dessert   25

3. A Little Light Sedition   40

4. The Screaming Duke   55

5. The Wolf of the Sea   67

6. Lost and Found   82

7. A Bounty   96

8. The Chalk Rule   111

9. Degrees of Closeness   122

10. A Ship of Sisters   136

11. A Meeting at the Gallows   148

12. The Garden of the Gods   168

13. The Forgotten Revolution   185

14. Sabers and Wine   204

15. The Power of the Press   224

16. The Power of the Law   242

17. The Echo Court   255

18. The Black Isle   270

19. The Shadow Queen   285

20. The Ageless Horror   303

21. Oranges   314

22. Breaking the News   332

23. Muhlemlo   348

24. The Vote   367

25. Solidarity   386

26. The Remembered Revolution   395

27. The Sea of Spirits   404

28. The Storm Breaks   416

29. Commander-in-Chief   430

30. Liberty and Death   442

31. Godspeed, Sister   457

Epilogue: Jetsam   476

Acknowledgements   481

THE FIVE SISTERS
CRAB ISLE
UPAILIT
KOSSI
NEW SOLADIS
MOONWHISPER ISLE
BROKEN HOOK ISLE
HIGH HILL ISLAND
Halston
N
THE ISLAND of KITES
The City of Soladis
THE GRAY ISLE
MUHLEMLO
0 mi   200   400   500 mi
NIGHT DRAGON ISLE
THE ISLAND of SOLADIS
DOGSHEAD ISLE
Port Dueno
THE SAPPHIRE ISLES

PROLOGUE: FLOTSAM

ON UPAILIT, IN THE LANDS OF THE SIX BROTHER CLANS. 17TH IUNOS-MONTH, YEAR SEVENTEEN OF THE GOLDEN REPUBLIC.

The Soladiseans say we should be reconciled to one another. They say both our peoples came to the Seaward Isles from far away, and, as we both cannot leave, we must share the land and the waters. Here is what we say: the great currents that flow between the stars and seas lead our ancestors to the Seaward Isles as a gift of trust. The ancestors of the Soladiseans did such evil that they choked off the spirit currents and poisoned the seas to make the Isles submit to their will. By no means can a thinking people be reconciled to this depravity, not without a great making of amends, and the Soladiseans who speak of reconciliation make nothing but noise. When they say 'reconcile,' they ask us to forget. We cannot forget. But, to their people, forgetting is the greatest pleasure.
–'Our History of the Golden Republic,' published in *The Dawn Beacon.*

A WAVE WASHED ACROSS a beach of brown silt and reeds and set a half-drowned woman on the shore.

Cevette Zarcanzi rolled onto her front and spat out a mouthful of brackish water. Her head spun. Her muscles ached. She pushed herself up onto her knees, sinking a half-inch deeper in the silty soil whenever she moved, and looked about her. *Where am I?* Rolling hills rose in the distance, gray clouds descending on them like a cloak. Pine trees covered their slopes. Reeds and cattails covered the shore in faded green. A small flock of pied ducks were plucking mussels off a rock. The air smelled of smoke.

Upailit. I'm on Upailit. The name of the island came back to her. Was this her home? She knew of this place, but she didn't know how she knew of it. She knew she called herself *Cevette Zarcanzi,* which was a Soladisean name, but many people had Soladisean names. She had come from—

The great emptiness howled in her chest. Cevette gasped. She hugged herself as if she was keeping in her own organs; she expected to see blood on her hands when she pulled them back but only saw the stained, damp sleeves of a plain linen shirt. Tears rolled down her cheeks. She could not remember the woman's name, or when they had met, or how long they had lived together. Now the very shape of her lover's face was threatening to slip from her mind.

With her fingers, she drew the shape of it in the silt: long nose, thin lips, high cheekbones. Waves erased the lines as quickly as she could draw them, but she traced them over and over, locking down every last detail that remained in her mind. Tying them down like cargo in a storm.

When she had grasped all she could, Cevette grimaced and stood. She rubbed the crusted salt and silt from her shaggy blonde hair, the collar and cuffs of her shirt, and the split knees of her brown homespun breeches. She was missing one boot; her stocking dripped as she trudged up the beach. Her chest felt tight. Her skin felt hot, both from the dizzying confusion of having memories snatched away from her and the sun beaming down through the cloudless blue sky.

(She had been in a similar state before. She did not remember that.)

Cevette pushed her way through the tall, thick green reeds, past the scraggly trees with their sparrow nests and the holes in the dirt where the shore-crabs dwelled. At last, she came to a narrow dirt path. A signpost indicated a village lay three miles to the east; she set off toward it. Burrs clung to her bare stocking foot. A wind stirred the reeds that rose to either side of her, but did nothing to lessen the heat or the humidity. A lone heron winged past overhead. The path twisted and turned.

She sorted through her memories, horror coiling in her guts like some great serpent. *Where did I grow up? Who were my parents? Do I have brothers or sisters?* She knew how to dive deep for clams and pearls, how to shift a stuck infant in the womb, and a dozen ways to kill a man, but she did not know who had taught her any of this. *Who are my people? My nation? My clan?*

She rounded a bend in the path and nearly slammed into two men.

They jumped backward, empty crab traps rattling on their shoulders. "My apologies," Cevette said. She tried to step around them. One man, who was shirtless, stepped into her path. The other, the one with the white beard, looked her over from beneath furrowed brows.

"Where'd you come from?" he said.

Cevette blinked several times, her mind racing. She said the first thing she could. "I came . . . from the sea."

She regretted those words as soon as she'd spoken. The crab catchers shared a look. They were tall men, both at least a head taller than Cevette, and both were well-muscled. Their sun-weathered skin, knee-length trousers, and callused bare feet spoke to years of familiarity with hard labor and the shore. But they had addressed her in Soladisean, and they had spoken far too sharply. One of them sneered at her, a vein throbbing in his neck. The other pressed his rifle to his shoulder. "Show us your hands," he said. "Both of them."

Cevette bit down a curse. These men were far north of the fishing grounds granted to the Golden Republic in their treaty with the Six Brother Clans of Upailit. Their people always took more than they could eat from the waters; everyone who came after them was left to starve. They had no right to treat her as if *she* was the threat. But anger would be no help here. She lifted her hands and spread her fingers wide.

"No webbing," said the man with the sneer.

"That doesn't mean they're not one of the Sea People," said the other. "Some of them look almost like us."

"She couldn't have been one of those who attacked the fort. Their women don't raid."

"How do we know they're not a man? They're dressed like one."

Cevette was one of the Sea People; she remembered that much, at least. They had been the first people to call the Seaward Isles home, and had

dwelled here for countless generations before the ancestors of the Soladiseans had invaded. But she could pass for a Soladisean, and, if that was what
got her out of this, she'd feel damn complicated about that all later. She was
a woman as well, but she wore men's clothing because she wasn't a woman
in the same way that other Sea People women were. She had no desire to
explain her culture to men like this.

The man with the gun cocked his head to the side. "We don't get many
strangers out here. Are you with the raiders who burned the fort, girl?
Where'd you come from?"

"I…" *I don't know.* Cevette opened and closed her mouth several times.
"I'm a sailor. I fell off my ship. The waves washed me here." A plausible
tale. It could have been true.

"Who do you sail for? A merchant captain? Commander Gavon and
the navy?"

Commander Gavon? Her nostrils flared at the name. Her jaw clenched
up tight. Her heart sped, fast as a military drum. Now she knew what had
happened to her. Everyone in the Seaward Isles knew Commander Gavon
could steal or alter memories. He insisted that he only used his magic in
times of great need, and only when authorized by a vote of the Assembly;
Cevette thought it more likely that he used his magic frequently, but in
subtle ways, shifting the memories of his supporters only just enough to
keep himself in power.

There was nothing subtle about this. He had ripped away her connections to her clan and to her ancestors. It was a profound and direct assault
on her person. Who had she been, to come to his attention? How had she
made him her enemy?

"You heard me," said the man with the gun. "Who are you? An honest
sailor? A Sea People raider? A pirate?"

Cevette drew a deep breath and stilled her trembling fingers. She gave
her reply by lunging forward. She ducked under the gun barrel, which
kicked upward as the man fired on empty air. The reeds rustled at the
boom. Cevette slammed into his hairy, unwashed waist and knocked the
wind from him. He dropped. Instinctively, he reached to catch himself.

The rifle fell from his hands. Cevette grabbed it and swung. It cracked it against the side of his head. He crumbled. Blood dripped into the dirt.

The other man swore and fled, rushing down the path to the shore. Cevette knelt and checked the wounded man's pulse. *He'll live.* She took his purse, counted out six brass pennies, and slid them in her pocket. The man moaned, rolled onto his side, and vomited.

"I'm a pirate," Cevette said. She didn't want him blaming the nearby Sea People for the robbery, and a well-armed ship could be quite useful to her. "Since you asked so politely."

Then she went to steal back her past.

The Gray Lady

Beginning Fifteen Miles West of the City of Halston, in the un-ceded territory of the Wichil Nation, on High Hill Island; Ending in the Halston Fortress, in the Golden Republic. 25th Kaspermonth, Year Twenty-Two of the Golden Republic.

The tyrants of ancient days would steal your sheep and your harvest. But, in the age of revolutions, a modern tyrant would do best to steal your mind. –'Citizens Beware,' published in *The Silver Sentinel.*

THE GOD HUNTERS SET their trap in the dip between two gray seaside cliffs, dusted with the dying summer's first frost. On the pale sand below lay the body of a traitor, his limbs stretched out like spokes. The philosophers had drawn symbols in his lifeblood; whenever a scavenging crab drew too near, it crumbled into ash. Even the lapping gray waves seemed to pull away from the corpse as the tide went out.

Evazina Gavon watched from the top of the eastern cliff. She was a pale young woman, her face long and thin, her eyes dark as night, clad in a gray wool hunting gown with thick petticoats. She had tucked her long black hair up into a bonnet; small strands flew loose, brushing along her high cheekbones. To be brought along on the hunt was her twenty-second birthday present from her father. She would have rather received throwing knives, books about boats, or forged identity documents and passage to Port Dueno, but she had enjoyed her almost-freedom since they'd set off yesterday. She was even almost alone, and her guard was her closest friend, one of the two people in all the world she trusted. For once, she spoke her mind.

"I thought Father saved us from tyranny." She tapped fresh powder down her flintlock, then pointed it down at the dead man. "They said he was a traitor. But there was no trial; he had no chance to defend himself. And my father had him *butchered*. Is that justice?"

Lieutenant Ezekiel Dare glanced all around before he spoke. Commander Gavon and his soldiers stood on the opposite cliff, over a hundred feet away. Windswept bracken and heather concealed both parties, rustling in the breeze. They would not be overheard. Zeke lowered his brow and whispered "I can't speak on justice. I'm only a soldier. But the philosophers assured him that this ritual would let him capture the goddess, and she must be caught. We need more officers in the Godreaper Corps. To protect the Republic."

Eva frowned. "The Golden Republic is the most powerful nation in the Seaward Isles. Its borders encompass not only Soladis, but half of the Five Sisters and the Sapphire Isles as well. What do we need protection from?"

"For one, the abominations. They feed off the misery of our people. We have to keep their numbers in check. And then there's the outlaws . . ."

"Outlaws and monsters. Is that what I should fear?" Eva gripped the barrel of her gun so hard her knuckles hurt. She rammed a ball down the length of it. Hard. "You know this is the first time Father's let me go anywhere in months."

"I know," Zeke said, and nothing more.

"Why does he always keep me so close?" She lowered her voice. "Is he planning to *split* me?"

"No. He would never. That man was a traitor. You're his daughter."

Eva had asked this question a hundred different ways. It had only one answer. Commander Gavon was a great man. He'd overthrown the Theocracy and liberated the Seaward Isles. He'd ushered in an age of freedom, prosperity, and democracy. Who was she, to question him? A fool, or, worse, (the response she'd gotten few times she'd been foolish enough to ask someone who wasn't Zeke or her brother) a traitor.

She knew what happened to traitors.

Down below, scavenging abominations emerged from the sea and the low caves on the cliffs. They stalked and slithered over the sand. A pack of wild dogs with the claws of lizards emerged from a chink in the rocks and gazed at the sacrifice with alert red eyes. A bull seal with the maw of a shark sniffed at a rune and roared in agony as its skin ignited; it turned and shuffled back into the sea. A flock of six-winged vultures, each pair of wings a yard or more in length, circled above it all. Crabs with iron shells ringed the ritual and clicked their claws, drawn by the reek of corpse-flesh and the magic in the air.

A fog rose from the sea, billowing and thick. "I think it's starting," Zeke said. The two of them lay down on their stomachs and slid forward through the bracken. Woody stems crunched beneath them. Eva lifted her gun and pointed it over the cliff. Their target was not *quite* a god, as a technical point, and it had not been a *whole* god in quite some time, but the scouts who had reported seeing it said it still had the look of one. The philosophers had assured the commander their methods would still work to capture the creature; if it was not quite a god, it most certainly was nothing stronger. But if something unexpected happened, Eva would need to act quickly. She would need to prove she wasn't on its side.

The fog rolled over the hungry crabs. They scurried beneath the sand as it caressed the cheeks of the sacrifice. The blood runes pulsed like a heartbeat, winding the fog around them like spools of thread as it turned an ashen black. The wind picked up, building into a howl. The dog-abominations turned tail and fled back into their den. Vultures screeched above. Eva's fingers drummed a nervous rhythm on her rifle stock.

The fog and shadows coalesced into a tall, arched doorway. Bits of human bone protruded at odd angles from its frame, and it had a skull for a capstone. Inside it was nothing but darkness and smoke, which then rippled like a curtain as the remnant of the goddess of death stepped through.

The vessel that held the power of Morghaia the Skullrunner stood ten feet tall. Ash-gray smoke gowned its pale skin. Its bony, near-skeletal fingers trembled as they reached for the sacrifice, its head and shoulders bent, exhausted, as if beneath an unseen weight. It sunk to its knees and touched the dead man's cheek, as if in benediction. Behind it, the portal into Death blew off into the mist.

Atop the western clifftop, someone lifted a golden pennant on a pole out of the bracken and waved it about.

Philosophers stepped out from the narrow crevasse between the cliffs. They wore robes of brown homespun, with heavy hoods, and they split into two groups to ring the Skullrunner on all sides. Swiftly and silently they moved; then, at the next flash of the pennant, one man threw a great white spray of salt in the air and the rest began to chant in the archaic tones of Classical Soladisean.

The goddess-fragment pivoted. Her head whipped back and forth. She lifted her hands. Two knives materialized from black smoke. She flung them, and two philosophers collapsed, screaming, as dark ash ate through their skin. Another philosopher knelt and lit a hidden fuse. Flames snaked through oil-soaked daisies hidden beneath the driftwood and sand. The Skullrunner howled in pain.

"Move it, soldiers!" shouted Commander Gavon from deep within the bracken atop the western cliff.

Soldiers in orange uniforms clutched rifles to their chests as they ran single-file down the small switchback trail in the cliffside. Tucked under their arms were wooden boards coated on one side with lead. Their boots threw up puffs of sand as they reached the base of the trail and scurried into position, forming a ring outside the philosophers' small circle. "Attention!" called the commander. The soldiers snapped to, their backs as straight as fishing lines, and saluted.

Commander Jonathan Junosi Gavon walked down the clifftop trail and marched toward the ritual circle. He was hardly the tallest or broadest of men, long-faced and pale, his eyes as dark as night, with lines of gray blooming at his temples and forking back through his neatly trimmed black hair. Handsome, Eva had heard him described as, though his orange coat did not flatter him. He held himself as tautly as a snake about to strike.

The commander added his voice to the chanting chorus. The phrases in Classic Soladisean were clumsy on many tongues, but each word from his thin lips cracked like a whip. As his feet reached the edge of the circle, the Skullrunner collapsed. Face-down in the sand, it convulsed, smoky limbs thrashing and snapping obscenely.

The commander's hands rested on his pistols as he approached the helpless Skullrunner; his weathered brow furrowed in concentration.

"Hello again," he said, and ground his boot into its pale neck. "Is that all the fight you've got left? How disappointing."

Eva ground her teeth together. Her stomach churned. *The gods were tyrants,* she told herself. Everyone said so. They had taxed their followers into poverty and forced them to fight in bloody wars. Whoever dared defy them had been burnt as an offering. And Morghaia had been the worst of them all. This was justice. What this one small, strange piece of a goddess deserved.

Tonight, the Republic would gain a new officer of the Godreaper Corps, a loyal champion to protect their nation, and the Skullrunner would be bound deep in their soul. This was all most certainly for the greater good. She could not—dared not—argue with that. But the commander would drag this god to Halston and have her executed at the birthday dinner in the great hall. All his guests would see what he was capable of. *Eva* would have to see.

And the goddess' face was an exact match for her own.

WHEN THE REBELS FIRST came for Morghaia, she had cut them down with daggers of black smoke, then commanded their lifeless corpses to attack their fellows-at-arms. Yet the rebels had refused to fall back. Instead, they had surrounded her palace and forced her to call out for aid. Her wife, Heraline, did not come to her—yet another failing in Heraline's long history of them—but Iunos, god of memory, had rushed to her aid.

Commander Gavon had planned for that. He had challenged Iunos to a duel, slain him, and drank his power. Golden marks had bloomed in his hands. Then he had marched into Morghaia's palace and unleashed magic he did not understand. It had sliced the goddess apart. Into two identical women. Then four. Then eight. Whenever her divine soul had split, what *was* fractured into *what might have been*, loosening the ethereal fabric of memory just enough for Gavon to pluck out truths and fill the gaps with his own tales. Over and over the pieces of the goddess had fractured, until each one of the women created in Morghaia's splitting was only a fraction of what they had once been.

They were called *echoes*.

And while the people of the Republic believed Commander Gavon did not alter any memories that day, that he only used his magic in times of great need and with the full approval of the Assembly—the echoes doubted. They could only trust his word that he was good, that he was honorable, and they knew he had hurt them once before.

Of course, they had deserved it.

Eva returned to Halston in a cramped, dark carriage. It bounced along the dirt roads, surrounded by the commander and his companions on horseback, followed by the cart that held the Skullrunner in the crate, and a troop of marching soldiers. Foggy meadows and scraggly trees passed them by. Eva sat uncomfortably on a moth-eaten cushion, reading a treatise on naval navigation as she fiddled with her petticoats. There was a loose lace in one she was trying to ignore. Zeke sat across from her, on the opposite bench, mending a worn stocking heel, humming a contented tune. The carriage was so small that their knees pressed together. Whenever they went over a bump—which was often, on these frontier roads—he bounced up and hit his head on the roof.

The third such jolt knocked his words free. He cursed, lowered his voice, and said "Surely you can't believe your father is *that* cruel. He adopted you and your brother. He's always looked out for your best interests."

Eva looked up from her book and frowned. She had never fully convinced him that her fears were justified (of course, she had never fully convinced herself), but, for so much of their friendship, he had at least listened patiently as she voiced them. That had changed in the last two years. He had grown more sympathetic to her foster faster. She had asked him what had changed, and if it had anything to do with how frequently her father now assigned Zeke to act as his personal bodyguard. He had replied that he could not divulge the secrets of his commanding officer; the conversation had ended there.

"He has never raised a hand against me," Eva said. "He has always seen me fed and clothed. Still. You must allow me to find it disquieting that he can do such things to something that shares my face."

"She's not you." Zeke shifted uncomfortably. His head and shoulders were painfully stooped under the low carriage ceiling, not made for a man six-and-a-half feet tall. "You're different, even if you all look the same."

Citizens of the Republic oft assumed the morality of echoes had been permanently tainted by their origin; that they were exceptionally prone to violence, discord, and cruelty. This, Eva could not dispute. Everyone knew of the echo pirate who styled herself the Demon of Dogshead; she and her all-echo crew were the bloodiest and most fearsome outlaws on the seas. But all because echoes had a predilection toward violence did not mean they had to act on it. Eva had never done worse than peruse a few illegal newspapers and think some seditious thoughts. She was nothing like the echoes the world feared. But she did not know if that mattered to her foster father.

Zeke softened his voice. "I truly believe he won't split you. And I swear to you, on my honor as an officer, if he ever tried, I would not let him."

"Thank you." Some of the tension in her chest ebbed. Zeke didn't make promises lightly.

But he was only one man. And her father had an army.

If I only possessed some small fraction of Morghaia's magic—but, no. She didn't. No echo did. The magic had all wound up in the smoke-clad not-quite-goddess chained in the crate. It was a creature of pure divine essence, released from Morghaia's soul as it fractured. The echoes were flesh and blood, subject to old age, sickness, and death. Like all the human folk of the Seaward Isles, they could claim magic by hunting and killing gods, but they held no innate power within them. *It's for the best.* Too many echoes would use such power for violence—and too many citizens of the Republic would see that as a reason to punish them all.

They reached the first wall an hour before noon. The palisade of saplings, some so freshly hewn they still smelled of birch sap, stood six feet tall, and stretched across the rolling hills as far as the eye could see. Long gray meadow grasses bloomed at its base. The gate, a wooden door lashed shut with leather ties, rolled open as they approached.

The soldier on guard duty saluted and waved the commander through. But he lifted his hand to stop the carriage and the cart with the god. Zeke and Eva both disembarked; Zeke reached into his breast pocket and had his papers well in hand by the time they reached the soldier on the gate.

"Lieutenant Ezekiel Dare?" said the guard. The spots on his face and his cracking voice put him at no older than twenty. "I didn't know you were still under a foster bond."

"The army holds my bond until my twenty-fifth birthday next year."

"It's an honor to meet you, sir. I grew up in the frontier colonies on New Soladis. We were all so proud to hear one of our own had been chosen to reap a god." He turned to Eva. "And yours, echo."

Eva reached into her petticoats and pulled out her papers. The date written for her bond expiration was three years hence, but the skull stamped atop the page would never go away. The soldier read them over several times. Eva's nails dug into her palms. She made herself smile. She did not want them to think she was one of *those* echoes.

The wall was meant to mark where the Wichil Nation of Sea People ended and the Golden Republic began. Eva had asked the commander if they had secured permission from the Wichil to hunt gods on their land.

He had answered that the treaty only forbade them from taking fish and game without permission; besides, the Skullrunner had been a Soladisean god, so Soladiseans should have the right to hunt her. She had not known what to say to that.

The inspection of her papers lasted only a few minutes less than the inspection of the crate on the cart. When the guard nodded, she ducked back into the cramped, dusty carriage. It trundled through the palisade.

Zeke reached inside his orange wool jacket and withdrew a stack of newspapers. He passed them to her; as he reached over, the white patterns of his godmarks shone on the light brown skin of his wrist. "Here. Another soldier smuggled me some. Thought you might be interested."

The first atop the stack did catch her eye. It boasted a woodcut illustration of a woman kissing the lip of a pistol. 'Be Warned Loyal Citizens – Notorious Pirate Captain Cevette Zarcanzi Seen Offshore.' A smile tugged at Eva's lips as she read. She loved stories about pirates, when they were not echoes, and Cevette Zarcanzi was a particularly notable one. She led a crew of pirates who had illegally become godreapers (to kill a god without the commander's approval was a hanging offense) and, together, they raided battleships and merchant vessels twice the size of her small ship *Sea Wolf*. Eva traced the drawing of her face with a fingertip, wishing she was her. Powerful. Unencumbered. And not an echo at all.

She leafed through the other headlines. They spoke of frontier farmsteads destroyed by rampaging abominations, vagrants camping on the Halston docks, missing bureaucrats found murdered, graffiti calling for her father's head. The *Silver Sentinel* boldly announced 'Horror and Intrusion – Eight Halston Men Jailed for Tax Protest – Disregard of Civic Rights at the Hands of Cdr. Gavon.' Eva frowned as she read. The *Sentinel* was the most widely read of all the illegal papers in the Isles, and its anonymous author wielded a pen sharp as a knife.

The commander will want this forgotten. It was not at all uncommon for soldiers of the Republic to raid libraries and archives, arrest journalists and destroy printing presses, burn seditious books and pamphlets on great fires. The commander claimed this was all necessary, to protect the Republic's citizens from moral corruption and sedition. But it also could permit him to conceal scandals that might cost him and his allies dearly in the next election. *How steep a price would he pay to erase this?*

The day grew no warmer as they went on. Orderly square fields and farmers' houses, some great and some small, rolled by them. Foster children as young as eight carried bushels of wheat over their shoulders as they walked down the road. Only one in three had shoes, and half of them had the skin webbing between their toes and fingers that marked them as Sea People. One of the fosterlings was an echo, a girl of twelve, her dress in tatters, her black hair shorn short. She shivered in the wind like the trembling birch groves clinging to the hillsides.

That might have been me, if not for the commander. He was a good man. A charitable man. There were other fosterlings whose bonds he owned, and he had sent them to labor on the farms. She had been spared that fate. *But why must he always keep me close?* Sweat prickled on her skin. Eva drew the ostrich-feather fan from her sleeve and wafted air through the window.

The second wall, which stood ten feet tall, was made of red-gray brick. It completely ringed the city of Halston, save for where the harbor opened out on the sea. Commander Gavon's party approached the western gate in the early afternoon; the iron-banded oak doors creaked as they swung slowly open. He and his soldiers marched through. Eva and Zeke climbed down from the carriage and passed their papers to the soldier on guard duty.

"No need for this, Lieutenant Dare." The guard passed Zeke's papers back with barely a look. "You saved our patrol from that seal abomination that came up from the sea. A hero, you are." He squinted down at Eva's. "Lieutenant Dare, does the echo have any amulets or magical devices in her possession?"

"None whatsoever."

"Nothing that could incite an abomination attack?"

Eva glared at him. "I have no desire to incite an abomination attack on the city where I live."

He flinched from her gaze. "Those eyes of hers are like death."

"And that paperwork of hers is in perfect order," Zeke said. "Let us through. And watch your tongue. Miss Gavon is a good woman."

The guard nodded, thrust the papers back into Eva's hands, and scrambled out of the way. Zeke and Eva returned to the carriage. The coachman cracked his whip, and it rolled through the gate and into Halston proper.

They trundled through the streets. Eva pressed her face to the glass, stealing glimpses of the world her father would not let her enter: barracks, stables, and smithies by the wall, where the air rang with bellowed orders and the clang of ironwork, the neatly whitewashed houses where families peered down from upper windows to cheer on the commander, tossing sunflowers and toad lilies on his path, and the courthouse, with its great cupola, where even the prisoners chained on the steps watched him with admiring eyes.

Gavon! Gavon! The shout of his name filled the city like a heartbeat. Eva tried to pretend they were cheering for her, even as a third woman glimpsed her pale face and turned to shield her children from the echo's gaze with her body. *Gavon! Gavon!* Commander Gavon was no king, no emperor, only a hero who had fought against tyranny, a man who won so much love from his countryfolk that they had voted him onto the Assembly in every election since the Republic was founded, and won so much love from the Assembly that every year they re-appointed him their chairman and the commander-in-chief of the army.

I could I do it, too, Eva told herself. *I could show them I'm no goddess, no monster, no tyrant. I could fight for them and keep them safe.* Perhaps they would never cheer her name. But at least they would not be afraid of her.

The city fortress sat atop a small hill. Its wall and keep were built of pale granite, quarried on the island of Soladis, brought north to High Hill Island at great expense. It stood fifteen feet tall and six feet thick, and the gate was two iron portcullises. They stopped at the outermost gate to present their papers one final time; the guards slapped Zeke on the back as they waved him forward, and only grunted at Eva as she passed. On the far side of the gate, a group of soldiers debated how to transport the god crate into the main hall for the ceremonial reaping. Eva left Zeke with his fellows and proceeded into the western courtyard.

Guests had already begun to arrive for the ceremony, and so the out-buildings bustled with activity; the grooms leading dozens of horses back into the stables, the housekeepers directing the visitors' servants to the kitchen and the staff quarters. The smell of roast meats and sweet potatoes drifted from the kitchen windows and everyone who passed it stopped to take a deep breath. The pale gray keep, four stories tall, towered over them all. It was built in the fashion of a Soladisean chateau, square with rounded towers on each corner and steep, slanting rooftops of gray tile. Its small windows peered down like countless watching eyes.

A stage about fifteen feet across had been constructed in the courtyard dirt. Aristocrats and wealthy nobles milled about it, clad in worn but well-made traveling skirts and breeches. They joked and laughed amongst themselves, silver coins flashing from hand to hand as they placed their bets. Eva walked around them and found a place to the back of the crowd, near the left side of the stage, where she could watch. Like all full-grown echoes, she stood only two inches below six feet herself, and she didn't want to block anyone's view, even if it meant standing closer to a manure pile than she liked.

A beam of afternoon sun fell in the center of the stage. To one side of it stood an older man, who had untied his brown ritual robe to reveal knee-length breeches and a blue velvet waistcoat. His wig of white curls listed slightly to the left. On the side of the stage closest to the keep, with bodyguards and sycophants close at hand, Commander Gavon stood beside his son. Both men had their heads bowed in conversation.

Andreas nodded as his father spoke. His hair, bleached white by metic-ulous dyeing, fell loose past his collarbone. He wore tight black breeches and a loose white shirt, the front of which had come unlaced, revealing the slight curve of his breasts. His face was as long and as narrow as Eva's, albeit more used to smiling. Only a handful of echoes decided to be men; Andreas Gavon was unique and he knew it. He had a taste for rum and smokeweed, but attention was his drug.

"Are you nervous, boy?" the commander said.

"Excited, sir. I look forward to making you proud."

"You always do."

Andreas nodded to his father, then turned to face the crowd. The onlookers murmured amongst themselves, heads lowered, plumed hats and bonnets casting their faces in shadow. In all the chatter, Eva caught one word. *Echo.*

The smile on her brother's face only widened. He lifted his chin and addressed them as if he'd heard nothing at all. "Citizens of the Golden Republic. Honored guests. In the name of my father, the esteemed chairman of the Golden Assembly and commander-in chief of its armed forces, I welcome you to our home. It is my honor to announce that, tonight, I will claim the Skullrunner's power and take my place on the Godreaper Corps. I pledge before you that, as long as I live, I will fight for your prosperity and your liberty."

Andreas will claim the Skullrunner. The crowd applauded. Eva joined in, clapping loudly as a wave of relief swept through her. *Thank the gods.* Andreas had told her privately that their father had promised him a god, but nothing had been publicly confirmed until now. Once her brother claimed the Skullrunner's power, he'd be far too valuable to sacrifice. Killing a god left their magic inextricably bonded to your soul, a connection severed only by death. If Commander Gavon made Andreas a godreaper, he would be safe.

When they were younger, Eva and Andreas had often gathered in dark corners to share whispered worries that their father might split them. Andreas had insisted that they needed to prove themselves valuable to him. *That way, even if he does split echoes, he won't split us.* He had done quite well at that; the gentry of the Republic regarded him as almost as good as one of their own. Eva had struggled. The norms and customs of polite society slipped through her mind like loose sand. She had a terrible tendency to say the wrong thing, or use the wrong tone of voice, or to say nothing at all when something was required. She knew quite well that, next to her brother, she was not the echo their father would choose to keep.

"Now," Andreas said, "it is my pleasure to have organized this afternoon's entertainment: a grand philosophical debate!"

More cheers rose from the crowd. Debate was a beloved pastime of Soladiseans, who deeply valued literacy and a mastery of rhetoric. The older philosopher cleared his throat. "Today, we shall debate an age-old question: the root of political identity. You may state your position first, Mr. Gavon."

"Oh, do go on, Professor," Andreas said. "My thesis can only be understood in the context of your work I build upon. I would never have become the third-youngest scholar ever admitted to the philosophers' guild."

The philosopher narrowed his eyes, as if he expected a trap. "Well, it has always been my position that the political history of the Seaward Isles can best be understood in terms of the centuries-long struggle between the primitive Sea People and the great civilization of Soladis. Our ancestors arrived in the Isles aboard the greatest fleet of ships the world has ever seen, each laden with riches, knowledge, and weapons the likes of which the Sea People could not hope to match, and so, in jealousy and rage, they called upon the sea goddess Heraline to sink our fleet beneath the waves. Thus, we were marooned upon the shores of the Seaward Isles. On the island of Soladis, we built the foundations of a prosperous empire, and sought to share our wealth and enlightenment with others. We founded great cities, from Port Dueno in the far south, to Halston itself—" A few of the young men in the crowd whooped and cheered at that. "Yes, yes. But even as we have fought for our civilization, the Sea People have challenged us at every turn."

As the man went on, detailing centuries of skirmishes and struggles, Commander Gavon stepped down from the stage and walked about the edge of the crowd. His nose wrinkled as he drew near Eva and the manure pile. "There you are," he said. "Smile. Be happy for your brother."

"I'm quite happy for him." Eva made herself smile. Her face often failed to match her disposition. Doing her best to sound earnest and humble, she said, "May I have the honor to kill the next god you catch?" Each godreaper could only wield one power. The commander couldn't give all of them to his favorite son.

"You'll have a god when you prove you can be of service to me."

"I can fight. You've seen me with my knives—"

"An officer should possess more skills than your average dockside brawler. Your brother is beloved by this city, a member of the philosophers' guild, and obedient besides. The maids don't find seditious papers in his room, now do they?"

"I didn't know they were there," Eva lied. She ducked away from his piercing gray eyes and stared down at her hands. "I'm sorry, Father. It's only . . . you're not going to split me, are you?"

His eyes narrowed. "What did you say?"

"You're not going to—"

"I heard you the first time." He placed his hand on her shoulder. His grip was tight as iron. She winced.

Up on the stage, Andreas cleared his throat and cracked his knuckles in his fists. The loose fabric of his shirt shifted to bare his collarbone. A girl whistled. He gave her a wink. The crowd laughed. "Allow me to make my rebuttal, Professor," he said. "In your many essays, you have argued that the fall of the Empire of Soladis and the cruelty of the Theocracy that followed is the work of the Sea People. Yes, Heraline is one of their goddesses, and she certainly played a role in the empire's collapse, but so did the gods and leaders of Soladis. And it was the gods of Soladis who divided the Seaward Isles between them in the aftermath of the empire's collapse, and established the warring kingdoms of the Theocracy. Only a fool would argue that the only political project of the Soladisean people is the advancement of civilization. By the same token, one cannot argue that the Sea People are only devoted to its destruction."

The crowd remained quiet at that point. It was not popular to publicly defend the Sea People. Eva wanted to clap, but her father's grip was like an iron vise on her shoulder.

Up on the stage, the old philosopher folded his arms across his chest. "No great civilization takes steps forward without stumbling. And yet, it was a Soladisean man leading an army of Soladisean rebels who overthrew the Theocracy and built the Golden Republic, leading us to new heights of prosperity and civilization. You cannot deny this."

"What I deny is your assertion that my father's politics are only informed by his Soladisean heritage. He is Soladisean, to the extent that he—and many of us here—are descended from those sent forth from the Empire of Soladis to colonize this island. But the Gavon family has dwelled on High Hill Island for generations. He grew up on land threatened by Morghaia and her armies. The nobles of Soladis did nothing to help them against the goddess of death; they refused to even grant him a military commission. So he called all the colonists of this island together to take action. The revolution spread quickly, but it started here. With him and his people. With Halston. With all of you." Andreas swept his hands out, gesturing toward the crowd.

That earned him some applause. "Gavon!" one man in the crowd shouted, waving his hat about, and a chant of *Gavon! Gavon!* rose from their tightly gathered ranks. Many of them turned to face the commander, smiling at him, and a nearby woman even slapped him on the back.

The commander nodded at the citizens, and bowed his head modestly. As they turned their attention back to the stage, he leaned in at Eva's ear and whispered, "Do you remember what Morghaia did, when she and her wife built their kingdom in the north?"

"I . . . I have none of her memories, sir." No echoes did. Shouldn't he know that?

"I meant, do you not listen to your tutors? Or even the speeches on Independence Day?"

"Oh." She did. Of course she did. "You said 'remember.' I thought that implied—"

"That *thing* you came from slaughtered thousands of innocents. She denied their souls rebirth until they served in her ghoulish army. She burned traitors and heretics at the stake. Half the north fell to her onslaught in the centuries before I stopped her. The fear of her haunts many to this day. Do you understand?"

"I understand."

The commander deepened his tone, though he still kept his voice hushed, so only she would hear. "It is illegal for me to split echoes without Assembly approval. I wrote that law myself, to reassure my people that I will never abuse my power as a godreaper. But these ugly accusations, should they plant themselves in the fertile soil of gossip and the jealousy of lesser men, could be grounds for the Assembly to remove me from my post. When you speak of such things, you not only undermine your own father. You jeopardize the peace and prosperity I have brought to the Golden Republic."

"I . . ." Her voice trailed off. She bit her lip. "I don't mean to cause trouble," she said, and meant it. She wanted to believe in him, the man who had adopted two infant echoes out of the kindness of his heart. The man who once had swept her up on his shoulders and carried her down the street while a band played behind them and the crowds cheered on the Independence Day parade. The man she'd once run to with her nightmares, who had held her, stroked her hair, and promised all would be well come morning.

"You don't mean to cause trouble, and . . ." His grip tightened on her shoulder. She stiffened.

"And you're a good man. The Republic is a good place. It's nothing like the Theocracy, and . . . and you're nothing like Morghaia."

He chucked, a dry, humorless sound. "That I know. Keep your mouth shut. Don't let anyone see her in you."

Eva flinched, then nodded. It was good advice, if bluntly given. He hadn't seen Morghaia in the little girl he'd treasured long ago. In those days, she had only been his daughter.

He wouldn't do that to his daughter.

Up on the stage, the old philosopher frowned at her brother. Sweat dripped down from under his wig. He mopped at his forehead with a handkerchief. "What is your point, Mr. Gavon?"

Andreas smiled. "The history of the Seaward Isles is more than a tale of two opposing cultures locked in conflict. Rather, it is a history of great changes, each of which opens new ways for the many peoples of the Seaward Isles to build connections and redefine themselves. For example, I am very fond of Soladis, but I am a Halston man to my bones, a man of High Hill Island and the Five Sisters. The Soladisean people have created the Golden Republic, not because of the ancestry we share, but because the desire for democracy unites us. We are the people of Halston, and by our votes we will define our own future."

Cheers swept through the crowd. Fists were thrust aloft; women blew kisses at the stage. Their enthusiasm. Eva thought, most likely stemmed from their pride in their city, rather than any intellectual insights they had gleamed from his argument. She found it hard to grasp. It was true enough to say that there were many distinct groupings among the Soladisean people, and that the Soladiseans of Halston were quite different from the Soladiseans of Port Dueno in the far south or even Soladis itself. But one could not simply choose which group they belonged to on a wish or a whim. An echo should know that better than anyone.

Andreas bowed to the crowd. Two men lifted him up on their shoulders; a third passed him a rum flask with a ruby stopper. He grinned and drank deeply. The crowd chanted *Gavon! Gavon!* and *Halston! Halston!* Sunlight gleamed golden in the sweat of his brow as his fellow philosopher stepped down from the stage with a huff.

"I thought that would last longer," the commander said. "But reason is a homely girl indeed beside her sister, flattery."

"Father?" Eva took a deep breath, and met his eyes. "I would be honored to serve the Republic in any way I could. If not as a godreaper, then as a naval officer? My tutors say I'm ready for the entrance exams—"

"You will stay here, obey me, and cause no more trouble. Do I make myself clear?"

"Father—"

"Do I make myself clear, Evazina?" He squeezed her shoulder. A stab of pain shot down her arm.

She winced. "Yes, sir."

"Good. I'll see you at the banquet." He let go of her shoulder, patted her cheek, and stepped into the crowd. It parted around him. The men carrying Andreas set him down on his feet before his father. Commander Gavon smiled and said, "Well argued." Andreas grinned.

An image tinted in crimson and scarlet swept unbidden through Eva's mind: her dagger pressed to her father's throat. *Answer me honestly,* she would say. *Do you split echoes?* Then, whatever came out would carry the sure weight of truth. All her rage, confusion, and denial could be put to rest with a flicker of steel.

And she would know herself to be the most wicked echo of them all.

DEATH FOR DESSERT

IN THE HALSTON FORTRESS, ON HIGH HILL ISLAND. 25TH KASPERMONTH, YEAR TWENTY-TWO OF THE GOLDEN REPUBLIC.

Great Gavon, wise and brave / his countrymen did save / A great god's life he took / Old Iunos, in whose book / lay memory of the nations. // Godreaper, he became / Godreapers, in his name / must each one slay a deity / to save us from depravity / and dark abominations. —Entry for the letter *G* in *A Children's Primer of the Golden Republic.*

WHEN EVA SET OFF for the great hall, she carried a slim, leather-bound book in the lacings of her bodice.

Years ago, she had discovered it behind a loose panel in her wardrobe. *From the diary of Korinne Gavon,* had been written on the first page. Korinne and her twin sister Ariella had been echoes, foster daughters of the commander. He had found them in the ruins of Morghaia the Skull-runner's palace, reduced by her breaking to two identical girls of thirteen. In his great charity, the commander had given them a home and a generous education. Korinne had been shy and quiet, passionately devoted to the study of natural philosophy, with a special interest in the prevention of abomination attacks. Ariella had been lovable and outspoken. She had wanted to follow her father into politics. Both of them had idolized him.

Korinne had been fascinated with the study of abominations and how their attacks might be prevented. Each year, hundreds died to the monsters that prowled the coasts, and the many impoverished citizens who left the

Republic's walls to seek their fortune on the frontier bore the highest casualties. But she had learned the Assembly had voted against funding research into how such attacks might be prevented. And she had asked her father questions. Why was the army more devoted to guarding the government's archives than fighting the beasts? Why did the government refuse to consult with the Sea People clans whose rituals successfully kept the abominations off their lands? And, as abominations spawned in response to human misery to spawn, why had their recorded numbers *increased* since the Theocracy fell and the supposedly-better Republic took its place?

Her inquiries had enraged the commander. He had insisted that Korinne did not understand matters of state, that the mere act of asking was seditious. Dangerous. He had said she was no better than Morghaia herself. But Korinne had done nothing wrong. She'd earnestly wanted to help him and his people. And Eva could not help but wonder—had her father been mistaken when he compared them to the goddess of death? Or had he only said such things to keep them quiet?

As Eva descended the servants' stair that would allow her to avoid the keep entryway (and potential conversations with her father's guests), her head spun with old, unanswered questions of her own. Why didn't she remember Korinne and Ariella, who seemed to have lived openly in the fortress until at least about when Eva and Andreas had turned twelve? Why did no one ever speak of their older sisters? Why had Korinne written, on the very last page, *if you find this, sister, don't trust the commander?*

Andreas and Zeke insisted the diary had to be a clever forgery, written by political malcontents. But Korinne understood so profoundly what it meant to be an echo, or at least, what it meant to Eva: uncertainty, powerlessness, and above all else the terrible weight of Morghaia's legacy. She had never realized other echoes might feel the same ways she did; indeed, her father had stopped her from ever meeting or speaking with echoes who were not her brother. She had asked Andreas to read the diary, if only so he might understand her better. He'd refused. Told her to burn it. *Father would be so angry if he found it.*

She'd kept it. The words on its pages were a promise. Even if the only soul who understood how Eva felt was another echo, she was not alone. And one day, she too might find the strength of conviction to write in thick black letters that her father could not be trusted. That, whatever dark potential that echoes carried in their souls, they were not wrong to fear the man.

Before Eva opened the door at the bottom of the stairs, she pressed her fingers to where the little book lay hidden in her bodice, and took a deep breath. *I am not alone.* Then she squared her shoulders and stepped into the great hall.

The long chamber, its high ceiling vaulted above her, stretched two hundred feet from the main entry to the polished white marble of the stage at the far end. Long tables lined its ashen floorboards, each one covered by gold-trimmed cloth and set with fine porcelain and crystal serving dishes. Servants in starched black uniforms bustled about, folding napkins and laying out silverware. Atop the stage, beneath a ten-foot-tall gold-framed portrait of Commander Gavon, a string quartet tuned their instruments. The severe lines of his face, caught in oils, gave the impression he strongly disapproved of the racket.

And from every windowsill and rafter hung orange banners marked with two interlocked black rings. The flag of the Golden Republic, waving in the late summer breeze that drifted through the windows. Eva shivered as she walked down the length of the tables, checking that each fork and soup spoon was in the right position.

The great oak doors at the front of the hall creaked open. Zeke ducked through. "Miss Gavon! I thought I might find you here." His polished boots clicked on the floorboards as he walked down to join her. Afternoon sunlight winked off his epaulets, which accentuated shoulders nearly as broad as he was tall. His well-trimmed curls sat neatly beneath his violet cap, and the cuffs of his orange wool dress jacket were pinned back to show his godmarks: an elaborate, tattoo-like pattern of whips and flails, broken chains and tumbling coins, running from his palms to his elbows, the white lines of which stood out neatly against his brown skin. Zeke had killed

Kothrin, the Pridebreaker, god of charity and humility, and from him he had taken the power to weaken the magic of his enemies.

"You even polished your cufflinks," Eva said.

He grinned. "Not bad for a boy who grew up on the frontier, eh?"

"Not bad at all." He fit neatly amongst the gentry of the Republic, at least, he fit a hundred times more neatly than she did.

She frowned, and checked her reflection in a silver plate. She looked well enough, she supposed. Her maids had done their best. Her cream-white gown was draped over a hoopskirt that was fashionably wide in the hips (four feet.) It was covered in lace and studded with crimson bows. Matching bows also adorned her high, powdered wig and long red gloves. Her bodice was embroidered with tiny snowdrop flowers. The thick layers of fabric were snug against her chest, a rather comforting pressure, but failed miserably at pushing her small breasts up into any semblance of a feminine shape. The rose blush her maids had painted on her cheeks only made the rest of her look corpselike. It was an echo she saw there; nothing more, nothing less.

"What's for dessert tonight?" Zeke asked.

"Maple custard."

"My favorite!"

"Yes, well, Father made me plan a whole menu. I thought I'd sneak one small bright spot in." Banquet planning was the latest role he had invented to keep her occupied. Someone more socially adept might have found power, or at least agency, in the position. Andreas had once given her a pamphlet on flower symbolism so she could encode subtle messages in the centerpiece bouquets. For two weeks, she'd ordered nothing but chrysanthemums, for justice, and been mocked so thoroughly that she'd given up trying to say anything at all.

"There you are!" The door creaked open once more, and Andreas stepped in. "Eva! You should come out to the reception—these planters from the Sapphire Isles have the most fascinating stories—no? Ah, well, happy birthday anyhow!"

Smiling broadly, he walked down the hall and brushed his dry lips to Eva's cheek. He wore a suit imported from Soladis: a waistcoat and jacket of pineapple-yellow, a cravat of ruffled lace, his cuffs embroidered with the Republic's joined rings in golden thread. His straight white hair poured down his back like a frozen waterfall. His newest paramour walked behind him, the panniers on her hoopskirt a foot wider than Eva's. Her name, Eva was almost certain, was Mary. She wasn't sure if she'd been told it or not, and, since she'd met the girl three times, it felt rude to ask now.

Andreas handed Eva a parcel. She ripped through the crinkly brown paper and pulled out a ring as heavy as lead, topped with a silver skull. The sight made her flinch. "I . . . I can't wear this. It's Morghaia's symbol."

"You're hard to buy gifts for, sister. I would have bought you some daggers, but it's illegal for echoes to carry weapons."

He gave her a wink. Eva shivered, and slid the ring on her left hand. She did not like it, but she loved her brother, and she did not wish to seem as if she was ungrateful.

"Why do you want to make trouble between your sister and your father?" Zeke asked Andreas.

"Why do you care?" said Andreas. To that, Zeke only folded his arms across his chest and glowered.

Eva sighed. There they went again, the two of them. Zeke thought Andreas was an arrogant bastard; Andreas readily admitted himself to be an arrogant bastard, but he thought Zeke was a bore. She had long since given up expecting her two closest friends to love each other as she loved them. But she had hoped they might at least behave themselves through the dessert course.

"Listen, Lieutenant Dare," Andreas said. "In the morning, I sail to Moonwhisper Isle for my first official assignment as a member of the Godreaper Corps: a six-week stint guarding a government archive. I want Eva to have some token of me while I'm gone."

"What about me?" Most Likely Mary said.

"Ah, love, you have nothing to fear. The moment I receive my pay as an officer, I will deck you in diamonds."

Eva decided to pull the girl aside later and let her know Andreas had made similar promises to his last three lovers. For now, it was all she could do to reach into the pocket of her heavy hoopskirt, draw out a small bottle of fine sherry, and press it into Andreas' hands. "Happy birthday."

"Delicious. My thanks."

"Why do echoes have birthdays if they were never born?" Most Likely Mary asked.

"We chose this date because I fancied it. To mark the dying of the summer. Poetic, isn't it?" Andreas kissed her cheek. She turned, as if to make their lips meet, and he ducked away. "Later," he murmured, and Zeke grunted his approval. Eva nodded, as if she also applauded his devotion to the virtue of chastity. In truth, it had been two years since she'd kissed a girl. She didn't want to be reminded of all the social graces Andreas had that she lacked.

As the sun set, their father's guests drifted into the hall and took their seats. Most wore orange and gold: coats of pale cream with buttercups embroidered on the lapels, hoopskirts with red and yellow ruffles, powdered wigs topped with golden ornaments. Eva and Andreas stood by the door, as their father had bade them, and greeted each new arrival. Pleasantries flew about them like twittering birds.

"Happy birthday, Miss Gavon, Mr. Gavon."

"You look lovely tonight, both of you."

"I heard you'll reap your god tonight, Mr. Gavon. Congratulations."

Eva's hands were shaken by dignitaries from every island of the Golden Republic. Every face was different; every conversation the same. *Thank you for coming. We're happy you're here.* When one guest left, she would pause, unclench her jaw, relax, then pull back on her smile for the next, and run through her well-practiced lines of small talk. *Take your seat. Enjoy.* Servants collected gifts from the guests and stacked them in a heap behind the echoes: pendants of diamond and pearl, ivory chessboards, feathered hats. A flute carved from a whale rib and a cloak made from a tiger pelt. A portrait of Eva that another echo woman must have posed for. She shuddered to see it.

"That would never fit you," Andreas said, pointing at a tiara of gold and emeralds. "You'll have to leave it for me. I'm the only one with a head big enough to wear it."

It was a bad joke. She knew it was polite to laugh, but Andreas would understand if she bent the rules, and her mind had jumped to some very important facts. "This isn't ours. It's all Father's. Echoes aren't citizens of the Republic. We can't hold property or vote, not even when our foster bonds expire. Did you hear, a judge ruled that we're not even people—"

"I know." He gave her a small, tight smile. "But this isn't the place to speak of it."

Her shoulders tightened. Her heart sped. She lowered her voice to a whisper. "He could split me. He could. You must admit, it's possible."

"You mustn't dwell on that. Not tonight. Smile. Make small talk. Please the guests. Show Father your value."

"I'm not as good at it as you."

"So follow my lead." He squeezed her hand. "There's nothing to fear."

Of course he would say as much. He was the echo worth keeping. She envied him for that, slightly, in a petty and childish way she knew she should move beyond. *I should trust him here.* Eva often relied on her brother's judgement. She was so often wrong, and wrong in a way that upset others. Perhaps she should simply accept that Andreas wasn't scared because there was nothing to fear. She was only making trouble for herself and others. That was what echoes did. What she'd been told they did.

She squeezed his hand back. Korinne's diary pressed against her chest.

Commander Jonathan Gavon was the last to arrive. The guests stood and clapped as he entered. Military medals glittered on his orange wool dress coat as he walked down the hall. His sky-blue sash of office, an honor he had awarded himself, lay wrapped proudly about his shoulder. Soldiers saluted as he marched to the front of the room and stood atop the stage, directly before the quartet. As one, every guest pressed their hands to their hearts and swore the Oath of Loyalty:

I pledge my house and my most vaunted honor to serve the Golden Republic. May my blade and dying breath preserve the land I love. And should my peer or kindred turn their coat on liberation, may my hand have the privilege to strike them down.

A singer took the stage, her gold skirts rustling, and performed the national anthem. Listeners sniffled and pressed handkerchiefs to their watery eyes. Eva stared down at her pale hands and told herself to feel grateful for the revolution that had broken her.

As the feast commenced, Andreas went to sit with a group of aristocrats he'd wanted to befriend. Eva sat alone, and silent, between a pair of elderly merchants. The servants brought in the first course: whitefish in a buttery broth, served with pale grassy wine. Her spoon trembled as she dipped it in and raised it to her lips. The delicate fish dissolved on her tongue. A salad of fresh spinach followed, dressed with olive oil. Then a pewter platter of cheese laid out in the Republic's interlocked rings was carried down the length of a hall, and the diners plucked off morsels with long forks as it went. Some made a game of it, laughing and poking their fellow diners. Down at the far end of the table, Andreas fed cheese to a man in a three-foot tall wig. Lest her shaking hands betray her, Eva let the tray slide past. The servants who followed piled her plate with sweet potatoes, roast duck, and a double helping of maple custard. She nibbled at the food, the sugar like ash on her tongue. Her stomach churned. Sweat prickled under her wig. Her lungs pressed tight against her stays.

Soon, she could not bring herself to eat another bite. Her hands fell into her lap. She fiddled with the ring Andreas had given her, turning the large silver skull around and around. *Why would he give me this? He knows it will make trouble.* It was nice to fidget with, though. Shiny and smooth, it spun pleasingly under her fingertips. Then she twisted a bit too hard, and the skull and ring moved separately.

It's on a screw. Eva frowned. *What does Andreas mean for me to do with it?* Holding her breath, staring down at her lap, she unscrewed the skull from the ring.

A small depression had been sculpted on the flat backside of the silver skull. There, a narrow strip of metal, three inches long, had been latched in place. Beside it was an inscription: *For you, Sister.* Eva pushed the little latch aside and let the instrument drop into her palms. There was a switch along one side of it. She pressed it. A three-inch blade sprung out.

Her eyes widened. She collapsed the knife by jabbing it into the underside of the table until the blade locked back into place, then slid it back into the ring and screwed it all back together. *Andreas gave me a weapon. Andreas broke the law for me.* He wanted to keep her safe. But that meant that he believed she was in danger.

She was almost grateful for the distraction of cannons booming in the harbor.

Nervous whispers spread through the great hall. Guests rose to their feet and flocked to the south-facing wall. Eva lifted her skirts gingerly and followed the crowd. They pressed against the windows, their ranks two or three rows deep before she drew near. Thankfully, she was tall enough to see over most of their heads, and her eyes were keen enough to spot the chaos churning down in the black waters of the city port.

Tentacles shot up from the foaming brine, their pale lengths lit by the setting sun. They grabbed small fishing boats, lifted them up, waved them about, and dragged them under like toys. Soldiers fired muskets and cannons at the beast, but they were merely gold-uniformed specks against the abomination's bulk and the dark power that drove it.

"Kraken," said Zeke, stepping up beside Eva's shoulder. "Someone drew it here." He passed Eva a spyglass. She pointed it at the harbor. Someone had upended a barrel of blood on a pier. *So much blood.* Worse, abominations would only seek out *human* blood. They fed off the essence of their suffering.

"Who would do that?" Eva asked.

"I don't know." He pursed his lips. His brow furrowed. "But they'll regret it."

"What's going on?" shouted an Assemblyman, turning from the window to face Commander Gavon, who had already returned to his seat, and was sipping his wine. "This is the sort of disaster I would only expect in a frontier port."

"Abominations can't read maps," the commander said. "They spawn, they devour flesh, the army destroys them. If you wish to take some action against the abomination attacks, you may authorize an increase in the military budget at our next Assembly meeting. For now, I shall have a godreaper eliminate it. Go, Lieutenant Dare, and godspeed."

Zeke saluted. "Yes, sir."

Andreas, watching the attack through a window, turned back to the great hall and sighed. "Damn. If it had come a few hours later, I might've been able to kill it myself." A number of guests laughed politely.

Zeke shook his head and said, "Best of luck with the deicide." He nodded to both Andreas and Eva, turned, and strode down the length of the hall, gesturing at a number of his fellow soldiers as he passed. They fell into practiced formation behind him. One push from his heavy hands, and the door sprung open. Half the soldiers present followed him out. As the doors creaked shut behind them, an uneasy hush settled over the hall.

"Very well," Commander Gavon said. "We move forward. Bring in the Skullrunner."

Eva frowned. The reaping had been scheduled for near midnight. *He must want to distract his guests from the kraken attack.*

As a footman ducked out the back with the commander's orders, the musicians lowered their instruments, bowed, and departed the stage. The guests returned to their seats. Commander Gavon climbed the stairs to the stage and waved to Andreas, who eagerly leapt up to stand beside him. Commander Gavon placed a hand on his shoulder and smiled a thin smile. He met Eva's eyes as she made to return to her seat; then gestured toward the foot of the stage and pointed at his lips. *Be happy for your brother.* Eva went to stand by the stage's foot and did the best she could to pull on a genuine grin.

The doors creaked open once more. Grunting and cursing, soldiers dragged the twelve-foot-long lead-lined crate of the Skullrunner's prison down the length of the hall. Sweat shone on their brows. Their fingers trembled where they gripped the crate's leather straps. Up the short set of stairs they went, onto the stage proper, where they set the crate down on one end and gasped with effort as they pushed it upright.

The philosophers entered after them, all mysticism and ceremony, their faces shrouded by the hoods of their heavy brown robes. They laid out a circle of salt and daisies about the crate, chanting in Classic Soladisean as they went. "Open it," Commander Gavon said. The soldiers lifted heavy iron pry bars, wedged them into the gaps in the boards, and pushed. The crate broke open. Boards fell—one philosopher was struck in the shoulder as he dodged—and the Skullrunner rolled out.

The gray phantom reached for the warding circle, and pulled her fingers back, waving them as if she'd been stung. She huddled on her knees and buried her face in her hands, shivering in her gray wisp of a gown, making no sound. The guests stared at her. They pointed, laughed, and tittered. One man pressed his palms to his face and moaned in mockery.

Eva's pulse sped. Her muscles tensed. A sheen of sweat glowed on her powdered cheeks. This was not the Morghaia who Commander Gavon had overthrown. It wasn't enslaving the dead or burning cities to ashes. It was only a small fragment of something divine, brought low for the amusement and profit of the Republic. *Is that what all these people see in me? What they hate? What they fear?* She wanted to comfort the creature. She wanted to sink into the earth and disappear.

The maids closed the curtains. The philosophers climbed down from the stage, then lit sticks of incense and placed them in the small braziers set out atop the long tables. A sickly-sweet scent filled the room. The soldiers retreated to the walls and stood at attention. Andreas strode forward and stood over the goddess, the light of a hundred candles filling his hollow cheeks with flickering shadows. He reached into his coat and drew out a knife with a twisted blade. The guests applauded as he lifted it high.

"Andreas Gavon," the commander said, though he faced the room, addressing the guests, not his son. "You had been chosen to ascend as a godreaper. Strike down this monster in the name of the Golden Republic of Soladis. Drink in her power and rise as a protector of the common good. For prosperity and liberty!"

"Prosperity and liberty!" Andreas shouted. He held the sacrificial knife above the goddess' head. Eva held her breath, willing herself to believe that she was nothing like this creature, that nothing like this would ever happen to her, that all of this was good and natural part of the world her father had built. She had to ignore the cracks in that reasoning. Ignore all the small scars on her soul.

A pistol shot rang out behind her ear.

Andreas dropped, clutching his shoulder. Blood welled through his fingers. The knife tumbled to the floor.

What? Eva's mouth fell open. She blinked, once, twice. *What was that?* Up and down the walls, soldiers reached for their weapons. Guests shouted and pointed. Slowly, Eva turned to face the doors—

And saw *her.*

Her fair skin weathered and ruddy, her face heart-shaped face and her short blonde hair chopped like straw, Cevette Zarcanzi frowned from behind a smoking pistol. Eva knew her on sight; the printed illustrations in the papers had captured her well. The pirate wore the stolen orange uniform of a soldier and held herself with all the gravity of the burning moon. She drew a second pistol from her belt and pointed it at Eva's head. "Miss Gavon. Don't move."

Eva froze.

Cevette marched down the length of the hall. Guests gasped and scrambled away from her, pushing themselves back against the wall. The soldiers struggled to push their way through them and their wide hoopskirts. The pirate lowered her brow and set her jaw. Sweat gleamed on her bare hands. Her *unmarked* hands, Eva realized. She'd come to kill the god and take its power. If it wasn't for the notorious inaccuracy of flintlock pistols, it would already be hers.

With the hand that didn't hold her gun, Cevette grabbed Eva around the waist and pulled her back into the pirate's chest. She was shorter than Eva had imagined her, and the closeness of her skin was much warmer, near feverish. Her broad-shouldered frame was as steady as a wooden figurehead. The cold lip of her gun pressed against Eva's ear.

"Commander Gavon!" Cevette shouted. "Remember me?"

"I can't say I've had the pleasure." The commander glowered. His fists were tightly clenched. His words were carefully controlled. Andreas knelt at his feet, bleeding and cursing. The commander did not even look at him.

Eva's breath came in short, shaky gasps. Her eyes widened as she looked to her father. *Please,* she thought. *Help me.* He did not meet her gaze.

In her left hand, she began to fiddle with the skull ring.

"You stole my past from me," Cevette said. "My childhood. My family. My home. The echo I loved. You split apart an echo and you took away who I am."

"How dare you levy accusations at a gentleman, sea scum?" shouted an Assembly member, an old man who brandished his walking stick at the pirate. "You have no right."

"I don't need a right. I have a gun." Cevette's voice dropped dangerously low. "Where did you put my memories? Tell me. Now."

Memory. Eva's breath caught.

"You'll find your memory at the bottom of the rum barrel where you left it," he said. "If I don't hang you first, that is. Let my daughter go."

"Very well," Cevette said. Her voice was hard as iron. "Send your guests and soldiers from the hall. We'll discuss this privately. When we finish, I'll kill the Skullrunner, take her power, and return your daughter to you."

Eva shivered, and wrung her hands together. Hidden from view, the silver skull dropped into her right palm. Her left hand undid the latch and plucked free the spring-loaded knife.

Commander Gavon frowned. "You must understand my position. I can't simply hand divine power to an enemy of the Republic."

"Sir. I have your daughter."

The commander paused. Heat flared in his eyes. His cheeks reddened. His lips moved, as if calculating under his breath. Save the life of one echo, or protect himself and prevent a pirate captain from reaping a god? He was a great man. A leader. The father of his country, not only her. She knew what choice he had to make.

But she did not want to be his sacrifice.

"No," she whispered, and shook her head. "Father, no!"

He said nothing. Cevette swore. And Eva saw there was only one way forward. He would not protect an echo. But he would protect a godreaper.

Eva pressed the hidden switch, and the blade extended in her left hand. She raised her head to sight her target, and her eyes met those of the god-fragment, whose thin gray lips curled into a smile.

A fierce wave of longing swept through Eva. It came so quickly and suddenly that she could barely put words to what it was before it consumed her. Her heart pounded in her ear. Her fingertips tingled. *I want this,* she realized, and the *want* was as much a part of her as her own left hand as she drew back the knife and threw.

The small knife flashed silver as it flew through the air and sank into the Skullrunner's throat.

The goddess-fragment fell on her side. Blood of black smoke rose from the hole in her throat. Andreas stared at Eva in numb shock, clutching his wounded arm. "What have you done?"

The fragment of the goddess of death dissolved. In a flicker of shadow, her shape collapsed into smoky black sludge. It raced across the marble stage, dodging the pool of Andreas' blood, pouring down the steps. Cevette swore. She dropped her gun and grabbed for it, but it slipped through her fingers. It surged up and over Eva's hoopskirt, over her bodice, and poured down her throat.

The Skullrunner tasted of cream pudding and maple meringue. It tasted like fall winds and the scent of the sea. The power settled in her, light as sunshine. *Death for the dessert course.* Eva pulled off her gloves. Black marks bloomed in the centers of her palms. Grinning skulls wreathed in coiling smoke.

Her hands trembled. She pressed them to her mouth. Countless feelings raced through her all at once, too quick to grasp just one, all threatening to sweep her away. She stumbled toward the stage, toward her brother *I won. I won.* The pirate wouldn't take the magic. The Republic would have its new godreaper. And she was now valuable enough that her father would keep her soul intact. At last, she could breathe easy in his presence.

The hush in the room was only broken by the sound of Commander Gavon's voice. "Seize them."

The soldiers pushed their way through the guests and surged forward. Eva turned to see Cevette Zarcanzi punch one in the jaw. He fell. Two more soldiers wrenched her arms up behind her back. She cursed and shouted, kicking at them. It took three soldiers to grab her legs. They lowered her to the floor. The two largest of their number sat on her back while the others bound her with rope.

"And my daughter," the commander said.

The rest of the soldiers gazed at Eva. Their eyes were as cold as if they faced Morghaia herself.

What is he doing? Eva took one step backward. Her eyes widened. Her voice shook. "Sir. I have the magic. You need me for the Godreaper Corps." She glanced over her shoulder at Andreas. Servants surrounded him, pressing a rag to his wound. He had no help to give.

"To kill a god without my permission is treason." The commander's voice was cold. "That you would defy me makes it plain that you carry the taint of Morghaia herself."

"No!" Eva tightened her fists. "I—she had a gun on me, Father—"

He nodded to his soldiers. "Take both women to the southwest tower. Lock them in. Hang the pirate at dawn. Hold my daughter until I decide her fate."

Eva looked up and met his gaze. *Am I truly no better than Morghaia?* She could not read his face. She could never read faces. *I wanted the power. But I also wanted to live.* She pressed her hands to her bodice, to her hammering heart, and felt the shape of the diary she had hidden inside it. *He told Korinne she was tainted, too, and all she wanted to do was protect the Republic from abominations. He uses the legacy of Morghaia against us, regardless of whether we deserve it or not.*

A soldier took her by the arm and led her to the door. She went, unresisting. Her heart fluttered. *Perhaps Korinne was truly right. Perhaps we cannot trust him.*

Perhaps she could now trust herself.

A Little Light Sedition

In the Halston Fortress, on High Hill Island. 25th Kaspermonth, Year Twenty-Two of the Golden Republic.

We have agreed in countless treaties that the walls mark where their Republic ends and the nations of the Sea People begin. Yet they tell their own people that the land beyond their walls is something called a frontier, a land belonging to no one, and send their poor and their criminals to this frontier to rob and murder the Sea People. When we ask the leaders of the Republic to take responsibility for their own, they tell us about the frontier, how they hold no power over the Soladiseans who live there, for these are people who answer to no laws. Yet the Soladiseans who grow rich from the plunder of our lands are honored as great men and women. There is no reconciliation needed or recompense required to atone for their lawbreaking; wealth pardons all. Thus we see the Soladiseans do not care for their own laws, save as tools to carve the world into the shape of their liking. –'Our History of the Golden Republic,' published in *The Dawn Beacon.*

The kraken had died too easy.

Lieutenant Ezekiel Dare had ridden into the harbor with twenty soldiers at his back. One blast of his power had left the kraken trembling; a second had left its tentacles melting into seafoam. The cannon crews had done the rest. Someone had lured the beast into the harbor, but they hadn't fed it enough suffering to survive the first coordinated counter-attack. Had it been a trick? A diversion? A messenger had ridden down from the fort and told him that a pirate had attempted to kidnap the commander's daughter. Zeke had left his soldiers to secure the harbor while he'd raced back to check on Eva. Questions had spun through his mind all the way: had Captain Zarcanzi unleashed the kraken? Or was something worse on its way?

The soldiers on the gate had told him the full tale. *The echo girl took the god. They threw her in the southwest tower. She grinned like Morghaia herself as they dragged her away.* He'd known right away that he had to go to her. His cap was missing, his curls were disheveled, and smears of dark red abomination blood covered his orange wool coat, but Eva didn't care for propriety. Not at all.

He was climbing the spiral steps of the southwest tower, taking them two at a time, a lantern in one hand, his own breathing loud in his ears. Two soldiers walking down had to push themselves against the pale stone wall as Zeke rushed up past them. "My apologies," he grunted, but he did not look back.

Memories swam through his head. His sister, screaming in the night. The dull thump of his father's body as it hit the floor. The violent orange blaze of fire glimpsed through the slats in the root-cellar door, where his mother had shoved him while she bled out from a pincer-stab. She had died leaning against it. *Mama! Mama!* That was his own voice. It had never left him.

Zeke drew a deep breath and squared his shoulders. *That abomination attack was ten years ago,* he reminded himself. The pale tentacles in the water and the corpses on the docks had brought the fear back to him. But he was a man grown now, a godreaper, and tonight he had lived up to the promise he'd made to his mother in that root-cellar, the words never spoken aloud but etched onto his soul. *I will make you all proud of me.* And he had. He had earned a place at Commander Gavon's right hand. His parents could have dreamed of nothing more than that.

One more turn of the stairs, and Zeke stood before two soldiers guarding a thick wooden door. They were passing around a smokeweed pipe, but they leapt to attention once they saw him. "Lieutenant!" one gasped.

Both were green boys, newly enlisted. Most likely fosterlings, recently arrived from the frontier, he guessed from how their orange coats hung loose on their scrawny frames. Admiration glowed in their eyes when they looked at him.

Zeke was the only officer in the army who was, at present, subject to a foster bond. All members of the Godreaper Corps held the ranks of officers; it was a military necessity, though Zeke could expect no promotion above the rank of lieutenant until his bond expired. Still, he was quite aware that status alone was an inspiration to boys like these. Fosterlings led hard lives; to be subject to a foster bond meant one had either been orphaned before eighteen, with no family to take them in, or that one's parents had been declared unfit to raise them. They could not vote, own property, or enjoy many other rights of full citizenship, and they were legally obliged to labor with no pay save food and shelter from their bondholder. Still, it was a kinder fate than starvation or vagrancy.

He gave the guards a firm salute. They grinned as they returned the gesture. "I'm here to see the prisoners," Zeke said, and they moved aside. He opened the door, stepped through, and shut it behind him.

The southwest tower had been built as a watch post to overlook the courtyards below. It held only two iron-barred jail cells, built into the back half of the room, though Commander Gavon said they were more secure than the fortress dungeons. Cold wind whistled through cracked mortar and the one small window. A small chest to hold the prisoners' personal effects was bolted to one wall and locked with an iron chain. In the cell to his left, Cevette Zarcanzi lay dozing on a bed of hay. To the right, on the far side of the bars between two cells, Eva stood trembling and staring at her hands. Straw and grime clung to her white skirt. She looked up when she heard him enter and rushed toward the cell door. "Zeke! Is the kraken dead? Were you wounded?"

"It's dead, and I'm unhurt." He hung his lantern from a hook in the ceiling. Godmarks—dark, grinning skulls—shone faintly on Eva's palms as she reached through the bars. He took her hands. They both squeezed tight.

"How's Andreas?" Eva asked.

"The last I heard, his wound was a shallow one. The doctors will stitch it up. How are you?"

"Ah." Her brows knit close together. She looked away from him, and cleared her throat. "I'm not certain. Did you hear what happened?"

He nodded.

"I believe I made the right choice. I'm not sure of it, though."

"You did," Zeke said. He glanced at the pirate. The woman had been stripped of her weapons, and she seemed half-asleep, her head resting against the bars dividing her cell from Eva's. "Her claims that he stole her memory were clearly false. She wanted to get him alone, and she wanted the Skullrunner's power. You put a stop to her plan. You protected him."

"That's not why I did it." She shuddered. "Do I deserve this?"

"No!" He squeezed her hands once more, harder, as if he could make her feel his certainty.

"Zeke, I wanted that power."

"Of course you did." He knew how it frustrated her, to live under her father's restraints. He knew she wondered if her desire for autonomy grew out of her connection to Morghaia. Zeke had spent his childhood in the frontier territories of the northern island of New Soladis, lands claimed by Morghaia in the dark days of the Theocracy. He had heard stories of corpse armies raiding the land and seen the abandoned and half-demolished shrines built in her honor. But he could not see the cruel and terrifying goddess in Eva, and he would not judge her for wanting to make her own way in the world. "You'll make an excellent officer. We'll be proud to have you in the Godreaper Corps."

She bit her cheek. "I . . . I don't know if I want to serve him as an officer. Not after this."

A wave of fear swept through Zeke. Hair prickled on the back of his neck. He licked his lips. For a moment, he could not speak. For a moment, he was that boy hiding in the root-cellar again. His fear was irrational, foolish, and he knew this, but he could not make it go away. He would rather face a kraken than a split between Eva and her father.

"Is something wrong?" Eva said.

"It's nothing," Zeke lied. He pulled on a smile, trying to think of what to say. How much he *could* say. He supposed it didn't matter what the pirate overheard. She would be hanged come morning. "I know how your father thinks. The ceremony was meant to be a show of power for his guests. He wants the Republic to see he's still the same leader who freed them from the Theocracy. He wants to reassure the gentry that he can keep the peace and build up alliances to secure his position in the Assembly—to keep the Republic stable. Andreas was meant to kill the god. You taking it embarrassed him; made it seem as if he has no authority in his own household. That could have political consequences. He might have felt it necessary to assert his strength."

"Oh," she said. "Politics. You know I'm no good with that."

"Listen to me. He can be unpredictable. But he needs to make you an officer, and he knows it. I'm certain that he only did this to teach you a lesson."

"How long does he plan to keep teaching me?"

"Only he knows."

Eva sighed. "Could you get the keys? They're right on that hook."

Zeke looked. So they were. A ring with three brass keys hung from a hook hammered into the mortar of wall beside the door. His first thought was it should be placed more securely. He'd need to have words with the guards.

His second thought was that the truth could be more cruel than a kraken.

"Zeke?"

He was a soldier. His was a place of honor and respect. And, in return, it demanded his full obedience. *I cannot free a prisoner of my commanding officer without his leave.* And it was more than duty that compelled him. It was a force that twisted his heart.

Zeke released Eva's hands and stepped back from the cell door. "I would need his permission."

"No. No!" Her voice rose. She reached for him. Her fingers fell just short of his. "You would let me sit in a cell for him?"

"I'll go to him right now." Zeke forked his hand back through his hair, then looked away from her and swallowed once more. "I'll convince him to let you out. He'll do it if I ask him, I promise you. This is the better way. For both of us. Trust me."

"I trust you," she said, quietly.

"Once you're an officer, we can train together. Travel all over the Isles. Defend them from abominations. This will all feel like a bad dream when it's over. I promise."

"I hope it will," Eva whispered.

"It *will*. I'll leave you the lantern." He smiled, and gave her one last nod. Then he left.

As THE DOOR CLOSED, as tears ran down Eva's cheeks, Cevette Zarcanzi said in a soft voice, "Miss Gavon. I'm sorry."

"He has his reasons." Eva wiped her eyes with her sleeve. "There would be trouble if he let me go. He's looking out for both of us." Two years ago, she had cut herself during weapons practice and taken a fever. She had spent weeks abed before she recovered. Her father had never visited her. Andreas had been distracted by society matters. But Zeke had come to her each day. He had sat by her side, brought her dinner, and read to her from banned newspapers. She was not sure of much, but she knew Zeke cared for her.

"Oh, I see what he means to do," Cevette said. "I meant that I was sorry I held a gun to your head. I hoped most dearly I wouldn't have to use it. I had assumed your father would be more protective of you." She stood, smiled, and stuck her hand through the bars. "Cevette Zarcanzi. Captain of the *Sea Wolf*. It's a pleasure to meet you."

Eva hesitated, then crossed her cell and reached through the bars to shake Cevette's callused hand. *It's only polite.* The pirate's grip was firm.

Her warm brown eyes widened as she looked Eva over. A shiver ran all the way down Eva's spine, toward the very depths of the sea.

"Congratulations," Cevette said. "On your kill, and on surprising me. That rarely happens."

Eva blushed. She pulled her hand back and touched her cheek, then quickly disguised the gesture by reaching up to remove her disheveled wig. Hairpins clattered to the floor.

"You're quite composed about all this chaos for a gentlewoman." Cevette picked up a pin, and bent it into a hook. She tied it to a lace from her shirt and tossed it at the keyring. It missed. But, Eva supposed, she had the rest of her life to get it done.

"I've never seen the purpose of panic," Eva said. "It's strange, I know it. I don't feel things how I ought to."

"Who is there to say how anyone *ought* to feel?"

"My father and all his associates."

Cevette nodded, and threw her hook again. Another miss. "It must be quite hard, growing up as a fosterling in Gavon's household. Hearing everyone decry Morghaia while he rips up echoes' souls to erase some minor scandal from memory."

Eva laughed, and clapped her hands over her mouth. "Gods, it's not funny. But it's good to hear someone admit the sacrifices might be real."

"Oh, they're real. That's why I came. To make him confess to taking my past, or at least to get the Skullrunner and turn it against him." Cevette wound in her hook. "I have better things to do than die tomorrow. Please don't scream for the guards, Miss Gavon. My quarrel isn't with you. Not unless you make it so."

"If the guards ask me anything, I'll say I was sleeping. If you can make the throw, that is."

"Well, now I must make the throw. I must prove myself to you."

A smile stole over Eva's face and stuck there. *Gods.* Was she truly enjoying the company of this pirate? A thief and a murderer? What did that say about her? *But her eyes are like freedom.*

As she couldn't quite sit on the bare floor in her hoopskirt, Eva leaned her shoulder against the bars between her and Cevette, tapped a finger to her lips, and thought on what Zeke had said. *An officer. He will make me an officer.* But the prospect left her spirits sinking like a ship in a storm. She was no longer certain that she wanted her father's protection, and it frightened her what that might mean.

The long minutes passed. The moon rose high against the clouds, a thin white crescent, its light beaming through the one small window. No demon-fire bloomed on its face that night. That meant good wind tomorrow, or so the old sailors said.

At last, Eva looked to Cevette, who still had not landed her hook. "Captain, may I ask you a question? I don't often have the chance to consider a fresh opinion."

"Of course. I can talk as I work."

"Is it wrong of me to be angry at my father? He's a hero. Surely he knows what is best."

"He's no hero." Cevette shook her head. "He calls himself a champion of the common people. But his family has been wealthy for generations, made so off the land they stole from the Wichil Nation. He calls himself a revolutionary, but his revolution left most of his people just as poor and desperate as they started. He calls himself the father of this country, yet he is not even a father to his own children. He locks them away when they've done nothing wrong."

Eva's eyes widened. She'd never heard anyone disparage her father so openly. She wanted. "But Morghaia was evil. She had to be stopped. And he's the one who stopped her." The words came quickly. They were an instinct. She was an echo. She had to make her loyalties clear.

Cevette shrugged. "Yes, the Theocracy had its problems. It needed to be brought down. But that he did it is no proof of his virtue. I can't tell you how to feel about Morghaia. But decades have passed since she was broken. Her deeds should have no bearing on how echoes are treated today."

But they do, Eva wanted to say. *We're still tied to her. Somehow.* She remembered how she felt when she had met the god-fragment's eyes. She would need to try her best to forget that. "It's not that simple," she whispered, and shivered as cold wind washed through the window. "I know he's hurting echoes. I don't know what to do about it."

"You're an echo, Miss Gavon. You'll know far better than I what echoes need. What you do with that knowledge—what you do with your magic—is your choice."

Your choice. Eva's eyes widened. She stared at Cevette through the bars, as if she'd misheard. She was so rarely given choices. Freedom was a dangerous thing in the hands of an echo. She had the power of a god written on her skin now—and Cevette Zarcanzi trusted her to use it as she chose.

The door banged open. Eva jumped away from the bars between the cells as Andreas entered. The moonlight shone in his hair. He wore only a thin shirt and breeches; his right shoulder was wrapped in thick bandages. His dark eyes, cool as the death of summer, met Eva's. He strode toward her cell as the door swung shut, and spoke with a knife's edge in his voice. "How could you? That god was *mine*."

"I'm sorry." Eva backed away from him, her slippers shuffling on the stone floor. "I'll make it right to you. I promise."

"What, will you buy me a caged god from a street peddler?"

Cevette had been winding her makeshift hook around her hand since Andreas had entered, with eyes only for his sister. Now she tucked that hand behind her back, stuck out her chest, and spoke. "How dare you address your sister so rudely, Mr. Gavon?"

"I—forgive me." Andreas squeezed his eyes shut. "I should mind my manners. I shouldn't let my more vicious side show. I'm only—" The lines of his neck tensed. His voice peaked, high and vulnerable. "I'm *scared*."

Cevette frowned at that, but said nothing. Eva's eyes widened. "Scared you won't get to be a godreaper?" She didn't understand. "He'll find you another, in a year or so."

"I don't know if I have a year." Andreas drew a deep, shaky breath. His eyes met hers. "Not if he decides to split me."

Oh. Her heart pounded. Had she truly put him in that much danger? She stepped back up to the cell door and gripped the bars tight. "He wouldn't destroy you. You're the golden son. You're his favorite."

"Not if he learns what I've done." His voice dropped to a whisper. "Listen to me. At the upcoming Assembly meeting, a group of representatives plan to call a vote of impeachment against him."

"What?" Her eyes widened. "Why?"

"The Assembly members who represent the city of Soladis are proud bastards who still think they rule an empire. They've never liked that a man from Halston leads them. And they don't think he's doing enough to protect their investments in the Sapphire Isles."

"Why would they think that?"

His thin lips curled into a slight smile. "I enjoy Father's parties no more than you do. All the Assembly members and aristocrats know what I am. They hate what I am. But, when I follow their rules, they hate me just a bit less. All the philosophy? All the ceremony? It means they listen to me. Especially when I start drunkenly blathering about how much my father despises them."

"What?" Eva's head spun. "By the gods. You . . . you've undermined him. It's only six weeks until this year's Assembly meeting begins. If the vote passes, he would lose his chairmanship, his seat on the Assembly, and his command of the military."

"We can't take away his magic. But we don't need to." His smile widened into a grin. "It's his political position that lets him to catch and control echoes. If he loses that . . ."

This plan could stop Commander Gavon from carrying out sacrifices. This plan could free them all. "Andreas, you're the smartest man I've ever met," Eva whispered.

"I know."

"Why didn't you tell me what you were up to?"

"I thought you'd try to help me."

Eva flinched.

"Oh, don't give me that. You're hopeless at subtle maneuvering. I knew you would have caused trouble. But that was my mistake. There's no worse trouble than what you caused tonight. You reminded everyone that you're a fragment of their worst enemy. And everything you do reflects on me."

"You gave me that knife!"

"To defend yourself. Not to murder a god." He sighed. "Ah, never mind. It's not your fault. Our minds are made from god-flesh sliced thin. Of course some of us struggle with . . . limitations. I shouldn't expect you to do things the same way I can."

"No. I can't." Her mouth went dry. A lump formed in her throat. She had endangered his position. His plan. She had endangered them both. "I'm sorry." His bluntness in pointing out her difficulties stung. Then again, she could be blunt as well. She had no right to hold that against him.

Andreas turned away from her, then crossed the small watchpost room to the hook that held the keyring. He picked it up, walked back to her, and held it out through the bars of her cell. Eva took it. Her fingers brushed his as he let the keys go. He smiled. "Go on. Get out of here."

"You want me to . . . leave?"

"I want you to help me. And this is how you can help me best." He stretched onto the tips of his toes, leaned through the bars, and kissed her forehead. His lips were dry. "Godspeed, sister."

Then he turned on his heel and left, closing the door tight behind him.

AFTER ZEKE DESCENDED FROM the southwest tower, he found a fresh lantern in the kitchens and climbed a servants' stair back up to the second story of the keep. The hall he walked along provided a convenient route for the housekeeper to bring dinner to the commander's office when he worked late, which was often. But there was also a door near the top of the stairs that led to a storage closet. Zeke entered, squeezed between two sets of wall-mounted shelves stacked with bedlinens, and knocked on the wall in the back.

The secret panel slid open. "Come in, Ezekiel."

Zeke stepped into the commander's bedroom, a plain yet comfortable chamber, the wallpaper a deep blue stamped with a pattern of sailing ships. The four-poster bed sported a thick goosedown mattress, the wardrobe door hung open to reveal three identical black wool coats, and a half-dozen bookcases overflowed with volumes, the spines uncracked and new. A simple desk sat across from the bed, the papers atop it stacked in two neat piles, six inkwells lined up sorted by size. Crackling flames leapt in the fireplace, filling the room with warmth and the scent of burning cedar.

And Commander Gavon stood right before him. He wore only a nightshirt, which fell to his knees, and his reading glasses, the golden frames shaped like two coiling snakes. Dark circles bloomed under his eyes. His hair was disheveled, his gray streaks unruly. His gray eyes traveled all over Zeke and his disheveled uniform.

Then he wrapped his hands around Zeke's neck and pulled him down into a kiss.

Zeke leaned in to savor it, drinking in the taste of sugar and wine. When it ended, Commander Gavon reached out and pushed shut the secret panel. The seam blended into the pattern of the wallpaper. Zeke put the lantern down on the bedside table. Commander Gavon opened it and pinched out the flame. *He wants me to stay.* Heat rose in the pit of Zeke's stomach.

"No one followed you, did they?" Commander Gavon asked.

Zeke shook his head.

"Good." He smiled. "No one can know how much I need you."

"They don't," Zeke said. "Not even Eva knows."

Growing up on the frontier, Zeke and the other children in his village had heard countless tales of the commander's heroic defeat of Morghaia, how the corpse legions had all dropped dead in a heartbeat, how the rebels had offered to crown him king in her stead and how humbly he had refused. They had heard of cities like Halston and Sheepgrave, where high walls and brave soldiers kept out abominations and Sea People, where the markets overflowed with food, where criminals were punished and the virtuous rewarded. And they had heard how, if they worked hard, brought in enough pelts and lumber from the frontier wilds, the Republic's borders would expand to include their towns and villages, and they would be rich and prosperous too. After all, the frontier settlers were Soladiseans, in language and culture, even though they had their small differences, living where they did. Commander Gavon was the man who would bring them their rightful due.

The morning after the abomination attack that had destroyed Zeke's village, the army had arrived. They'd pulled him from the ruins of his family home and said he had no choice but to become a fosterling, to labor in bondage until he was twenty-five, as Ministry of Child Welfare had decreed. But, unlike most fosterlings, who were sent to labor on farms or in the households of wealthy citizens, his bond had been assigned to the army so that he might train for a chance to join the Godreaper Corps. Something in the waters of the part of New Soladis he'd been born in caused one child in twenty to grow to exceptional size and strength, while rendering one in every ten sterile. Zeke, who even from a young age had desired a more masculine look, had always seen his size as a gift. On that day, that gift had offered him not just a chance to fight abominations, but the honor to serve Commander Gavon himself.

The army had sent him to Halston. The next four years had been a near-ceaseless blur of training and classes. He'd learned reading, writing, mathematics, and military theory. He'd learned five ways to kill a man and countless ways to kill a monster. Commander Gavon had watched the potential godreapers train. He had rarely spoken with them, but his mere presence had pushed Zeke to run faster, study later, fight harder. He had wanted to be everything this man was: in his courage, in his courtesy, in his virtues. The day Commander Gavon had chosen him to claim the Pridebreaker had been the grandest day of his life, second only to the day a year and a half ago when the commander had invited Zeke into his bed.

No one can know how much I need you. Of course, the relationship had to be kept secret. Commander Gavon had explained this to him a dozen times. When their ancestors had left Soladis to colonize the northern isles known as the Five Sisters, they had sought to distance themselves from the libertine frivolity of the island they had left behind. The Soladiseans of the Five Sisters frowned on any sort of sexual pleasure outside of marriage. But Zeke would not be free to marry until his bond expired. The scandal, if they were exposed, might be so great as to jeopardize the support of the voters that kept the commander on the Assembly.

Zeke dared not run that risk, even it if meant keeping a secret from his closest friend. He had to protect Commander Gavon. He could not remember a time he had not loved him.

The commander ran a hand back through Zeke's disheveled curls. "I'm told you went to see my daughter before reporting in to me. How is Eva?"

Zeke sighed. He knew better than to lie to soften the blow. "She is frustrated. Uncertain. Frightened. And quite angry."

The commander frowned. "As angry as Morghaia?"

"I can't say. I don't remember Morghaia. But any one of us would be angry to be locked up like that. You would be. You fought a revolution for your freedom."

"I fought to be free of tyrants."

Sweat built on Zeke's palms. He licked his dry lips, struggling for words. "Eva is the furthest thing from a tyrant. She's brave, loyal, and powerfully determined. If you make her an officer, she'll do her duty."

"You believe that?"

"Yes, sir."

The commander smiled. His gray eyes caught Zeke's warm brown ones. The two of them still stood quite close together, so close Zeke could feel the heat rising from his skin. It surprised him still, whenever he realized this man was flesh and blood. A man of flesh and blood could be wounded.

"Eva is your friend," the commander said. "But you didn't free her."

Zeke shook his head. "I know my duty."

"You are a rare sort of man, Lieutenant Dare. Anyone can serve his country when it pleases him. Few indeed will risk angering a friend to do so. But, to build a civilized nation, we must place the wellbeing of society over our personal desires. Your magic makes you a useful asset to the military, but it is your honor that makes you a credit to your country. You are the very image of what a man of the Republic should be. You are everything that I love."

Heat flooded his cheeks. His pulse raced. His stomach fluttered. This was nothing like the dalliances he'd had with other soldiers, men and women alike. *He loves me, too.* The commander had said it a few times before, but it was sweet indeed to be reminded.

"There's no reason to hold Eva overnight," Zeke said. "Let her go back to her rooms."

"Ezekiel," he said, almost teasingly. He smiled, a slight, thin thing, then reached out and put his hand on Zeke's hip. "I'll make her an officer. In the morning."

He's a great leader. A great man. He knows what to do.

"In the morning," Zeke said, and lost himself in another kiss.

THE SCREAMING DUKE

IN THE HALSTON FORTRESS, ON HIGH HILL ISLAND. 25TH KASPERMONTH, YEAR TWENTY-TWO OF THE GOLDEN REPUBLIC.

A company of distinguished philosophers has arrived from Soladis to lead a symposium on abomination physiology at Carreton. When I arrived with my research notes to request admission, they told me nothing good would come of an echo's interest in such dangerous creatures. I would not be admitted, and furthermore, I would be banned from the university grounds until the symposium concluded. "Good sirs and ladies," I told them, "I did not choose to be an echo. Were it in my power to make myself something else, I would do so forthwith." They did not believe me. I had spoken too honestly to be trusted. –from the diary of Korinne Gavon.

EVA CLUTCHED THE KEYS to the cells tightly in her fist. She stared at the door Andreas had just left through. A cool wind wafted through the narrow window of the tower; the flame of the lantern flickered. The air smelled of frost and straw bedding. In the cell beside her, Cevette whistled. "That's your brother? That's how he speaks to you?"

"He's upset," Eva said, heart hammering. She could still feel Korinne's diary pressing against her chest. *Echoes. Only echoes understand this. The fear. The desperation. How it drives you.* "For a number of good reasons, not the least of which is that you shot him."

"I was aiming for the god. Damn flintlocks. Well, if I get out of this, I'll write him an apology letter." Cevette leaned up against the bars that divided their cells. She brushed a loose lock of blonde hair off her forehead. It was too short to tuck behind her ear, and so it flopped back where it had been right away. "Listen to me, Miss Gavon. I have a godmarked friend who knows many things. Among them, how divine power manifests in human flesh. How it's always weaker than when the god had it. How it manifests in predictable ways. He told me that, should a godreaper take the Skullrunner's power, they would gain the ability to travel through Death to any place they pleased."

Eva pictured the goddess-fragment they had caught on the hunt, gliding out of an archway of bones from the realm called Death. "It's truly that easy?"

"A portal into Death can only be opened at a spot where someone has died. Recently and, preferably, through violence. That leaves more of a mark. Has such a thing happened recently in this tower? You should be able to tell."

Eva furrowed her brow. Did she feel anything different? Then she hesitated. "What do you want from me?"

"My freedom, if you would be so kind." Cevette's eyes flickered to the keys. "You handled the situation downstairs quite well, Miss Gavon. You have a cool head on your shoulders, and you're a decent shot. Help me get back to ship, and I'll give you a place on my crew. What do you say?"

Eva clutched the keys to her chest. For a moment, they felt as heavy as a body in a noose. Her stomach sank. Her lips opened and closed. No sound came out.

This woman was a notorious pirate, thief, and murderer. The blood of Republic soldiers covered her hands. The law demanded she should hang. That was justice. But the law also said that echoes couldn't vote. That the crimes of Morghaia meant they could not be trusted. *Will I be proving them right if I help her escape?*

"Your choice," Cevette said.

Eva closed her eyes. Tried to sort through the numb mess of her emotions. Find something in the darkness she could put a name to. Cevette had spoken to her kindly. Cevette had shown her respect. Cevette had offered her a place in the world. *A place as a pirate. Stealing and killing.* As an echo, she should not contemplate such a thing.

But, as an echo, she would be foolish indeed to serve the man who could split them.

She bit her lip. A faint booming sound rose in the distance. *Cannonfire?* The wall shattered.

Eva screamed. She and Cevette both dropped to their knees and threw their hands up over their heads. Wind and heat washed over them in a fierce wave. Dust filled the air. The tower swayed, groaning on its foundations. Eva coughed, stumbled, and nearly fell over as she stood.

"We're under attack!" yelled the guard outside the door.

"Leave the prisoners and run!" shouted his fellow. Their footsteps pounded on the stairs as they fled.

Eva's ears rang. Her heart pounded. Cevette also stood, brushing dust off her clothes. Both women turned to face the fresh, gaping hole in the wall. Brick and mortar crumbled along its edges and fell to the ground.

"Captain Zarcanzi." Eva lifted the keyring in one trembling hand. "I won't leave you here. Let's go."

It was the work of moments to open her cell, then Cevette's. The captain stepped out and rewarded Eva with a sparkling, wicked grin. Eva gave her an awkward nod, then reached for the main door. She opened it a crack, then hesitated. "There'll be a dozen guards at the bottom."

"Give me the keyring," Cevette said. Eva nodded, and tossed it to her. It landed precisely in her hand. Cevette unlocked the chest full of confiscated assets; she grabbed her guns and slid them back in her belt, then dug out a coil of rope and began tying it to the bars of her cell door. "We'll have to climb," she said. "One moment. Let me secure the knot."

Eva ran to the hole in the wall and peered out. A warship had entered the harbor. She was as large as any in the commander's fleet, her sails black as midnight, her flag a silver skull. Her cannons flashed. Glowing orange shells streaked through the night. Dust flew up wherever they struck the walls. The fortress trembled.

"Oh, she's powerful," Eva said. She blinked, then squinted, trying to get a better look. She stretched her hand out, as if the ship was a model she could pick up and hold. She should've been terrified. Neither her body nor her mind was delivering terror. She so liked looking at boats. "She's not yours, is she? That's a ship-of-the-line. I read your ship was only a barque."

"She belongs to the woman who lured the kraken into the harbor."

"I thought that was you."

"I don't play with abominations." There was something dark in her tone. Cevette secured her intricate knot, then tossed the free end of the rope through the hole. "We'll have to climb. Fast."

Eva looked down and shuddered. It was quite a long way. "Have you done this before?"

"Of course." She knelt, gripped tight to the bricks at the bottom of the hole, and slid her legs out into the open air. "The rope is for you, Miss Gavon." Down she went. Her fingers and toes found small handholds in the moonlit sides of the tower as she descended, as nimble as a monkey.

Eva swallowed. She looped the rope about her right arm and swung herself out through the gap. The cold wind whipped around her. She pressed her feet against the side of the tower to still herself. The wicker hoops of her skirt rested atop her legs.

Step by step, she told herself, and let more rope slide through her grasp. Her forearm ached. Her raw skin burned where the rope raced through it. She walked backward down the side of the tower. *I hope no one sees me,* she thought, letting up more blood-spotted rope. But her father's soldiers had greater problems to attend to.

Cannons fired. Heavy lead missiles whistled through the air and crashed against the walls. Footsteps pounded through the night. Screams rose all about the fortress. Something tugged at the edge of Eva's awareness, shifting about like water in her ears. *Death.*

Her nostrils flared. Her teeth ground together. Whatever these raiders were after, innocent people had already died for it. A wave of anger at the injustice of it all seemed to knock her sideways. Her foot slipped. She swung through the open air and slammed into the brick. Pain shot through her cheek. She gasped out.

"Easy there," Cevette whispered from below. "Let go. It's a short drop."

Eva took a deep breath. She grabbed the rope with her left hand and unwound it from her right. *Trust her. Trust her.* She let go. Gravity snatched her down—and then firm arms caught her. "Well done," Cevette said as she set her down on her feet. Her hand lingered on Eva's waist. She might have said something more, but she was cut off by a piercing scream.

The two of them stood atop the narrow inner wall that enclosed the keep's treasury building. Grappling hooks gleamed atop the fifteen-foot-high outer wall. Pirates were climbing atop it. The woman who had screamed stood atop the southern gate, lit by the moon.

No. Eva shuddered. Her heart sank. *An echo.*

The echo wore a black coat, black breeches, and a necklace of shining silver beads shaped like skulls. In place of a right hand, she sported a three-fingered steel talon. In her left, she held a bloody sword. Godmarks shimmered on her arms. Her long black hair flew unbound on the wind. Her pale skin gleamed in the moonlight. She grinned.

She was the picture of death.

Cevette cursed. "That's the Demon of Dogshead."

Eva bit down a curse. Cevette Zarcanzi, at least according to the newspapers, only robbed wealthy merchants and nobles. The Demon of Dogshead would hit anyone, even frontier villages and fishing ships washed out to sea, and she announced her presence to her foes by screaming until their ears bled. Eva's skin crawled just to look at her. *Dangerous. Repulsive.* She had to put distance between them. For more reasons than one.

Behind her, more echo pirates were climbing up the wall, more pale and dark-haired women who all shared the same long face. *My face.* Eva vividly remembered the tales she'd heard of Morghaia and her army of the dead. Orange-clad soldiers charged toward them, racing along the top of the wall from the direction of the western gate. They hoisted their rifles and bayonets, shouting to their fellows and urging them forward. The echo leader faced them and screamed once more. The air rippled with the force of her magic. Soldiers flew backwards. Some fell off the wall and dropped into the night. Bones cracked. The echo smiled. Two soldiers died. Eva *felt* that, like ripples in a cup, and reached for her magic. Willing the door to open into Death.

What am I doing? she thought. She had decided to get Cevette out of the crumbling tower; not to run away with her. Still, her instincts were screaming at her to put distance between herself and the Demon. To run, as fast and as far as she could, wherever she could go.

"You can go to her," Cevette said. "You're an echo. She'll grant you mercy. I've seen it."

"No," Eva said. She shivered at the thought. Instinctively, she looked down at her hand; her skull ring was gone, the silver band taken by one of the soldiers who arrested her, the screwed-off skull lost in the banquet hall. She was glad to not be wearing it now as she took Cevette's hand. "Follow me."

Eva guided the pirate to the narrow staircase built into the north-facing side of the treasury wall. They descended into the eastern courtyard. There, only a few outbuildings clung to the wall, and they and the yard were both deserted. But torches still blazed in the night, marking off the corners of the beast pit and warning all about the threat that dwelled within. Eva led Cevette up to the edge.

"Down here," she said, pointing to a ladder. Cevette nodded.

Down they climbed. Eva's battered dress slippers were the first to hit the sand. Cevette followed behind her; she had taken a torch from up top and now held it aloft. Eva was grateful for the light. Down in the pit, all was silent. It was dug ten feet deep into the earth. Cannons ringed it on all sides. Abomination dens had been dug into the walls, great iron gates keeping the beasts imprisoned within. It had been five weeks since the last soldier was ripped apart in a training exercise. Eva hoped that would be bloody enough to count.

She strode into the center of the pit, reaching out with a sense beyond sense. Her heart pounded. Her eyes darted about. She felt alert, but not afraid. Still not afraid. "One moment, please. I need to concentrate."

Cevette nodded. "Take your time."

Eva took a deep breath. Minutes ticked past. Back up on the walls, swords clashed, guns fired, and an echo screamed once more with the force of a god. Death hung all around her, as vivid as flashing daggers, as smothering as a shadow. Darkness tugged at her chest. Smoke rolled out from under her feet. The screams in the night grew closer. For a moment, she felt the world ready to break open and weep.

"Good evening, Captain Zarcanzi," said a clear, sharp, familiar voice. The voice of an echo.

The Demon dropped down into the beast pit, a rope in her one good hand. Her steel claw shone in the moonlight. Above her, three other echoes smiled down, faces blood-spattered and bone white. *Do I look like that?* The Demon whistled. The pirates shoved an orange-clad corpse over the edge. It slammed into the sand of the pit.

With a bang like a firebomb, a two-headed wolf threw itself into the bars of its cage.

Eva jumped. The wolf howled from both throats. Its heavy paws dug wildly at the earth below the cage gate. In another den, a fan of red eyes flickered open. Something hissed.

"Don't provoke abominations," Cevette said contemptuously. She folded her arms across her chest and lowered her chin. "You never know what they'll do."

"I know they'll make trouble. That's good enough for me." The Demon smiled. She studied Eva, her black eyes unblinking. "Hello, little sister. Those are quite pretty marks."

Eva's pulse sped. Sweat shone on her godmarks. She cracked her knuckles. "I'm not your sister. If we were family, you wouldn't attack my home."

"Your home, or your prison? You'll see it for what it is, soon. Once you set foot outside it. Once you sail the seas." The Demon took two steps closer to Eva. "I planned for one of my crew to take the magic. It seems the commander moved up the ceremony. You did well, to claim it for us."

"There is no *us.*"

The Demon laughed. High above, her crew joined in. The chuckling blended together, one sound in the four throats. "There's us, and then there's everyone else. Don't be a fool. It's as plain as the nose on all our faces. Come with us. We'll get you out of here."

Eva narrowed her eyes. *Does she want me dead?* No. When a godreaper died, the god bound to their soul made their way back into the realms of the living in time, but the philosophers said that took years. If the Demon wanted the Skullrunner on her side, she'd have to keep Eva alive.

"What do you want me to do?" Eva said.

"I want you to help me free the echoes." The Demon took one more step, and put her remaining hand on Eva's shoulder. "I want you to help me kill Jonathan Gavon."

My father. The Demon's casual tone and too-familiar voice sent shivers down her spine. It could have been Andreas saying that. It could have been her. Eva stepped back. She shook her head. Her mouth opened and closed several times before she found words. "No."

"No?" The line of the Demon's jaw tightened. "Do you still believe him when he says he doesn't split echoes? Is his grip still that tight on your mind? Where do you think you came from? Why do you think there are so many of us?"

Eva shook her head. Her head spun. Her heart hammered hard. All her words seemed to stick in her throat. "I . . . I know what he can do. And I do think he does it. But . . ." *There is so much wrong inside us. How can we judge if it's right to kill him?* She dared not say that out loud. Not to this terror of an echo.

"I know who you are. Evazina. I've known of you for years. I know your brother was to board a ship for Moonwhisper Isle once he was invested. He was assigned to guard a government archive."

"How did you learn that?"

"I came ashore on a dinghy, dragged some sailors into a back alley, and made them talk. Do you know what the commander keeps in his archives?"

Eva thought back to Korinne's diary. The young echo had been interested in the archives, how they were spread all throughout the Isles, how heavily the Republic invested in keeping their locations and their contents a secret. She had been looking for government records to study patterns in abomination attacks; she had asked her father what was hidden inside them. He had ordered her not to pry. "I . . . I don't know. He keeps his secrets close."

"Here. Let me show you." The Demon reached into her pocket and withdrew something that resembled a piece of paper. She held it out; Eva picked it up. Its surface was ragged, printed with words she could not read in the darkness, and it felt more solid and sturdy than she'd expected. "The ship to Moonwhisper was carrying a crate of these. The sailors gave it to me, in exchange for their friends' lives. Burn it. Then you'll know why it's so important that you come with me."

You aren't my sisters. I don't know you. Or perhaps she knew this woman too well. She was everything the Republic feared in an echo. "Perhaps later." Eva slid the scrap into her bodice, into the small leather diary. Death pressed against her eardrums, a terrible pressure that grew and grew as the souls of soldiers tumbled between worlds.

Up on the edge of the pit, the echoes flung down another corpse. A python-like creature, glimmering blue, wrapped its tail around the bars. It squeezed and pulled. Metal creaked and bent. White-furred paws as big as Eva's head curled through another gate. Twisting. Crushing. Howls and bellows rose through the dark, blending with the pounding bootsteps of soldiers and the screams of dying soldiers. The crude, ugly cacophony grated against Eva's ears, as overwhelming as the scrape of a flaying knife. She bent double, pressing her hands to her ears.

"Come along, Eva," said the Demon. "These beasts will cover my retreat. You don't want to be in the way when we set these free."

"Miss Gavon." Cevette placed a hand on her shoulder. "Listen to me. My ship is right off the coast. You'll be safe there. But we must go."

Eva grabbed Cevette's hand and squeezed it tight.

Black smoke bloomed up where her feet met the sandy soil. Eva stepped backward, her heart pounding in her throat. The smoke rose up over her head and formed itself into an archway. Its frame was made from a jumble of intertwined bones, femurs and ribcages tangled together. Its capstone was a grinning skull. Only swirling shadows lay within.

Eva pressed the fingers of her free hand to her lips and grinned. *I did that.* It felt like half a dream.

"Beautiful," whispered the Demon.

Eva stepped across the threshold, pulling Cevette with her.

All color vanished as she stepped into the realm called Death.

A great hallway stretched out before her, as solid as stone beneath her feet, fading into gray smoke in the distance. The walls were carved with the shapes of countless bones, jumbled and overlapping in a pale mélange. The arched beams that held up its ceilings were covered in finger-bone embellishments set in the shape of curling rose-vines. Colorless embers floated through the air, tossing off pale light. To either side of her, tall windows looked out on black-and-white visions of suffering—a soldier with a sword through her chest, a servant clutching a bullet hole in his gut.

As Eva reached toward one, it broke, shards of maybe-glass drifting past her face and dissolving into smoke. The dying soldier tumbled into Death, or at least her soul did; what came through was a half-transparent shade, devoid of color. She remained curled up and silently weeping until a sparkling silver mist coiled about her, lifting her like a leaf on the wind and pulling her off to where the hallway vanished into smoke.

Eva shuddered. She knew little about the mechanics of this place. The gods of Soladis had once told their people that Death was merely a place for souls to rest before they moved on to their next life. But there was clearly more to it than she'd been told. Her chest tightened. She took a deep breath. Her skin crawled at the cool sensation of breathing air that was not quite air. *What is this place, truly?* Perhaps a philosopher could tell her. But here, she could only ask that question of herself.

Cevette. Eva glanced over her shoulder. The captain stood behind her, unmoving. White smoke tendrils encased her from head to foot, binding her like a spider's web, holding her frozen. *Life,* Eva realized. *The stuff of life clings to her. For now.* She grabbed Cevette by one frozen arm and tugged her forward. The captain bobbed along, still frozen, like a buoy in a current. Odd, but workable. She could run with her.

Behind Cevette, a bone-framed window opened onto the training yard. *Safety.* Her prison. The only life she'd ever known.

Eva swallowed hard. *The Godreaper Corps need this magic.* With it, she could reach remote abomination attacks in a heartbeat, transport soldiers to defend frontier villages, carry food and medicine to wounded survivors. And yes, she would be serving her father, but the people who needed her help were not to blame for his cruelties. What sort of person would turn her back on them? An echo. The worst sort of echo.

No. She'd seen the worst sort of echo tonight. Whatever she was, she wasn't the Demon of Dogshead. She had no wish to unleash chaos and destruction, only to put a thousand miles between the Demon and herself. But when she imagined life as an officer, it felt hollow. Empty. She wanted more.

She would see where this path led.

Eva grabbed Cevette's arm, opened up her stride, and *ran.*

Her worn dress shoes struck the floor of the hall. It was stone—no, it was jumbled vertebrae, worn smooth with time. Puffs of smoke flew up under her feet. New windows appeared in the distance as she let the first ones fall behind her. The floor seemed to move of its own accord, speeding her on. In one hand, she held up her gown, the skirts tangled and torn. With the other, she dragged Cevette's shade like a ship towing cargo.

The great hallway of Death narrowed as she went. Souls drifted past, on currents fast and slow. The light that filled the corridors was as flat and gray as twilight. Windows and archways flashed by, framed in carved bone, some vivid with imminent death, others dark and reeking of atrocities. Each portal hummed with a different resonance, a note of music that carried *where* and *when* and *how many.* But some part of her knew that none of them was her destination.

Eva laughed. After years of struggling to match Andreas, at last something came naturally to her. *Is this part of the magic I claimed? Or part of*

Morghaia within me? She wasn't sure. But she could not see any evil in this. Only the open path ahead.

She pushed harder. Her thighs burned. Her chest ached. She closed her eyes and told herself to focus. *The sea just off the coast of Halston. A ship called* Sea Wolf. *A godmarked crew, and the riches of the Isles in their hold.* Every story she'd ever heard of Cevette Zarcanzi ran through her head, fueling her will where her own strength could not. She didn't even know which tales were true, but she only needed one to be. *Let her have killed at least one person on that ship of hers.* Eva imagined Cevette, a dead sailor at her feet, her hands red with blood. Confident. Powerful. *Free.*

With Cevette as her compass, Eva leapt between worlds.

Her palms struck weathered wood. Her head spun. She rolled over onto her back.

Before the darkness claimed her, she glimpsed a thousand stars.

THE WOLF OF THE SEA

Aboard the ship *SEA WOLF*, forty miles west of Halston. 26th Kaspermonth, Year Twenty-Two of the Golden Republic.

They call me the first godreaper. I find it difficult to believe that no one before me ever stabbed a god in the back. Perhaps Iunos took the memories of when it happened before. They say the Sea People have legends about heroes eating gods, though I would not hold those in equal weight with our factual histories. I consider myself to be the first to kill a god in service of a good cause, and I have found that virtue is an achievement to prize above all others. In your last letter, you asked for insight into my experiences during the revolution. My hope in writing this is to satiate your curiosity. Yet there are certain truths I dare not put to paper. There would be much upheaval if they were known. –Letter from Commander Jonathan Gavon to Lord Mykil Merris, Minister for Childhood Welfare.

A headache pounded at Eva's temples like a hangover or divine curse. The world swung, left and right. She reached out, instinctively, for balance, and found knots of tangled hemp rope. *Oh. I'm in a hammock.*

Then she remembered *why* she was in a hammock.

Eva cursed. She blinked her eyes open and rubbed her aching forehead. Godmarks lined her arms, running from her fingertips to her elbows like gloves. Little black bones wreathed skulls with mocking grins. Twisted coils of funeral smoke framed them all. She spread her fingers wide and twisted her wrists back and forth. Her mouth went dry. The marks were real. "Oh, gods."

She had killed the Skullrunner. No fortress could hold her now.

"I'm free," she gasped. An uncontrollable giggle bubbled up in her throat, like backwards champagne, making her laugh over and over, until she was short on breath and hiccupping. For a moment, nothing else mattered.

"Quiet," someone grumbled.

"My apologies." Slowly, wobbling like a newborn colt, Eva rolled her way out of the free-swinging hammock. Her feet hit the wood of a deck. The *Sea Wolf* rocked beneath her. She stumbled. Instinctively, she grabbed the post the foot of the hammock was tied to for balance. Her hand nearly grazed the blade of an axe. Her eyes widened. Weapon racks covered the posts that held up her hammock, bristling with pistols and knives. Someone hung her torn and filthy gown from a hook on the post by her head; Korinne's diary, with the odd almost-paper the Demon had given her stuck in it like a bookmark, sat on a small shelf beside it. Eva wore only her shift and stockings. Her shoes were missing.

What do I do next? she wondered. Her guts gurgled painfully.

First, she had to relieve herself.

The lower deck was a dark and cluttered place, lit only by handful of lanterns, a forest of support posts with hammocks slung between them and sea chests chained at their feet. The posts were wrapped in garlands of dried flowers and coral beads (and one garland of rat skulls); quilts and blankets dyed in a rainbow of colors hung from the hammocks. Three cannons pointed out the gun-ports at port and starboard; someone had painted an obscenity on one of the rolling wooden cannon mounts in black tar. The chains that held them in place creaked in time with the ship beams as the *Sea Wolf* rolled and tossed.

All about her, pirates slept and snored. The air about them smelled of sweat and rum. More than a few had arms covered in godmarks, colored emerald, crimson, or violet, shaped like swirling spirals of leaves and ancient runes. One sweat-drenched pirate had a pattern running down his chest past his navel. They had killed gods without the commander's permission, a capital crime. Yet no one seemed to care there was treason written on their skin.

Eva made her way to a narrow set of stairs. Up she went, clutching to the rail, her steps swaying. She stumbled out onto the upper deck, blinking in the blinding light of the day sun as it flashed off the ocean. Sails flew above her, hard yellowed canvas snapping in the wind, and the ship's flag was a skull weeping blood. Small altars of candle stubs and chips of mirrors sat embedded in the rail, throwing smoke and sunlight. Barely ten feet away from her, a cluster of pirates sang bawdy tunes as they mended nets, passing around a bottle of rum. They cursed and smiled chipped-tooth grins.

It was so different. So new. *New* didn't always sit right with her stomach. She'd been told all her life that everyone outside the Republic's borders was uncivilized and dangerous, and pirates were the worst of them, as likely to kill you as to shake your hand. She had never quite believed that, knowing Zeke had come from the frontier, and now she saw it all for falsehood. Joy hung in the air, alongside the smell of salt and tallow, a wild joy for the tossing seas. A smile stretched across her face. Her lips parted. She pressed her hands to her cheeks, beaming as she drank it all in.

Sea Wolf was a lovely ship, a barque one hundred and twenty feet in length. She had three masts and gun ports for twenty-four cannons, though only half were in use. She sported three masts: foremast, mainmast, and mizzenmast, named from bow to stern. The captain's cabin lay to stern as well, situated neatly below the quarterdeck; atop the quarterdeck sat the ship's helm. Crates and boxes had been lashed to the rails, both for use as benches and for (Eva assumed) the storage of stolen goods. She had read dozens of books on ship construction; she was pleased her education had not failed her.

Cevette stood before the mainmast, which was about twenty feet from the stairs Eva had come up, near the ship's geometric center. The captain was polishing an already-spotless pistol. Her long coat was white leather, a match for the snowy ostrich plumes in her tricorn hat. Broaches studded her lapels: pearl, gold, and glistening diamonds. In crisp linen trousers, a blue cravat around her neck, she drew Eva's gaze like the rising sun.

"Good morning, Miss Gavon," she said as Eva staggered toward her. "It may cheer you to know we spotted the Demon's ship at dawn, racing northwest to rejoin her fleet. Halston was not burned. It seemed she withdrew the moment she realized she wouldn't get her hands on you."

So her family was safe. Eva let out a deep breath. She put a hand on the mainmast to steady herself. "Thank you for telling me."

"Of course. How did you sleep? I was quite worried after you collapsed last night, but the ship's healer assured me you had merely overexerted yourself."

"Yesterday was a . . . a long day," Eva said. "But I slept very well, thank you. Though . . . I did note you tossed me into a hammock. Surely saving your life would merit me better accommodations?"

"That was the best hammock we've got. No holes. At least, no holes where there aren't meant to be holes."

Eva flushed. "Oh. My apologies. I didn't mean to insult you."

"You'll have to work harder than that to insult me." Cevette laughed. "You're welcome to stay with us. But you don't have to. I owe you a good deal. I can pay you back in gold; then you can go wherever you like."

Eva pressed her lips together in a slight grimace. She ran a hand back through her hair, thinking hard. What was she doing here? These were dangerous people. Thieves and killers. *Evil people?* The soldiers of the Republic killed hundreds. What was the difference between them and the pirates? The weight of law and custom? Crisp orange uniforms?

Perhaps she should keep running. Find some small island where she could live out her days. But then she would be utterly alone. And what place would she find for herself there?

What place do I have on a pirate ship?

"I'll think it over," she said.

"Oh. Good." Cevette smiled. She pressed her fingertips to her lips. A warm glow filled her eyes. There was a depth of gratitude in that look that Eva found slightly incongruous with the fact they were near strangers. But she liked the deep warmth that flooded her whenever their eyes met.

"Where might I . . ." Eva hesitated. "Where might I relieve myself?"

"If you've got a cock, off the side. Elsewise—" Cevette held up a bucket. "Don't worry. It's our best bucket."

EVA FELT A MODICUM more steady once she was dressed.

A pirate named Naeri de l'Havre led her to her sewing nook on the lower deck. Sectioned off by weathered floral drapes, lit by a single swinging lantern, it was almost peaceful. Hooks held bolts of fabric and leather. Beads, sequins, and armored plates overflowed from her heavy chests. Naeri fitted Eva for a pair of high-waisted breeches, fastened with brass buttons, and a weathered, loose-fitting V-neck shirt of white, then gave Eva a pair of leather boots: well-worn, midnight black and fastened with brass filigree. She adored them.

"I hope I'm not too much trouble to dress," Eva said, turning about to check her reflection in a dented silver mirror. "I know I'm a bit taller than the average woman."

"You're no trouble at all." Naeri, who stood an even six feet tall, wore a gown of sea-blue silk that fell in ruffled tiers like a foaming wave, adding shape to her slender form. She had a darker complexion, a cool undertone to her skin, and her countless small braids were bound back in a clip of silver and sapphire. Her face was long, her full lips painted a deep burgundy. Her godmarks, royal blue, were of needles, thread, and a fine tangle of lacework. She spoke with the accent Eva associated with the city of Soladis, and smiled with each word. "There's rags in that bucket, if you need them. Wash them before you put them back."

A brief moment passed before Eva realized what the rags were for. Right. "Echoes don't have bleeding weeks. We can carry children, I've been told, but we only fancy women, so we only get to test that when we meet women with . . . the capability."

"Well, as a woman of . . . the capability, I also make the most ingenious little enchanted stockings that you slide on down a penis. Puts a firm stop to childbearing and the pox." She tapped a small wooden box. "Wash them before you put them back. Thoroughly."

"Thank you," Eva said. "It's good to know. I've never wanted children."

Among the peoples descended from the Empire of Soladis, gender was a quirk of language and custom left over from the ancient days before the empire rose. Soladiseans varied greatly in physical sex and fertility; Zeke made use of monthly bleeding rags, though his courses only came once or twice a year, which he thought was most likely the result of the physical condition that had granted his height and strength. The Soladisean custom, as Eva had learned it in Halston, was to address folk as men and women based on their matter of dress and the style of their hair, unless they stated otherwise, for there was no certain way for Soladiseans to categorize sex, and even if they could, it would be of little use to them. Zeke and Andreas had always asserted themselves as men; as for herself, Eva was a woman in the sense she'd been told she was one and thought that fit well enough not to dispute it.

She had been told sex and gender mattered somewhat more among the Sea People and the peoples of the Sapphire Isles. Many Soladiseans insisted that the Sea People treated their women oppressively, keeping them close to their home villages while their men travelled to hunt, fish, and trade, though no one who had ever said this to Eva seemed to care much for the Sea People at all.

"How did you decide you wished to join Cevette's crew?" Eva asked.

"She's a good leader," Naeri said. "Pays well, fights bravely, and shows her crew respect. She's made this ship a haven for people who have nowhere else to go. And, when she offered me the chance to sail with her, it was do that or hang."

Respect. She liked the sound of that. Though she was not quite certain Cevette would offer it so easily to an echo as she had to the beautiful Naeri.

"How did you kill the Skullrunner, if I may ask?" Naeri said.

"I had help from my brother."

"That was kind of him. Will you miss him, if you stay at sea?"

Eva frowned, and thought that over. Once, she and her brother had been inseparable, identical. They had shared a language of nods and gestures, books and tutors and past-times, and equaled each other in all things. But, around their twelfth birthday, he had begun to excel, both at school and at manners. Their father had crowned him the favorite, and a chasm had opened between them. She did not know how to reach back across it.

Perhaps it was necessary to put some distance between them. To get out of his way. To discover her own. To be more than only his echo.

Another woman ducked into the tailor's nook, short and plump with light brown skin and a chip in her front tooth. Her skirts and sleeves were tied up with colorful scarves, and wavy hair stuck out of her bun at all angles. "Lizeth fucked their shoulder," she said. "They're a mess. I need help on the pumps."

"I'd be happy to help," Eva said, and offered the woman her hand. "Evazina Gavon."

"The new Skullrunner."

Eva frowned. Every god had a sobriquet along with a personal name. *Kasperos the Crownbearer. Kothrin the Pridebreaker. Morghaia the Skullrunner.* The sobriquet passed to whichever person wielded the god's power. But she did not want it given to her. A philosopher might very well say that she was the *old* Skullrunner, Morghaia reforged. She did not wish to invite that comparison.

"She meant it kindly," Naeri said. "You won a great victory. You earned the title."

That was also true. Zeke had slain a god. Her father had slain a god. They had mastered their power; it had no mastery over them. But they were not echoes. And she did not think their gods had smiled at them right before they struck them dead.

"Well," said the pirate with the chipped tooth, "if that's the most I ever offend her, I'll count it an achievement. I'm Donya Breamtide," She shook Eva's hand, and, instead of letting go, pulled her towards the stairs. Her fingers were connected by light pink webbing. "I took my magic from the god of brutal honesty."

Eva couldn't tell if she was joking, but laughed so as not to look rude.

Donya led her to a small ladder. They climbed down into the cargo hold. The ship's belly was as damp and hot as an abomination's asshole, with only one lantern for light. Trunks swung above them, suspended in nets. Far toward the bow end of the ship, a line of iron bars sectioned off the brig. Water sloshed across the wooden floor. They waded through it to reach the pump, the valves and pistons concealed within an iron box and the rusty lever of the handle sticking out the top.

"You found someone else to pump?" said a voice. Atop a stack of barrels, what Eva had taken for a mess of rags rolled over and revealed a scrawny person even shorter than Donya. They wore a long black robe, which hung open in the front; the scars on their chest said they'd had breast tissue sliced away. Red godmarks covered the brown skin of their wrists, a pattern of clouds, lightning bolts, and eagles soaring on updrafts. Their curls were shaved flat along the sides of their head, their eyes were lined in black paint, and they were spinning a golden bracelet around their wrist.

Eva waved to them. "I'm Evazina Gavon. I'm here to join the crew. Potentially."

"Hello," they said. "I'm Lizeth. The quartermaster."

"What's your magic?"

"I summon storms." They attempted to slap their chest, in what seemed to be a boastful gesture. When they lifted their right arm, they gasped in pain and squeezed their shoulder with their left hand. "Argh. Donya, do you have more numbing cream?"

"Not much." Donya said. "The captain told me to save it for when we truly needed it."

"I can't believe that I killed a god and still lost a battle with a pump."

Eva broke in. "Quartermaster, forgive me if this is rude, but—"

"How did I kill a god? Easy. My god was Toponomitl. The Storm-braider, the Soladiseans called him. He was a Sea god, or a demon, depending on who you ask, but I won't get into that now. What matters is he was never part of the Soladisean pantheon. He led the resistance against the Empire in the Sapphire Isles."

Eva nodded. She had heard stories about Toponomitl, and they had not framed him favorably. She had often wondered what separated the rebellion he had led all those years ago from Commander Gavon's revolution, but she had been told that was a foolish question to ask.

"All my life," Lizeth said, "I'd loved the stories about him. When I was sixteen, I'd heard rumors that Toponomitl had been spotted at a ruined temple outside Port Dueno, that the army of the Republic planned to capture him. My father told me not to interfere, but I couldn't let those bastards take a god who means so much to the people of my island and turn him against us. So I took a horse, and rode all night, and tracked him to his temple, and shot him with my father's pistol. He smiled as he died. I think he was glad that I got him and not one of the soldiers."

"That's incredible," Eva said. Relief washed through her. *I'm not the only one whose god smiled.*

"Don't feed their ego, Eva, it's bigger than they are."

"And cynicism makes you small." Lizeth hiked up their robe and jumped down, barefoot, into the bilge water. They winked at Donya as they waded past her. As they grabbed the ladder with their good hand, they shouted, "I'm going to see if there's any food left in the mess!" Eva watched them climb up, nimble as a dancer even with one bad shoulder.

Donya slapped the rusty lever on the pump. Eva turned back to face her. "Come along. You can pump while you talk."

They stood side by side to work the lever, lifting it up and then forcing it down, pushing bilgewater through the floor-level valves and down and out through the pistons. The handle creaked. Soon, Eva's arms burned. Her tutors in seamanship had explained the task, but this was the first time she'd attempted it herself. Sweat dripped down her brow. She wished fervently for a handkerchief and cursed herself for possessing the determination of an ox and the strength of a cucumber.

Donya also had no great gifts of strength. Godmarks shone on her straining arms as she pushed the lever to Eva. Water droplets and a dozen differently-shaped leaves, broken bones and curved ulu blades, all shimmering teal, wrapped up her arms like gloves.

"What do you do here?" Eva asked her, forcing the lever back over to Donya's side.

"Nothing important." Donya lowered her head and pushed. Water sloshed around her boots. "I'm just the ship's healer."

"Oh. How did you get your magic?"

"I grew up on Kossi. Small island southwest of Upailit. Heard of it?"

Eva nodded. Upailit was the smallest of the five islands counted as Five Sisters. There were smaller islands than it in the region, of course, but islands like Kossi had never been counted as full sisters for the purposes of the mapmakers. "The Island of Poets."

"I was never much of a poet. Small islands like Kossi, they stamp a reputation on you when you're five or six, and that's it, that's you, for your whole life. I dropped my grandma's best knife off the pier once. That was it. I was the fuck-up. Now, my older sister, she was golden. We're Sea People, didn't knew if you noticed—"

"I saw the webbing on your hands."

"—but my sister is *proper* Sea People. Doketty. Better swimmer and diver than me. Knows all the traditional poems. All the elders love her. Our grandmother taught her all the rites of Hewia. She's our goddess. The goddess of healing."

"I thought the Sea People all worshipped Heraline." Though Eva would be the first to admit she did not know much about their beliefs. The Sea People who dwelled within the Republic kept quiet about such things; after all, Commander Gavon had outlawed religious practice of any kind after the revolution. But she knew Heraline, the goddess of the ocean, had been a Sea People god long before the Soladiseans had prayed to her. Their world was more sea than land, and the goddess who embodied its mysteries and its rage was mighty indeed. The tales Eva had heard as a child framed Heraline as the primal ignorance Iunos had conquered to build the Empire of Soladis, the rage that lit the demon-fires on the moon. She had also been the wife of Morghaia. Eva wondered, every now and then, what that marriage must have been like. What had they talked about at dinner?

"Heraline is the most well-known," Donya said. "She's the goddess of the ocean, and also the currents that connect us to each other, so she's hard to keep secret. Even some Soladiseans worshipped her, back in the days of the Empire. All the different Sea People nations have their own connection to her. Some see her as a teacher, a protector, or a mother. Some pray to her, some give her gifts of respect, and some of us only greet her nicely if we meet her at sea. She matters a great deal to the Six Brother Clans on Upailit. On Kossi, Hewia is closest to us. But we keep quiet about our local gods. We don't want the Republic coming after them."

Eva nodded. "Quite reasonable."

"After the Republic rose," Donya continued, "when the revolutionaries trespassed into our lands to hunt gods, Hewia hid away in a cave on the island just south of us. It was a sacred place. Only my grandma and the women she'd chosen could go there, and they didn't go often, because they didn't want soldiers seeing them. One night, my grandma had a dream. She said that Hewia had decided to bind herself to my sister—"

"She decided to die?"

"We don't see it how the Soladiseans do."

Eva thought the term *Soladisean* for herself was a bit inaccurate, as she had never set foot on the island of Soladis, and had spent her life in the Five Sisters. But she supposed the term *Sea People* was a bit inaccurate as well, for while many Sea People were skilled swimmers and sailors, they spent most their time on land. She supposed Donya could use whatever terms she wished. After all, her people had been here first. "How do you see it? The act of godreaping?"

"Gods die and come back like the summer becomes winter and then becomes spring. Sometimes a season lasts too long and needs changing. Then the gods choose to bond with someone who can set things right."

Eva shivered. *What if the Skullrunner wanted me to kill it because it wanted me to use its magic for evil? To harm the Republic and try to re-establish the Theocracy?* The sight of that shadowy smile flashed through her mind again. But surely her father wouldn't have hunted down the Skullrunner if there was the slightest chance of that.

Donya's tone grew heavier. "Now, a fever came to Kossi. Lots of people got sick. Grandma had it bad. So did my sister, and her oldest son. I was looking after them. Grandma knew she didn't have long, and my sister would go soon after. So she said to me, real quiet, that she'd lied about her dream. The goddess didn't want Doketty. She wanted me. Grandma had planned to send her Doketty anyway, but now my sister couldn't go. So I had to go kill Hewia and bring her power back to the village."

"She lied?" Eva said. "About a dream from her god?"

"She lied," Donya said. "But I think the second story was the lie. She would say anything to save my sister. And I would do anything, so that's on me. I thought Hewia would be looking for my sister to come. So I took her parka, her boots, and her mittens. They were too big for me, so I stuffed them with scraps of seal skin. I took her favorite canoe over to Hewia's island. I prayed, too. I didn't know the rites, but I whispered over and over, the whole way across, how grateful I was for her sacrifice, how much we needed her, how I hoped Hewia would be happy with me. She met me on the shore. And I took my sister's knife and . . . did what I did."

Donya fell silent. Hesitantly, Eva asked, "What happened next?"

"I went home. I saved my sister's life, and my nephew, and three of the elders, too. But it was too late for my grandma."

"I'm sorry."

Eva could not read what was written on Donya's face. It was a tangle of feelings. The healer lowered her brow and threw her weight into pushing the pump handle back to Eva. The loud metal creak filled the hull. "No one would believe me if I said she had blessed my going," Donya said. "And so I left, before they could exile me for what I'd done. I met Cevette in a port on Upailit a few weeks later. She was meeting with elders from the Six Brother Clans to see if they knew something about her family."

"Oh. Does she belong to one of the clans?" She had not known Cevette was one of the Sea People, but she supposed the captain had good reason to keep her kinfolk a secret, with how the Republic wanted to arrest and hang her.

"Cevette's family is her story to tell. But if you hear us speaking Kossket, or calling each other cousin, that's why. So, with her, I have a little bit of home on *Sea Wolf.* But I haven't been back to my island in the five years since I left."

Eva reached out and squeezed Donya's hand. "I'm sorry to hear that. Truly. Would you like a hug?"

"Do you have any food?"

Eva dug around in her pocket and pulled out a bundle of dried beef she had found in the sea chest at the foot of her hammock. Cevette had told her those chests, which had belonged to a sailor who had left the crew to get married, could be hers. Eva had decided to assume that all the contents could be, too. She'd found some copper pennies there, too, which were in her other pocket, along with Korinne's diary. She still wanted to keep it close. It was a comfort. A reminder she was allowed to have her fears.

She passed the dried meat to Donya. "Thank you," the healer said, and bit down.

They pumped until mid-afternoon, when the ship bell rang out the watch change, and then they limped back up to the upper deck. Donya introduced her to more of the crew: notable among them, the rotund Mr. Smoke, the ship's cook, who had godmarks of dancing golden flames on his arms and a round, hairy belly covered in tattoos of dancing women. He urged her to guess what his power was while lighting his pipe with a fingertip. The pirates passed it around, laughing as they sunned themselves and mended nets. At the center of their ring, which had assembled just outside the door to the captain's cabin, at the foot of the quarterdeck, a pile of coins and tokens lay on a woven-reed mat.

"Join us for dice!" Mr. Smoke said. "We're celebrating."

"What are we celebrating?"

He paused. "I got new shoes." He lifted a foot to show off well-made dress slippers, Halston leather with silver buckles.

Eva raised an eyebrow. "Where'd you get those?"

"From my new friend." Mr. Smoke slapped her on the back and offered her a cup. Three bone dice rattled in the bottom. "Bet your coin, and roll. The highest number takes the pot."

"Is that all?" Eva asked, deciding to let the shoes go. She needed friends on this ship, and she preferred the boots she had now.

"Pirates can't play complicated games," Donya said. "If we argue about rules, someone'll get shot, and I'll waste my time fixing them."

Eva pulled a coin from her pocket and dropped it on the mat. Everyone else tossed in scraps of gold; one man adds a crimson parrot feather. "You'll had to excuse me if I'm bad at this," Eva said. "I've never gambled." She bit her tongue, then, afraid that had been the wrong thing to say.

Mr. Smoke slapped her shoulder. "First time? Gather round, everyone, it's her first time throwing dice!"

Cheers rose from bow to stern. Sailors clustered around, sweaty, hot, and eager, elbowing for a view. Some slid down from the rigging; some ran up from below. "Roll!" they chanted, as Eva shook the cup theatrically. Her pulse kept pace with each clatter of the dice. "Roll! Roll! Roll!"

A pistol fired. All eyes went to Cevette, high up on the quarterdeck, gunsmoke wafting from the lip of her pistol.

"Do none of you have work?" she bellowed.

"Captain," Eva said. "We can take a few minutes. You run this ship better than any Republic naval commander. We're far ahead of schedule."

Cevette narrowed her eyes. "How do you know my schedule?"

"Well, I can see the angle of the sun at Smallfoot Point." Eva waved to the rocky peninsula off to starboard, thinking back to her lessons in Halston. "We're southwest of Halston, but we've just turned northwest, to round the crest of Soladis. Once we pass it, we'll be en route to the Lonely Isles. The Republic navy will be hard-pressed to catch us there."

Cevette paused, studying her. Eva shivered. No one had ever quite looked at her like that. Like the captain's eyes were searching for treasure in her own. "You know your way around a navigational chart."

"Well enough to know when the winds favor me."

"We may yet want to keep our speed." A teasing note crept into her voice. "We've caught a lucky wind. Can we count on that to last?"

Eva held up the dice cup. "Give me two minutes, and we'll see where our luck stands."

Cevette grinned. "Very well, Miss Gavon. Throw."

The moment stretched out between them, as delicate as a spider's thread. Eva turned back to Donya, Mr. Smoke, and their circle of friends. The cup rattled. Dice tumbled about its insides. She sank to her knees. Everyone held their breath.

She threw.

Six. Six. And one more six.

All around the circle, pirates leapt to their feet, shouting and whooping. The cheers spread across the upper deck. Two celebratory pistol-shots fired in her honor. Eva pressed her hands to her cheeks, giggling. Maybe this was a good omen.

"Were those dice loaded?" Donya muttered.

"You think I'm a cheat?" An irate Mr. Smoke folded his arms. Then he grabbed at something before it could fall from his sleeve.

Cevette descended the steps from the quarterdeck. *She's coming to speak to me,* Eva thought. The noon sun shimmered on her hair, the leather epaulets of her shoulders, the crook in her nose where a break didn't set. Eva smiled at her. But the captain walked right past her, moving at a brisk clip. Her shoulders trembled, as if she was on the brink of tears.

Something's wrong, Eva thought. Perhaps it was none of her concern. But she could not bear the sight of Cevette's discomfort. Not after Cevette had so kindly welcomed her aboard. *And perhaps I can help her.*

Cevette stepped through the door of the captain's cabin. All thoughts of propriety deserted her as Eva followed Cevette inside.

LOST AND FOUND

ABOARD THE SHIP *SEA WOLF*, FORTY MILES WEST OF HALSTON. 26TH KASPERMONTH, YEAR TWENTY-TWO OF THE GOLDEN REPUBLIC.

When my only daughter showed an aptitude for language, I sent her to join the current women. As a mother, I weep for her, as a woman of the Wichil Nation, I know it must be done. The Sea People are divided in many matters, yet we do not forget what history has taught us. Our sisters who travel between the nations and speak all tongues connect the Sea People as the currents connect the islands. –'Our History of the Golden Republic,' published in **The Dawn Beacon.**

"CAPTAIN?" EVA SAID, PUSHING the door shut behind them. The knob was shaped like a brass swan. The cabin itself was small but opulent. Blue velvet rugs, trimmed with gold tassels, covered the beams of the floor. A candelabra swung above a plush bed with a gilded frame. In one corner stood a claw-footed wardrobe; in the other stood a mirror. A glass window looked out on the bright sea.

And everywhere, *everywhere*—was clutter.

Nautical charts engulfed one wall, tacked atop each other with daggers, scrawled with the inkings of a fast and frantic hand. The other wall was covered with paintings that depicted scenes from every corner of the Isles, so many they were also stacked atop the floor. Half a dozen sculptures stood there, too, covered in Cevette's clothes. Pillows, papers, and a belt lay scattered across the rug. The captain's desk was bolted to the nearest wall;

Cevette sat at it, frantically sketching a pair of pied ducks in reeds with a charcoal pencil.

"You shouldn't come in here without my permission," Cevette said. Something shone on her cheek.

"I'm sorry," Eva said. She took another step toward the captain. "Are you crying?"

Cevette set down the pencil, turned to face Eva, and smiled. Eva, who almost never picked up on hints like these, realized the smile was false. "I owe you my apologies as well. I should be welcoming you to the ship, not running off to—"

The ship tossed. A small, framed portrait fell off Cevette's desk and landed near Eva's foot. She picked it up.

"No! It's not you!"

But it was. A hand-sketched portrait of a woman with a long face and thin cheeks, dark hair and a soft smile. Cevette's signature lay in the corner. Eva pressed a hand to her mouth. Heat flooded her cheeks. The back of her neck prickled. Cevette had drawn her with the gentleness of a lover. She had never felt more beautiful. More *wanted.*

"My sincerest apologies." Cevette snatched the portrait back. Their fingertips brushed. Sparks tingled up Eva's arm. "I drew this long before I met you. She was—dear—to me."

"What was her name?"

"I don't know." Cevette lowered her head. Strands of her chopped blonde hair flopped loose over her forehead. "Whatever the commander did to my memory was targeted, and powerful. A great deal of my past is lost in fog. Some nights, I lie awake and try to remember the first time I saw the sun set into the ocean. The memory pours through my mind like sand through my fingers. I don't know who my parents were. Where I was born. The name of my clan—I'm one of the Sea People, though I don't look it—"

"Donya told me," Eva said. "If you don't mind me asking, ma'am, how do you know that?"

"I don't mind," Cevette said. "It's a tricky thing, how we know what we are. My earliest memories are of washing up on a beach on Upailit, five years ago. I was confronted by a group of trappers. They thought I might have been part of a Sea People raiding party. They would have shot me if they'd found webbing on my hands. And I knew my fear was that they would see who I was."

"That must have been terrifying," Eva said.

Cevette nodded. "Then I made it to the Republic fort that warriors of the Ya Tonim Nation of Crab Island had just burned. A group of Upailitan women were guarding the ruins. The soldiers had been forcing them to build ships for the navy. They had invited the Ya Tonim to attack, and given them the ships as a gift of thanks. They were wise women, with no reason to trust strangers. When I approached the burned-out fort, they spoke to me in Kossket first. I answered in the same. I later learned there were three women waiting to ambush me in the undergrowth."

"There was a Republic fort on Upailit?" Eva frowned. "But that would violate our treaty with the Six Brother Clans."

"That it did," Cevette said. "So we burned it. Commander Gavon erased it from the memory of the citizens of the Republic. But his power does have its limits; it seems he lacked the strength to take the memory from us as well."

Eva nodded. Yes, that all seemed like something her father might do. To lose a battle to the Ya Tonim would be a great embarrassment to him. She had often heard him rage about the Sea People and the treaties the Assembly had negotiated with them. He did not seem to think of them as full people; many in the Isles did not, citing their poverty as proof of some innate lack.

But Eva had learned differently. One of the illegal papers Zeke occasionally smuggled her was *The Dawn Beacon,* written and distributed by the Wichil Nation on Broken Hook Island. It described life in their villages, their ceremonies and celebrations, their folktales and their jokes. It had also described the long history of their struggles, peaceful and otherwise, against the waves of colonists who had planted their banners on their shores. The citizens of the Republic would rob the Sea People of their wealth, then use their poverty as justification to rob them more. It was a disgusting way to see the world and one she wanted no part of.

"So you knew the language," Eva said. "And you knew the fear. You must be from Upailit, or the nearby islands. That duck you're drawing—they live on Upailit. I've seen pictures in books."

"Anyone can learn to draw a duck," Cevette said. "I have ties to Upailit, but I can't be certain I'm *from* there. You see my short hair? It's the mark of a current woman. Do you know what that means?"

Eva hesitated. "I know that most Sea People women stay close to the villages where they were born. It can be dangerous for them to leave, and they're needed to care for their villages and their families while the men travel and trade. Some say it's an archaic way of doing things. But I've read that, in most Sea People cultures, the female elders are the true leaders." She felt briefly excited to share what she knew; then her cheeks burned as she realized that, of course, Cevette knew it as well.

"That's the broad way of looking at it," Cevette said. "Though, of course, there is a good deal of difference between all the Sea People nations. One tradition we all share is that of the current women. When our ancestors first arrived in the Seaward Isles, very long ago, they knew we would split into separate nations and clans. So they made an agreement to send girls with a gift for language to travel the nations, learning the tongues, tales, and traditions of them all. The current women travel with the men of the clan and serve as translators and diplomats, and they speak with the authority of their elders on distant islands. Because the flow of the currents affects not one clan, but all of them, the current women serve as diplomats and advocates, connecting us so that we may face the challenges that threaten us all."

"How many languages do you speak?" Eva asked.

"At least seven. More, depending on how one categorizes languages."

Eva's eyes widened. It was a prodigious feat. "So all because you know Kossket doesn't mean you're from Upailit or Kossi or any of the nearby islands. It must be tricky indeed, to discern your past, if you have so much knowledge from so many places. But that's how it was clear to the Sea People women you met on Upailit that you were one of them. From your hair, and from your skill with tongues . . ."

"There's more." Cevette hesitated. "The women gave away all the ships save one. An elder had dreamed that the goddess Parha—Heraline, the Soladiseans call her—needed them to keep the *Sea Wolf* for a time. When they heard my story, that I needed a ship to find everything I'd lost, they gave her to me."

"The goddess sent them a dream about you?" A hint of awe crept into Eva's voice. "I see. So that's how you know you're one of the Sea People."

"No," Cevette said. "The Sea People women who bled to build this ship trusted me with it. That's how I know." She smiled. "I'm sure the rest of the tale is widely told through the Republic. I travelled the port towns of Upailit and built my first crew—that's where I met Donya—and we raided the Soladisean settlements north of the treaty line, raising our strength. Most of the first crew went back to Upailit when I decided to sail south and cast a wider net for my answers, but some stayed."

"They all seem quite close," Eva said.

"It's a good crew I've built over the years," Cevette said. "Many of them are as close as family to me. But I still need to find the family and the people I've lost. And I've seen beautiful women all over the Isles, but none of them . . . none of them are her."

Eva didn't quite know what to say to that. How to comfort that heavy a sorrow. "That must be awful," she whispered.

Cevette bit her lip. The ship creaked and shifted. A leather-bound book slid several inches across the floor. "You do and say all these small things that . . . resonate . . . with me. Around you, my buried memories stir. I've met dozens of echoes, but no others draw me like you. Is it possible that you could be . . . ?" She trailed off. Scared to ask.

"Hardly possible. Not unless your ardor enabled you to break into Father's fortress each night. Besides, I was seventeen five years ago. How old were you, Captain?"

"That, I don't remember," Cevette said. She looked to be several years Eva's senior, though it was hard to tell how much of that was simply due to time spent with her face in the sun. "But I was a woman grown then, and I think my girl was of an age with me."

"So I don't fit." Eva wished she did. Years had passed since she'd last held another woman. And Cevette was the most handsome woman she had ever seen. But the captain had painted an echo. Not her. Not in any way that mattered. "You must had loved her a great deal."

Cevette closed her eyes. "I loved her like how a drowning man loves the sea: in the utter darkness, she was all I could trust to be there."

Something broke in the captain's manner. She lowered her head. Eva didn't know what to do. She reached out for her. Cevette took her hand and squeezed it, steadying herself. A smile spread across Eva's face and vanished when she thought *is it* my *comfort she wants, or is it* hers?

"One moment," Cevette said, pulling back from her. The captain squared her shoulders and took a deep breath, composing herself "There's someone who can help us." She went to the door, opened it, leaned out, and shouted, "Mr. Lovett!"

A tall, scrawny, sunburned man with a scraggly beard, thick glasses, and violet godmarks stepped into the cabin and shut the door behind him. He gave Eva a jerky nod. "Mr. Selig Lovett, at your service."

Eva curtsied. The ship lurched. A carved whale tooth fell off the top of a bookshelf and struck her by the ear. She reached out and caught it before it could hit the ground. "And I at yours," she said, setting the tooth on Cevette's desk. "It's quite something to see so many godreapers in one place. Even my father only has a handful at his command."

"He had a fair number of them ten years ago," Cevette said. "But the Demon killed most of them, and the commander has erased their names from memory."

Eva shivered. "How do you know that? How can you be certain what's altered and what's true?"

"We think most of what he does is conceal information that would damage him and his allies politically," Lovett said, his voice scratchy but deep. "Once you know and accept the truth of what he does, you'll have a better sense of when he's shifting your memory. You'll be able to resist his efforts, keep the shape of the truth in your mind. He mostly targets Republic citizens, people whose perceptions matters to him, but he does occasionally change things for us. His magic varies in power: the older an echo, the stronger the sacrifice, and an echo's age is cut in half whenever she's split, so he tries to save older echoes for when he truly needs them. And how he focuses the power matters, too. If he's shifting the memory of just one person, he can do much more than if he means to shift it for thousands."

"Mr. Lovett has the power of the Lorekeeper," Cevette said. "He can view any book ever written from afar. He serves as the ship's first mate and as my expert philosopher. Do you still have the object that the Demon gave to you?"

Eva nodded. She reached in her pocket and pulled it out from between the pages of Korinne's diary. It looked like a newspaper that had gotten wet and dried clumpy, though it felt strangely dense in her hand. The ink on the surface had blurred together, making it hard to read. She did see *Evazina Gavon* printed on one line and *tunnels* printed a bit further down.

"Fascinating." Lovett tilted his head to the side. "A memory."

"Excuse me, what?" said Eva.

"It's a memory. Caught in physical form. One of yours. The Demon must have been serious about recruiting you, even before she knew you had taken the Skullrunner."

"But I'm not missing any memories. I would know."

"Burn it. Take it back." Cevette took a candle off her desk, lit it with a flint, and held it out to Eva. Lumpy tallow wax ran down the sides. "If it's nothing, then it's nothing. You'll know."

Eva held the flame to the not-quite-paper. It ignited. Flame swept through it in a white-hot wave. It crumbled into ash before it could as much singe her fingertips.

"Wait!" Cevette shouted. "You should probably sit *down*—"

A memory seized her. She stood shivering in the darkness, breathing in a claustrophobic fog that smelled of mildew and decay. A lantern shone in her fist. She took three steps down a dirt-floored hallway. A door carved with a skull hung open in the brick wall to her right. *The mortuary.* She was in the dungeons, deep beneath the fortress. The undertaker was scheduled to come the next morning and haul away the corpses. His cart was one of the few that the soldiers wouldn't search. She meant to slip aboard, ride it all the way to the harbor, and find a ship that would carry her far away.

"Eva!" a familiar voice said behind her. She turned. There was Zeke, holding a lantern of his own. "There you are. I thought you'd been kidnapped. We've been searching the whole fort for you."

She cursed. She hadn't told him of her plan. He had been acting so strangely in recent months, and had become so much more sympathetic to her father. She hadn't trusted him. She hadn't realized he'd come looking for her.

"What are you doing down here?" Zeke said. "Eva—"

"Get her," the commander said.

Three soldiers rushed at Eva. One punched her in the gut. She doubled over, retching, gasping for air. The lantern fell from her hand. A boot slammed into her ribcage. Stars flashed before her eyes. She slammed down in the dirt.

"No!" A *crack* rang out as Zeke's fist connected with a jaw. "What are you doing? Commander—sir—call them off! Call them off now! You—Stanton, Byway, leave her alone!"

And they did.

The soldiers turned on Zeke. He was taller and stronger, but they had the numbers. Two struck him in the stomach; another kicked his legs out from under him. He slammed down into the earth. Dust flew. The soldiers laughed. "Frontier trash. Men like you are barely one step up from Sea People." They kicked at him, stomping on his chest and arms. Zeke grunted and cursed, reaching out for Eva with one hand. She pushed herself up and stumbled toward him. A soldier knocked her down once more and laughed.

Commander Gavon watched, gray eyes unmoving. He carried a squirming burlap sack on his shoulders. "Bind them," he said, as Zeke spat out blood and Eva struggled in the dirt. The soldiers tied their hands.

When the commander set down the bag, an echo girl, perhaps six years old, tumbled out. She wore a long white dress and was missing one shoe. "Where's Mama?" she shouted, gazing up at the soldiers. "Mama! Help!" The commander lifted his hands. A cold light gathered in his palms.

"No!" Eva shouted. "Please—take me! Not her!"

"I have better uses for an echo of your age. But I'm certain your time will come, Evazina." He grabbed the child by the collar. "Don't be afraid, little one. This won't hurt."

A shining beam shot out from his palm and struck the girl in the side. The light stretched out to wrap her in a glowing cocoon. Threads of power poured back into the commander. He smiled, soaking it in. Eva screamed. Zeke cursed. Even the soldiers who had beat them looked uneasy, though they said nothing.

The cocoon pulsed. Wiggled. Slowly, it pulled apart. What was left of the echo were two babes, perhaps three years old each, screaming and wailing. The scraps of the cocoon were hardening into rough clumps of not-quite-paper.

"What have you done?" Eva gasped.

"Their discomfort is temporary. They only need me to create a past for them. It won't take long." The commander cupped her chin in one glowing hand. "I will give you and Ezekiel one more chance. Show me your spirit, Eva. Show me all you can do for me."

The light filled her mind. Words of black ink bloomed across the cocoon. Eva screamed.

"Miss Gavon!"

Her eyes flew open. She was back in Cevette's cabin, doubled-over and gasping. The captain had grabbed her shoulder. "Miss Gavon, are you well?" Cevette passed Eva her handkerchief. Eva twined the scrap of silk through her fingers as she straightened, still trembling. "What did you remember?"

"I was right," Eva whispered. "He does sacrifice us. I was truly right to run." She knew the truth now; she could not deny it. Yet it brought her no comfort at all.

"Let me get you something to drink," Lovett said, and dashed out the cabin door. It swung shut behind him.

Cevette gazed up at her. "Was that all?"

"All?" Her head was spinning. That memory had taken place only a few months ago. She'd previously remembered her injuries as the result of her and Zeke getting drunk and falling off a stable roof. "Oh. No. I'm sorry. I didn't recover any moments with you. I wish I had. It would be more pleasant than . . . than the truth."

"Very well." Cevette nodded. For a heartbeat, she looked as if she were about to cry once more. Then she drew a deep breath. "It's good we've kept to a firm schedule. The Demon said there's a Republic archive on Moonwhisper Isle. We'll stop in and raid it. Burn the stolen memories. And, if I'm lucky, I'll get back some scrap of what I'm missing."

"And the people of the Isles will get back some of what my father took from them."

"Indeed." Cevette nodded. "I would much appreciate your assistance on this journey, Miss Gavon."

Eva hesitated. She quite liked this plan of Cevette's. She would be much more at ease, sailing with pirates, now that she knew there was some justice in their aims. But . . . "I've never been much of a help to anyone. It's Andreas you want for that."

"I'm not asking him. I'm asking you."

Eva hesitated. The warm brown of Cevette's eyes caught her gaze. She realized they were the same color as the timbers of the ship.

The *Sea Wolf* lurched.

Eva's stomach flipped. Cevette swore. "Follow me," she said.

They raced out of her cabin. The ship tossed back and forth. Eva leaned against the cabin door to steady herself. Cevette remained balanced on the balls of her feet. All across the upper deck, sailors cursed as they slammed into one another. Lovett, carrying a clay cup, shouted as a shifting crate knocked his legs out from beneath him. Something green flashed in the sea—off to port, then off to starboard, then all about them. Eva braced herself.

And the entire ocean heaved up in a spray of foam.

"Serpent!" bellowed Cevette.

The beast reared up at the bow, high enough to rival the mainmast. Fanlike fins covered its neck and protruded from its sides, its skin a mottled green and brown like a kelp forest. The jaws of its lizardlike head opened, flashing yellow fangs. The smell of rotting flesh washed over the upper deck as it roared. Hooks, harpoons, and barbs stuck out from the fresh wounds on its face. *Sea Wolf* wasn't the first ship it tangled with. Eva dearly hoped it would be the last.

Sailors ran toward the bow and drew their guns. A barrage of pistol-shots cracked through the air. Bullets bounced off its scales, leaving behind grazes no deeper than cat-scratches. The serpent growled. The ship lurched once more. Eva stumbled forward and nearly fell as a green tail emerged from the waves off to port, topped by a fan-like fin ten feet across.

"Mr. Lovett, take the helm!" Cevette shouted. "Gun crews, take the starboard cannons! Mr. Smoke, coordinate the lower deck." The crew divided, some running across the deck, some racing down the stairs into the hold. Cevette glanced back over her shoulder and met Eva's eyes. "Miss Gavon, go below."

Eva nodded and sprinted for the lowered deck. The masts, sails, and maze of rigging towered high above her. Planks creaked. The scent of salt and tar washed over her. The ship pitched. She grabbed a rope for balance, and winced as the rough hemp fibers rubbed against her uncallused palm.

Run. Run. She scrambled down the stairs to the lower deck and pushed her way through a maze of hammocks and flailing garlands that had come loose from their posts. Three cannons stood at the ready, powder, ammunition, and rods chained to the wall beside each one. Mr. Smoke and his friends manned two; Donya waved Eva over to hers. Someone had painted flowers up and down the wooden frame of the cannon mount.

"Prime your shots!" shouted Mr. Smoke, his voice raspy. Eva rolled a ball down the cannon's barrel, grunting a bit from the weight. Cevette hadn't told her to help, but she hadn't told her *not* to, and she wanted to do her part. Donya stepped up beside her, ramming the round home with a tamping rod. "Hold it! Hold it!"

Sea Wolf wheeled about, nimble as a dancer. The serpent clicked and hissed. A mantle of magic hung over it, a fog that whispered to Eva in the wordless language of Death. *A half-dozen sailors have died in that throat.* She had to prime the shot. She braced herself against the cannon, shielding the powder-horn with her body as waves slapped through the gun ports. Water drenched her shirt, soaking through to her stays, but the powder stayed dry as it tumbled into place. She stepped free.

Outside the gun ports, the green coils of the serpent flashed into view.

"Plug your ears!" shouted Mr. Smoke. "Fire!"

Sparks flew from his fingers. Three *boom*s rang out. Each one pounded through Eva's chest like a drumbeat. Cannons recoiled, flying backward, chains jingling as they stretched taut. The serpent's back fin evaporated into crimson. It howled as chunks of red muscle were exposed to the air. Donya slapped Eva on the back, and Eva pulled her into a hug. Every pirate on the lower deck cheered, voices blending with the serpent's screams.

"Fire!" Cevette shouted. Cannons boomed out above. Glowing missiles streaked across the day and slammed into the beast's belly. It thrashed wildly. Its guts spilled into the sea, reeking of bile and rot.

Sea Wolf lurched sideways. So did Eva's heart.

They were still in danger.

"That thing's still moving!" Eva shouted. Its blood-streaked, fan-shaped tail slapped the sea in punctuation, throwing up a wave of crimson foam. "It's going to swamp the ship!"

"I could try to heal it!" Donya yelled.

"Clear the cannons!" Mr. Smoke shouted. "Reload!"

But it would take a minute or more to fire a second volley. The cannons had to be cleaned of debris between each shot. Eva looked to Mr. Smoke. "Do you have a grenade?"

He reached into his baggy trousers, pulled out a small bomb, and tossed it to her. It was a small, thin iron sphere, packed with gunpowder and, no doubt, shards of iron so that the blast would rip into flesh. "Always. Why?"

Eva snatched up a flint and lit the fuse. It sparked. She sprinted up the stairs, into the sunlight, focusing with all her might on the spot where Death touched the deck. Cevette stared at her. "What the—"

A bone portal opened. Her instincts took over. She leapt into Death, out the nearest exit—and slammed into a wall of flesh and darkness.

Eva gasped. Something *crunched* in her chest. She gasped in pain, and slime flooded through her lips, hot and coppery. All was wet, and all was dark, save the light of the fuse. The walls of the serpent's throat wrapped tight about her. They pushed with bone-crushing strength.

Eva closed her eyes and dropped back into Death.

She hit the deck just as the serpent's head exploded.

The ship bobbed back and forth as the dying serpent sank beneath the waves. Eva's ears rang. She tried to stand, and stumbled sideways with a gasp of pain. Cevette wrapped an arm under her shoulders and hauled her up onto her feet. Every sailor on the upper deck turned from their cannon to face her; more came up the stairs from below and stared at her with wide and awestruck eyes.

Donya ran to Eva's side and pulled a jar of ointment from the pocket of her skirt. She pushed up Eva's shirt and cut the laces on her stays with a knife. "Don't think this means I like you," she said, and slathered the waxy substance on Eva's chest. Her fingers glowed blue as she rubbed the medicine into Eva's skin.

Eva cursed. Hot streaks of pain flew across her vision. She leaned into Cevette, bracing her forehead against the warmth of the other woman's neck. The captain held her steady. Eva focused on that, on the heat of her. Healing magic washed through her like the sea. At last, the pain died away.

"Your rib is fixed," Donya said, wiping the goo from her hands onto Eva's loose stays. "Excuse me. I need to go smoke." She strode off toward the rail.

Cevette led Eva to a pile of crates that had slid back to nearly the quarterdeck, on the starboard side. She helped her to sit and said, "Are you well? Truly?"

"Yes, ma'am," Eva said. "Truly."

Cevette clasped her the forearm. Warmth glowed on her eyes. "Thank you. *Thank you.* By the gods, Miss Gavon, you're the most audacious woman I've ever met."

Yes, Eva realized, somewhere in the haze of her spinning thoughts. She could be quite audacious indeed. That was the strength she could bring to this ship. That was why Cevette wanted her aboard. These people needed her courage, and she wanted them to have it.

"I'll help you find and free the stolen memories," she told Cevette. "Listen to me. I . . ." *I only ask for your respect,* she almost said, but she didn't need to. She already had it.

And, for that, she was profoundly glad.

"Welcome to the crew of *Sea Wolf.*" Cevette squeezed her wrist and turned to face the crew. "Miss Gavon sails with us!"

The crew cheered. Mr. Smoke whooped and leapt into the air. Even Lizeth tried to lift their fist aloft before wincing in pain.

With that, Evazina Gavon was home.

A Bounty

Beginning eight miles to the east of Halston, on High Hill Island, and also aboard the ship Sea Wolf, *three hundred and fifty miles west-northwest of Halston. 30th Kaspermonth, Year Twenty-Two of the Golden Republic.*

This honorable reporter is of two minds about piracy. Firstly, I consider myself to be a virtuous man. As such, I cannot hold with thievery and violence. And yet, many of those who turn to piracy do so because the Republic has no place for them. If I am to denounce the violence of pirates, must I not also denounce the violence that makes them? –'A Pirate's Life,' published in *The Silver Sentinel.*

Ezekiel Dare loved making the children smile.

Not that it was particularly challenging. He had but to flex his chest and make his shirt ripple, or bend over to play pony, or pretend to take tea with their dolls. Commander Gavon often visited the orphanages, to make certain the Republic's foster system was functioning as intended, but he did not warm easily to the children. He had asked Zeke to help him with this, and Zeke had eagerly agreed. Hunting down the abominations the Demon of Dogshead had released to cover her retreat from the fortress had worn away at him. It was good to remember that duty could lift his spirits as well as drain them.

The Halston city orphanage lay outside the city proper, in the rolling hills of the farmland. They had ridden an hour to reach it on that cloudy morn. It was a tall building, all red brick, slanting rooftops, and square windows that peered down like watchful eyes. Smoke rose from its chimney. Gray leaves overflowed from its gutters. The hills that lay behind it had been left gray by the harvest; scrub forest covered their crests, where the gentry hunted deer and foxes. The brick wall that ringed the orphanage was topped by iron spikes every foot, and six soldiers guarded the only gate.

A safe place, Zeke thought, as he ran across the browning grass lawn that stretched out before the orphanage. A pack of children followed at his heels, laughing and grabbing for his clothes. His hat had flown off in the cool autumn wind. A smear of mud ran down his cheek. As he passed a gnarled old oak tree, he spotted a small girl hiding in the shade. She was spindly and pale, with long dark hair and darker eyes. *An echo.* She was entirely alone.

Zeke knelt down to meet her eyes. "Do you want to play?"

The little echo shook her head.

"You don't have to," Zeke said. "Here. Take this." He pulled a packet of honey candy out of his jacket and pressed it into her hands. She pressed the paper close to her heart and ran, darting off toward the orphanage door.

As she went, Zeke caught sight of bruises beside her ear.

Fury bloomed within him. But the other children were catching up to him, and he did not want to frighten them. Zeke stood, and pretended to trip over a root. Dropping to his knees and rolling in a practiced manner, he let the delighted children rush about him and jump on his back. Once he had two in grabbing range, he hoisted them up, one on each shoulder, and sprinted back toward the orphanage doors. The other children followed, shrieking in delight.

The orphanage doors swung open. Lord Merris, the Minister of Childhood Welfare, stepped out into the day. He was a short, pale man who wore a tall wig, and he was quite prone to shivering. Commander Gavon followed him outside. As was his fashion when out of uniform, he wore black from head to toe. He looked down the lawn, a slight frown on his lips, and said, "Lieutenant Dare."

The commander's voice caught him like a snare. Zeke quickly set the children down. They ran off as he snapped to attention. "Yes, sir?"

"Walk with me," Commander Gavon said. "There is a matter I would discuss in private."

"Right away, sir."

The children gave Zeke disappointed looks as he followed the commander down the lawn. Lord Merris shot Zeke a glance that he desperately hoped was not jealousy; he did not need that trouble at present. The soldiers at the gate saluted, then opened the lock. Zeke pushed the heavy wooden gate open with his shoulder, then followed the commander out onto the dusty road.

Instead of following the road to the east or west, the commander set off to the north, following a trail that wound up a hill covered in farmers' fields and led to a small grove of birch trees. Dry chaff from fresh cut wheat stirred on the wind and crunched under his boots.

"I must confess, I feel much more myself outside the city." Commander Gavon peeled off his black leather gloves and revealed the golden godmarks shining on his wrists. "My family made its fortune here, in the wilds of High Hill Island. This place is home to men like you and me. It's something we share."

"I do appreciate the quiet," Zeke said, and fell silent, biting the inside of his cheek. He did not always know what to say to a man so great.

Their relationship had begun last year, when they had sailed south together for an Assembly meeting in Soladis. Along the way, the commander had plied him with gifts: fine wine, sugar candies, knives with jeweled hilts. The man had invited Zeke to his cabin and asked for help removing his wig; the next day, he'd needed strong hands to rub a knot in his lower back. It had proceeded on that course, a nighttime thing, a shadow thing, with little room for sunshine and conversation.

He followed the commander into the birch grove. The trees were slender and as narrow as silver spears. Their branches rustled and waved on the wind, the leaves only just turning yellow. The air smelled of dying earth. As a child, Zeke had heard folktales of a warrior goddess who turned the men who trespassed into birch groves into abominations. *We shouldn't be here,* he thought, for he had known himself to be a man from early in his youth, all his other parts be damned. Still, here they were.

"Thank you," Commander Gavon said, when they were finished. He fastened up his breeches, then steadied the angle of his hat. "Now. Have you thought on what it means that Eva has not yet returned to Halston?"

Zeke nodded, cleaning twigs and grass off his breeches as he stood. "I'm quite concerned for her. The soldiers who survived the Demon's attack on the walls have assured me that they witnessed her using the Skullrunner's power to flee with Captain Zarcanzi, but we have no way of knowing where she went or if she reached it safely—"

"Her power means she can come and go as she pleases. But she went off with that pirate and she has not come back. So I must assume she has joined her."

Joined her? No. Not even Eva would be that foolish. Piracy was a hanging crime, and the commander could not ignore that his own daughter had turned to it. *That would ruin her.* But she believed in the conspiracy about the sacrifices. She might believe herself safer at sea. Even Zeke had experienced a moment of doubt several days ago. He'd fallen into a terrifying daydream about his own fellow soldiers beating him senseless while the commander ripped a young echo girl apart. But such dreams were mere mist. The Republic was a truth set in steel.

"Sir . . ." Zeke hesitated. "There's no need for us to assume the worst of each other. Captain Zarcanzi must have forced her to help. She'll send us a ransom letter, surely. Pirates always do."

The commander sighed. "There's a possibility, I will allow it. I hope this pirate keeps her expectations modest. My wealth is not unlimited."

"Eva is your daughter."

"She's my foster daughter. Oh, don't look at me that way. It's not cruel. It's correct. I hold the bonds of hundreds of fosterlings, most of whom I lease out to labor on farms in the south. Compared to them, Eva has always lived in luxury. Fosterage is better than most echoes deserve."

The hair prickled on the back of Zeke's neck. He licked his lips, once, then twice. His shoulders tensed. He took a deep breath and willed himself to stay calm. "There was an echo girl at the orphanage. Someone hurt her."

The commander waved his hand dismissively. "She likely brought it on herself. Those creatures are barely one step removed from godhood. They're dangerous."

Zeke frowned. "How are they dangerous? They don't share Morghaia's magic. They don't share her thirst for conquest." Or, at least, he had never met one who did. "Do you really think Andreas and Eva are dangerous?"

"They most certainly could be dangerous, if they so chose. I have made it clear to my children what side they should be on."

"Sir, Eva is afraid of you."

"She should be. Oh, Ezekiel. Don't look at me like that. I'm responsible for the wellbeing of the entire Republic. My people are terrified of echoes, and so it falls to me to keep them in their place."

But what about your family? He had his duties, yes, but did he not have a duty to them? When Zeke thought of his parents, he thought of mending socks with his mother and his father slapping him on the back after Zeke shot his first elk. Their frontier cabin had been small and cramped, but it had been warm and full of love. Eva deserved a family like that—even Andreas deserved that. *Of course Eva hasn't come home. What does she have to come back to?*

"Your daughter deserves better from you," Zeke said.

The commander stared at him. His eyes widened. His mouth opened once or twice before he spoke. "You forget yourself."

"Eva deserves better. Your family deserves better." Zeke shook his head. "How can I build a life with a man who does not care for his family?"

The air whistled.

Zeke, who knew the sound from growing up on the frontier, threw himself at his commander and knocked him to the ground.

The arrow sunk into Zeke's side.

Red pain shot through his chest. His heart jolted. His nerves screamed. And his training took hold. "Stay down!" he shouted at Commander

Gavon. The commander obeyed, lying, stunned, in the dirt. *Good.* Zeke checked his wound. The arrowhead had punctured the wool lining of his coat and sunk into the fat of his stomach. It was in securely. It wouldn't move.

So Zeke turned and sprinted in the direction it had come from. Silver birch trees rushed past him. His boots crunched in the undergrowth. He held up his arms to knock branches aside. Each step was agony. He let his body scream at him. It was only pain, and he deserved it. *Fool,* he told himself as he went. *We rode slowly. Our horses were visible from the road. Anyone could have seen us.* There were no reports of rebels in this area, but all a would-be rebel had to do was hop over the wall from the frontier side. But Zeke had never seriously considered the potential of an ambush. This was the Golden Republic. Here, Commander Gavon was loved.

The would-be assassin had started running the moment Zeke had turned. His legs churned as he fled down the hill, out of the birch grove and into the open grass of a fallow field. His quiver bounced on his shoulders. His clothes were ragged, his boots worn, and he had the look of one who had not eaten well in weeks. As the sound of Zeke's footsteps drew closer, he turned and drew his belt knife. He looked up to Zeke with sharp defiance in his eyes.

Zeke slammed into him. More pain shot through his wound. He broke the assassin's knife arm with his first strike and his neck with the second. The man fell to the ground with a dull thud.

Is he alone? Zeke looked about himself. No movement in the long grass of the field. No movement in the trees. He took a deep, steadying breath, and took a second look at the corpse.

A rainbow of ink tattoos covered the assassin's skin. *He must have grown up on the frontier, too.* The frontier folk of the Five Sisters sometimes wrote spells and symbols on their bodies, though such witchcraft was frowned upon in the cities and among the elite. Zeke did not recognize these symbols. But the lines on the dead man's arm reminded him of a map.

He leaned down for a closer look. The world lurched. Darkness swallowed him.

FOUR DAYS AFTER HER arrival on *Sea Wolf*, Evazina Gavon robbed her first ship.

The Seaward Isles were situated in three distinct geographic regions. Most central was the large and temperate island of Soladis, home to the great city of the same name. To the south of Soladis lay the Sapphire Isles, famed for their blue waters, white shores, and the diverse peoples who dwelt upon them. The southern Sea People and the Soladisean colonists had fought many bitter battles on their shores; the Terraloro people, who shared blood with both, quarreled with both as well. To the north of Soladis lay the Five Sisters, the cold, gray, forested islands of Eva's childhood.

But there were other, more remote and less populous isles—the fangs of volcanic black rock that jutted out from the sea, impossibly high, to the northeast of Soladis, the swampy southwestern isle called Dogshead, and the bare and scattered Lonely Isles, to the southwest of the Five Sisters, which *Sea Wolf* approached one frigid afternoon. At least, the maps said that Moonwhisper, the third-largest of the Lonely Isles, was near; the sea and sky were both a cloudy, heavy gray, hiding all from sight. Eva was peering off the starboard rail with a spyglass, searching for whatever she could find, when she spotted the sloop.

It was a small vessel, thirty-five feet in length, with a single mast. Six sailors bustled about the upper deck, shouting and arguing among themselves as they tried to position the sail to catch the wind. A few crates rested on the deck, but it did not have the look of a cargo ship—no, this was a messenger vessel, built to carry news swiftly from island to island.

"Ship ahoy!" Eva shouted. All across the upper deck of *Sea Wolf*, pirates set aside their mending and tidying and rushed to the starboard rail, lining up beside her. On the sloop, a man shouted "ahoy!" back at her, and his crew mates shouted and waved their arms, beaming in relief, jumping up and down. A young man in a pale blue coat clambered up from below deck and began to dance a jig.

Then the wind shifted. Canvas snapped. Cold blew across Eva's cheeks. The flag of *Sea Wolf,* the skull weeping blood, billowed out on the wind. The sailors on the little sloop cursed and drew their pistols.

"Pirates!" shouted an older man with a thick mustache, who had to be the captain. "Give no quarter!"

"We surrender!" shouted the man in the pale blue coat. His loose ginger curls blew on the wind. "We'll give you anything you want! Don't hurt us!"

A sharp whistle rang out across the deck of *Sea Wolf.* The crew turned. "Good," said Cevette, who stood before the mainmast, the tails of her white coat billowing in the breeze. "You're already lined up." They fell silent, waiting on her command. Cevette marched up to them and strode along the row, her shoulders back, her chin held high, her boots clicking in an orderly pattern. "Listen to me, sailors. When we board, someone down there might try to be a hero. If we kill him fast, the rest will get the fear in them, and no one else has to die."

Kill him. A shiver ran down Eva's back. She'd killed a man three years ago. He'd broken into the commander's study, brandishing a pistol. She'd slashed his throat with a letter opener. The commander had praised her for her quick action, thrown his arms around her while the man's blood was still wet on her cheek. *My brave daughter.* For weeks after that, he had adored her. Then Andreas had been admitted to the philosophers' guild and it had all become *my brilliant son, my brilliant son.*

Eva had told herself she'd killed that man to save her father's life; that it had been a just action. But she'd also done it, in part, for his approval, and the knowledge of that clung to her like sea scum. How easily she could be moved to do violence. How clean and simple it felt for her to send a stranger into Death.

"Ma'am," Eva said as Cevette walked past her, "their ship is struggling."

"I know." The captain paused and turned to face her. "But they have cargo. We'll take the valuables. The rest we'll leave up to those poor bastards down there."

"Even though we could sail away?" It was a foolish question, she felt sure of it. But she would run the risk of looking foolish to save a life. Especially when she could also show the crew that *this* echo was merciful.

"Even though we could sail away. Five years ago, I washed up on a beach with nothing but my name and my two fists. Since then, I've killed two dozen people with my bare hands, and more with my cannons. It's a hard world. This is how we fight to live in it. I'm not opposed to mercy, but I put my people first. I do what's necessary to protect you. I mean to be the leader you deserve."

Eva hesitated, then nodded. "Yes, ma'am. Of course." She would watch and see how Cevette did things. She would try to understand before she levied judgement. *Or before I participate.*

In the end, Cevette selected Naeri, Lovett, Mr. Smoke, and a trio of other pirates for the boarding party. They slid down a rope to the struggling vessel. Donya, Lizeth, and Eva stayed back, leaning over the starboard rail. Each one of them held a pistol trained on the small ship's crew.

"Cevette should have let me board," Lizeth said. They had painted their eyeliner on thick that day, to help with the sun's glare, but still squinted down at the little ship. "I could use the bonus pay."

"She let you board last time," Donya said. "And you wound up summoning a lightning storm that nearly sank both ships."

"That's the cost of my magic. When I set the weather in motion, it does what it will. The wind wishes to be free."

"And I wish to remain undrowned." The wind had pulled a curl of the scarf that held Donya's hair. She pushed it back into position. "What do you need all that bonus pay for anyways? You've never owned more than three outfits."

"I wear proper tarkalma garb." They gestured toward the robe they wore. It was simple black linen, with no sleeves, wrapped around their small frame and tied with a scarlet sash. Embroidery of blooming red flowers lined the edge of the garment, running down the right side of their body from shoulder to toe.

"What's tarkalma?" Eva said. Down on the sloop, the stranded sailors dropped to their knees and lifted their hands high. Their voices wavered as they begged for mercy. Eva's stomach churned. She looked back to Lizeth.

"It's a third gender we Terraloro have. Tarkalmas cultivate a life of the mind through research, writing, and prayer."

"Oh. Do you do that?"

"Not at present." Lizeth shrugged. "I never said I was a good tarkalma. Just that I was one. Didn't you know? You've been addressing me right."

"I was mostly following Donya's example in the grammar. I didn't want to be rude."

Donya laughed. "Following my example is an *excellent* way to be rude. Especially to Lizeth." She reached out and tousled their curls. They rolled their eyes.

"Regarding the Terraloro," Eva said, "I know they're not considered Sea People by the eyes of the law, but do you count yourself as one of them? Or do you see yourself as more Soladisean?"

Lizeth sighed. Their fingers drummed on the ship's rail. "I'm Terraloro. So is my father. We have blood from a dozen Sea People nations. My mother was Hoca. She had finger webbing, and I was born with it." They lifted a hand and spread their fingers. Looking closely, Eva could see faint white scars lining the inside of each digit. "If I'm not Hoca, it's because it was cut out of me."

"What happened?" Eva said.

"My father's mother didn't approve of him bringing Hoca blood into the family. When I was four years old, she drugged me with rum and cut my webbing away with a knife."

Eva flinched. "By the gods, Lizeth. I'm so sorry."

Quietly, Donya said, "It's not the finger webbing, or any other part of your look, that says who your people are. It's your kinship ties. It's who welcomes you in when you come home."

Beneath them, Cevette and the pirates checked the stranded sailors for weapons and valuables, taking pistols from their belts and rings from their fingers, then binding their wrists and ankles with hempen cords. The youngest sailor, a mere boy, wept as Cevette took the locket from his neck. Eva's nails dug into her palms. She supposed all robberies were a bit cruel. But she felt more than a bit cruel herself for taking part in it.

She turned back to Lizeth. "Why did you turn pirate after killing your god instead of joining the Godreaper Corps?"

"Oh, fuck the Godreaper Corps. They destroyed my family's farm. Said my father was plotting a rebellion against the Republic. Which he wasn't. Not then, at least."

"Is that why you're saving up gold? To help fund a rebellion?"

Lizeth looked her over, as if weighing up what to say. Their brows narrowed. A silver hoop glittered in one of them. "Perhaps," they said. "Or perhaps I just like gold."

After the fall of the Theocracy, the people of the Sapphire Isles, of which the Terraloro had the greatest numbers, had been divided on whether or not to join the Golden Republic. The Republic had offered them seats on the Assembly and close trade ties with the northern isles; still, many people of the Sapphire Isles feared that, as had happened in the past, tying their fate to the north would lead to economic exploitation. Those in favor of union had won out, but those against had not given up the fight, and they had grown in support over the years. The assignment of seats in the Assembly had left the Sapphire Isles with fewer representatives, proportional to their population, than the regions to the north, and the seats they were allowed in the Assembly were often filled by Soladiseans who owned vast farms in the Sapphire Isles. In the illegal newspapers, Eva had read dozens of stories about the horrifying conditions those laborers faced. It did not surprise her to learn there were those in the Sapphire Isles actively conspiring to break away.

Down on the sloop, a flicker of motion caught her eye.

A cargo hatch flew open. A man leapt up from below. His lips were pulled back, baring his teeth, and his eyes were so wide they looked white. A sword flashed in his hand. The world slowed as he lunged, aiming dead at Cevette's heart.

"No!" Eva shouted. Her instincts took over. She jumped onto the ship's rail and shot. Her gun kicked upward. Her bullet flew over the man's head.

But Cevette turned at the sound. She side-stepped the blow and grabbed the man's wrist with one hand. With her free arm, she drew her pistol and shot. Blood burst from his chest. He flew backward and fell to the deck. A few gurgled gasps, and his soul dropped cleanly into Death. Cool contempt glimmered in Cevette's eyes as she gazed at the body.

Eva could not look away from her. But her leap onto the rail had left her balance off-center. Gravity took hold. Her desperate, reaching fingers closed on air as she fell forward. The world spun as she tumbled downward, over and over, wind whistling about her.

The sea hit her with a cold, wet slap. Her heart hammered in her ears. Water poured into her nose and mouth. She kicked, flailed, screamed—

"I've got you." Naeri's hands closed about her one arm. Lovett grabbed the other. Together, they plucked her from the sea and lifted her up onto the sloop. On her knees, Eva coughed and spat, hacking half the ocean out on her boots. "There you go. All's well."

"Are you hurt, Miss Gavon?" Cevette said. Concern flickered in her warm brow eyes.

"I don't think so," Eva said, and stood. She squared her shoulders and tried to appear dignified, even though she was dripping with water. *I shot at him so easily,* she thought. *Like it was nothing.* But that hadn't been because of any innate violence in her, surely. She had been protecting Cevette. Any other member of the crew would have done the same. She'd just been quickest.

The redheaded man in the pale blue coat had watched Cevette kill a man from his seat atop a water barrel. Up close, Eva could see his coat was shimmering satin, and his cravat was a plume of white lace. He was three inches shorter than her, a plump figure, his cheeks smoothly shaven and his green eyes lively. His wrists were bound, but he gripped a quill in both hands, and took clumsy notes in a book open on his knee. Eva walked up to see what he was writing. *The echo pirate fell overboard. She cannot swim.*

Eva wrung out her hair and made sure to let a few drops fall on the page, turning the ink to a black smear.

"I can't believe it," Cevette said, rummaging through a shipping crate. "You dress that richly, and you're only carrying *this*." She strode over to the barrel and thrust a handful of paper in the nobleman's face. Eva recognized the byline. *The Silver Sentinel.* "No gold, no gems. Only newspapers. What are you doing out here?"

"I was sailing back to Soladis after investigating a story in the Five Sisters," the man said. "Our ship went off course in the currents."

"You're that anonymous journalist?" Eva's mouth fell open. "You're a nobleman?"

"As a teller of truths, I consider myself one of the people—"

Cevette said, sharply, "Are you worth a ransom?"

"My name is Tomis Augustis Beauchamp, Marquis of Thistle Bay and Count of Centois. I can pay a large ransom. Please don't kill me."

"Very well." Cevette gazed down into a crate of newspapers once more, then closed it. "These are worthless to me. Naeri, leave these sailors a dull knife. They'll be able to cut themselves free by the time we're out of sight. The current will carry them to the Crest of Soladis. But we'll take the lord with us. He's worth a good ransom."

Lovett slung Tomis up over his shoulder. "Don't worry, Lord One-of-the-People. This will be a good story for your paper."

A good story, Eva thought. A good story, and a cruel deed.

A WEATHERED, DRY, AND callused hand had threaded its way between his fingers. *Father,* Zeke thought, but he opened his eyes and it was Commander Gavon who sat on the chair beside him.

"Where am I?" he whispered, his throat dry.

"Back at the orphanage," the commander said. It was a dusty attic room they'd put him in, beneath the high eaves of the house. Trunks and baskets of abandoned toys and clothing lined the walls. Wind whistled through an open window. The cot Zeke lay in had not been built for a man of his height, and his feet stuck out over the end. Someone had piled quilts on top of him. Sweat clung to his skin. Zeke pushed them back and saw a crisp linen dressing wrapped about his wound. "They have a doctor on staff. He cut out the arrowhead with a clean knife and stitched the site closed. You should make a full recovery."

"Are you hurt?"

"I strained my shoulder dragging you back to the road. But they gave me some whiskey."

"You . . . you brought me back?"

"But of course. A true leader never leaves a man behind."

He saved me. Zeke closed his eyes. Another kind of warmth filled him, one he hadn't felt in far too long. The tightness in his chest eased away. He drank in the moment, pressing it into his mind like a flower in the pages of a book. A talisman of protection to cling to should he ever doubt the commander again. *He saved me even after I stood up to him. After I told him he was wrong for how he treated Eva.*

"You have eight months left on your foster bond, correct?"

"Yes, sir."

"Good. Once it expires, I will bestow on you all the honors, titles, and properties befitting a senior officer of the army. Twenty thousand acres on New Soladis, if not more. All the Republic will honor you for the heroism you have shown today."

Zeke stared up at the commander. This time, it was not only the dryness in his throat that stopped him from speaking. *Twenty thousand acres.* That was more than anything he had ever dared to dream of. A hundred times what his parents had sought to claim on the frontier. With that much land, he would be wealthy enough to adopt every last orphan here. But why was he so shocked? This was what the Republic was meant to be. A place where merit, not birth, dictated who could rise high.

He tried to sit up. Pain shot through his chest. He remembered the impact of a boot in his gut. He heard an echo girl, screaming in the dark, and saw Commander Gavon, reaching out with a glowing hand.

"Careful there, Ezekiel." The commander squeezed his fingers. The sunlight trickling in the window cast a golden halo across the older man's lined forehead "You see what this means, don't you? When your bond expires and when you hold this land, there will be no question of impropriety when I marry you."

Zeke blinked. His voice shook. A tear rose in the corner of his eye. "You . . . you will?"

"Of course." The commander leaned in and kissed Zeke on the forehead. His lips were as dry as paper. "I need you."

I need you, too. That was why he had thrown himself over the commander, in that moment when he heard the arrow's flight. This was the man who had made his world. Zeke was nothing without him.

The commander smiled. "Do you remember what we were speaking about before you were struck? It's no trouble if you don't. It was of no great importance."

"No," Zeke lied. "I don't remember at all."

THE CHALK RULE

ABOARD THE SHIP *SEA WOLF*, EIGHT HUNDRED AND THIRTEEN MILES NORTHWEST OF HALSTON. 4TH HERALMONTH, YEAR TWENTY-TWO OF THE GOLDEN REPUBLIC.

Love is the sweetest gift / known in all lore and myth / bringing many great pleasures / so we take great measures / to secure a lover. // Love makes the heart wild / as a fosterling child / Govern it well we must / lest our manners be dust / and society suffer. –Entry for the letter *L* in *A Children's Primer of the Golden Republic.*

AFTER MORE THAN A week aboard *Sea Wolf,* Eva had adopted a routine. The first thing she did each morning, when she slid out of her hammock to dress, was to affix hidden sheaths at her wrists, ankles, hips, and armpits. She had taken a dozen daggers from the ship's armory, clean steel with hilts wrapped in black leather, near invisible under her shirt and inside her boots. After loading them, she tested the release switches in her bracers, checking that each knife drew smooth and quick. Then she donned a belt with a pair of pistols, loaded and ready, tucked into the small of her back.

"Why did you learn knife fighting?" Donya said as Eva dressed. She lay in her hammock, swinging it back and forth by kicking the support pole.

"Knives are swift, decisive, and easy to hide." She did not speak of the woodcut printing she had once come across in an old book, of Morghaia flinging knives of black smoke into her foes, not how her fingers had run over the page as if they could catch and hold true power. "What's not to like about knives?"

"They make all these little holes in people and then I have to fix them."

"Eva!" Naeri ducked out of her sewing nook and handed Eva a bundle of fabric. "It's finally ready. Wear this. To keep you safe."

Eva unfolded a long, heavy coat. The coal-black fabric drank in the in the lantern-light: skulls embroidered in red metallic thread shimmered in and out of sight. The fasteners were brass filigree; the inner lining a shocking crimson. Within the chest, shoulders, and tail were stitched thin layers of chain mail, lightweight and brimming with Naeri's magic.

"Naeri, I could kiss you for this." Eva pulled on the coat and whirled around. Its tails spun out behind her. She flipped daggers down into both her hands. Then she spun a knife on her fingertip, bounced another off her bracer, and caught both by the hilt. Naeri clapped. Donya nodded. Eva grinned.

Gods, it feels good to have friends. The thought surprised her. She'd known Zeke for eight years; she'd had Andreas by her side since she'd learned to walk. But this was different, somehow. She had always struggled to make friends. She didn't quite connect to others in the way they expected her to. But the pirates did not judge her for those failings. With no other echoes nearby, she could be the best one they knew. With no other echoes nearby, she could seem as if she was just like the rest of them. There were parts of her that could be liked, and liked well, and aboard the *Sea Wolf,* those parts of her could finally be seen.

Eva climbed to the upper deck, into the crisp, clear calm of morning. The sky was cloudless; the air smelled of the seaweed Mr. Smoke was drying over the quarterdeck rail for soup. Over by the port rail, Cevette, clad in a loose white shirt and breaches, sawed at a board mounted between two crates. A broken cannon mount lay beside her; the cannon itself was chained to the mainmast, so as not to roll about the deck while Cevette made repairs. Sweat ran down the captain's brow, the heaving muscles of her shoulders lit by the morning sun.

Eva cleared her throat. Cevette set down the saw and turned, flicking wood dust off her fingers. Eva noted her nails were neatly trimmed and quite short.

"What do you think?" Eva said, spinning in her new coat. "Naeri made it for me. Isn't it lovely?"

"You could make a burlap sack look lovely. But that coat is quite fine work." Cevette patted Eva's hip. "Adjust your belt, Miss Gavon. That pistol nearly fell out."

Eva checked her belt. The pistol hadn't budged. *Oh. She wanted to do that.* Eva smiled. "Are you going to paint that mount when you're finished? Donya has flowers on hers."

"Maybe I'll add a sea serpent. See if that scares my enemies more than a massive gun."

The crew assembled on the upper deck for weapons practice. Cevette made them stand shoulder to shoulder, lined up against the starboard rail, eyes on her, sabers lifted and at the ready. "Listen closely!" She paced down their line, a sword in her hand. "Republic nobles have deep pockets. Their ships will have dozens of mercenaries guarding their cargo. Don't assume they'll crumble at the sight of our flag. Be ready to fight. Ready to kill. Put your main foot forward and your blade up. Show me your fencing stance." The pirates fell into position, looking about themselves to mirror the stances of their neighbors. "Tuk!"

"Yes, ma'am?" said the man, who was one of the Upailitian sailors, as he stepped forward.

"Your guard is wide-open." Cevette slid forward, hitting three neat strikes to his shoulder, hip, and heart. "Keep your sword near your chest. Here, watch me."

"Donya," Eva whispered as Cevette demonstrated the correct footing. "Could you—discreetly—detail who on this ship is romantically attached to whom?"

The healer grinned, sunlight dancing off the brown curls that had escaped her bonnet. "Oh, yes, I can."

She dove into the tales with the eagerness of a bird plucking fish from the sea. Since Donya had come aboard, she'd broken three sailors' hearts, two men and a woman. Naeri wished for Lovett to marry her, but he had yet to ask for her hand. Mr. Smoke had convinced two of his fellow pirates that he was theirs alone. Two loosely-arranged coupling circles had nearly split the crew in half until Cevette threatened to strand all the quarreling lovers in a dinghy and make them all row to shore.

"That's glorious," Eva whispered. "To hell with manners. Pirates can love as openly as they wish."

"They can. That's where all the trouble starts."

"Miss Gavon! Miss Breamtide!" Cevette snapped her fingers, sharp as a gunshot. They bolted to attention. "You're discussing weaponry, correct?"

"Yes, ma'am," Eva said. "I was telling Donya about . . . throwing knives."

"You are quite skilled with a knife," Cevette said. "Could you show me again?"

Eva nodded. She stepped forward from the line. The rest of the crew watched her intently, but she paid them no heed. She walked to the mainmast, then paced ten steps back toward starboard, taking note of where her foot landed. Blades dropped into her hands with a flex of her wrists. She cocked back her elbow and whipped her arm forward, letting the knife fly with practiced spin. The air whistled. Silver flashed in the sun. The blade sliced into the heart of the mast.

Eva did it again. Just to make sure the captain knew it was no accident.

"Hmm." Cevette gave her a small nod as she retrieved her daggers. "How do I do that?"

"Stand where I stood," Eva said. Cevette fixed her feet into position as Eva moved behind her. The breadth of her shoulders pressed into Eva's chest as she lifted her arms into position. "Release the blade when your arm is level. Let it spin."

Cevette threw. The knife hit the mast sideways and clattered down to the deck. Eva gave her another. The pommel struck the mast, bounced off, and nearly hit a sailor as it fell.

"Not to worry," Eva told her. "It took me a good deal of practice to get it right. You need to build up your body's memory so that you can weight a knife, judge a distance, and know in your bones how fast you need to throw to hit your target."

"Quite the skill. And here I thought I was teaching you." Cevette smiled. "Back to the others, Miss Gavon. Perhaps I'll have you show me tricks more later."

"Yes, ma'am." Eva returned to the line with the crew, grinning like she'd won a prize.

"So that's why you want to know who's fucking who," Donya said. "You know, she won't stop looking until she gets her memories back. And there's a girl in there."

"An echo girl," Eva said. "So I know she likes the look of me. And, unlike this girl of hers, I'm *here*."

Donya pursed her lips, and blew a puff of hair off her face. "You might be swimming with the sharks."

"Or swimming with dolphins." The world felt so bright with possibilities. Why couldn't Cevette Zarcanzi be one of them? "The only way to find out is to dive in."

They drilled for another hour or so. Cevette gave most of the crew permission to disperse and go about their other duties. Some clambered up into the rigging; some ducked below deck to cook and clean; and some set about mending a torn sail. She waved for Eva to follow her; together, they climbed the stairs to the quarterdeck, where Lovett had the helm.

"Mr. Lovett has been doing research on the Republic's hidden archives," Cevette explained as they climbed up. The pair of them strode across the quarterdeck to the helm. "Their locations are carefully-guarded secret, often only written of in code, but we have discovered at least one more we can sail to after Moonwhisper Isle." Lovett stepped aside, and Cevette gripped the helm with practiced ease. The warm golden wood of the wheel fit neatly in her hands as she held the ship steady on its course. "While we sail, I mean for you to master your magic. Lovett, do you know anything that might help her?"

"She seems to manage well enough."

"Only when there's some threat."

"No shortage of threats on a pirate ship."

"But if I master this magic," Eva said, "I could fetch us goods from anywhere. Even from down in the Sapphire Isles. You know, I've never eaten a fresh orange."

"Neither have I. You're right. We should get some. Let me see what I can do." Lovett took a few steps back from the helm. Magic shimmered up his hands and wrists. He tilted back his head—and was immediately engulfed in a plume of white flame. Behind his glasses, his eyes glowed like two suns. His jaw fell wide open, and his tongue cracked like molten stone. Eva swore and threw her hands up to shield her face.

"Show-off," Cevette said.

Lovett snapped his fingers. In a heartbeat, the fire vanished, the rail and deck beneath him unburnt. Once again, he was only a scrawny man, sweat gathered on the sunburned skin of his brow, his clothing (they were all thankful for this) intact. "Right," he said, pushing his glasses back up his nose. "Try reaching out your hand, like you're opening a door. The arcane senses mirror the physical."

"You lit yourself on fire to learn I should move my hand?" Eva said.

He shrugged. "Why not?"

A plume of water billowed up from the distant sea. "Whales!" Cevette shouted, and pointed out at blue-gray shapes nearly as long as *Sea Wolf*. "Look! They've got a calf!" A half-dozen pirates rushed to the rail. Cevette leaned down over the quarterdeck rail, passed them her spyglass, then turned back to watch the magic lesson.

Eva had no time to watch baby whales frolic in the sea. She whipped her hands through the air, picturing Death and all its shadows. "What about the souls within Death? What happens to them?"

"The souls of the Sea People go into the spirit waters," Cevette said. "The current where the boats of our ancestors travel. I don't think you'll encounter that—even the greatest priests and shamans can't access the spirit waters without months of preparation and prayer—but you must avoid it at all costs. It is a great and sacred thing, but not a safe one. If you see water in Death, turn around."

"Death has many strange corners," Lovett said. "Different cultures and religions brush against it in their own way. In the Soladisean cosmology, Death is where souls purge themselves of the burdens accumulated in life. They atone for past misdeeds and find healing for their wounds. They release their memories back into the universe and are reborn. Death and memory are quite intricately tied together; that's why your foster father must break an echo's soul to fuel his magic. You're all linked to Death, even if only you can walk in it."

Eva shivered. She didn't like the thought of that. Of the distance between echoes and other folk. Quickly, she asked another question. "Could a soul attack me?"

"Some souls do refuse to re-enter the cycle," Lovett said. "They linger as spirits and ghosts. Some of them do find the strength to leave Death and return to the lands of the living. But the truly dangerous dead are few and far between, and, should you encounter one, you are quite well armed."

"Would I have to fight the . . . the damned?" Korinne had written of them in her diary. *Damned* was an ancient word, one repurposed in the modern era to refer to the souls that crawled out of Death to become abominations. But Korinne had known nothing of what they did within Death itself.

"According to myth, they dwell deep within Death, bound to something called the Hell's Eye. It can touch the world of the living wherever there's sufficient suffering for abominations to bloom, but it hides itself away from the rest of Death. With luck, you'll never see it."

"With luck." She wondered what might happen if she met a soul who needed her help, a ghost lost on its way. In the stories, Morghaia took them and shoved them into corpses and made them fight wars for her, but she most certainly did not want to do that, and she did not even think that she could. She barely knew how to make her own way in the world. For now, the dead would have to fend for themselves. "Right. I suppose if I want to learn, I have to run."

"Take a deep breath," Cevette said. "You've done this twice already. You can do it now."

Eva climbed down the quarterdeck stairs and stood before the door to Cevette's cabin, where she had opened a portal before. She breathed in and straightened her back. Braced herself. Then she extended her left hand and reached out with that new sense of hers, feeling for where the fabric of Death touched the deck. Wisps of smoke played around her fingertips and vanished as she jumped and gasped in excitement.

"Congratulations," Lovett said, once she had climbed back up the stairs to the quarterdeck. "You've accessed the third-most-dangerous force in the continuum of existence."

"When do we play with the other ones?"

"When we have a mile-wide blast radius."

Eva looked to Cevette and smiled. "Anything you want me to pick up in Halston?"

"Grab some of those gossip pamphlets about me. They're always good for a laugh."

"I know. They say you're six feet tall."

Cevette leaned over and tapped Eva's chin, which she barely stood level with. "How many have you read?"

Blood rushed into Eva's cheeks. "Oh, one or two. Just for a laugh."

"I see." Mischief sparkled in her eyes. "Good luck, Skullrunner."

Eva hesitated. *Skullrunner.* "Don't call me that, please. It's an insult, to compare an echo to Morghaia."

"My apologies. Thank you for telling me."

"Of course," Eva said. She descended the steps once more, then squared her shoulders and reached deeper into her magic.

Smoke bloomed at her fingertips. It fell to her feet and billowed up over her head, coalescing into an archway made of femurs and twisted spines. A glowering skull capped it all. Darkness swirled within the portal.

Someone cursed. Eva glanced back over her shoulder. Half a dozen sailors were watching her, seated atop the rail or standing atop spars in the rigging. Eva flinched. *Do they see Morghaia in me?* But some of them thrust their fists aloft and cheered, and she knew they were cheering for *her.*

"Good luck, Miss Gavon," Cevette shouted.

Eva let that wash over her like a wave, then stepped into Death.

The hallway of gray bones, with its arched ceiling and narrow walls, stretched out before her, vanishing into the distance as a puff of gray smoke. Already, the sting in her lungs from breathing almost-air felt familiar to her. She took one step forward, then another. All was quiet. All was still. *Right. Time to run.*

A few moments, and she glimpsed the first window back into the living world: it looked out onto another ship, a fishing vessel. *Not Halston.* Souls floated past her, gray figures with unfocused gazes, drifting on tides of silver mist. But one or two smiled as she passed, and Eva smiled back at them. She felt as if she stood ten feet tall. A glow lit up her face. It took a moment for her to recognize the feeling as pride.

Her target was the dockside jail in Halston. She hoped the locus of suffering would draw her like a magnet. Soul after drifting soul vanished behind her down the corridor of bones. Once more, she stretched out her hand, reaching for pain, loss, and death. *Punishment.* The dark window on her right called to her, as beckoning as the edge of an abyss. It urged her to jump in. To swim or sink on the sea of human misery.

It fit what she wanted so neatly that she did not look twice before leaping through.

Eva emerged from Death into a musty room, quiet as the grave save for the scratching of quills on paper. A dozen students, heads lowered and brows furrowed, scrawled answers on an exam. Two quietly wept in frustration; another had chewed his quill to a nub. Not one looked up to notice her nor the elderly proctor slumped over at his desk. The smile on his wrinkled lips said he'd died doing what he loved.

Well. Cevette never had to know she'd got lost.

"I can get to Halston," Eva told her captain when she returned to the ship. Several hours had passed, but Cevette still sat near where her portal opened, checking how the glue had dried on the crossbeam of her cannon mount. "I'm almost sure of it."

Cevette looked up at her and quirked an eyebrow. "Almost?"

Eva nodded. "Yes. Almost." She was glad for the uncertainty. Morghaia must have never gotten lost. Eva held her magic, nothing more. In that, she was no different than any other godmarked sailor aboard. And she was learning, and improving, and she could already see the potential of the power she carried. *Just what will I do with this? And how much will I do?*

"Right, then." The captain set down her woodwork, stood, and waved for her to follow. "Let's count how we're off for replacement spars. I haven't stopped in at a shipwright for months, but now I can send you to buy them. I want *Sea Wolf* to be well-equipped in case our masts take damage in a storm."

They climbed the stairs down to the lower deck, then descended the ladder into the darkness of the cargo hold. In the belly of the ship, beneath the crew quarters, wood creaked with every passing wave. Both wrinkled their noses at the scent from a large puddle of bilge water. Cevette lit a lantern and nodded toward a crate. Eva pushed it aside and—

"Gah!" Lovett and Naeri rolled apart, him fumbling with his breeches, her pushing down her skirt. Eva leapt backwards, splashing in the puddle. Cevette cursed.

"Chalk rule, sailors, chalk rule!" Cevette swung her lantern toward the ladder. "You chalk an X on the top rung, then erase it when you're done."

"Captain," Naeri said, "We're so sorry. Donya ground up the chalk to make potions."

Cevette sighed. "Right. Mr. Lovett, Miss de L'Havre, you'll take the late watch. On different ends of the ship." Abashed, they nodded, ducked away, and climbed up the ladder. "Miss Gavon, please add chalk to your shopping list."

Eva knelt to count the long wooden poles tied in a bundle in the corner. They would be needed to repair masts that cracked from battle or bad weather, but *Sea Wolf* only possessed two extras, and one had split down the middle. Worse, they were running low on planking, and the iron screws and nails had begun to rust. She would need to remedy that before they took any damage to the hull.

Cevette cleared her throat. "I'm quite serious about the chalk rule, Miss Gavon. There's no foolishness permitted in the bunks when other sailors are sleeping, and no breaking into my cabin for a private spot either."

"I haven't done *foolishness* for years." She thought of the soldier she'd dallied with a handful of times three years ago; they'd understood each other well enough, but the girl's unit had been sent away to the far north, and Eva had found it most difficult to make that sort of connection since. "The face of the goddess of death is . . . dissuading, to all but the most brave. And, even if some girl *does* want me, I may not notice. Books and poems make it sound as if you look at someone and simply—understand. I once met a man who could not tell red from green. Me, I struggle to tell a mannerly gesture from a desirous one. So, if a woman were to desire me, she would do quite well to make her feelings clearly known."

"I see. Do all echoes only desire women?"

"All the ones I've met." Eva said. To make herself clear, she added, "Myself included." She wasn't sure if the captain had been asking about her, specifically. But she did want her to know.

"Thank you for telling me." Cevette smiled. "That is quite good to know, indeed."

DEGREES OF CLOSENESS

BEGINNING AND ENDING IN THE HALSTON FORTRESS, IN THE GOLDEN REPUBLIC, AND ALSO ABOARD THE SHIP SEA WOLF, EIGHT HUNDRED AND NINETY MILES NORTHWEST OF HALSTON. 5TH HERALMONTH, YEAR TWENTY-TWO OF THE GOLDEN REPUBLIC.

You ask me if I ever had an echo like Andreas and how we might get more like him. He is an exceptional creature; he came from exceptional stock. But echoes are more difficult to breed than cows and horses. Each one will only produce two more, and one of that pair—as you can see with Evazina—is most likely defective. –Letter from Commander Jonathan Gavon to Lord Mykil Merris, Minister for Childhood Welfare.

IT WOULD NOT, STRICTLY speaking, be fair to say Andreas Gavon shared none of his sister's struggles when it came to the finer points of socialization. But he, as he told himself, put in the effort. While Eva hid in her room and threw knives at posts, Andreas attended university lectures and wrote essays. The Soladiseans who had colonized the Five Sisters deeply valued education. (Andreas thought this was most likely due to the inability to do anything in the Five Sisters' freezing winters but read.) His thesis on the mutability of political self-identification (which, he explained to Zeke and Eva, meant the ability of groups and individuals to change how they perceived themselves as a tool to achieve collective goals) had earned him a place in the philosophers' guild of Soladis, the most elite intellectual society in the known world.

Andreas was not a godreaper, not yet, but he did not need to be. He was an excellent scholar, and an excellent spy. His academic credentials opened doors for him to host debates and symposiums where he might exchange small talk with the gentry. At these, he studied people as if they were an ancient text. He spoke loudly and freely, yes he did, and tried his best to be seen as friendly and affable. But he listened, too, and he remembered every word ever spoken in his presence, and he put what he remembered to very good use.

He had organized a small luncheon in honor of a number of wounded veterans who had recently received degrees from Carreton, the premier university in the city of Halston, from which Andreas himself had graduated (in only three-and-a-half years.) It was held in the great fortress, in the bluebird parlor, so named for the dozens of taxidermy bluebirds sitting in tiny cages about the edges of the room. The cream-colored wallpaper was stamped with fluttering bluebirds; the rugs woven with patterns of feathers. The plush chairs that filled the room had carved wings on the armrests, and, paradoxically, no stuffing in the cushions. The wounded veterans in attendance, many of whom could not walk without canes, sat upon them uncomfortably, shifting their weight from side to side.

Andreas had shaken their hands when they had entered, and thanked them for coming, all on the behalf of his father. He had congratulated them on their achievements and asked them what they had studied. He had pretended not to notice how some of them refused to meet his deep black eyes. *They think I'm beneath them, when they rely on sympathy for their wounds to pass the simplest exams.* They were nothing to him, and were useful only to his father as a symbol of past victories. The servants were keeping them well-supplied with fine whiskey and small platters of cheese. He was free to fully attend to his more elevated guests. At present, that meant standing by the wall and nodding along as important people spoke, with slightly more life in their voices than the watching glass-eyed bluebirds.

"The Sea People are encroaching on my territory," Lord Marston said, sipping tea in a plush armchair, which he had ordered hauled in from the room across the hall. He was one of the few aristocrats in the Republic who still formally styled himself as such. The accolades had gone out of fashion since the revolution, especially among the practically-minded people of the Five Sisters. "Those web-fingered bastards sunk three of my fishing boats. The crews are refusing to go out on Greymarket Bay."

"You think that's bad?" said Assemblyman Varney. "My fosterlings rioted. Burned down a whole mill. Ungrateful children. You give them a home and a family. All you ask is that they work for their keep. They refuse to even do that."

Andreas pulled on a small, tight smile. His first instinct was to propose a debate on the merits of the foster system (or, in his opinion, the lack of them.) He would win; the facts all supported his position.

The foster system was one of the key innovations that had built the Republic; for implementing it, Commander Gavon had been praised as a savior of poor orphans, another brick in the wall of his heroic legend. Any child without living kindred or competent guardianship could be fostered by a Republic citizen, or the army, or a number of trade guilds. Their bondholders would pay to feed and clothe them; in return, the fosterling would labor for their bondholder until their twenty-fifth birthday. Commander Gavon owned the bonds of hundreds of fosterlings, whom he often allowed his allies to employ as cheap labor. In theory, fosterage prevented youth vagrancy, educated the poor, and relieved the strain of overpopulation on the frontier. In practice, it enabled the kidnapping of impoverished children for forced labor and provided an easy legal mechanism for newly-split echoes to be kept in Republic households where Commander Gavon might reach them.

If it came to a debate on the merits of fosterage, Andreas would win. But, even in victory, such debate would only serve to remind his guests of his fosterling status. And he tried very hard to not be seen as a fosterling. He was meticulous about his dress and mannerisms, to comport himself as an heir to the Gavon name, not some orphaned. He always called the commander 'my father' and spoke of him with pride, even when he wanted nothing more than for his father's empire to collapse around him.

"Assemblyman Varney," he said, "I quite admired that essay you published on my father's refusal to name himself a king after his victory in the revolution. 'A greatness by which all other greatness shall henceforth be measured.' Wise words, sir, wise words."

"Thank you, Gavon," said the assemblyman. "Though I confess, I've had second thoughts of his greatness since that disaster with your sister. Is it true she joined a pirate crew? I suppose one can expect very little indeed of an echo."

One would expect a gentleman not to say such things to my face. But, he hoped, perhaps the assemblyman did not see him as an echo, or at least, not that sort of echo. That was why he spent several hours each month using alchemical concoctions to bleach the color from his hair. He hoped it would come easier now that Eva had left and they did not have her at hand to compare the two of them.

Of course, that hadn't been why he encouraged her to flee. He knew his sister. She wasn't capable of building a full life in the Golden Republic. Few echoes were. She would be happier far away from it. He wanted her to be happy. If he benefited from her absence in some small way, he need not say so out loud.

"Lord Marston." Andreas nodded to the aristocrat. Marston returned the gesture. He was a short man, his wig disheveled, the gold trim on his suit coming apart on one sleeve. His head bobbed forward and then back again as he ate sweets from a small tray. *How utterly pigeon-like.* Andreas stepped forward to stand beside his chair; Assemblyman Varney moved on to speak with a one-eyed veteran, leaving Andreas and Marston to speak alone. "A pleasure to see you. I was so glad to hear you'd recovered from your cough."

"Thank you, Mr. Gavon. How's your shoulder?" A note of laughter crept into his voice. "That was quite dramatic, that birthday of yours."

"My shoulder is healing cleanly. Thank you for asking." The doctors had urged him to use his right arm as little as possible. He could not seem to stop clenching his fist.

"If you'd actually killed the god, would the commander have given you a commission?" Marston mimed a salute. "Lieutenant Echo. Imagine that."

Andreas forced himself to smile. He had to take a few deep breaths before he could speak calmly. "It's military protocol that all godreapers are commissioned officers of the army. The nature of their unique position means, in certain military scenarios, they will need to be obeyed without question." *And it would have been Lieutenant Gavon, you nitwit, and you would have shown me the respect due a gentleman and my father's son.*

"It must be quite the disappointment to be trapped here with us."

Laugh. Laugh. Andreas made himself laugh. He hoped it rang true. "Now, why would it ever be a disappointment to remain in such honorable company?"

"Honorable? Surely you jest."

"Why would you say that, my lord? You do these wounded veterans a great service here today."

"No greater a service than Assemblywoman Westport." Marston glanced at a woman in a gray gown, over by the parlor door, chatting with a journalist from one of the deadly boring Assembly-approved newspapers. "She's bedding one of them. A one-legged horse groom. Such a scandal. Can you imagine?"

"The nerve," Andreas said, shaking his head. He had no desire for men, but even he knew Mr. Westport to be a poor specimen. "For how long?"

"Three years. Ever since that business with her husband. Did you hear of it?" Lord Marston gestured at the small plate he held. "These are excellent biscuits. You know, I too have a very good chef."

"Do you?" Andreas let the topic of the Westport family slide. The gossip was useful, but there would always be more where that came from. What mattered was making a connection.

"She has a fiendish way with roast quail. You should come to dinner next week. My son is preparing to attend university. He would quite enjoy the opportunity to debate a member of the philosophers' guild."

"It would be my honor." Andreas lifted his chin. His dark eyes gleamed. This was what passed for friendship among the elite. He would ignore the jibes about echoes. Such barbs were common enough in polite society. He was learned enough to know he had no choice but to face them all and smile gladly.

Not many echoes would see that as a strength. That was their weakness.

In five long years, Cevette Zarcanzi had never faced a challenge quite as fearful as Evazina Gavon.

Cevette was used to girls fawning over her. Occasionally, one would catch her eye, but she wanted more from a woman than a quick tumble in the sheets. She wanted to be close to a woman, in every way she could be, and she wanted a woman who wanted the same.

Eva was as subtle as a knife in the gut. She was obviously and profoundly inexperienced in the ways of love. But she was no fool. She had snatched the power of the Skullrunner right under Cevette's nose, where all the gentry of Halston could see her. She had slain a sea serpent from inside the beast's throat. She was brave, and she was capable, and Cevette couldn't help but wonder what might happen if she gave Eva a chance to act on her desires.

A warm shiver rolled through her at the thought.

But she needed to be *responsible*.

"I don't see why this is a problem," Naeri said.

"Because the captain makes it a problem," said Donya. "She makes everything much more complicated than it needs be."

Cevette sighed. "All I ask for is your advice on how I might navigate this impulse of mine with dignity and respect toward all involved."

The three of them sat together on the forecastle, atop a pile of crates. Cevette was trimming her hair in a small hand mirror, Naeri was embroidering the sleeve of her new gown, and Donya was smoking a pipe. The evening was warm, and the pink of the sunset was like the blush of a cheek. *Sea Wolf* slid gracefully through the blue-gray waves that splashed up against the figurehead of the carved wooden orca. Down on the upper deck, Tuk By-Water, who had sailed with her all the way since Upailit, was practicing duck calls on a wooden whistle. A chorus of quacking filled the peaceful night.

"You should go kiss her," Naeri said. "Right now. Why wait? You fancy her, and I can see how she looks at you."

Cevette glanced down the length of the ship, reassuring herself that Eva was still with Mr. Smoke on the quarterdeck, learning how to clean and fillet a fish. She kept her voice low all the same. "She's not the woman I'm looking for. I may yet find her. If I do, and if I let this go further, Eva might get hurt."

"Even you can only control so much," Donya said.

"What if my first girl and I were married? What if she learned I broke my vows, and—"

Donya stood and met Cevette's eyes. "You, cousin, are the most fish-brained fool on the sea, and if I didn't love you so much, I would toss you off the ship and let the sea freeze some smarts into you." She said all this in Kossket, which only the two of them knew, and which meant they were speaking as equals. "On Kossi, no one would care if a current woman had two wives. It's the land folk who have all the rules about who can love who. They make themselves miserable. We know better."

"We?" Cevette said, also in Kossket. "Didn't you just say I had the brains of a fish?"

They both laughed, then. Naeri cleared her throat and spoke in the common Soladisean they all shared. "Well, I don't know what Donya said, but I know that, if I loved someone, and then we were parted by forces beyond our control, and they didn't know if I was alive or dead, I would want them to be happy. Captain Zarcanzi, wouldn't your girl want you to be happy?"

Cevette sighed, and answered in the Soladisean tongue. "I can't know."

"You can't know a good number of things," Naeri said. "What if you find her and she doesn't even want you back? What if you get your memory back and learn the two of you ended things years ago?" She met Cevette's gaze with her rich brown irises. "What if you and Eva are happy together?

What if you find this girl and she's glad for you? What if all three of you wind up together? Claim your happiness. You deserve it."

Do I? Cevette thought, and frowned.

A quiet tune drifted into her ears, a chant sung in a deep voice that cracked with pain. She turned to look out at the upper deck once more. Nukit, son of Nowi, stood by the starboard rail near the mainmast, a fist curled around the seal tooth pendant he wore. He was tall, for a Upailitian man, his black hair trimmed in a bowl cut, clad in a smooth hide vest and simple trousers. A bracelet of traditional dot tattoos wrapped around his wrist, marking him as a warrior of the Otter Clan who had survived three battles. Tears rolled down his cheeks as he squeezed his eyes shut. Somehow, Cevette heard his nearly-whispered prayer. *Give me strength, Parha, heartbeat of the currents.*

Cevette doubted his goddess would be listening. She did not think highly of Parha, or Heraline, as the Soladiseans knew her. *But I can help him.* Cevette stood. "I'll be back," she told the others.

She descended the steps from the forecastle, walked halfway down the length of the deck, and reached Nukit's side. As she leaned against the rail beside him, he blinked and met her eyes, rubbing the tears from his cheeks. "Yes, captain?"

He was addressing her formally, as a Soladisean sailor would address a superior officer. The Sea People men on her crew often treated her that way, with deference and respect, and a hint of distance between them. Current women rarely led trade expeditions or war parties, but they directly advised the men who led them, and most Sea People men grew up under the authority of female elders in the villages, so she was commonly assumed to be a step above them in leadership. She valued the respect they showed her. Still, something in it saddened her. It had crept in from Soladisean culture: there, leaders were expected to *command* their people, to demand their service or make them suffer.

"What's wrong?" she said, in Kossket.

A hint of light flickered in his brown eyes. He answered in his first language. "I miss Upailit. I miss my mother. I miss my grandmother. I miss my son. He's almost four now. I haven't seen any of them in two years. I know they all look after each other. I know they need the money from our raids. But I want to be there." Another tear slid down his cheek. It fell down into the sea.

"The oceans connect us all," Cevette said quietly. It was a hard thing that was expected of the Sea People men of so many nations, that they separate themselves from their homes and families for months or even years so that they might earn some money or fight to defend their kin. "Your family will know how much you miss them. Your son will feel your love every time he goes to the shore." Tears prickled in her eyes as well. Every now and then, she would feverishly check her stomach for stretch marks, terrified by the thought she might have a child somewhere she had forgotten. Her body bore none of the signs. But that did not mean she did not have a family that had been stolen from her, parents and siblings and grandparents, or a family of choice as dear as a family of blood. "You are not alone. None of us are."

"Thank you," Nukit said, quietly. "May I hug you?"

Cevette nodded. They pulled each other into a tight embrace, kin to kin, heartbeat to heartbeat.

There came a quacking sound. Tuk walked up. He was shorter than Nukit, with a bit of a belly, and he wore his dark hair in two long braids. He held the whistle he'd carved out to Nukit, who took it and gave it a quacking blow. Both men laughed. Tuk stretched up on his toes and kissed Nukit on the cheek.

"We're all here to help our families," he said. "And I will help you, too."

Cevette smiled at them. It was common for Sea People men to take each other as husbands on a long voyage, in addition to any wives they might have back at home. She had presided over the ceremony herself, a blend of Upailitian and sailors' traditions. She was glad they had each other. Still, she could not help but feel a pang of loneliness.

It would not be wrong, for me to love Eva. She glanced up at the quarter-deck, where Eva and Mr. Smoke were laughing over some joke, elbow-deep in fish guts. *There's so much joy in her. So much life. So much hope.*

What Cevette had not told anyone—what she'd been afraid to share—was that, over the years, she had come to remember some bits and pieces of her last conversation with her girl. It had been an awful conversation, rife with pain that cut at her like an obsidian knife. She remembered leaving, though not where she had left, and she remembered the sea. When all else failed her, she always turned to the sea. They had been parted by a great distance when her memories had vanished. If they'd been together, they might have found a way to hold on.

She told me something was wrong. Between them. Inside Cevette. *She asked me to leave. To heal what was broken in my soul. She said that we should not be anything to each other until I had.* Only Cevette had forgotten what it was that she needed to make right inside herself. All she knew was that she had not done it yet.

She owed it to her sailors to be the woman who kept them safe. She especially owed it to Eva, who was new to this life, new to the ways of love, who trusted her so deeply. If there was something in Cevette, or in her past, that might hurt her, then letting her come in close might break them both.

She had to reclaim her past. Only then could she steer a clean course to her future.

Three times, Andreas wrote to his father and asked for a meeting. Never before had he needed to ask twice. He waited, read several books he had meant to get around to, and composed a long letter to Tomis Beauchamp continuing a debate they had begun at the philosophers' guild in Soladis in early spring. His girl Mary sent him a half-dozen letters, and he went to her for a night, only for it all to dissolve into an argument about how he asked too much of her, so now he no longer had Mary to distract him from his growing fear.

Five years ago, Andreas had won the citywide debate tournament. His father had hoisted him on his shoulders and carried him about the great green park at the heart of Halston as the crowd cheered his name. Then, news had come via courier. It had been bad. Andreas couldn't remember what, specifically, it had been. He remembered how his father had looked at him afterward, though. The calculation in those gray eyes.

This man would tear apart his own children if he deemed it necessary. He had not chosen it that day, but he was capable of doing so. He would never love them. And, no matter what Andreas did, his father would never fully see him as his son.

So Andreas had decided to tear him down. Not with sword, or ship, but strategy. When Commander Gavon had first privately promised to make him a godreaper, Andreas had begun to maneuver the members of the Assembly toward impeachment. He had assumed, by the time the vote occurred, he would be on military duty in some far-flung corner of the Republic. That was necessary. After all, his father would be desperate once the Assembly stripped him of his elected position and his military command. He would target what echoes he could, echoes without means or a roof to sleep under. He would try to claw his way back into politics. Andreas would need to keep his distance from his father; to master the magic of a godreaper so he might keep the defeated commander out of power for good.

But he had not planned for Eva to reap the Skullrunner. So he needed to shore up his place in his father's affections before they sailed south for the Assembly meeting. He had to make certain that the next echo split would not be him.

At last, nearly two days after sending his first missive, he secured an appointment to speak with his father.

The guards made him wait an extra half-hour outside the door to his father's bedroom. At last, they let him in. Heat filled the room; though the fire was burning low. A scent of whiskey hung in the air; *two* glasses sat on the table beside his father's bed, and the sheets were disheveled. He wrinkled his nose and quickly looked away from that, then closed the door behind him and cleared his throat.

The commander sat behind his desk, simply clad in a white shirt and black breeches, squinting down through his reading glasses as he perused a paper. His forehead had furrowed in concentration; the gray at his temples shimmered in the faint firelight. He did not look up at his son. "Right. What do you have for me?"

Andreas took a few more steps into the room and stood at attention, his shoulders back and his chin high. "Lord Marston received a bribe of ten thousand pounds from the Viridian League to sway his vote on the fishery bill. Assemblywoman Westport has betrayed her husband, but he betrayed her first with their fosterling, a boy of twenty-three from the frontier." Such goings-on among the members of the Assembly were hardly un-heard-of. The eighty-odd members of that body, each elected to represent a certain territory, were meant to serve as a beacon of democracy and justice. But there were not enough echoes in the Seaward Isles for Commander Gavon to erase the memory of all their petty disagreements. "With this leverage, I believe you can convince both of them to vote yes on the army appropriations bill."

The commander did not look up from his papers. "Thank you, Andreas. You may go."

Was that all his father would say to him? No clasp on the shoulder? No 'my brilliant son?' *Fool. He's not your father. He created you. Ripped apart a soul to make you.* He could play the role of the commander's son, but it was only a role. They both knew it.

Andreas cleared his throat and said, "Sir, has there been any movement in the matter of finding me a new god to reap?"

"I have more pressing matters to consider," the commander said. "Are you aware that the Assembly is planning to surprise me with a vote of impeachment?"

"A vote of impeachment?" Andreas pitched his voice upward. He made sure to put a hand to his chest in surprise. "How could they? You . . . you're a war hero."

"Yes, well, that was twenty years ago. The members of the Assembly have short memories."

Andreas took a small stool from the foot of his father's bed, slid it over to the desk, and sat down beside him. He smiled a humble, helpful smile and met his father's eyes. Commander Gavon arched a brow.

"There's no chance it passes," Andreas said. "None at all. The people of the Seaward Isles . . . they love you. They would never stand for their representatives to deprive you of your privileges." *It's me,* part of him wanted to say. *Look what I did. Don't you see I'm so much more than just some echo?* He'd expected his father to weep or curse when he learned of the Assembly's impeachment plan. He seemed to be only resigned. As if nothing his son accomplished mattered much to him at all.

"We shall see," the commander said. "On the matter of gods, I have ordered my philosophers to tell me when they next believe one of those divine bastards is near enough to catch. It may take months or a year, but you will have one. My gift to you."

My gift to you. Andreas pressed his hands to his chest. Sweat prickled on his palms. His stomach fluttered. Once, this had been all Andreas wanted. Some flicker of warmth from his father. Some proof the man cared. That he truly saw the worth of his own son.

The door creaked open. They both turned to face it. "Just what you asked for, sir," said a soldier, and pushed through a girl, no older than seven or eight. She stared about the office with wide, stunned eyes.

An echo girl. Andreas froze.

She's so young. With the same terrible haircuts the maids would give him and Eva at that age. They had been a matched pair back then, indistinguishable from each other. Life had been simple, even joyful. Their father had adored them. They had not yet heard of the sacrifices. (His memories of those days were a bit blurry. He did not like to think of what that might mean.)

"Take her to the barracks," the commander said. "I need more time to work out my plan for her."

The soldier nodded. He grabbed the girl by the arm and pulled her from the room. She looked to Andreas. He could not break away from her wide and terrified eyes until the door shut.

This is a test, he realized. This girl was one of his sisters. He wanted to break her out of the barracks and let her run. Eva would. But if he did, the commander would know who had done it. *He means to learn if I will defy him.*

And he would. But he would be smart about it. One common echo was not worth risking the plan that could deliver them all. One common echo lacked the strength to do anything that mattered.

So Andreas turned, met his father's eyes, and said nothing.

At last, the commander shook his head. "Off with you," he said, and gestured to the door. "Go on, boy. I need to work out how to get the Skullrunner back."

A Ship of Sisters

Moonwhisper Isle, nine hundred and sixty miles northwest of Halston. 6th Heralmonth, Year Twenty-Two of the Golden Republic.

What is the difference between abominations and natural creatures? Some would argue it is a matter of viciousness. But the great sea serpents are vicious, are known for hunting ships, and they are natural creatures. Some would argue it is a matter of life cycle; abominations are not born from other abominations, but from mats of sea-sludge that take on living form when tragedy draws the souls of the damned into them. Still, jellyfish are born from strange polyps; and the reproduction of eels is a mystery to us all. Some would argue it is a matter of organ structure; but the organs of abominations are inconsistent, with some possessing an internal structure that mirrors that of higher creatures while others only possess sludge. Myself, I would argue it is a matter of diet. Abominations devour the stuff of life; not only flesh, but pain and loss. Natural creatures must consume material matter; abominations can subsist for years of the anguish that radiates from human suffering. –from the diary of Korinne Gavon.

Two days after Eva learned of the chalk rule, she found herself gazing through a spyglass at Moonwhisper Isle.

The rough white stone of the island's cliffs rose in a curve about a natural harbor. Wiry green plants grew from crevasses in their sides, where seabirds flocked for shelter, and goats grazed in the patchy grass on their heights. It was a small island, barely fifteen miles in length. Cevette had told her that once, hundreds of Sea People had gathered there to trade with the Ya Tonim Nation. But, over recent years, soldiers of the Republic had forced them away from the island. They had built a fort in the harbor, and a village around the fort, and an archive up on the cliffs, all to hide the memories Commander Gavon had stolen memories from his own people.

Cevette and Lovett had discussed attempting to dock in the harbor. With his power, Lovett could read the fort log book, and he had discovered there were only fifteen soldiers in the fort, compared to *Sea Wolf*'s crew of nearly forty. But a fight would still mean casualties, and Cevette had decided the course was too risky. They had sailed north, tossed by slapping waves that threw white foam up against *Sea Wolf*'s flanks. Pushing through them had taken the better part of a morning. When they dropped anchor around the backside of the island, the sun was noon high, but the day was no warmer for it.

Eva could not help but shiver as they set about their preparations to venture ashore. The wind howled about the white clifftops with inhuman fury, like an evil spirit in a tale. Seabirds watched the ship with dark, unblinking eyes. Mr. Smoke climbed up into the crow's nest, lifted a curious hand-made cannon, and fired. A grappling hook shot across the day and caught itself on the top of the cliffside.

"Command of the ship is yours, Mr. Smoke," Cevette said, when he climbed down from the crow's nest and offered her the rope. "I'll want you here until we return. I don't trust you not to start a fire in the undergrowth."

"Very wise, ma'am."

Cevette tied the rope to her belt, wrapped more rope snug around her waist, climbed onto the port rail, and leapt. She flew across the gap, her short hair flying back in the wind, and struck the wall boots-first. She grunted. Dust billowed up about her. Birds flapped up and flew away. Hand over hand, Cevette climbed. Sweat ran down her back. The muscles of her shoulders strained against the thin white fabric of her shirt.

"What are you looking at?" Donya asked Eva, who was leaning against the port rail, looking up with eager eyes.

A slow smile crept across Eva's face. "Nothing," she said.

Cevette slid herself over the top of the cliff and went to work. With a hammer and pins, she anchored the rope more securely, then tossed down three more lines. Naeri followed her up, though she took the time to swing about on the rope, her long braids and her blue skirts flying out behind her. Lovett showed Eva how to tie a bag of chalk to her belt to keep her hands dry as she ascended. Donya had no skill at climbing, and had two of the other pirates haul her and her backpack of medicines up the whole way.

In the space of an hour, they were all assembled on the clifftop. Cevette checked their position with her map and compass, then led them into the undergrowth. She and Tuk cleared the path before them with machetes. Branches dropped with every beat of their rhythmic chopping. Lizards and snakes scuttled for cover in the earthy undergrowth. The humming of pearl-winged dragonflies filled the dank, stagnant air. Onward the crew went, clambering over rocks and fallen roots. Eva kept a tight grip on her pistols, peering through the shadows for a foe.

At last, they glimpsed daylight. Cevette hacked through the last few branches, and a dirt trail stretched out before them. She held up a hand to warn them against advancing. "Stay to the shadows. According to Lovett, there'll be two soldiers guarding the entry to the archive. Nukit and I have the best aim. We'll get closer to the archive and find a good sniper position. Donya will stay safe with us. The rest of you will sneak down five hundred feet down the trail. Lovett, use the duck whistle when you're in position. We'll take the shot. If we miss, you stop them before they reach town."

"Yes, ma'am."

Stop them. Eva rubbed her ear. Scratched at her neck. If all had gone as planned, Andreas might have been one of the guards. One of Zeke's friends might be stationed here. *They're complicit in what my father does. They're guarding memories that belong to all people of the Isles*. But did they know what they were guarding? *Does that matter?* She shuddered. Of course it mattered. This was life and death.

Morghaia wouldn't care. So she had to. Perhaps, if soldiers came running down the road, she should let the others handle them. But what if she did, and a one escaped, and alerted the fort, and they were caught? There would be great bloodshed then. Would that be on her? Would that—

Cevette frowned. "I smell smoke."

She led them out onto the trail. Fresh footprints covered the dirt. Lots of them, and hoofprints too, all aimed at the archive. Threads of smoke coiled through the air. Eva shivered at the scent of burning. The captain drew an ivory-trimmed spyglass from her sleeve and peered down the trail, back toward the harbor.

"The fort is on fire," she said. "We need to get to the archive. Now."

She turned and ran up the trail. The crew followed after. Pebbles and dust flew up under their heels. Their arms pumped; their breathing sped. As they turned a bend, they caught sight of the archive: a squat, square, windowless brick building with a single door that clung to the cliffside like a barnacle. Two soldiers in orange coats lay dead in the mud before it. A dozen echoes, their blades drawn, stood between the crew of *Sea Wolf* and the archive door.

The Demon's crew. Eva froze at the sight of them. Glimpsing the echo pirates had been strange enough in the dark of night—in the day, to see her own face repeated over and over like a pattern in lacework embroidery left her dizzy, her mind insisting that the evidence of her own eyes could not be. She had glimpsed other echoes before, echoes who were not her brother, through carriage windows, at a distance, but never before had she seen them gather in such large numbers. Some were older than her; some were younger. Some had tattoos, and all had a different assortment of scars. But, clad in black shirts and breeches all cut from the same cloth, to look on them was to see something unmistakably wrong. As terrifying as the goddess of death.

"Captain Zarcanzi. Beat you here."

The Demon of Dogshead emerged from the archive door and leaned causally against the wall. Her chin was high; her eyebrows arched in satisfaction. In the light, she appeared to be in her early thirties, sallow-cheeked and gaunt. Her godmarks were silver: singing birds and notes of music, the pattern distorted about the stump of her right hand. She wore a long coat of midnight black, with her hair down across her shoulders. The necklace of silver skulls shone at her throat.

The pirates of the Seaward Isles had little in the way or hierarchy or formal organization between them, but it was common knowledge that the strongest among them ruled from Dogshead Isle as the Demon, keeping peace and facilitating trade between the captains, and uniting them for war if the navy pushed too far into their seas. This Demon had held the title for six years. Eva shuddered to think of what terrible things she must have done to gain and hold onto it. What terrible things the people of the Seaward Isles must believe of echoes thanks to her.

Two abominations crouched at the Demon's feet. They were snake-shaped, with the heads of seagulls, and long, venomous fangs that curled down from their beaks. With unblinking, adoring eyes, they watched the Demon. More echoes from her crew walked out of archive past her, dragging open crates through the dirt. Black-and-white almost-paper spilled out of them. The Demon grabbed a clump of memory and flung it to her beasts. They leapt at it. One caught it in its fanged beak and tossed back its head, swallowing it down. A wave of energy pulsed through it. Its body shivered and contorted as it grew, stretching out an additional three feet in length over its brother.

"What are you doing?" Cevette said. "That's someone's past. Does it—does it go back to the owner—"

"Only if you burn it," the Demon said. "If the abominations eat it, then it's gone. The loss of it makes more suffering to fuel them. They're not smart creatures, but they remember who feeds them. And they obey."

"You can control them?" Eva said.

"No, not completely," said the Demon. "But I can handle them as well as anyone. I've studied them all my life. Do you know how they spawn?" She went on without waiting for a reply. It was clear that sharing the information brought her great pleasure. "At sites of great loss and pain, damned souls escape Death into deposits of living tissue that build up in the seas. They take on monstrous forms to cause and feed off the pain of the living. Now, all sorts of pain can do the trick. But these memories accelerate their growth like nothing I've ever seen."

Eva thought of the slim leather diary now secured in her sea chest. *No. It can't be.* But she was about the right age, and had a touch of the Halston accent in her speech. And she had that same passion for the study of abominations. *I should have seen it back when we first met.* But she hadn't wished to imagine just how far an echo could fall.

"You . . . you're Korinne Gavon," Eva whispered. "The commander's old foster daughter."

Korinne scowled. "How do you know that?"

"I have your diary. You hid it in my bedroom."

"Oh," she said, a bit quieter. "I'd almost forgotten about that."

Eva wrinkled her nose. Her skin crawled. Her stomach twisted. She thought of the Korinne she had met in the diary—thoughtful, inquisitive Korinne, who had written *how I hate the part of me that is the goddess of death, for she is the worst part, most unworthy, and brings much trouble on my sister and me.* Now she gleefully sauntered down Morghaia's path, monsters at her heels and murderers at her side. "What happened to you?"

"By the gods. The way you look at me, girl, you'd think my guts were hanging out of my stomach."

"You were . . . quieter, back then. Softer. More kind."

"I was a child," Korinne said. "I'm not one now."

Will I be like her one day? The thought hit like a gut-punch. *No. Never.* But Korinne, too, had once wanted to be the best echo she could be.

"Commander Gavon must die for the echoes to live freely," Korinne said. "The man is too well-guarded for my crew alone to bring him down. I need an army." She patted an abomination on the head with her metal hand. It snapped at her. She pulled back just before its jaws closed. "So I'm making one."

"This is wrong," Eva said.

Korinne pursed her lips. "Why?"

Why? It was wrong. She knew it in her gut. *If it's a debate she wants, she should talk to my brother.* Of course Eva wanted to end the sacrifice of echoes. She had lived with the fear of sacrifice all her days. And she had grown up in Halston, hearing tales of the revolution that had brought liberty and justice to the Seaward Isles, of the moral righteousness in overthrowing a tyrant. But this did not look like justice. Only destruction.

"This will . . . cause chaos, and violence," Eva said. "A great deal of it. There must be other ways to stop him."

Korinne's thin lips quirked up in a smile. She seemed almost amused. "And what would you propose?"

Eva hesitated. She wished Andreas was here. He always had a clever plan, or, at least, clever words to describe one. He had already set their father up for a vote of impeachment. The Assembly would gather and decide whether to expel him from his position. *It's a chancy thing, though. If he can find another echo, make them forget their concerns . . .*

Like a flash of lightning, she saw the answer. He had stolen decades of memory from his people. But what if she could burn them faster than he could take them away? Cevette was already looking for the stolen memories. With a fast ship like *Sea Wolf,* they could expose decades of scandals in the weeks leading up to the vote. When the citizens of the Republic truly realized what had been done to them, what had been kept from them, they would go to their Assembly members and demand justice. The vote Andreas had orchestrated would be almost certain to succeed.

"We could make the Assembly push him out of power," Eva said. "Listen to me. He already faces a vote of impeachment. If we release enough memories—"

Korinne laughed. A number of her sailors joined in, the near-identical chuckles blending into a mocking chorus. "You truly think the Assembly will stop him?"

"They'll have no choice. What he's done undermines the democracy they've fought so hard to build. No one can vote freely when one man has so much power to deceive them."

Korinne's brows narrowed. She folded her arms across her chest. The silver buttons of her long black coat flashed in the sun. "They built their democracy on land stolen from the Sea People. With the labor of the children they call fosterlings. With the shattered souls of echoes as the glue that binds it together. I would not take their elections as proof of their devotion to the cause of freedom."

"I don't mean to say the Assembly is perfect. But that does not justify what you mean to do." Eva took a step forward. "I know the rage, the powerlessness, the loneliness of being something very few people understand." Some of the echo pirates exchanged heavy glances at that. "I've read your diary front to back a dozen times. You leaving it for me was a great kindness. There . . . there must be good in you, Korinne. Surely there is."

"I left that behind for if he ever put another echo in that room. Because I wanted that girl to know that we look after each other. You must know that, too. You took the power of the Skullrunner. You must have known how much it would mean to us to have that power back in our hands."

"It's only magic," Eva said. "The god-fragment I killed to take it—anyone could have killed her. It didn't have to be an echo—"

"But it was. And that matters. We don't have much power, sister. We have to use what we've got for us all." Korinne took a step toward Eva, hands held high. The abominations followed at her heels. "Right. I'll ask more mannerly this time. Come with us. These memories can only feed so many abominations. But the commander has larger vaults. Some even contain the memories of the gods themselves. With you at my side, I can have them all open in a fortnight."

"Come with us," said an echo with her hair cut short. "The Demon's a good captain. She looks out for us."

"We get the best scores with the Demon," said an echo with an eyepatch. "We have the best cook, too."

"We all get to share clothes," said an echo with a blue feather in her cap. "You'd like it!"

How do you know what I'd like? Eva struggled to find words. She filled her cheeks with air, then blew it out again. *Family.* What sort of family was this? One that would command an army of damned souls bound in flesh? A force to rival Morghaia's legions of walking corpses? They would, if they could. She could see it in their faces. The sisterhood they offered was a foul, corrupting thing. They brought out the worst in each other. And Eva was determined to be better than that.

"No," Eva said. "I sail with the *Sea Wolf*."

"You honor me, Miss Gavon." Cevette stepped in between her and Korinne, her shoulders back and her chest held high. She caught the older echo's gaze. "By all the customs of the sea, it's her choice who she sails with. I trust you'll respect her decision."

Korinne frowned. "She's my sister, not my slave. I'm not our father." Her dark eyes met Eva's. "Just try to remember that."

Our father isn't the tyrant that I see in you.

Two echoes walked up the dirt trail. They led a pair of weathered gray mules hooked to a three-wheeled cart. The beasts stopped a hundred feet from the abominations and refused to move closer, even when one echo jabbed them with a stick.

Korinne sighed. "Load up!" The other echoes dragged memory crates through the dirt and, grunting, to hoisted them aboard. Cevette stared at the crumpled memories as they went past, running her fingertips along her collar. Her lips moved in silent calculation. Eva had already counted herself: Korinne's echoes outnumbered them three to one.

Naeri leaned in at Cevette's ear and whispered, "Captain, your memory might be in the next one."

The captain's lips pressed together in a slight grimace. She scratched her neck, then ran a hand back through her short hair. At last, she nodded. "Right, crew. Off we go."

THERE WAS LITTLE CONVERSATION as they trooped back through the undergrowth. They returned to the cliff they'd climbed, and descended down it. Eva shimmied down the line, the rope burning in her fingers. She kicked off the side of the cliff, swung, and jumped down onto the deck. She wanted to put this place and its echoes behind her.

The moment Cevette's boots touched down on the upper deck, she called, "Lift anchor!" Eva ran to the crank by the starboard rail and joined two other pirates in pushing the wooden wheel round and round. Slowly, as their backs ached and sweat ran down their brows, the chain rose up from the sea. The ship creaked. Spars shifted in the rigging. Mr. Smoke pulled a rope, and the rolled-up sails opened once more. The canvas billowed in the wind. Wild waves slapped against the hull as Lovett steered their course back into the open sea.

Cevette came up beside Eva, who was leaning against the crank, and clasped her by the shoulder. "Want a smoke?"

Eva nodded. The captain waved for her to follow. With the white tails of her coat blowing out behind her, she led Eva her up the full flight of stairs to the quarterdeck, and then up the second, shorter flight to the poop deck. The flag of the skull weeping blood snapped in the wind above them. Once they were seated, side by side, atop one of the crates lashed to the stern rail, Cevette pulled a bundle of smokeweed from her pocket, packed it in a pipe, and lit it. She took a deep breath and passed it to Eva, who followed suit, and slowly felt the heavy lump in her throat dissolve.

"For years, I've searched for my true identity," Cevette said, her voice so soft that Eva thought at first she was talking to herself. "I've asked myself if I was one of the Upailitan women forced to labor in that shipyard, perhaps one who broke away and went to the Ya Tonim for aid, or if I was a Ya Tonim current woman who had travelled south with the raiding party. I might have been a current woman of the Wichil, smuggling guns out of the Republic for sale in the north, or even one of the Turtle Trappers, seeking allies against the Soladiseans on the rivers. I know their languages, their prayers, their customs, as if they were songs I heard long ago. But I don't know my part in the music. And it makes it quite hard to sing along."

Eva's heart twisted. "I'm so sorry, Captain," she said. Not knowing what else to do, she passed back the pipe.

Cevette took it, and breathed deeply. "It is my sorrow to carry. Not yours. But before today, I thought, well, it must be a blessing for echoes to know where they come from. They can all be kindred to one another. I did not realize that the knowledge of who you are could be as heavy as the lack of it."

"It is heavy," Eva said. "I . . . I often fear that the taint of Morghaia dooms me to cruelty and violence."

Cevette frowned. "Why turn pirate, then?"

Eva hesitated. Some of her reasons, she dared not put in words. They were as ephemeral and frightening as the desire that had surged inside her before she'd killed the Skullrunner. But some were easy to speak of. "I sail with you because you seek justice for my father's crimes. Not so that I might be like *her.*"

"Her? Korinne or Morghaia?"

"Is there a difference?"

Cevette passed back the pipe. Eva took it and inhaled. The sweet spice of the burning leaves eased the racing of her heart. Out to starboard, the sun was setting in the western sea. Red and gold striped the sky, like the work of a painter's brush. The colors made her think of the two dead Republic soldiers, blood staining their orange coats. She shuddered.

"I've known the Demon a few years now," Cevette said. "She's a good leader, and she loves her crew fiercely. She keeps her people on the right side of the pirates' treaty line with the Tarwik. And, yes, when she wants a thing done, she does it with violence, and her violence goes beyond what I would do myself."

"Beyond what I would do, as well." She noted Cevette had not said *you could never be like Korinne.* But the captain was still speaking with her, and had not run screaming, so perhaps that was implied. "Do you remember . . . do you think your echo girl ever did something that hurt you? Or was she . . . good?"

Cevette slumped forward, resting her chin in her hands, her elbows propped up on her knees. The back of her neck was sunburned raw. "I was the one who hurt her," the captain said quietly. "Maybe she hurt me, too, at times. Things can sometimes be that way in love. But there was something wrong with me, something that might be wrong still. I don't remember what it was. Only that it pushed us apart."

Oh. Eva's face softened. Her eyebrows drew together. She reached out and wrapped an arm around Cevette's waist. Beneath the thin fabric of her shirt, the captain was unexpectedly soft. Eva tugged Cevette closer. The captain's lips parted, a small round O of surprise. As slowly and deliberately as a general, she leaned down to rest her head on Eva's shoulder.

Cevette took the pipe from Eva's fingers, her hand callused yet gentle in that touch. She took another deep breath of the smoke and blew it out in a ring. "Thank you for listening, Miss Gavon, and for not condemning me."

"There's nothing condemnable about you." A slow smile crept across Eva's face. She trembled as Cevette looked up at her, her brown eyes as warm as the wood of the ship. "You're stubborn. You're quite hard on yourself. But you have my good opinion of you, and you always shall."

And some part of her was glad to hear Cevette and her girl had pulled apart from each other. That their love had not been perfect and irreplaceable. That Eva could perhaps offer Cevette something better.

"I shall make your faith in me my battle flag." Cevette smiled as well. "And, before the next raid, I suppose I should teach you to swim."

"Thank you. I would truly appreciate that. What does one wear to a swimming lesson?"

"As little as you're comfortable with. I shall wear nothing at all. If that's acceptable?"

"Quite acceptable." Eva's heart leapt. Warmth filled her chest. It had been years since she'd flirted with anyone. Why would she bother, with Andreas around? He was the one girls liked, the young gentleman with the silver tongue and the favor of the gentry. Next to him, Eva was nothing but an undeserving echo.

But she was not the worst echo in the Seaward Isles. Not yet. Perhaps there was something worth liking in her after all.

A Meeting at the Gallows

Beginning aboard the ship *Sea Wolf*, nine hundred and ten miles west of Halston, and continuing to the City of Halston, on High Hill Island. 7th Heralmonth, Year Twenty-Two of the Golden Republic.

Hellbroken Heraline, wife of death / A weeping mother left bereft / Tears that fill the empty seas / Grief that brings her to her knees / Her only son betrayed and caged // Nations rose beneath her hand / People of the sea so grand / By her will they united / Yet the seas were too blighted / And her peace became lost in the rage. –Entry for the letter *H* in A Children's Primer of the Golden Republic

Come dawn, the sea was a calm, glassy gray, turning violet where the sun kissed the horizon. Pale gray clouds hung low over the waters. The air smelled of snow and salt. Lovett and three other pirates winched Eva and Cevette over the side in a dinghy. It splashed down into the current, where it rocked gently back and forth, connected by a rope to *Sea Wolf*'s weathered flank. The world was so quiet that it felt like they might be the only people left alive.

Cevette removed her weapon belt and set it down in the boat's belly. She stripped off her vest and trousers; she wore naught but a man's long undershirt beneath. Eva removed her coat, and hesitated.

"I, ah, I only have two shifts," she said. "I'd like to not ruin this one. Do you mind if I . . . disrobe?"

"Not at all. Most Sea People swim nude, especially down south, in the warmer waters. We don't hold with Republic notions that one must wear fifty damn layers to be moral."

"I see. So . . . would it mean very little to you if I did?"

"I distinctly suspect that every inch of you is beautiful. But I desire your comfort more than anything." As Cevette spoke, she slid off her shirt. Eva's breath caught. Warmth swept through her. Her heart pounded heavily in her ears. Her eyes shone as she took in the sight of her captain. Her breasts were round and low-hanging, as full as moons. Strong lines of muscle ran like rigging lines through her forearms, shoulders, and back; the pale skin of her stomach was a soft curve about her naval. *Don't stare, Eva. You mustn't stare. This is for swimming. Well, no. For flirting, too. A bit of flirting.* There were scars, too, thin pink lines from stabbings and white puckers from bullets, angry red burns and even the deep rings of teeth marks that must have come from abominations. She wanted to run her fingers along them all, to memorize the heat and texture of them, to be grateful for each time her captain had faced the enemy and survived.

Cevette saw her staring and nodded. "Go on."

Cheeks burning, Eva disrobed completely. Cool air tickled her bare skin. Cevette was watching her, but Eva could not tell what her look meant. Kicking off her boots, she slid her feet into the sea, then turned around and lowered herself, inch by inch, clinging to the side of the dinghy. Her teeth chattered. Goosepimples rose down her bare chest.

Cevette dove in a neat arc. The sea sprayed up around her. She surfaced, tossed her head back, and began to tread water. Her skin flushed pink as her eyes met Eva's once again. "Hold your breath. Put your head under. Get your hair wet." Eva did as she said. The cold was a shock on her cheeks, but, when she came up, it was easier to bear. "Very good. Now, paddle and kick." Cevette demonstrated, swimming a swift circle around the dinghy. "Like this. Hands cupped. Turn to the side to breathe."

Eva did her best to copy the captain's movements. Her legs jerked like a toad's. Her arms flailed like a water wheel.

"Kick. Kick!" Cevette shouted. "Breathe to your side! There you go, just like that, there—"

Salt water flooded Eva's mouth. She coughed and sputtered. Cevette wrapped an arm around her chest, pulling her upright. Both of them grabbed hold of the dinghy.

"Are you well?" the captain asked.

"Yes. Thank you."

"Paddle a few yards out, turn around, and come back to me."

Eva lowered her head into the water. A shiver ran down her spine. *Cevette. Do it for Cevette.* She kicked and paddled, moving with all the grace of an elderly mule. "I might just prefer drowning! How do I look?"

"Alive! That's something!"

Eva turned about. With all her might, she strained to swim back to Cevette's side. The captain was treading water beside the dinghy, her grip loose on its side. Eva grabbed her by the shoulders and shoved her under.

Cevette came up laughing. Droplets of water flew as she shook out her short fringe of hair. "I'll do a swim about and demonstrate the technique. You can dry off for a bit and watch."

Eva nodded, and pulled herself back into the boat. As she wrung out her hair, Cevette lapped *Sea Wolf*. Her strokes were short and efficient, and she barely needed to come up for air. Muscle rippled in her shoulders. The shining sea sluiced off her bare skin.

Then, only yards from the captain, an abomination breached the surface in a white spray of foam.

Eva's breath caught. Her heart pounded. From the waist up, the creature resembled nothing as much as a large otter. But, as it dove through the waves, racing toward Cevette, she saw its hindquarters were that of a shark, and its fangs were yellowed and bloodied. It splashed back under the water, and Cevette reached for the dinghy. But its sharp gray tail fin brushed her chest, and she froze.

Eva drew her gun. "Stay still."

"Don't shoot. You know those things aren't accurate at close range."

"Captain, it's right atop you."

"I know. Wait." Cevette reached out a hand.

Ripples radiated across the sea as the beast reared up.

Eva held her breath.

The abomination butted its head into Cevette's chest, its wet fur shining. Its deep, dark eyes met hers. It cocked its head with a quizzical look.

Fangs aside, it resembled nothing as much as an eager puppy.

Cevette scratched the beast between the eyes. It made a chittering noise, its tail wagging and churning in a wash of white foam. After one last pat, it turned and dove deep. Swiftly, Cevette climbed back in the boat. It tossed from side to side as she sat on the wooden plank bench at the stern. Eva set down her pistol and sat beside her.

"That was … sweet," Eva said. "I thought all abominations were bloodthirsty killers."

Cevette shook her head. "Creatures like that one are rare and ancient. They dwell far out to sea, watching over the waters. They're not abominations; the word *abomination* refers to the perversion of the ancient practice that created them."

"Truly?" Eva said. "How did that go? If it's not prying for me to ask. I read a good deal about the study of abominations in Korinne's diary. She knew they were tied to the Sea People in some fashion. She was in correspondence with scholars of the Wichil Nation, who confirmed that the abominations originated at the same time our ancestors invaded the Seaward Isles, but they said the full history of those days had been lost in the chaos that followed."

"You should know what I can tell you," Cevette said. "You walk in Death. But let me start at the beginning. The universe is made from countless great rivers of energy, with no beginning or end, set in eternal motion. The Sea People often speak of the Three Currents: the flow of friendship between peoples, the flow of souls from one life to the next, and the flow of waters in the sea. We believe—broadly, mind you, many clans and nations share this philosophy, some do not—that what we pour into the currents is carried out to the whole sea. For good or ill, every choice we make has great power to affect the lives of others. What concerns this, and what concerns you more broadly, is that the current of the spirit waters, where the souls of the Sea People swim and sail, flows near the edge of the realm Soladiseans call Death."

"You told me to run away if I ever saw water in Death," Eva said.

"For good reason. The spirit waters are dangerous." Cevette sighed. She leaned over the rail of the dinghy and trailed her fingers in the water. Ripples spread across the calm, gray sea. "They used to be a safe haven, where souls could rest. From where they could reach out to their descendants, in dreams and omens, in wind and water, all the things of nature. And if an ancestor was needed for some great deed, the goddess Heraline would guide their soul through the spirit waters into a vessel of flesh and blood, so that they might return to the world and fulfill their purpose."

"Like the shark-otter?" Eva said. Cevette nodded. "What . . . what changed?" She hesitated as she finished asking. She already knew.

"When the ancestors of your people invaded this world, their ancestors invaded the spirit waters. They churned them into a great maelstrom, one that still spins, with the evil called the Hell's Eye at its heart. Its malevolent glare opens the way for those wicked souls to invade the Seaward Isles. And the spirits of our ancestors must struggle to withstand the storm it has brought upon them."

"It sends abominations into our world," Eva said. "And it hinders the spirits of the Sea People from connecting with their living kin." She cocked her head to one side. "If the souls inside the abominations are the long-ago ancestors of the Soladisean people, why do they attack us, too?"

"They have no love for their children. They *cannot* love. They sought to kill all Sea People to take this world for themselves. And the hate they poured into the Three Currents poisoned them, too."

Eva shivered. A cold wind washed across the surface of the still and glassy-gray sea, the fingertips of winter brushing her neck. This truth was a heavy thing to know, especially when she did not know what she could do about it. "Korinne spent years searching for the truth of where abominations came from. Do you think she would have come across this story?"

"I doubt it," Cevette said, quietly. "Not many of us remember. I couldn't even tell you where I learned it myself."

Eva studied the captain. How droplets of water shone on her bare skin. How the brown of her eyes was like the timber of *Sea Wolf,* or the pelt of a seal, or the richest of ambers. *There's something different about her.* Something Eva could not put words to. She had first assumed it was because she was one of the Sea People; a small difference in her mannerisms or accent, in how she saw herself and the world. But she had grown close to Donya, and had spent some time fishing with Tuk and Nukit, and she did not think Cevette's difference was simply a matter of culture.

She put a hand on Cevette's shoulder. Her skin was warm and slick with seawater. "Are you glad that you at least remember all these stories?"

"Very glad indeed," Cevette said. "But there are many sad ones."

"Your people will tell a story about you one day. How you fought to find them. How you came home. And it will be the happiest story of all."

"You truly think so?" Cevette looked up and met Eva's eyes. A small note of hope returned to her voice. "You don't believe they'll be angry with me? That I took so long?"

"Of course not. You've fought so hard to find them. They'll be so proud of you and all you've accomplished. It takes a great leader to unite people audacious enough to kill gods. I don't know what I did to deserve you."

"Thank you, Miss Gavon." Cevette reached up and squeezed Eva's shoulder. Her palm was firm and callused. "You deserve a great deal of good. I hope you never forget that."

WHEN THE MOON ROSE that evening, it was a waning sliver, the light of a demon-fire glowing green along the outside of the crescent. The stars were shrouded in fog. The crew milled about the upper deck, all of them gathering around a stack of crates near the foremast to drink rum. As they passed around bottles, Mr. Smoke told the story of how he fell in love with a star-maiden and travelled to her palace on the moon. He described his amorous affair in lurid detail; when the third sister of the star-maiden showed up, the others tossed their empty bottles at him.

"Can't believe I sail with this great lot of children," he grumbled. "No respect for romance." He scratched at his hairy neck. A distinctive scent rolled through the night. Eva wrinkled her nose.

The subject of bathing sparked some debate amongst pirates. Mr. Smoke insisted it weakened his powers; Lovett would wash thrice a day if he could. For her first bath aboard *Sea Wolf*, Eva had stripped down in a tiny wooden tub and spent half an hour tossing a small pail of water over her head and scrubbing with a lump of soap no bigger than a coin. It had been hard, cold labor. Still, she was firmly on the side of bathing, and dearly hoped Mr. Smoke could one day be persuaded to join them there.

"I'll tell a story," Lizeth said. They hopped down from the crate where they had been sitting next to Eva and cracked their knuckles. The black paint around their eyes had melted in the day's heat. It ran down their cheeks in ribbons. "In the height of the Soladisean invasion of the Sapphire Isles, the wicked Emperor Aurendros Augustis lay siege to the capital of the Kingdom of Serpent Riders. Their armies were decimated. Their people were desperate. Aurendros Augustis marched his legion up the narrow mountain road. Then, from the sky, he heard the cry of a great eagle. The bird dove from the sky. The mountains trembled as it landed. It took the form of Toponomitl, the Stormbraider, ten feet tall, with wings of razor-sharp obsidian. He charged, one god against a legion. And you know what he did?"

"He killed them all," Donya said, and yawned. "You've told that story a thousand times."

"It's a tale worth telling. It's how my people brought down the Empire of Soladis."

"The Empire of Soladis brought itself down," Lovett said.

Lovett and Naeri sat together on a pair of embroidered cushions across from the stack of crates. She leaned against him, her head resting on his cheek. The night wind stirred the lace ruffles on her sleeves. "You're so intelligent," she whispered. Lovett scratched his nose. Eva, though she liked Lovett well enough on his own, could not help but occasionally question her friend's taste in men.

Lovett went on. "The war the Empire lost to Toponomitl is what led to its fall. But only because that loss gave Morghaia and Heraline the leverage they needed to unite the gods of Soladis around their plan for peace between Soladis and the Sea People. They had a son together, Kasperos, the Crownbearer, and put him on the emperor's throne. He was meant to lead everyone into a new age of peace."

"Only he was a rotting bastard," Donya said. "So he fucked it all up."

Eva frowned. She drummed her fingers on the rough wood of the crate where she sat. All her life, she had heard tales of the empire's fall. Of the wars in the Sapphire Island that had decimated the forces of Soladis; of Kasperos, the young emperor who had carried on his shoulders the last chance for peace. But she had never heard a telling that did not place the blame for the collapse squarely upon the goddess she had come from.

She looked to Cevette. "Is it true that Morghaia summoned a legion of corpses to burn the city of Soladis to the ground?" He heart leapt as she spoke. If Morghaia wasn't a monster—

"She did that," Cevette said. The captain sat on the highest crate, a head above all the others. She held a lantern in her lap. Light danced off her chin and the folds of her long white coat. "Our histories measure the facts much the same as the Soladisean ones. Morghaia and the other gods fell into a bloody civil war after the Crownbearer was overthrown. The Empire of Soladis collapsed. Most of the gods knew nothing of life before it; it was a devastating blow. The only way they could keep themselves from each other's throats was to divide the Isles into separate kingdoms, each one ruled by a different handful of gods. The Theocracy. It was a dark age, marked by ignorance, violence, and disease. Morghaia played her part in it, and Heraline stood beside her."

"Oh," Eva sighed. Another pirate passed her a jug of rum. She took a hearty sip and handed it to Mr. Smoke, who tipped it down his throat and finished it off.

"If it helps," Cevette said, "I believe the hatred for Morghaia, within the Republic, at least, is rooted not in the violence she did, but the peace she tried to build. She was cruel and demanding, but she acted to help the Sea People where she could. She pushed the Empire and the governments that followed it to adhere to their treaty obligations and not expand past their set borders. The Soladiseans of today would love her more dearly if she had simply given them what they wanted."

Eva frowned, thinking that over. She had never made that connection between Morghaia's attempts to help her wife's people and the hatred that the Golden Republic still bore her. The citizens of the Republic would be horrified by the insinuation. But Eva could not help but think it made a degree of sense.

"Whatever good Morghaia did the Sea People," said Donya, who leaned against the side of the crate Cevette sat atop, "it was Heraline who pushed her to do it. I'll never forget that. Heraline left her people to join her wife and the other Soladisean gods in the capital. For centuries, she stood alone, doing everything she could to convince the Empire of Soladis to spare us. Yes, her wife stood with her. But Heraline had the hardest struggle, and she did it all with no one by her side who truly understood what she had lost."

"Heraline was a coward," Cevette said. There was a sharpness to her tone Eva had never heard before. "Everything that made her what she was, she surrendered it without even a fight. Once, she had a thousand names, a thousand faces, a world of worshippers who called out for her guidance. Then she married Morghaia. She took a Soladisean name and a Soladisean look. She could have fought for our freedom. Instead, she stood beside the gods of an Empire that hated us and negotiated treaties that left us with nothing but crumbs. What good did that do us?"

"We're still here," Donya said. Her fingers curled around a nearby rigging line. The pink membrane between her fingers shone in the green-tinted moonlight.

"Splintered. Divided." Cevette frowned and pushed her hand back through her hair.

"I don't see why you're so hard on her," said Donya. "She was never the most important god back on Kossi. She's a traveler. She looks after the waters that connect us. But my grandmother taught me, if I saw her in the water, I should show her the same respect I would show any current woman. She's one of them. She should matter to you."

"I'll change my opinion of Heraline if and when she does something for the Sea People. She's been hiding ever since she lost her wife. Our people deserve better than that."

"I won't argue with that," Donya said. "And you know how much I like to argue."

Donya then said something in Kossket; Cevette answered in the same. They laughed. The captain pulled a pipe from her pocket, lit the smoke-weed, and breathed deep. She leaned down and passed it to Donya, who took a deep hit, then smiled and passed it to Lizeth.

"Your turn." Lizeth blew out smoke and passed the pipe to Eva. She slid it through her lips, took a deep breath, and thought, *do I have the right to form my own judgement of Morghaia?* She passed the pipe back to Lizeth, her head spinning. Morghaia was gone. There was no putting her back together. What Eva thought of her mattered very little, in the practical sense. *But there are echoes who would follow in her footsteps. Echoes like Korinne.* And if Eva came to see the shattered goddess in a kinder light, it might make it all the easier for her to follow Korinne into dark waters.

Pressure built at Eva's temples. A fog stole through her head. She felt a sensation like fingers rustling through papers, but deep inside her mind. Her heart raced. She stared down at her godmarked fingers.

A memory swept through her, as vivid as if it were the night of her birthday dinner once more. The words Commander Gavon had spoken, low in her ear, after Cevette Zarcanzi had been dragged from the great hall back in the Halston. *Well done, daughter. You made me proud.* He had kissed her cheek, and squeezed her shoulder, and explained what she must do: help the pirate escape, infiltrate her crew, learn of their strengths and weaknesses—then drive a dagger through Cevette's heart. This was her first mission as an officer of the Godreaper Corps. And it was time she saw it through and went home.

Her fingers crept toward the knife in her boot.

Cevette jumped down from the crate she sat atop and grabbed Eva's wrist. Eva froze.

"I know that look in your eyes, Miss Gavon. Don't do anything foolish. We're all friends here."

"I'm not doing anything—"

"You don't truly wish to do this." Her voice was low. Steady. Reassuring. "The commander has split an echo. He's altered your memory to pull you back to him."

The sacrifices. Cevette believed they were real. Just like she did.

Eva shook her head from side to side. Her lips pressed together in a tight grimace. *Father loves me. He wants to honor me.* No. He had only ever wanted to honor Andreas. *I could be an officer. I could show the Isles that echoes can be good.* But nothing good would come of her serving him.

"How do I fight it?" Eva said.

"You already are. Remind yourself what matters most."

What matters most. Eva met the captain's deep brown eyes. They were wide and worried, the thick lines of her eyebrows knit together, her lips pursed in concern. *Father is lying to me. He must be lying.* She could never raise a hand against someone who looked at her like that. She could never believe that she would be better off in the fortress than at sea with Cevette.

The grip of magic clinging to her lessened. She had made no such plans with her father. He had ordered her dragged from the great hall with barely a word. She could see both the true and false memory together, and she knew them for what they were.

Eva breathed deeply. Her racing pulse stilled.

"Better?" Cevette said.

She nodded. "Everything's come back, I believe."

"Good. We're lucky, all things considered. Whatever echo he sacrificed, it seems he didn't draw a great amount of power from them. Nothing like what he did when he took my memories from me."

"I'm glad we have you around, captain," Donya said. "You have a knack for telling exactly when Gavon's doing it."

"He's a predictable man."

He's a tyrant, Eva told herself. *Whatever evil might lie within echoes, we don't deserve this. No one does.* That was the truth, and it was the sort of truth that demanded action of her. Korinne had answered its call in her own way.

She needed to speak to her brother.

The next morning, Eva ran to Halston.

She ran through corridors of twisted bone, northeastward, crossing the sea and frontier in a few short steps. As she went, the hall grew wider, stretching from five to fifty feet across. In their own peculiar fashion, the halls of Death mirrored the realm of the living: each place within its walls of smoke were as (relatively) large as its graveyards. Souls milled about, wreathed in clouds of silver smoke, bent-backed farmers who died of age or exhaustion, youths struck down by mischance or the ague. A small number of them looked to her; but then they looked away again, and did nothing. Eva had some vague idea they might expect the Skullrunner to do something for them, but, as she did not know what that was, she avoided their gazes. She would work that out later.

The city called to her, a howling void of living and dying that pulled her forward like a towline. As Eva drew near Halston, she passed windows bordered in tibia and scapulae, each one a small round eye, rising up into the vaulted ceiling. Her fingers brushed the bone lintels of the nearest portals. They hummed with fear and pain. But none were quite what she was looking for.

Show me the docks, she thought as she peered through the windows, glimpsing anonymous bedrooms and back alleys. The docks would be where she'd have the best chance of finding Andreas. He would be preparing to sail south with their father for the Assembly meeting, as he did every time the Assembly gathered. *Docks. Docks. The Halston docks.* She needed drunk drownings, workers crushed as they unloaded cargo, the gallows where the pirates swung. *Come to me.* She turned her head, willing Death to guide her. The windows seemed to spin about her. She glimpsed a portal unfurling like an opening blossom, framed with a black-smoke lattice of human ribs. Beyond it hung a row of fraying nooses.

Eva didn't break her stride as she crossed through. Around her, the world opened into gray fog.

She stood beneath the wooden platform of the gallows, which rose eight feet off the ground. There were no hangings scheduled for today; the air was quiet and there were no soldiers about. Eva took a deep breath, and stepped out into the day. Quickly, before she could be noticed, she ducked into the shadow cast by a city wall.

The harbor and the dock market lay where the city wall opened like a bell onto the sea. Ten feet high, the red-gray brick enclosed the harbor to the east and west. The ships lay still, only four in number today, anchors dropped and lines bound to the docks, their sails drawn up. Smaller fishing vessels were tied to the docks beside them, bobbing in the current. The harbor buildings were tall and whitewashed, their square windows shuttered and the doors barred.

The people were just as closed-off. A group of fosterlings in gray rags, the youngest of them barely ten, hammered new planks into the dock smashed by the kraken attack. Passerbys in brown homespun walked around the children, heads low. Only the shouts of fishmongers could be heard, ringing out from the market stalls where the docks met the land, holding up their glassy-eyed catches. Even the banners with the Golden Republic's emblem hung limp.

Halston was just as she had glimpsed it whenever her father had let her take a carriage into the city, which had been rare enough. But what caught her eye were the notices. They covered the wall, the sides of buildings, the fronts of market stalls. Hundreds of them, the paper freshly printed, not yet swelling in the cool dampness of the air. He must have ordered them placed the moment she had not responded to his gambit in her memory.

Cmdr. Jonathan Junosi Gavon has Issued a Reward of Ten Thousand Pounds for the Brave Soul who Captures and Returns the Rebellious Echo Fosterling, Evazina, Twenty-Two and Thin, who Departed Halston without His Express Permission.

A sheen of sweat rose on Eva's skin. Her nostrils flared. *The Rebellious Echo Fosterling.* That was her crime. Not piracy, not kidnapping Tomis Beauchamp, not freeing a prisoner. Leaving. *He would see me in chains for that.* Her skin flushed. Her pulse raced. Her fingers curled into fists, itching to pull the daggers from her sleeves. If she had her father in front of her in that moment, she might have opened his throat.

This was not the rage of a monster. Commander Gavon had freely and eagerly brought her rage on himself.

A clatter of hoofbeats filled the air. Three army officers in orange coats rode down the main avenue into the harbor proper. A troop of soldiers followed them. As the officers shouted orders, the soldiers spread out along the docks. Most went to the ships and the crates loaded off them; with iron pry-bars, they forced them open, digging about, looking for . . . something. Eva looked them over. Then her breath caught. *There.*

One of the officers was Zeke. He had dismounted from his horse and gone to inspect the base of the demolished dock; he was speaking with the fosterling laborers. Andreas stood behind him, clad all in black, fiddling with the hilt of his sword. *Oh, good. They're getting on decently, for once.*

Eva ducked under the gallows and stepped into Death.

It was a quick few steps across the harbor. Three soldiers had died during the confrontation with the kraken. She went to the window one had left behind and waited. Andreas and Zeke walked past her, their heads buried in earnest conversation.

Eva reached through the window, grabbed each man by one wrist, and pulled as hard as she could.

Caught off-guard, they stumbled backward. White smoke wrapped around them as they fell into Death. They went still as statues and as light as feathers. She tugged them along behind her for a few quick steps and pulled them out of Death into the shadows beneath the gallows.

"Eva!" Zeke gasped as he stumbled, reaching out to steady himself against a nearby support post. Andreas fell to the cobblestones. "What—how?" He looked to her. For a moment, Eva wondered if she'd made a mistake. In the orange wool coat of his uniform, his eyes wide and alert, he was looking at her in the way a soldier looked at a foe. But then he shook his head, smiled, and he was Zeke again, crushing her into a hug. "You're safe!"

Love and warmth washed through her like a wave. She squeezed him back, as hard as she could. He gasped in pain. "What's wrong?" Eva said, and let him go.

"Still recovering." He stepped backward, still smiling. "I took an arrow for your father. By the gods. It's so good to see you."

"Someone tried to kill my father?"

"Don't worry. He's unharmed."

Eva frowned, and bit her lip. It was a cruel thing to think—something *Korinne* would think—but if that archer had struck home, a good number of her problems would be solved.

Andreas stood, brushed the dust off his long black coat, and gazed up at the open trap door above him. "We're all the way over at the gallows. Did you just tug us through Death? Gods, that's unnerving."

"You're unnerving," Eva said, and stuck her tongue out at him. "I'm glad you two are getting on. Have you finally decided to be friends?"

"Hardly," Andreas said. "I needed to take my trunks to the docks, and Zeke decided to come along so he could check the ships for hidden assassins for the third time. What brings you back to Halston?"

She drew a deep breath. "Father's conducting sacrifices. He tried to shift my memory last night. I was able to resist, and . . . and I believe that means the echo he sacrificed was quite young. All I could think of last night was how I could have saved her."

Her brother's cheeks flushed red. He looked away from her. Eva didn't understand. *Is that shame I see?*

"You might be next," she said. "I had to warn you."

He laughed. There was a hint of a bitter edge in it. "I'm certain he's saving me for something special. Perhaps he'll need me to erase a lost battle or an outbreak of plague."

"He wouldn't," Zeke said.

Eva turned to face him. Sweat had beaded on his forehead. "The sacrifices are real. And I can prove it." An autumn wind whistled through the harbor. The gallows trapdoors, hanging open, swung on their hinges. "Recently, did you remember a night when I tried to slip out of the fortress? You and Father found me hiding in the dungeons. He brought soldiers with him. When they grabbed me, you tried to stop them, and he had you beaten black-and-blue."

Zeke's mouth opened and closed several times before he said anything. He looked away from her and straightened his cuffs as he spoke. "It . . . it was only a dream."

"Then how do I know of it?"

"I . . . I assume pirates have all sorts of strange magic."

"Enough, Ezekiel," Andreas said. He put a hand on Eva's shoulder and pulled himself in closer to her. "The sacrifices are real. Even you can't be foolish enough to believe my father has clung to power so long thanks to the goodwill of the voters alone."

Zeke frowned. Eva went on, encouraged. "He targeted my memory. He tried to convince me I'd been sent to *Sea Wolf* to kill Captain Zarcanzi and that I should do so and come back to join the Godreaper Corps."

"And you say that's the commander's magic?" Zeke shook his head. "Eva, that sounds like your good sense speaking. Kill the pirate. Tell your father that Captain Zarcanzi kidnapped you. He'll forgive—"

"I don't want his forgiveness." Her words cracked like a gunshot. She folded her arms across her chest. Her heart pounded in her ears. "I've seen what he does when provoked. Jailings, wanted posters, sacrifices." Anger burned inside her like the fuse of a lit bomb. What would be left of her if it went off? "He must be held to account for what he's done."

Zeke took a step closer to her. "You *must* come home."

"No." She shook her head. "I'm here to warn my brother. Andreas, if you need to leave, I can take you far away from here. We can go now."

Andreas pursed his lips. He turned his head, glancing out from under the gallows at the soldiers milling about the harbor. No one seemed to have noticed that Eva had snatched the pair of them away. She had been lucky. Andreas might not have that much luck left.

"No," he said. "I have business to settle while the Assembly meets."

The vote of impeachment. He would go south for the Assembly meeting, and he would make certain it passed. Eva smiled. The squeezing pressure in her chest ebbed away. She was proud of her brother. He always seemed to know the right thing to do. "I can help you," she said.

He leaned in close to her ear. A lock of bleached hair had escaped the tie at the back of his neck and fallen down across his forehead. His dark roots were beginning to show. She could not read his face as he said, quietly, "What do you propose?"

With a twist in her heart, Eva realized she could not let Zeke hear her.

In a low voice, she whispered, "I can release the memories. Reveal what he's done."

"What?"

"When he steals them, they take on physical form. He's hidden them all over the Isles. Cevette and I—we're looking for them. We can set them free. Will that help you win the vote?"

He pursed his lips, thinking it over. A light sparked in his eyes. "Do it," he whispered. "Godspeed, sister."

Eva gave him a tight hug. Beneath the thin fabric of his shirt, he was so slender she could feel his bones poking into her. She wanted to tell him about Korinne. She wanted him to reassure her that the two of them were not on the same path as her. That all they shared was a look, the same eyes, the same stature, and that many ordinary people looked alike as well. But, when she held him close, all she could think of was that she held the other half of her own splintered soul.

She squeezed him tightly once more, then let go.

"Eva," Zeke whispered. She looked up at him. "Please. Come *home.*"

She frowned. The pain in his voice took the edge off her frustration with her old friend. "Zeke . . ."

"I've spoken with the commander. He's ready to have you as an officer of the Godreaper Corps. He's offering you a place of honor."

"These notices insinuate I'm facing criminal charges."

"Yes, I know. But he only had those posted because you ran away. If you come back, they'll disappear. We'll all be happy again. I promise you."

She wanted to believe him. That, if she only served the Republic, all her turmoil would vanish into mist. She would be safe from the sacrifices if she went back to the commander and pledged her loyalty. He would rip apart other echoes instead.

"Please," Zeke said. "I know your father is a . . . a difficult man, yes. He's stern, and demanding. But he cares, and he tries, and he . . . you don't know him as I do, but trust me, as your friend, when I promise you that your father has a good heart."

"Zeke . . ." She hated to see the tears brimming in his eyes. *I'm hurting him.* She didn't know what to say. *I'll come home.* But her lips went numb before she could speak.

Andreas broke in. "By the gods, Dare, are you fucking him?"

The words cracked like a whip, petty and cruel. It was the sort of careless jibe Andreas might toss out at any moment. But Zeke froze. His mouth fell open. His shoulders slumped. He blinked, slowly, and licked at his lips. He said nothing.

"Oh," Andreas said, softer now. "That second glass of whisky on his bedside table."

A few moments passed before Eva realized what he meant, and a few more passed before she truly *understood.* Reflexively, she shook her head. *It can't be.* But of course it could. For all the power her father held over echoes, he held nearly as much over a young man tied to the army by a foster bond. Her guts churned. She bit her lip until she tasted copper. Her hands curled into fists.

She shook her head. "Zeke, I'm taking you out of here."

"What . . . what do you mean?"

"I'll take you anywhere in the Isles you want to go. You don't have to join me on *Sea Wolf*, though Cevette would welcome you. You could go to Soladis, or the Sapphire Isles, or home to Greymarket. But you're not staying here. You're not staying anywhere near him."

"Eva," he said. "You don't understand. We're in love. We're going to be married."

"He's lying to you," she said, and took a step toward him. "He sacrifices children, Zeke. He can't be trusted."

"He doesn't! He would never! The whole world knows what a great man he is."

"The echoes know different." She grabbed for his arm. He jumped, and scrambled backwards.

"No closer," Zeke growled. White light pulsed at his fingertips.

Eva hesitated. *His magic.* "You wouldn't." If he struck her with his power, she would not be able to enter Death for hours. He would be free to arrest her and haul her to the fortress in chains.

"Please." His voice trembled. "Come home. So long as you evade your father, you are an enemy of the Republic. You are *my* enemy."

Eva closed her eyes. *An enemy of the Republic.* Every legend she had ever heard of Morghaia swept through her. The legions of the dead that had once terrorized the Five Sisters. The great city of Soladis burning as an empire collapsed into divine chaos. The stories seemed to wrap her throat like a noose. Strangling her. Holding her back. She thought of Korinne and her crew, following the path of Morghaia to death and destruction. *They only fight for themselves.* Eva would do this for Zeke, for Cevette, and for everyone whose mind had been violated by her father.

"I am your friend," Eva said. "And I intend to free us all."

She turned her back on him and lifted her hand. Gray smoke blossomed at her fingertips. An archway of bones and swirling darkness yawned open before her. She squared her shoulders and drew a deep breath.

"Eva, down!" Andreas shouted. Instinctively, she ducked.

A bolt of Zeke's magic flew over her head. It struck the gallows and vanished in a flash of light.

"Go!" Andreas shouted. "I'll take care of things here. Go!"

Eva lunged into Death. Her feet hit the bone floor hard. Her pulse hammered hard in her ears. Down the hallway she sprinted, darting around spirits, tears of anger and rage running down her face. *Fuck you, Ezekiel Dare,* she thought. *I will help you. Mark my words.*

The power of the Skullrunner was hers now. She would make her own path with it. One that led to justice.

THE GARDEN OF THE GODS

ON THE ISLAND OF KITES, WHICH THE SOLADISEANS ALSO CALL GOD'S GARDEN, ONCE THE HOME OF THE WIND DANCERS, FIVE HUNDRED AND FIFTY MILES SOUTH OF MOONWHISPER ISLE. 11TH HERALMONTH, YEAR TWENTY-TWO OF THE GOLDEN REPUBLIC.

My father, who for a time studied at the Carreton in Halston, said that, while he was there, the Soladiseans would always ask what he thought of Kasperos. He would say that he hated him. Many Soladiseans would agree with him. They hated Kasperos because the ancient god-emperor was the son of a Sea People goddess and yet he had claimed the throne of the empire as if he had the rights of a full-blooded Soladisean. But some Soladiseans would tell him that he did not judge Kasperos fairly, that he did not take into account the difficulties of his position as the first and only emperor of mixed heritage. To that, my father said that family was not a difficulty, but an obligation. He hated Kasperos more for what he had done to his own. –'Our History of the Golden Republic,' published in *The Dawn Beacon*

CEVETTE HAD BEEN THE first person Eva had told of what had passed between her and Zeke, and she had been furious on Eva's behalf. "After all those years of friendship, he owed you better."

"I understand his anger," Eva had told her. "That's what comes of being close to my father. All the world calls him a great man. When he hurts you, you don't know what to think. So you think what he wants you to."

"You're very forgiving." Cevette had said. "I find it an admirable quality. But be cautious, Miss Gavon. Many people do not deserve your grace."

The next day, Eva had pushed her power once again and had run to Port Dueno, where the posters had yet to appear. She had purchased spare rope and spars, and, in a novel feat, had dragged a rented oxcart through Death behind her. Silver smoke had bound the ox and kept the weight feather-light until she re-emerged on *Sea Wolf*. The ox had panicked. Mr. Smoke had shot and butchered it. He had seared steaks for the crew over his glowing palm.

"You're not the only one to get chased out of the Republic with your tail between your legs," he had told Eva. "When I was your age, my ma and I got ran out on account of witchcraft. We would tell fortunes and read the weather, make cures for folks who couldn't afford the doctor. When the Republic got started, the soldiers told us we weren't fit for citizenship. Chased us out, the bloody bastards." He had spat over the rail, taking care to get none on the meat.

Several weeks after Eva's arrival on board, they sailed past the first of the Whitestones. The great alabaster pillars dotted the seas between the Lonely Isles and Dogshead. Wind whipped about the stone monoliths. Seabird nests packed the chinks on its sides. Crew members lit candles and tossed handfuls of nuts in the sea, beseeching forgotten gods for safe passage. Cevette peered down from the rail of the poop deck, supervising the sailors who had the helm. Just behind her, Eva and Lovett sat atop a crate, studying a navigational chart. All were being moderately distracted by the ongoing debate between Lizeth and Tomis Beauchamp.

"It is the press that holds the greatest power to remedy the flaws of the Golden Republic," said the captive journalist. Stripped of his finery and clad in only a simple cotton shirt and breeches, his red curls flying back on the wind, he carried himself with the ease of a man for whom discomfort was still a novel adventure. "Through our work, we inform the citizens so they might hold the government accountable for their failings through their votes."

Lizeth shook their head. They paced tighter and ever tighter circles across the small poop deck. The tails of their violet coat, another of Naeri's armored creations, snapped each time they turned. Eva worried they might fall down. "I'm Terraloro. From the Sapphire Isles. The Soladiseans see us as lesser, as mixed-blood. We vote. We have Terraloro members of the Assembly. But whenever the Terraloro need something from the Republic, the Assembly members from the Five Sisters and Soladis band together to vote it down." They shook their head. "What good is a vote if it doesn't count? What good is a voice if no one listens?"

"If enough voices are raised—if enough papers are written—"

"Some people can only hear the sound of guns." Lizeth tapped the pistols at their hips. "Eva, you understand, don't you? Echoes can't even vote. But there's a better, faster path to claim our rights."

"Don't ask me to join in," Eva said. "I'm no good at debating."

Tomis sighed. "The press can play a powerful role to remedy the flaws of the Republic. But it has its limits. I've spoken with Andreas Gavon about the plight of the echoes—"

Eva raised an eyebrow. "You know my brother?"

"We're both members of the philosophers' guild. You're Andreas' sister? I thought you might be, but I didn't want to assume. We meet whenever he comes to Soladis. Did you ever travel south with him?"

Eva shook her head.

"The citizenship laws are powerfully unfair," Tomis continued. "As is the allocation of Assembly seats that dilutes the votes of the Terraloro. I've written about that in my paper. My articles spark conversations in the greatest houses of Soladis, among the members of the Assembly themselves. I believe they are willing to listen. Not all of them, and not all right now, but in time—"

"People need change *now*," Lizeth said. "We shouldn't have to wait on a group of old Soladisean politicians to decide that they'll treat us better."

"Well," Tomis said, "I do agree with that. Perhaps we differ in our preferred methods, but I am glad we all understand that the world should and will become more just and equitable for us all."

"Will it?" Cevette said. It was a low, bitter whisper, and in it Eva almost felt the nearness of Death. The captain then shook her head. She looked over her shoulder at Eva and gave her a tired, genuine smile. "Miss Gavon, Mr. Lovett, how's our heading?"

Lovett unrolled the largest of his charts, which fell all the way to his feet. The salt-weathered paper showed nearby landmarks, the flow of the currents, the location and depths of nearby harbors. He had scrawled calculations across it in a messy hand, now, as he read it, he cleared his throat twice and adjusted his glasses. "We're almost there."

Cevette peered at the chart. "Let me check the harbor depths." She took the chart from him and paced across the deck, working out the math with a charcoal stub. Tomis and Lizeth resumed their debate. Eva, seeing a chance, grabbed Lovett by the elbow and said, "This morning, I found Naeri crying in the crew's mess. About *you*."

He winced, and looked away from Eva, running a hand through his close-cropped curls as he stared out across the endless gray of the sea and low-hanging clouds. "I am most certainly not worthy of her."

"Your behavior does you no credit. Lovett, why will you not simply marry her?"

Lovett drew a deep, shaky breath. "Have you read the myths of the Lorekeeper? The god I killed was a well-read creature, but a lonely one. And never in all his tales was he brave enough to defy that fate."

"Why does that matter?"

"The shadow of the Lorekeeper has always eclipsed my own." Lovett frowned. "When the Theocracy fell, the Lorekeeper took his closest priests and fled to a remote island. Two of them were my parents. He held them all in his grip. We dared not speak against him. All throughout my childhood, I was taught that questioning him was a sign of wickedness, one I deserved to be punished for. I learned to hate my own mind."

"It sounds as if you were well justified in killing him."

"I thought I was freeing my family," he said, quietly. "But they saw the marks on my arms and said he had chosen me to reap him. That I had to take his place. They held me prisoner in the temple and prayed to me, day and night. Their voices crept into my mind, and with them came the knowledge that I might have infinite power if served their desires. I escaped in the end; I snuck aboard a trader's ship and reached Soladis. But I still hear their prayers, in the dark of the night, and I still feel the urge to answer."

Eva frowned. She met his dark brown eyes, which was the sort of thing she almost never did purposefully, but she needed to make her point clear. "We are not the gods we've killed."

"They live inside us. Perhaps they slumber, deep within our souls, but sleeping or waking, our fates are joined. There is joy in connection, but there is horror in it, too. And the Lorekeeper would not be a fit husband for any woman."

"You're a fool," she said. It came out sharp and swift.

"Perhaps," said Lovett. "I would rather be a fool than what I fear. But I think you know this fear too, Miss Gavon. You hold the power of the god from whence you came. Have you never wondered what that might mean for your fate?"

"No." Her skin crawled. Her stomach churned. "It's power. Only power. It means nothing more to me. Nothing at all."

He gave her a piercing look. She turned away from him.

A swift breeze parted the clouds. "Ah, there it is!" Lovett said. He jumped to his feet, crossed the quarterdeck, and went to stand by Cevette at the starboard rail. A small island poked out from the sea, a tall green hill ringed by pillars of alabaster, the stone rising from the sea in perfectly octagonal prisms. "God's Garden. There's an archive on those shores."

Eva had spent a good portion of her time in Halston studying naval charts and current maps. She had also read tales of all the voyages that had set out to learn what lay beyond the Seaward Isles, which had found nothing but open water, Sea People ruins, and disaster. She knew a great deal of sailors' lore. The tale of what had happened on God's Garden was heartbreaking. A cold shiver crept up her spine.

"The Republic lost track of this archive long ago," Lovett said. "I could only find it referenced in one book, and no records indicate there's any presence of soldiers."

Cevette frowned. "Their government is only twenty years old and it's already losing track of its secrets?"

"The Assembly is quite sloppy." Tomis trotted up to the rail and leaned on it with one elbow. "Captain, may I have leave to go ashore with you and your crew? I would like to see this archive for myself."

"Do you understand what we're after?" said Cevette.

"I've been interested in the archives for a good while. The Assembly is so secretive about them that I always assumed they were where Gavon placed his stolen memories."

Eva froze. "You also believe that he's stealing them?"

"I've heard all the rumors about him and his sacrifices, yes. It makes a good deal of sense as to how he stays in power. He's quite terrible at governance."

"What?"

"Oh, yes. He and his allies on the Assembly have drained the public coffers by authoring laws that exempt their land holdings from taxation. He has pilfered what little remains from the public hospitals and ferry services to fund his army—an army with no enemies save abominations and outlaw bands, neither of which said army has displayed any true skill at defeating. He has turned the Ministry for Child Welfare into a vehicle for the enablement of forced labor. His one political skill is propaganda; he is an expert in making himself appear to be a hero. But that only means his greatest weakness is the truth. And I intend to expose it all. What he has done to his people, and what he has done to the echoes."

Eva stared at him through narrowed eyes. He spoke like an ally. But could she trust him? A wealthy landholder who, by all accounts, had profited greatly under her father's government. What did he stand to gain by this? She wanted to know.

"He should come," Eva said to Cevette. *So I can keep an eye on him.*

"Very well," Cevette said. "Tomis, can you row?"

"I've never tried," Tomis said, "but how hard can it be?"

Swiftly, Eva prepared herself for the expedition ashore. Ducking back down into the crew's quarters, she donned a shirt, stockings, good wool breeches to fend off the rising chill, a waistcoat of amber satin embroidered with dancing harts—a gift from Naeri after Eva had fetched her silk ribbons from Port Dueno. She worked a comb through her hair, braided it, and tucked it up beneath her soft leather tricorn hat, then donned her armored coat. Her eyes were bright; she climbed back to the upper deck with a quick and eager step. For far too many years, she had been penned up in Halston. Every inch of her buzzed like a hummingbird at the chance to see something new.

Eva climbed aboard a dinghy with Donya and Tomis; Cevette and Mr. Smoke had taken the other one, and theirs was already zipping toward the shore at a good pace. Lovett and three other pirates turned the winch to lower the second dinghy down. Ropes creaked. The dinghy scraped against the hull. Tomis sang a tune. "'I have won a starry crown, I have won a silver throne. And the children laugh and play in the garden I have grown—'"

"Oh, that's a dark one," Donya said gleefully. She sat perched in the small boat's stern. The wind was plucking the curls free from her sky-blue bonnet. "'Yet the harvest rose up high and my fields were full of bones. And I curse the gods I stand alone here at the red dawn.'"

She sang about murder and hungry gods as Tomis and Eva took up oars and tried to row in unison. They couldn't keep a rhythm, so they drifted in circles, barely two hundred feet from *Sea Wolf,* until the watching crew had all laughed their guts out and Cevette and Mr. Smoke were nearly at the shore. At last, with Donya drumming her palm on her knee, they found their timing. Schools of shimmering green fish flocked about the dinghy's sides as they rowed their way through the surf.

"Why were you out at sea when we grabbed you?" Eva asked Tomis.

"I was sailing back to Soladis. To cover an important movement in the Assembly." The wind had turned his red curls to a bird's nest; smears of sun-ointment, which Donya brewed from grease and fat, covered his sweaty cheeks. His brown eyes were bright and alert. "A vote of impeachment in Commander Gavon. One orchestrated by your brother."

Eva raised an eyebrow. "He told you?"

"No. I don't blame him; he has good reason to keep his involvement a secret, though I'm sure he wants nothing more than to brag of it to all the Isles. But I know him well enough, and I have eyes and ears."

He was no fool, this Beauchamp. "And you mean to write an article to help the vote pass?"

"I mean to write an article that will help the people understand why the vote *should* pass, and trust them to follow their consciences and petition their Assembly representatives to make certain it *does*. A journalist shares truth, not opinion. For the people to freely decide, they must freely receive information. That requires an unbiased press." Tomis paused. "I must admit, on a personal level, I would be quite happy to see the vote pass. Does that make sense to you?"

"Oh, I understand," said Donya. "It's that Soladisean nonsense where the less you feel, the more you know."

GOD'S GARDEN ROSE OUT of the sea, its hill a steep peak that curved slightly, like a bull's horn. The sides were green, lush, and grassy. A switchback trail, marked by pale waystones, wound up to its summit. At the top, a walled-off orchard seemed to beckon Cevette, the tops of pear trees waving in the wind. A warm breeze washed over her cheek and toyed with her short blonde hair, smelling of fruit. The sea turned from gray to azure. Even the sunlight brightened as they drew near.

She despised that. What the gods of Soladis had done here went against the very order of the world.

Once, they called it the Island of Kites. The Wind Dancers had lived here. They had skimmed across the surface of the seas atop silver skiffs with tall sails, hunting great fish and serpents in the waves. Their homes had covered the curved horn of the island, small round buildings with countless kites flying from the bamboo poles in the garden. The homes and bamboo groves and gardens were gone now. Centuries had passed since the Wind Dancers had raced through these waves. Most had been forced to go to the Crest of Soladis to eek out a living on its stony shores.

"Ma'am?" said Mr. Smoke. "You're crying."

"I know," she said, and dabbed her cheeks with a handkerchief as they rowed into a small, shallow cove beneath the curve of a cliff. The pair of them took off their weapon belts, to keep their powder dry, then leapt out into the shallows. Water washed about their boots as they pulled their dinghy ashore. They walked across the rocky beach and to a great boulder, where Mr. Smoke tied the dinghy. He fastened his weapon's belt back on beneath his bare, round, hairy belly. Vivid red flame marks shone on his fingertips.

Cevette buckled her own belt back in place and looked about her. Over the years, many travelling Sea People had built memorial cairns from the stones on the beach. Beside them lay shell necklaces, blades of copper and obsidian, silver coins, and a carved walrus tusk. She reached into her pocket, drew out a gold ring, and laid it beside the other offerings. She pressed her hand to the side of a cairn, the stones cold and smooth under her fingertips, and wondered about who had built it, and if they also had felt this great heaviness on their shoulders and hollowness in their chest. *I want to go home. I want my people.*

Her stomach twisted. Her head spun.

She had been here before. She *remembered.*

It was not a full memory. Only a small scrap that drifted through her mind as if it were a handkerchief caught in the wind. She squeezed her eyes shut in desperate concentration, fighting to grab more of it—

"Ma'am?" Mr. Smoke said. She jumped, and turned to face him. "We're not alone." He pointed at the dirt trail, perhaps eight feet across, that led up the hill. The pale soil was marked by dozens of footprints.

Cevette cursed, and rushed to his side. She counted at least four distinct pairs of shoes, and two sets of bare feet. *It rained last night. These are fresh.* She saw no other boats, but there were other harbors on this island. The back of her neck prickled. A bead of sweat slid down her forehead. Her guts knotted up tight. "Let's go on ahead."

"You don't want to wait?"

"No," she said. Her voice wavered. She took a deep breath, steadied herself, and continued. "Your magic is sufficient to guard us both. If we must burn someone to death, I'd rather not make the others watch."

"Ah, you're protecting that Gavon girl," Mr. Smoke said. "That's sweet. I like that."

"I'm protecting all of us." Including, she had to admit, herself. If this memory meant what she feared, she wanted to face it alone.

At long last, Eva and Tomis steered their dinghy into the small, rocky cove where the other one rested. Eva leapt out to drag it ashore. As she splashed through the water, she looked about and realized Cevette and Mr. Smoke were nowhere to be seen.

"I thought your captain would wait for us," Tomis said when she said as much out loud.

"And I thought you would be faster at rowing," said Donya. She looked around. Her face grew somber when she took in the cairns and memorial offerings on the beach. "Look. Tracks. On the trail."

Eva knelt at the base to the trail for a closer look. *Those are from Cevette's boots.* Her tracks led up the trail, as did an unexpected number of others that preceded them and led in the same direction. "Someone else came through here recently. She must have gone ahead to look for them. But why wouldn't she wait for our boat?"

"To protect us," Donya said. "My courageous fool of a cousin."

"I admire her courage," Eva said.

"You'd admire the contents of her chamber pot. You're not the one who has to stitch her up whenever she gets herself shot."

"Fair enough." Eva pointed up the pale dirt trail. "We should follow them. They can't be that far ahead."

Donya nodded. Lifting her skirts in one hand, she stepped down from the dinghy, and waded barefoot to join Eva on the stony bank. Tomis clambered out behind her, wincing as the water soaked his pinch-toed black leather shoes. He tried to unload the heavy pack that held Donya's medical supplies, then nearly dropped it. He kept it above the water, but fell to his knees in the doing. Eva waded in, snatched it up, and slung it over her shoulders. She tripped as she tried to return to shore, and soaked her breeches up to her waist. Donya had another good laugh at that; after a heartbeat, they all did. They tied the dinghy to the boulder with the other and set off up the trail. Eva and Tomis both trailed water behind them.

Up the hillside they climbed, the trail winding back and forth, past sprays of yellow flowers and tumbled-down fallen fieldstone walls. Bees buzzed and floated from blossom to blossom, fat and longer than Eva's thumbs. "Oh. It's like springtime here," Eva said, and pulled off her coat to toss it over her arm. The air was just a bit too still, though, and she felt like she should be able to smell the flowers and she couldn't.

And, as she went on, the nearness of Death swept over her like the shift in the air before the storm. The barrier between worlds felt as thin as tissue paper. *Could that many people have truly lived and died here? How long ago was that?* She had heard the tale of how Iunos had demanded the island for use as a garden, how the god-emperor Kasperos had granted it to him, and how Morghaia and Heraline had turned against the empire and their own son in response. But the histories did not dwell on the lives of the Sea People who had called this island home, nor what they had lost when had been forced away.

"Iunos *did* something to this island," Eva said, and shivered. "Something that trapped it in . . . in this false spring. How could he?"

"How was he capable, or how did he become so disdainful of the order of nature?" Tomis plucked a flower. He pressed it to his nose, took a long sniff, and tossed it away. "Iunos is a difficult god to understand. I myself always wonder how it came to be that he dueled Commander Gavon in defense of Morghaia. The two of them never got along."

Eva nodded. "It is quite strange. But I suppose the gods do things quite differently than humans do."

"The philosophers say that all gods begin their existence as humans. They lived such worthy lives that ancient peoples began to worship them;

the raw power of that belief transformed them. The histories say Iunos was once the king of a nomadic shepherd clan, born with the gift to cure ailing minds with a touch. His people prayed to him, and, in his fortieth year, he ascended to godhood, with his warrior queen Kemamis beside him. Their power came from faith. I believe their great arrogance came from it as well."

"My grandmother said our gods are the children of the Three Currents," Donya said. "We see some great force of power in the world. Over the generations, we tell stories about it, and those stories blend with myth and history to give that god a face, a name. The more stories we tell, the more likely it is that a god will be born. They come from nature, from our ties to each other, and our ties to our dead."

"Fascinating. That does line up more closely with what we know of the origin of Morghaia. Most sources agree she was never human—rather, that the followers of Iunos and Kemamis already worshipped a death goddess with a long, pale face and black eyes, and she began appearing to her worshippers in the flesh at the time the Empire of Soladis was founded. Some pottery fragments indicate the myth of Morghaia might have been inspired by the legends of a earlier warlord—"

"She should have stayed a story," Eva said. She shook her head. Donya's pack bounced about on her shoulders. "She did such horrible things."

"She wasn't as horrible as Iunos." Donya shook out her skirts, shooing away a pair of large bees. "That's a hard way to speak of your own family."

Eva wrinkled her nose. Her lip curled. She wished she had the bathing bucket on hand. It felt as if there was something unclean inside her.

"We're not family, Morghaia and I. I'm not family to any other echo but Andreas. None of the other echoes are my family. We share a face, and some common history, but that's all. A family is a thing of birth, or law, or custom. That's why I call Andreas my brother. It has nothing to do with . . . with what we are."

"A family can also be something you choose," Tomis said. "I don't have many living relatives. I found my family amidst the folk who work on my newspaper with me."

"Very well," Eva said. "But I don't choose them. I have no tie to echoes I don't know, like, or trust. *What* I am is not *who* I am."

"It's part of who you are." Donya gave her a look she couldn't quite read. "You couldn't put that aside even if you wanted to. I've tried."

Eva frowned. She did not like the thought of that.

They turned left about a bend in the path and paused. A wall of white stone eight feet tall rose before them. One of Cevette's grappling hooks was anchored in the top, but the rope fell down on the far side of the wall. The captain wasn't making any of this easy; still, Eva liked a good challenge. She slung off Donya's pack and pressed her fingertips against the sun-warmed, weathered stone. There was a somewhat decent grip. Her toes slid into a chink in the mortar.

"Catch me if I fall," she said, and scrambled upward. Her arms burned. Her grip did not shake. Two quick reaches, and she grabbed the top of the wall. She dragged herself forward on her belly, grateful that Naeri's magic protected the embroidery of her waistcoat, and pulled her legs up behind her. Taking hold of the grappling hook, she stood.

The wall enclosed a ring about the hilltop, five hundred feet across. Within, an orchard bloomed. Delicate trees, their branches as thin and interwoven as lacework, grew at regular intervals along a white gravel path, which wrapped about the round walls in the shape of a spiral labyrinth. Golden pears, impossibly ripe, dangled from the boughs. Eva's mouth watered at the heady scent of rotting sugar. *Where's Cevette? Where's Mr. Smoke?* She didn't see them. But she was hungry.

"Come on up," she said, anchoring the grappling hook and tossing the rope down to Donya and Tomis. "There's lunch."

It took Donya and Tomis several more minutes to make it atop the wall and to haul up the pack. Eva dropped down on the far side as they were still navigating the descent. Her brass-buckled boots crunched on the gravel as she landed. She strolled to the nearest tree and twisted a pear on the stem. It broke off in her hand. She rubbed it on her shirt and bit down.

Juice filled her mouth, sweet and summery, and then—

A memory swept her up like a crashing wave.

Snow blew all about the central square of the small village. It covered tiny one-room cottages with thin wooden walls and thatch roofs, piling high atop a small stone chapel with the Lorekeeper's book and quill icon carved over the door. A fire blazed before her. Grim soldiers in leather vests and chain mail piled bodies atop it. They were old and rotting, flesh melting off their bones in yellowed strips. Yet the arrows sunk into their ribcages were terribly fresh.

A woman lay at her feet, still bleeding sluggishly from the wound left by a dead soldier's pike. Eva knew she was dead, but the girl whose memory this was still hoped. "Help us!" she shouted to the soldiers. "My mother—she's hurt!"

"Run, girl," said a grizzled one-eyed man. "There's more of them coming. Leave her and run!"

The girl fell to her knees. "Please," she whispered. "Please, Skullrunner, don't take her." She wept and prayed. Distant screaming reached her ears. Then came the clicking of metal on bone. The soldiers cursed and drew their weapons, fanning out in a line across the square.

When the girl looked up, a legion had surrounded the chapel. The soldiers were bone and rotting flesh and empty eye sockets. Flies and maggots crawled over their skin.

A woman led the attackers. She stood ten feet tall, with a long, pale face and eyes as dark as a moonless night. Her gown was red silk, dark as old blood, and she wore a surcoat of silver scale mail above it all. In one hand she held a knife; in the other, a twisted hunting horn. Her black hair billowed out behind her like a cloud of smoke.

She pressed the horn to her lips and blew. A note rang out through the village square. The sound filled the girl's ears, as low and ancient as the turning of the world, and she wrapped her hands around her head to drown it out. The soldiers dropped to their knees. Some begged "mercy!" But the fist of terror held the girl too tight to think.

And then her mother's corpse looked up at her and smiled.

"Ah!" Eva stumbled backwards. The pear fell from her grip. She pinched her wrist as her heart hammered, reminding herself that she stood in the orchard of endless spring, not in the corpse-filled snows.

"What was that?" Donya said. She slid down the rope from the top of the wall and ran to Eva's side, wrapping her hands around Eva's gut in preparation to *force* the morsel out of her. "Spit! Now!"

Eva spat twice. "It's out," she said.

"Good. What happened? Are you hurt?"

"The pears are full of memories," Eva said. "Old ones. That was from the time of the Theocracy." Her face reddened. A sheen of sweat covered her palms. "Iunos must have put them here. Memories he wanted to hold onto." *So the world might never forget the crimes of the Skullrunner.*

Tomis strolled over to them, Donya's pack now resting on his shoulders. "Ancient memories. How fascinating." He plucked a pair from a bough and bit in.

Then he screamed. The sound rang off the orchard walls. Wide-eyed and white-faced, Tomis flung the pear away and spat the remnants into the dirt. His fingers trembled.

"What did you see?" Eva asked.

"I saw a sea full of corpses. A tide of fangs and teeth. I saw a ship transform into a sword and bury itself in the flesh of our world. I saw *her*. The goddess of death. Smiling as the very ocean screamed in pain."

Donya frowned. "Right. No more pears."

"Agreed," Eva said. She checked the gravel for prints. "They went along the path." The pear trees wove together so tightly that they had no practical way of forcing their way into the center of the labyrinth without a machete, and she had no wish to see what would happen if she took a blade to these trees. "Let's go."

They continued down the path, walking side by side, their shoes clicking on the gravel. "I can't believe you put those things in your mouths," Donya said. "If you get killed here, I will never, ever forgive you."

"Curiosity is a virtue," Tomis said, "I applaud the courage Miss Gavon showed to pick up a pear and try."

Eva narrowed her eyes at him. "Why is a nobleman being so courteous to an echo?"

"I've met a number of echoes. One of my governesses was an echo. I always thought it was unjust that you were treated so poorly. Some common courtesy is surely the least you are owed."

"Many citizens of the Republic have echo servants. They treat us like shit. They think we deserve it. That we're just like *her*. Why not you?"

"I don't know." He shrugged. A warm breeze washed over them and set the tree branches to bobbing. "When I was a child, I saw how echoes and Sea People and everyone who wasn't a full citizen was treated. I decided it was wrong and I would do what I could to stop it. I made a choice. The right choice. I can't explain why I made it. Frankly, it's shocking that more people don't."

A choice. She mulled that over. Was that all that mattered? A choice?

"May I ask you a question?" he said.

"You may."

"Don't you believe that the echoes deserve better from the world?"

She sighed. "Some of us deserve better. Most of us, even."

"Don't you believe that *you* deserve better?"

Eva hesitated. What could she say? She knew beyond all doubt that she had the capacity to cause great pain and suffering. Growing up in the Republic had hammered that truth into her; but she had known it the first moment she'd drawn breath.

"I believe that I must earn the right to ask for something better," she said. "And I may only do that if I do all the good I can."

Tomis nodded. Donya frowned, and looked as if she was about to speak.

Then five people climbed atop the garden wall behind them.

"You there!" one bellowed. "By what right did the owl claim the fox?" Their clothes were made of leather and tattered homespun cloth, stained with salt, in the fashion of frontier settlers or common sailors. Tattoos covered every inch of their bare skin. Infantry rifles hung over their shoulders; tendons stood out in their necks. Their eyes were wide with fear.

"Pardon?" Eva said. "I don't understand." Beside her, Donya swore.

One ragged man, his fingers shaking, grabbed hold of his rifle. A bead of sweat ran down his forehead as he pressed it to his shoulder and took aim. "He said, by what right did the owl claim the fox?"

"Look at their hands," said a woman, and cursed. "The marks! They're Republic soldiers—with the Godreaper Corps!"

A shot rang out. Eva leapt sideways. A burst of gravel struck her legs.

"Run!" she shouted, waving at the others. They scrambled off the path, ducking low, and flung themselves under the tightly-interwoven branches of the pear trees. On their hands and knees, they crawled along through the mulch and grass. Bracken caught at their clothing. Pears bobbed all about them, golden and ripe.

A second shot rang out. Above them, pears exploded. A howling scream filled the air, rising off the wounded fruit like steam. "Stay down!" Eva told the others. She reached into the small of her back and drew a pistol. Keeping low, she rolled onto her knees and aimed through the branches. *There.* She had the shooter in her sight. She pulled the trigger. A dry click.

"Here. Let me." Donya reached deep into her skirts and pulled out a gold-trimmed blunderbuss with a muzzle wider than her hand. Eva stared at it. "It was a gift from the captain." Donya took aim and fired. Pears burst. The air howled with magic. A human scream joined the chorus.

"Enough!" bellowed a low, familiar voice. Eva peered through the branches just in time to see Cevette sprint around a curve in the labyrinth. Mr. Smoke followed behind her, his hairy belly bare to the breeze, his fists full of fire. "We're not with the Republic, you fools. We're pirates. You can burn, or you can put up your weapons and let my healer treat you."

"Hold your fire," said a quiet voice. The oldest man atop the wall lifted his hands. Blood ran in rivulets down his leg. Silence fell over the orchard. "A healer, you say? Let's talk."

THE FORGOTTEN REVOLUTION

BEGINNING IN THE CITY OF HALSTON, ON HIGH HILL ISLE, THEN RETURNING TO THE ISLAND OF KITES, ONCE THE HOME OF THE WIND DANCERS, AND CONCLUDING ON SMALLFOOT POINT, IN THE UNCEDED TERRITORY OF THE WICHIL NATION, FORTY MILES WEST OF HALSTON. 11TH HERALMONTH, YEAR TWENTY-TWO OF THE GOLDEN REPUBLIC.

The latest attack on my life appears to be the work of the True Ink Movement revolutionaries. I knew the archer for what he was the moment I saw the tattoos on his corpse. Their insistence I am some sort of tyrant disgusts me. No graver insult could be made against my person. I have devoted my life to the defeat of tyranny; they are dedicated to nothing but chaos. I have come to believe they are motivated by a perverse sense of envy. They cannot match me for achievements or virtue and so they have devoted themselves to destroying all I have built. I have encountered a number of such individuals in my years. It is unfortunately common. Not all of us may become great, but we may all be wise enough to accept that truth with humility. –Letter from Commander Jonathan Gavon to Lord Mykil Merris, Minister for Childhood Welfare.

COMMANDER GAVON'S FLAGSHIP WAS called *Kembrielle,* after his mother, and it was as handsome and formidable as the woman herself had been. A ship-of-the-line with gilded railings and three great masts, forty-eight guns and a golden flag ten feet in length, the sailors loading its cargo looked small as ants beside its bulk. The crisp white sails, the canvas and rope all fresh, snapped in the morning breeze. Gray waves lapped against the warm brown wood of the hull.

A pretty ship, thought Lieutenant Ezekiel Dare as he followed his commander down the dock. He dearly hoped he wouldn't get seasick this time.

Kembrielle was moored to the largest dock still intact after the kraken incident. It had been brought into the harbor with all haste, as the commander needed to be swiftly away to attend the yearly session of the Golden Assembly in Soladis. Andreas and his many trunks were already settled aboard. Soldiers, sailors, and common workmen stood at respectful attention as their commander passed. Jonathan Gavon had dressed for a sea journey, in a simple coat of crisp black wool, the buckles on his shoes polished, his silver-streaked black hair tied with a ribbon at the back of his neck. Zeke stood on guard at his back, clad in his orange uniform, his sleeves pushed up and his godmarks on display.

With narrowed eyes, Zeke scanned his surroundings, his chin high and his jaw set. One could never be too careful. He saw no sign of trouble. Only posters advertising the reward for Eva's capture, nailed to every surface.

He swallowed once, then twice, and looked away from them. His chest felt very tight. His guts were churning. *I turned my magic against my closest friend.* No. He had attempted to capture a pirate. That was all. He had done right. The Oath of Loyalty said *and should my peer or kindred turn their coat on liberation, may my hand be the bloody one that strikes them down.* He had sworn that oath a hundred times. He would abide by it. But part of him was glad she had gotten away.

He fervently hoped she would keep away from the docks, from Halston, from her father, from him. Stay out at sea. Never test his loyalty again. If the commander directly asked *have you seen my daughter,* then Zeke would tell him the truth. But, until then, he would behave himself as if that meeting had never happened. Both he and Andreas had agreed to keep the encounter a secret. As Andreas had said, it would surely cause the commander to question his worth.

Commander Gavon glanced back at Zeke over his shoulder and said, in a low voice, "Before we sail to Soladis, we have a stop to make along the way. There is something I need you to do for me."

"What is it?"

"A rebel must be brought to justice. She hides in a frontier village at Smallfoot Point. You will take a number of soldiers, arrest her, and bring her to me."

"Yes, sir. What has this rebel done?"

"Does it matter?"

"There's many kinds of rebels. Weren't you a rebel, once?" The commander did not often speak of the revolution, or much of his own past at all. Zeke supposed that was a sign of modesty. But he did wish to learn more of the commander's past, and of his thinking in the present.

"Was I a rebel?" Jonathan paused mid-step and turned to face Zeke. He shook his head and stepped in closer, shooting a wary glance at the public. Most of the watchers gave them a respectful distance, save for the seagulls flocking about their heels. He spoke, firmly but quietly. "Rebels are impoverished, uneducated, illogical, passionate fools. Most of them do little else in life beside grumbling. The few that do act are more likely to shoot themselves in the foot then bring down nations. And the small fraction of those who succeed . . ."

"They make the world a better place for us all."

"Don't be naïve, Lieutenant. The rebels who claim power claw their way toward it over the corpses of a thousand more decent and honorable souls. The masses enjoy a good tale of rebellion, yes, but they like it as a story. Not the truth." He smiled, and lifted his chin. A light gleamed in his eyes. "A revolution that is both just and successful is the rarest thing of all."

"What you have accomplished in the Republic is truly great," Zeke said. "Perhaps, as we sail south, you could tell me more of the revolution. Of what you thought at the time, and what you think of it now."

The commander laughed. "There's a dozen biographies of me. I prefer the one with the green cover."

"I read it. It was flattering, but lacking insight." Every biography of the commander began with praising the Gavon family for their bravery and industriousness in colonizing High Hill Island, then discussed in great measure the tyranny faced by the young Jonathan Gavon when the god Iunos advanced the Soladis-born officers in the army ahead of him. A number of revolutionary victories were covered in the books, but in very general terms, and there was little written at all of the commander that made Zeke feel as if he truly *knew* the man.

"What more insight do you need?" The commander put his hand on Zeke's forearm. "You are closer to me than anyone. Listen to me. During this session of the Assembly, I want you inside the Hall with me for the deliberations. There are lessons you can learn, and I want a good man to watch my back. In truth, I trust you far more than any of them."

"You want me in the inner chamber?" His breath caught. The invitation was a rare honor. For the sake of security, non-members were rarely permitted to watch the Assembly debate.

"Of course I do. I am always glad of your company."

Zeke looked away from him. Heat rose in his cheeks. He bit his lip. *He trusts me. And I'm lying to him about his daughter.* His throat felt dry. He licked his lips. "Tell me . . . tell me more about this rebel I'm meant to arrest. What am I needed for? Does she have some magic I may need to nullify?"

"She might," the commander said. A seagull bit at his shining silver shoe buckle. He kicked it away. "That's why I must send you. One never knows with echoes."

An echo. Zeke shivered, and nodded. *Don't think of Eva,* he told himself. *She made her choice.*

And Zeke had chosen this man, and everything that he stood for.

THE INJURED MAN INTRODUCED himself to Cevette as one Sebastian Thimmely, formerly of Halston. Short, rotund, dark-skinned with his tight gray curls styled up in a puff reminiscent of a gentleman's wig, he had the manner of a kindly grandfather. However, what kept her on guard were his tattoos.

As Thimmely and his fellows clambered down from the top of the wall, she could see that the rainbow tattoos covered every inch of their bare skin. Their accents said most of them had come from the Five Sisters, and, in those islands, the Soladiseans who most commonly practiced tattoo art were the settlers who crossed treaty boundaries to rob her people of fish% and land. Cevette placed a protective hand on her pistols as Donya knelt to check Thimmely's bleeding leg, as the webbing between her fingers shone in the sun. Two of Thimmely's rebels stared at her, but they said nothing, and Cevette decided to let them live.

Those aren't typical settler tattoos, Cevette noted as the rough-dressed folk fanned out protectively around their injured leader. Some of them wore naval charts, others squiggling characters of code. One man had a woman's face captured on his bare chest. Thimmely's wound was covered in wobbly lime-green script, spread and faded over the years. *Your name is Sebastian Thimmely. Cmdr. Gavon shot your father Peter. Your wife was*—the shrapnel had taken out her name. What remained was *remember.*

Despite her initial misgivings, she felt a drop of pity for them.

Donya smeared ointment over Thimmely's wound and ran her glowing palm over its surface. The skin knit itself shut. She prodded a mole at his collarbone. "Ugly, but harmless." A tattoo lay beside it; an archway with a star in its center. "What's this?"

"An old symbol from the banners the rebel forces carried in the revolution. Commander Gavon replaced it with the two linked rings when he took power. We adopted it for our own. All members of the True Ink Movement have one."

"What does it represent?" Eva said. "It strikes me as familiar."

The old man sighed. "That truth, and many others like it, have been erased, I'm afraid."

Donya pushed up his shirt, checking the scrape on his belly, revealing the stretched shape of a map. Lines and numbers wrapped around it. "What's this?" she asked.

"It's a puzzle," Thimmely said. "Showing us the way to our base camp."

"Us?" Cevette asked. "Who's *us?*"

"The True Ink Movement," said one of Thimmely's fighters. "The resistance against the tyranny of Jonathan Gavon."

"You're rebelling against the Republic?" Tomis said.

"We do what we can," said Thimmely. "In truth, we haven't made good progress in years. Not since I was young."

"When was that?" Eva said. "The Republic was only founded twenty-two years ago."

"Maybe," he said. "But my first tattoos about Commander Gavon were already starting to fade twenty-two years ago. His magic can change what you remember, and his soldiers can burn books and papers. But even he can't make old ink look new."

Unsettled murmurs rose from Cevette's crew. Even she shivered. She had assumed Commander Gavon primarily used his powers to erase embarrassing scandals and losses. She did not want to think what he could achieve if he was *creative.*

"A friend wrote to me several months ago," Thimmely said. "She had recently decoded a tattoo she had forgotten the meaning of and discovered the location of an unguarded Republic archive. She was too old and frail to travel, so she wrote letters to every member of the True Ink Movement she remembered. We arrived on God's Garden three days ago; docked around the far side of the island, where we wouldn't be seen. We've been searching ever since."

"We came for the memories as well," Eva said. "We mean to burn them all and set them free."

Thimmely nodded. "Burn them we shall." Two of his fighters helped him to his feet. He stretched, twisting from his waist up, then bent down to touch his toes. "Shall we carry on?"

"We shall," Cevette said. She didn't trust these people, but she also had no wish to lose sight of them. "My sources—" being Lovett "—tell me the memories are hidden in a cistern under the garden. It should be at the labyrinth's heart."

"Thank you for letting us know," Thimmely said.

"But of course." Cevette nodded to him. "Go on. Lead the way."

Thimmely and his fighters went ahead of them along the gravel way. Stone crunched underfoot. One man whistled a tune. Mr. Smoke and Tomis Beauchamp joined in. So did Eva, who, for some reason, carried

Donya's pack on her shoulders. *She's building some real muscle there.* A warm breeze stirred the air and sent her black hair whipping out like a pennant. Cevette let herself study the corner of her smile for a scant handful of heartbeats before she went back to watching the so-called revolutionaries, her hands on her guns.

Donya leaned in at her side and addressed her in Kossket. "What, by the ancestors, were you thinking when you went off without us?"

"I'm sorry," Cevette answered, in the same language. "We saw the tracks on the trail. I wanted to burn out the danger before it could get anywhere near you. We were searching the labyrinth when those fool rebels came over the wall."

"You went after them alone? Cousin, how does it protect anyone if you get yourself killed?"

Cevette winced. She had been foolhardy. Every Sea life was a hard-won victory in their centuries-long war for survival. She owed it to her people to keep breathing. "In all honesty, it was more than the tracks that scared me. I . . . I've been here before."

"What?" Donya's eyes widened. "What were you doing here?"

"Mourning," Cevette said, quietly. She remembered the grief. How her hands had trembled as she had knelt before the cairns at the shore, all those years ago. How heavy her heart had weighed in her chest. How she had been so hungry and yet unable to eat. How the passage of hours had slipped from her mind until the moment that a woman with long, dark hair had put her hand on Cevette's shoulder.

"Your sorrow still weighs so heavily upon you," she had said.

Cevette had turned to her and whispered, "Help me."

"I've tried." The woman had sunk to her knees beside Cevette. The skirts of her black gown had spread into a dark stain on the rocks of the beach. "I don't know how. You must go back to your people. You need a healer who knows your ways and can understand this wound you carry on your soul."

"I can't go back. I've become too Soladisean."

The memory of saying it churned her stomach. She wanted nothing more than to find her connections to her people again. How could she have once turned away from them?

"I will not force you to go back to your people," the woman had said. "But you can't come home with me."

Something had broken in Cevette's voice. "You're sending me away?"

"There has been no love between us for a very long time. And I am tired. Something must change. Not only between us—in the world."

A silence had fallen over the both of them. The last thing Cevette had ever said to the woman who had once held her heart had been, "There's only one way to set this right. Promise me you'll go to Jonathan Gavon."

"Commander Jonathan Gavon," Cevette whispered to Donya. "I trusted him. I thought he could help us. "

"Many Sea People think that. Republic propaganda is everywhere."

"I . . . I was living like a Soladisean. I was so far from home . . . "

"You wouldn't be the first one of us to do that. It's a way to survive."

"I need to do more than survive. I need to . . ." Grief and guilt washed through her, two tides blending in a brackish wave. *I need to make this right.* But the *this* was *everything.* And how could one captain, one current woman, do all that?

"Maybe you were working with the navy. They sometimes hire current women as translators and guides."

"They hire traitors," Cevette said. Her stomach heaved. She pressed her hands to it, as if holding her guts in. "I . . . it's only a fragment, what I uncovered. There must be something more here. Some . . . context. We need to find and burn those memories. Now."

Cevette sighed. She looked about her, at the pear trees, at the orchard wall, at the twists of the labyrinth as they walked through an about-face turn. Searching for a sign of what it had once been. Of what had been obliterated. *By Kasperos.* Her fingers curled into fists at the memory of the name. *He betrayed his mother's people.* The god-emperor had embraced his Soladisean heritage whole-heartedly, with all the violence it entailed. *I would never do anything like it. Would I?*

"The past is the past," Donya said. "What can I say? Sometimes we hurt each other."

Up ahead, Eva laughed at a joke told by one of the ragged revolutionaries. The sun shone in her dark hair. Cevette felt a sudden urge to bury her face in it and hide.

"How do you know that language?" One of the younger revolutionaries looked back over his shoulder, addressing Cevette in the common Soladisean tongue. "They say that Sea tongues break the teeth of non-natives."

"She's my cousin," Donya snapped, in Soladisean as well. The rest of the party paused to look at them.

"Really?" said the young man. He scratched his brow. His rifle nearly fell off his scrawny shoulder. "Your cousin? She doesn't look it?"

"You look like a man who knows when to keep his mouth shut," she said. "Looks can be deceiving."

"Enough," Cevette said, in Kossket. "Let them see what they want. I'm a pirate. There's a price on my head. I don't want the world knowing I'm one of the Sea People."

Donya glared at the man, but stepped backward. Eva gave Cevette a raised eyebrow and a tilt of her head. Her fingertips were on the switches to drop the knives from her bracers. Cevette shook her head. *All's well.* Eva nodded, and relaxed.

"Forward," Cevette said. She spoke in Soladisean, her voice taking on the cadence of a military officer. She was quite conscious of how naturally the shift came to her. "We'll find these memories and be gone."

The two groups trudged along the curving path. The branches of the pear trees trembled in the wind. No one spoke, except for Eva and Tomis Beauchamp, who were singing old tunes together, off-key. Cevette was glad that someone, at least, had brought a hint of life back to this island. As they turned a final curve in the labyrinth, the white gravel path expanded into a flat circle five feet across. Another twisting path led away from it in the opposite direction. Pear trees surrounded them in a great ring. Cevette frowned, and rubbed her eyes. "It should be here."

"Maybe it's hidden somewhere?" Eva swept her hand through the air. Black smoke followed her fingertips. "This whole island is touched by death. I can step inside and look."

"No," Cevette said. "The dead of this place are Sea People. The Death you enter here may not be the one you're familiar with. I . . . here." She stepped into the center of the labyrinth and stomped her foot. There came a hollow thud. She dropped to her knees and scraped at the gravel. It slid aside. Beneath it lay a wooden panel. She got to her feet and quickly stepped back off it.

The revolutionaries, all save old Thimmely, knelt and helped the crew clean off the hidden door. They lifted it up—it came easy—and set it aside on the gravel. Beneath it lay a deep, dark well. The sound of a bubbling spring rose up from below.

"Heraline's gift to the Wind Dancers, who once lived here," Cevette said. "The spring is part of a cave. It was a temple to her, once. The memories must be down there." She didn't know how she knew it—surely no Sea People were still alive who could pass that knowledge down—but she did. *What if Commander Gavon told me? What if he sent me here to desecrate this place?* She had more than enough reason to loathe Heraline, but to turn her temple into a dumping pit was an insult to the memory of everyone who had once called this island home.

"Only one way to find out." Mr. Smoke tied a rope about his waist. "I'll go, captain. I'll take care of them."

Cevette nodded. They all had to burn; burn them he would. The four of them and three of Thimmely's rebels held the rope and slowly lowered Mr. Smoke into the dark. A flame glowed in his fist as he descended.

Eva, who stood directly behind Cevette in the line of rope-holders, leaned in at the captain's ear as they fed the hempen line through their worn and callused hands. "Captain, before we all got here, did you eat any of the pears?"

"Why would I eat something that's so clearly cursed?"

"Oh, good. I had one. I wouldn't want you to see what I saw." She smiled and blushed, wide and earnest, and it was like sunshine sneaking through the clouds. The very air in Cevette's lungs seemed lighter.

"I shouldn't have left you." Cevette took a deep breath. "My apologies. It was a mistake, and you might have been sorely hurt by it—"

Eva shrugged. "You came back when we needed you. We all make mistakes, captain."

How many mistakes have I made?

"I found the memories!" Mr. Smoke shouted up. His voice boomed strangely from the bottom of the well. "Heaps of them. Absolutely everywhere. Should I burn them?"

"Burn away." Cevette said. "Just don't hit the rope!"

A warm yellow glow shone in the depth of the well. Flame crackled. Smoke rose up from the depths. One revolutionary rubbed the tattoo on her arm, an ink portrait of a young child. A moment later, she slumped forward, weeping. One of her companions pulled her into his arms, holding her tight.

"Damn my father," Eva whispered. Cevette glanced back at her. There was a violence in her eyes, sharp as the point of a compass. Cevette wondered where it would lead her.

"Thank you," Thimmely said. He looked to the pirates, a true warmth in his voice. "My mother—I've remembered more of my mother."

"We're honored to be of assistance," Tomis said. "Well, I wouldn't say I assisted. This is mostly the captain's work."

Cevette closed her eyes. She pictured the icy islands of the far north, the villages hewn from pinewood and hides, ringed by dog kennels and tundra blossoms. She imagined the great temples of the Kingdom of Serpent Riders in the Sapphire Isles and the secret tunnels of the Ketil Yata in Soladis. Songs and tales and languages swirled through her mind. *Show me where I belong. Who I belong to.*

Show me that I have always fought for the Sea People.

She clung tight to the rope. Blood dripped from a torn callus. Her head spun. *Come to me.* She tried to force it. She had tried this so many times. Nothing came. Nothing good. Nothing bad. Nothing at all.

She tilted her head back and screamed.

Eva had done her best to give Cevette privacy as she spoke with Donya, but her captain's exhaustion and pain swept her up like the tide. Without words, she could tell Cevette had recovered nothing from the burning memories. Still holding the rope, she lowered her chin onto Cevette's shoulder and whispered, "I'm sorry."

"Thank you," Cevette said, her voice raw. "I . . . thought for certain I would find something here. But I remember *nothing*."

Old Thimmely, watching from the far side of the open well, nodded gravely. "Commander Gavon must have used a great deal of power on you, captain. An older echo."

"My age?" Eva said.

He shook his head. "She'd have to be at least twice as old as you. Echoes don't often last that long. Those who do, he tries to use sparingly, and only against his greatest enemies."

"His enemy," Cevette whispered. "I . . . I must have been his enemy. Why else would he have done this to me?"

Thimmely nodded. "Whoever you are, you must be someone that he truly fears."

Eva smiled. She had never even pictured her father afraid. The thought of his dark eyes wide and sweat pouring down his face was a welcome one.

"He must be keeping a close eye on your memories, Captain," Thimmely said. "You should try to raid one of his more secure archives. The True Ink Movement doesn't have the strength. But you have some godreapers with you. They might be enough."

"That's the last of them!" Mr. Smoke shouted. "Haul me up!"

With the revolutionaries beside her, Eva set her teeth, dug her heels into the dirt, and pulled. "Heave!" Cevette shouted. "On my call. Heave!" Eva did her best to pull on the mark. Sweat ran down her brow. Her back burned. Her arms trembled. Foot by foot, the rope slid upward.

Mr. Smoke pulled himself up over the lip of the cistern. "Should have worn a shirt," he said, dusting grass and gravel from his chest. "There were dozens of them. Boxes everywhere. Gods. I knew he'd taken a lot. But that much? The man's a better thief than I am."

Donya nodded. "I don't know why no one's shot him yet."

"We've tried," Thimmely said. The other revolutionaries grunted and grumbled in agreement. They set down the rope and went to stand around him, grim expressions on every face. "But we've been unlucky. The poison always fails. The bomb only scorches his clothes. We sent a sniper after him, once. She took three shots, each with a clear line of sight. All three bullets missed, or so she thought. She couldn't quite see what happened to them from that distance."

Eva thought of the attempt on his life that she had foiled, several years ago. *If I had only stepped aside . . .* She had wanted to prove herself to him. *I should have let that man do to him what he would have done to me.* Her fists tightened. She set her jaw. For a moment, she imagined leaping into Death, running back to Halston, and shooting her father in the head. Her stomach churned. He deserved it.

But should she be the one to do it? An echo? Who would she be if she went that far?

"No," Eva said. "He should be punished. But he should be arrested and put on trial. He should be made to stand up and answer for his crimes. He should be publicly judged and condemned so that he, his victims, and all the people of the Seaward Isles can know that justice had been done."

"A good dream," Thimmely said. "But it may not be possible."

Eva shivered. She did not wish to think of that.

"What does your revolution do now?" Tomis asked Thimmely.

"Well, our resources are quite limited. There is little we can do effectively. But, what we do have, we share with those most affected by the Republic's failures of governance."

"So you're a charitable endeavor?" the journalist asked.

Thimmely shook his head. "Charities are beholden to their wealthy patrons. They make large, visible gestures to gain the sympathy of the public. They do very little of the lasting, needed work. We dig trenches and raise foundations in flooded fields. We erect palisades and insure crops near abomination blooms. It's a hard life, not in the least because Gavon has made several powerful sacrifices to target us, but, if we follow our tattoos, we can hold together well enough to be effective."

"Why do you choose to follow the tattoos after he steals your memory away?" Eva said. "If it means going up against the Republic itself?"

Thimmely smiled. "It's never been the Republic that's looked out for me when I needed help most. It's always been the people here beside me."

Eva thought of Korinne, and the crew of echoes she had gathered around herself. Was that similar to this True Ink Movement? A community standing together to support one another in the face of the failings and horrors unleashed by Commander Gavon? *They're violent people.* But Thimmely wasn't opposed to violence. It cheered her, to think her fellow echoes might not be uniquely bloodthirsty in their desires, even if their methods horrified her.

"Wise words," Tomis said. "Justice is coming. I can feel it in the wind. The people of the Republic will remember what has been unleashed here. They will demand the Assembly pass the vote of impeachment for Commander Gavon—"

"And then he'll just split the nearest echo and make them forget," said one of the revolutionaries, gesturing about with his rum flask as he gave Tomis a skeptical look.

"It will be harder than he thinks," Tomis said. "He can shift minds, but not words written in ink. If I write about what he's done, if I can get my papers around the port authorities and the government censors, every household in the Republic will have access to the truth."

"And the more we burn," Eva said, "the more difficult it is for him to make us forget. This is decades of work he's done. He can't re-do it all in just a few weeks." She considered the journalist; his weathered tricorn hat, his messy red curls, the scrubby mustache on his upper lip. For all his optimism, he did not strike her as a fool, and she liked the picture he painted. *All the people in the Seaward Isles, rising as one to demand justice.* "Lord Beauchamp. I believe we can help each other."

He grinned. His green eyes danced with light. "I would be honored to work beside you, Miss Gavon. Once my ransom to Captain Zarcanzi is paid, of course." He tipped his cap to her. "Here's to truth!"

She tipped hers back. "Here's to justice."

Before turning south to Soladis, *Kembrielle* stopped in at Smallfoot Point, ten miles west of the nearest Republic border. There was no harbor along the rocky peninsula deep enough for a ship of her size; instead, they dropped anchor below a steep cliff and lowered the ship's dinghies. Zeke took twenty soldiers ashore. They hid their boats beneath fallen pine branches; then marched up the narrow, winding trail that led to the village on the clifftops. The scent of drying hides and maple sap brought Zeke back to his childhood. He straightened his violet cap and held his head high as his soldiers approached the palisade gate.

The woman atop the watchtower just inside the gate shouted a command. A moment later, the heavy wooden panels swung outward on creaking hinges. "Welcome, welcome!" boomed a large man in a deer-hide coat as he strode out to greet the soldiers. His hair was greying and his pale face was lined. "My name's Carter. I'm the headman of this settlement."

"Lieutenant Ezekiel Dare." Zeke held out his hand.

Carter took it and shook vigorously. He smiled at the sight of the godmarks on Zeke's skin. "Oh, I've heard of you. A man born on the frontier of New Soladis who became the bodyguard of Commander Gavon himself? It could only happen in the Golden Republic. Come on in. You and your soldiers are welcome to eat, drink, and rest. We're humble folk here, but all we have to share is yours."

A bitter chill filled the air that gray morning, and yet Zeke still felt a spark of warmth in his chest. The frontier settlers were not as rich or as well-spoken as the aristocrats of the Republic's cities, but they were hospitable and generous to a fault. He was proud to have come from a village like this one. He was proud to serve a man who raised up others, no matter how low their birth.

"Perhaps another day," Zeke said. "We're here to deal with a serious matter. I have a warrant for the arrest of one Dorothea Bly."

Carter nodded. "We thought you might be coming for her when we saw your sails. Follow me." He waved Zeke forward, and Zeke looked over his shoulder and nodded to the troops ranked behind him.

"With me!" he shouted, and they marched through the gates.

Ramshackle huts, tents, and makeshift shelters lined the frost-dusted soil of the village road. Villagers clad in worn homespun and thick fur caps watched them pass with wide eyes. Dogs, cats, and chickens ran by underfoot. Children chased after them, and then, upon seeing the soldiers, chased after them.

"That's Lieutenant Ezekiel Dare!" one boy shouted. "He saved the commander from assassins!"

"I'll reap a god, too, one day," said a girl with sun-bleached ribbons in her hair. "I'll fight for the Golden Republic!"

A woman darted up and pressed bouquet of flowers into Zeke's hands. "Thank you," he said, and no sooner did she back away, blushing, than did a man rush up to give him a larger one still.

"You make us proud!" shouted an old greybeard, shaking his cane aloft on the edge of the road.

Zeke gave him a respectful nod. Heat prickled in his cheeks. He turned to Carter. "How do you all know about me?"

"We've read about you. In the papers."

"What?"

"I suppose a busy man like you doesn't get much time to read." Carter nodded to another woman who stood along the roadside. She wore a large broach of copper and pearls as a cloak-fastener. It reminded Zeke of one his mother had owned. "Nelly, do you have another copy of the *National Standard?*

Nelly nodded, and ducked inside the small square cabin behind her. The words 'News and Gossip For Sale' had been painted above the door. A moment later, she emerged, clutching a newspaper, and pressed it into Zeke's hands. As he fumbled with the flowers, trying to find a coin to pay with, Carter slipped a penny into Nelly's hand.

"A gift," he said. "It's the least we can do for you, Lieutenant."

Zeke looked over the paper. It was the *National Standard*, which he had never thought worth reading. The article was glowing flattery. It discussed the assassination attempt in broadly incorrect terms, suggesting it had been a dozen assailants, Ya Tonim warriors from the far north, and Commander Gavon had slain four of them himself, with Zeke accounting for the others. Still, it made him grin and chuckle, to see his name and the commander's so close to each other in print. Then he saw the headline beneath it.

Servants Reveal the Rogue Echo Evazina Was a Terror to the Household of the Charitable Commander.

Zeke frowned. The *National Standard* was a state publication. The government paid for its printing and distribution, to ensure that it was cheaply and widely available. The intent was to ensure that poorer citizens could make educated decisions when they voted, not to feed them lurid lies. *I need to tell the commander about this.*

"Old Madam Bly lives right there," Carter said, and pointed to a small hut. The walls of the lower half were packed earth; along the upper half, rough-hewn lumber beams supported a framework of thatch. Smoke coiled out through a vent in the roof. Along the walls, beans grew on a trellis, with tomatoes and honeysuckle blooming below. Swirling symbols painted in red covered the door. Zeke had once gathered madder root so his father could make just that color of paint.

Two villagers stood on guard at the door. Sharp bayonets glinted on the tips of their rifles. They did not look in the least bit surprised to see soldiers.

Zeke frowned. "You're quite prepared for this."

"Yes, we are," said Nelly. The news dealer had walked along with the soldiers. Half the village had followed along behind them. Parents were hoisting their children on their shoulders to watch. One young woman scrawled numbers down in a betting book as the onlookers passed her coins. "Bly and her wife used to be the town healers. But her wife died last year, and her hands are too stiff for much work. Folk didn't wish to throw an old woman out in the cold. But if the commander needs her, we're happy to serve."

"Needs her?" Zeke frowned. "I'm here to arrest her for treason."

"She's a rebel?" Carter said. "Ah, well, if we'd known that, we would have taken care of her ourselves and saved you the trouble." As Zeke scrambled to find words, Carter shrugged and continued. "Well, you know. She's an echo. It's not unreasonable to think the commander might have a use for her."

Zeke glared at Carter. "You insult the honor of a good man."

"Never! Commander Gavon is a good man. A great man! But we all understand that, sometimes, a great man needs to make sacrifices for his country." Carter nodded to the guards by the hut's cheerfully-painted door. They forced it open.

"How could you?" came a shout. A younger woman stormed out of the hut. "Shame on you! Madam Bly brought us food and medicine for years. She set your arm when you fell off your horse. She's the reason three families in this village didn't starve last winter!"

"She faces charges of treason," Zeke said. "She will have the opportunity to defend herself at trial. If she is as good a woman as you say, then justice shall win out."

"Fuck your justice," said the young woman. "Fuck you, and—"

"Enough," said a low voice. "I will go with them."

An old woman walked out of the hut, leaning on a cane. Her skirts were worn, patched, and threadbare. Tattoos covered her from her fingertips to her neck, a faded, wrinkled rainbow of color. Her hair was pale white. Her eyes were black as death.

Eva, Zeke thought, even though this echo was nearly eighty. He bit the inside of his cheek. *No. She's a traitor. We have proof.* He had read the warrant once *Kembrielle* had left Halston. She had written letters to a wanted rebel known as Sebastian Thimmely, urged him to steal government property from an archive. A clear enough crime. But the way she looked at Zeke said he was the one in the wrong.

He closed his eyes and saw his village burning. Heard the scream of his sister in the dark. He knew how it felt to be hunted by a power you could not fight. *But the abominations are monsters. I'm here on the behalf of the greatest man in the world.* His family would be so proud if they could see him. The people of this village were cheering him on. He had done what they all dreamed of. He had become everything a citizen of the Republic should be.

"Take her," he told his soldiers, and turned so he would not have to see the woman's face.

SABERS AND WINE

ABOARD THE SHIP *SEA WOLF*, FOUR HUNDRED AND SEVENTY MILES SOUTH OF THE ISLAND OF KITES. 15TH HERALMONTH, YEAR TWENTY-TWO OF THE GOLDEN REPUBLIC.

I watched death today. Father's philosophers have summoned several abominations for the purpose of military training; some soldiers from the eighth regiment were fighting one in the pit. A snake-gorilla made it around the wall of bayonets and ripped three soldiers apart before an officer of the Godreaper Corps forced it back into its cage. Two of the soldiers died quickly, but the third lingered for several of minutes, screaming. I felt a queer warmth in the aftermath, as if my father's arm was wrapped around my shoulder. I hope dearly that means nothing of note. Ariella asked me if something was wrong, but I dared not even speak of what I felt to my own sister. –from the diary of Korinne Gavon.

ONE MORNING PAST DAWN, as *Sea Wolf* raced southward through the warming sea, the lookout shouted "ship ahead!" and every pirate aboard leapt to attention.

"The *Pleasant Mary*," Cevette said, peering off over the bowsprit with her spyglass at a speck on the horizon. Eva stood at her captain's side, loading her pistols. The sun was rising bright and hot over the waves; a crisp wind filled their sails and a pod of whales glided through the waves off the starboard bow. Up on the foremast, a crew member played a jaunty tune on the pipes. "What do you know of that ship, Miss Gavon?"

Eva searched her knowledge. There was a public government registry listing all vessels owned by citizens of the Republic; she had read it back to front a number of times. "It belongs to Lord Mykel Merris. He's the Republic's Minister of Childhood Welfare. He's also a member of the Assembly; his district is directly west of my father's in Halston, and he's been re-elected twice." She cocked her head, thinking it over. "He might have memories aboard."

"Memories, or information." Cevette passed Eva the spyglass. "Every foster child in the Republic moves through his custody. He keeps extensive records of echoes. He might know something of . . . her."

Eva nodded, and tried to ignore how her stomach churned at the thought of Cevette with her lost echo. "He might know something about the archives as well. How we might access the more well-guarded ones. We have to get to them before Korinne does."

"Frankly, I would be inclined to attack under any circumstances," Cevette said. "I've seen how his ministry treats fosterlings. They go after Sea People children, too, the filthy kidnappers. It's settled. We strike." She raised her voice. "Lower the sails, crew! Get the wind at our backs!"

The ship named *Pleasant Mary* was a large carrack built from warm golden oak, one-hundred and fifty feet in length. It sported three masts, all of which flew the flag of the Golden Republic, and had two tall cabins built into the bow and stern. Carved panels of leaping dolphins covered its sides; its figurehead was a laughing woman with her gown sliding free over one breast. She was not a mere luxury vessel; she had eighteen cannons to *Sea Wolf*'s twelve, and soldiers in gold uniforms stood guard on her upper decks.

But Eva was quick to discover her weakness.

As *Sea Wolf* sped toward the Republic vessel, Eva stepped into Death. A plague outbreak had once killed twelve sailors on *Pleasant Mary*. She assumed Lord Merris had acquired the ship after that incident; if he knew how death haunted his cargo hold, he might have posted guards inside. But, when she stepped out of her portal, she was the only soul in that darkness. She had acquired three small gunpowder charges from Mr. Smoke;

she nailed them to the hull and lit them all, blowing holes as wide across as her palm in the hull. The sea trickled in. She opened the portal once more. The crew would find and patch the gaps soon enough, but the ship would be slowed and its crew would be distracted.

"We'll be in striking range within the hour," Cevette said when Eva returned to forecastle, watching *Pleasant Mary* through her spyglass. "Well done, Miss Gavon."

Eva smiled. "It's my honor to serve you, ma'am."

"Good. You'll be joining us in the boarding party."

Eva's grin widened. She drew a small bottle of sun-ointment from her pocket and started rubbing a new layer on her cheeks. Then she remembered: the boarding party would have to slice through the *Pleasant Mary*'s guards and capture Lord Merris by force. Soldiers would die on her sword. Her heart raced. Her stomach fluttered. *Death. Today, I deal death.* The thought filled her mind. With a stroke of horror, she realized she was almost eager for it.

No, Eva thought. *Why? Why do I wish for this?* Perhaps it was because Merris had information they needed, or perhaps it was because she sought to bring justice for the mistreated foster children under his care. It did not mean there was some dark goddess working inside her.

"Mr. Lovett!" Cevette shouted. She leapt down from the forecastle and marched across the deck, waving at the helmsman. "How long 'til we close on them?"

"At our speed?" he shouted in reply. "I give us twenty minutes to cannon range."

"Bring us in." She cupped her hands around her mouth and shouted to the crew. "Load the guns. Watch your fire. I want Lord Merris alive."

Pirates bustled about the deck, rushing to their assigned cannons. Eva climbed down from the forecastle and went to the second starboard cannon on the upper deck. *Where's Naeri?* Her cannon partner was nowhere to be seen. Well, she wouldn't need her to help clean the barrel until after the first shot, when there was a risk of flying embers. Eva unhooked the sponge pole from the rail and shoved it down the barrel. Any debris left inside might cause a misfire. When the barrel was clear, she opened the metal locker chained to the rail and lifted out a heavy lead ball. Carefully, she rolled it down the mouth of the cannon.

"Eva!" Naeri ran toward her, weaving nimbly around bustling groups of sailors. When she reached the cannon, she thrust a bundle into Eva's arms. "Here. Your armor. It's ready."

"Thank you," Eva said. "That's quite kind."

"Thank me when you survive this," she said, and proceeded to show Eva how to pull it on.

All of *Sea Wolf's* boarders wore armor in the same style: chestplates made from panels of thin wood and metal shaped like corsets, with bracers and greaves made of padded leather enchanted to halt bullets. Each set was painted with a different set of signature colors: Naeri's was a rich indigo and Cevette's was as white as her coat, making her a beacon on the battlefield.

In her armor, Eva was ash, blood, and death. She wore her dark coat with the embroidered skulls; the red inner lining would flash brilliantly when she lifted her daggers to strike. Her chestplate went beneath it, and atop it went the armor to guard her lower arms and legs, all the plates a deep red bordered with painted swirls of gray smoke. A dozen daggers lay right within her grasp. Her heart pounded as they raced across the sea, as if she could already taste battle in the cold salt of the wind.

The *Pleasant Mary* drew near, so close that, even without a spyglass, Eva could glimpse the sparkling gilt on its rails. Men as small as minnows darted about its deck, racing for their battle-stations. Their shouts rose on the wind as *Sea Wolf* sprung across the sea at ramming speed, its bow aimed at the *Pleasant Mary's* port side.

"Helmsman," Cevette bellowed, "bring us about!"

It took Lovett and another man to force the wheel to turn. They groaned and cursed as the very beams of *Sea Wolf* creaked in protest. The deck tilted sharply to port. Anything not nailed down slid and toppled. Eva and Naeri grabbed hold of the rail next to their cannon, their fingers scrabbling over the rough wood as they fought for balance. Cevette leaned artfully against the mainmast. The ostrich plumes in her hat flew back in the wind. Sails billowed out above her. Nimble as a dancer, *Sea Wolf* wheeled about in an arc of foam. Her bow pointed away from the *Pleasant Mary*'s course by thirty degrees.

"Starboard cannons, clear!" Cevette shouted. Every sailor on the upper deck scrambled to distance themselves from where the cannons would roll back. "Mr. Smoke, fire!"

Mr. Smoke waved his hands. Sparks flashed. Glowing lead balls flew through the bright blue sky. Cannons rolled backward. The chains connected to the wooden mounts went taut. The ship shuddered as *booms* filled the air. The scent of gunpowder washed over the upper deck.

Eva braced herself to hear the splintering of wood, the screams of dying soldiers. She heard only splashes. The shells had hit water. *We shot too soon.* But had they?

"Reset!" Cevette shouted.

Naeri grabbed up the sponge pole and shoved it down the barrel. Eva pressed her thumb over the vent to lock in air and prevent flying embers. "Ma'am?" Eva looked back over her shoulder and met Cevette's eyes. "What's going on?"

Cevette smiled. "What's the first thing the Republic's naval officers taught you about ship-to-ship combat?"

"You should draw up along a ship's broadside before you fire." Eva drew two parallel lines in the air with one hand. "To maximize the area you can hit with your cannons."

"Precisely. Lord Merris will think we misjudged and overshot our turn. He will try to turn as well, and make his course parallel to ours. But he will need to turn at a sharp angle, and his ship is longer than ours." Cevette grinned. "And, thanks to you, a good deal heavier."

Across the waves, there came the loud shout of an order. The helmsman of the *Pleasant Mary* spun the wheel. But his ship now maneuvered like a drunk manatee. She entered the turn—and lurched to a halt, as the weight of the water in her hull slowed her momentum. Sailors shouted at one another, and the soldiers raced to load their guns. Their cannons wouldn't save them now.

And the failed maneuver had brought the bow of *Pleasant Mary* just close enough to *Sea Wolf*'s stern.

"Boarders, to me!" Cevette shouted. She raced for the stern. Eva, Naeri, Lovett, Mr. Smoke, and a half-dozen others followed her up the stairs to the quarterdeck, and from there to the poop deck. Rope lines dangling from the mizzenmast had been looped around the rail there. Cevette wrapped one about her wrist. The rest of the boarding party followed suit.

Sweat built on the back of Eva's neck. She and Cevette had briefly discussed having her run them all through Death into the ship's hold, but the captain did not want to put so much responsibility on her for her first boarding. Through the air they would go. Eva gripped the rope with one hand and her pistol with another, heart pounding in her throat. Mr. Smoke winked at her, a cutlass in his teeth. Cevette leapt stop the poop deck rail and shouted "Away!"

The captain jumped and swung into the open air. Eva leapt a heartbeat behind her. Salt wind whipped across her cheeks as she flew across gap between ships. Her coat billowed out in a flash of red. The sun bore down behind them, one more weapon in Cevette's pocket.

A dozen gold-uniformed soldiers stood on the bow of *Pleasant Mary*. They squinted upward and lifted their rifles, taking aim at the borders. Gunshots cracked. Their shots went off wildly in all directions; the closest ball hit the armor on Cevette's thigh and bounced off.

Cevette dropped onto the forecastle and landed in a neat crouch. She ran a man through as she rose, then pulled her blade from the corpse and shot one more man in the jaw. Eva dropped down beside her, slamming chest-first into a soldier. The impact jolted through every inch of her body. He reeled backwards, found his footing, and reached for his saber as he lunged at her. Instinctively, Eva shot. Red bursts across the man's chest. His soul dropped into Death like a plunging stone.

I just killed someone, thought a distant part of her. She was already holstering the empty pistol and drawing her knives. The boots of her crewmates hit the deck behind her. Lovett stepped forward and ignited. He shone like a beacon of horrors. Wide-eyed, sweating soldiers backed away from him—only to meet Naeri, on his right side, throwing knitted tangles of yarn that bound and tripped whomever they touched, or Mr. Smoke, on his left, who wielded twin cutlasses, each burning orange.

"Forward!" Cevette shouted. The crew of *Sea Wolf* fanned out behind her like the point of a spear. They advanced, pushing the soldiers back toward the stairs that led up to the forecastle. Eva, heart hammering in her throat, positioned herself to her captain's right, her daggers lifted high.

Soldiers fled down the stairs to the upper deck. One, braver than the rest drove his bayonet at Eva. It flashed silver in the sun. She blocked with her daggers and forced the weapon upwards, then pivoted and kicked him in the chest. He plummeted back down the stairs. Four other soldiers fell beneath him.

"Well done, Miss Gavon!" Cevette drove her sword through a soldier's throat. Righteous fury shone in her eyes. The blood slid off her coat like sheeting rain. Eva's head spun. Death surrounded her on all sides. Its nearness was comforting, welcoming, like a warm blanket or a lover's embrace.

She could not stop her lips from twitching up in a smile.

"I'm with you, ma'am!" Eva shouted. Time flowed like pouring honey as they descended the stairs. A sailor on the poop deck lifted his pistol. She flung up her hands to shield her face as it flashed. The pistol ball bounced off her bracer. It hurt like a punch. Eva set her jaw and shook her wrist.

Cevette's gun cracked. The man who'd shot at Eva fell, screaming. Cevette looked back over her shoulder at her. "Stay close to me."

Eight soldiers had formed a sloppy battle line on the upper deck; four in front guarding four behind with their bayonets as they reloaded. The pirates reached the bottom of the stairs and fanned out, standing shoulder to shoulder. Drawing her spare pistols, Cevette dispatched two soldiers approaching from the bow. Eva flung a knife. It sank into the throat of a man reloading his gun. Her godmarks caught the light, ink black on her pale hands, spiraling over her hands and down her wrists. Sailors shouted

"Skullrunner! Skullrunner!" and "Morghaia! Lady Death!" until the howls of dying soldiers drowned them out.

Lovett and Naeri fought back-to-back, fluid and graceful as the tide. His pistols and saber guarded her from attack; her fingers wove spells of thread and rope to bind their enemies so he could cut them down. They smiled whenever their eyes met. Whenever a soldier surrendered, Naeri bound them, hand and foot. Mr. Smoke stopped to rip off the prisoners' rings. The rest of the crew followed Eva and Cevette onward.

Soldiers screamed. Soldiers died. Their souls drifted past Eva like leaves on a breeze. The world faded into a crimson fog. She and Cevette struck in tandem, cutting their way across the upper deck as the enemy fell back. "Mercy!" shouted soldiers and sailors on the quarterback. They fell to their knees. "Take what you want! Mercy, mercy!"

"Drop your weapons!" Cevette bellowed. "Hands on the rail! Double-cross me and I'll feed you to the sharks."

Guns and swords clattered to the ground. Trembling hands were lifted aloft. The pirates rushed upon those who yielded, binding their wrists and searching their pockets. Cevette left the crew to the plunder. With her head held high, she marched across the blood-slick upper deck to the door of the grand cabin. She levered it open with the tip of her sword.

Lord Merris stumbled out, cursing and stumbling, a small and pale man clad only in his dressing gown. Eva recognized him from her father's parties, but there was no revelry in him now. His wig was gone; his limbs were trembling. He collapsed to his knees. Rage shone in his eyes as they found her.

"You," he growled. "Echo. Monster. Abomination."

Echo. Her nostrils flared. Her lips curled. Death was all about her. Souls flowed into her place of power, and from their passage, she drew a sense of certainty and strength. She was a power to be respected. So she flipped around her dagger and slammed the pommel into Lord Merris's jaw. A tooth crunched and shattered, like a broken egg. Flecks of white and red fell to the deck.

"It's the Demon of Dogshead!" gasped a cowering sailor.

The crew of *Sea Wolf* broke into cheers.

THE HOLD OF *PLEASANT Mary* was stocked with treasures: eight thousand pounds in silver, two chests of fine jewelry, sixteen crystal wineglasses, a long ivory tusk carved with dancing foxes, twelve barrels of rum, three barrels of wine, and a small, locked chest full of memories. Lizeth took note of each item as it was loaded aboard *Sea Wolf*. Cevette dropped the memories in a brazier and lit it. Her frown widened as they went up in smoke. "Anything?" Eva said, and Cevette shook her head. *No.*

Mr. Smoke burned a number of *Pleasant Mary*'s sails to ashes, and the crew broke the spars on the mainmast; with the damage to the hull, it would take days for the survivors to make repairs and reach port. *Sea Wolf* sailed off, smoothly gliding through the open sea, Lord Merris locked in the hold. Sharks passed as they continued their southward course, racing toward the wounded ship. *They must have started throwing bodies in the water.* Lovett said a small prayer as they passed.

Donya had a shark shot and hauled aboard so she could grind up the teeth for powder. Lizeth divided the takings into even shares and passed them out to the crew. Boarders were entitled to a bonus, but Eva wouldn't receive hers until she'd served six months. *More treasure* was an impossibility for her to imagine. Lizeth placed a chest in her hands, and she opened it and reached in, letting silver coins run through her fingers. *What will I spend it on?* She had never possessed money of her own. Eva stashed the chest with the rest of her gear belowdecks, then busied herself by cleaning her knives, reloading her pistols, and tidying up the crates that had slid about during the pivot that had baited the Republic ship into that risky turn. She wanted to be busy. She wanted not to think about the warmth she'd felt when her bullet hit that man's chest in a spray like red rain.

"We're well enough away," Cevette said as the sun set into the sea. "Have at it, sailors. I have work to do."

As Cevette vanished down the stairs to the lower deck, the crew of *Sea Wolf* gathered around the mainmast. Two pirates opened a barrel with an axe and poured sparkling golden wine into the stolen crystal goblets, Eva downed hers, tasting grass and sunshine. Another crew member took up a pair of pipes, another a set of drums. Music spilled across the upper deck. Pirates pressed together, their footsteps pounding as they took up a wild jig. Eva finished off her wine and considered joining in; she had only learned a few of the slower dances, back in Halston, so she might make a fool of herself, but she quite wished to feel foolish in that moment.

"Eva!" Mr. Smoke thrust a coconut husk cup into her free hand. Dark rum waited within. "I'll race you to the bottom, girl!" They both tipped theirs back and drank. Mr. Smoke threw his empty cup down first. Eva coughed and sputtered as the last rich, sugary sip poured down her throat.

The liquor was strong; she felt it creeping over her right away. The deck spun. She tilted back her head and watched the first few stars flicker to life in the night sky. Three bright fixed points of light and one dim green wanderer. *The stars are still here. So am I.* A wild, cruel joy swept through her. She had survived her first raid. She told herself the joy was *only* because she had survived. She could let the alcohol keep everything else at bay.

She ran into the dance, clapping and stomping her feet in the best approximation of rhythm she could muster. Some of the crew gave her a pitying look; but Tuk grabbed her by the hand and pulled her into a ring of dancers. Round and round they wheeled, shouting and laughing. One pirate passed her a pipe full of smokeweed; she took a hit, passed it on, and next received a flask of some minty alcohol. A few deep swigs left her stumbling backward out of the dance. Someone shouted that she should, perhaps, sit down.

"We're rich! We're rich!" Donya clasped Eva's fists in hers. Thick silver bracelets glistened on the healer's wrists. An amethyst the size of a hen's egg hung at her throat. She twirled Eva around and around, and Eva laughed until she tasted bile in her throat. "Here. Pierce my ear!" Donya pressed a pearl stud into Eva's fingers.

"I've never pierced an ear."

"Just shove it in. I'm drunk."

Donya grinned. "I'm drunk, too!"

"Congratulations!" Eva grabbed Donya by the ear and shoved the stud into her cartilage. Donya gasped, grabbed Eva's ear, and forced in the matching one.

"I didn't even feel that!" Eva said.

"Because you're drunk!" Donya shouted back gleefully.

"Watch this!" Mr. Smoke waved his arms. The whole crew stilled to watch him. A flourish of his wrist, and plumes of fire flew up into the night. They burst apart in vivid explosions of color. The first was a spray of shimmering purple. The next was pink as dawn; the third, aquamarine. Eva and Donya clapped, cheered, hooted, and stomped their feet. One stomp went a bit wrong, and Eva stumbled backwards and smacked her head on the mainmast. She grabbed hold of it to stay upright.

"Eva!" Donya rushed over to her side. "Don't knock your brains out. I don't have a potion for that."

As Eva fumbled for a clever retort, a cold wind blew in from the north.

Death brushed her cheek like a thread of spider silk.

"Naeri!" Before the foremast, Lovett dropped to one knee and took her hands in his. "Lovely as the western stars, diamond of the sea—"

"Yes?" she gasps, voice high and expectant. Her golden gown shimmered in the light of the rising moon.

"I—ah, sorry, I've had too much to drink." Leaning all his weight on the foremast, he pulled himself back up to standing. He lowered his brow and looked away from her.

Naeri caught his hand. "Yes. The question you're trying to ask—my answer is yes."

"You must be drunk, too." He shook his head. "I love you with a human heart. But the prayers to the Lorekeeper whisper in my ears, and it was his doom and his curse to be forever lonely. We are all of us caught in the tide of history, and it runs in circles. I cannot let myself fail you."

Naeri shivered, the sort of shiver that ran through her whole tall frame. "Selig. Sweetheart. You're failing me now." With a sob in her voice, she turned on her heel and walked away. Lovett only stared after her.

You fool. Eva wanted nothing more than to shout that in his ear. She hesitated, though. Could she truly say she had no link to Morghaia? That the goddess was nothing but a source of power to her? No. Not tonight.

"Oh, gods," came a thin voice. Lizeth stumbled up and leaned against the mainmast. Rum slopped from the cup they carried onto Eva's boots. They pressed their hand to the stomach. "It's all so *uncomfortable*."

"I don't know how to face it, either," Eva said, with a sudden rush of gratitude. Perhaps she was not alone in this. Perhaps all those who reaped gods felt this way. "We killed eighteen soldiers, and yet I didn't feel distressed, in the moment. I felt—"

"I mean Naeri. She deserves better."

"Right," Eva said. "Naeri." She looked about for her, peering through the dancing, drinking, laughing crowd. No sign of Naeri de l'Havre. Perhaps she'd gone down to the crew's quarters. Eva took one step in that direction. Her head spun. She grabbed the mainmast to keep from falling. Bile rushed up her throat. She bent double.

"Eva!" Donya gasped. She grabbed a bucket and held it out. Eva grabbed it and vomited.

"I would help," Lizeth said, "but if I let go of the mast, I think I'll throw up too."

"Both of you, stay here," Donya said. "I'll go find Naeri, and I'll get both of you the drinking cure. Don't move." She took three steps away, glanced back to make sure they hadn't moved, and, satisfied, stumbled off toward the stairs.

Eva straightened up as much as she could. She clung to the mast with one arm; with the other, she pulled out a handkerchief and wiped her lips.

"My father would be so mad to see me drunk like this," Lizeth said. "He'd say I made us look no better than Sea People."

"Really?" Eva said. "He sounds nearly as foul as mine."

"Ah, well, it isn't quite like that. Your foster father is an evil bastard." Lizeth scratched the side of their head. Their curls were growing out. They'd have to shave again soon. "I'll be blunt—there's nothing worth salvaging between you two. My father is kind, and brave, and he'd do anything for his family. It's only . . . it's hard to explain. Anyone can sound awful when you only know the worst parts of them. My father, my family, my people . . . they're still my people. You know what that's like, don't you? You have your people."

My people. The crew of *Sea Wolf* were her people, she wanted to say. But that wasn't how Lizeth had meant it. "People? I . . . I have echoes."

"The echoes. Your people."

"We're not a people in the way the Terraloro are. We're not all born in one place, or in one family. We're . . . split. Divided. Literally, yes, but also geographically. We're far apart. If we want to find each other, we have to look. And we don't always like what we find."

"It's not the same," Lizeth said. "But it's close."

Eva bit her lip. Her stomach was still churning. The world was spinning a bit less. "Maybe," she allowed. She thought of Korinne and her crew. They would have enjoyed breaking the teeth of Lord Merris. They would have done that and more to him. No, they weren't her people. They couldn't be. Perhaps they could understand her, but she didn't *want* them to. They would only bring out the worst in her.

Eva and Lizeth fell silent. They clung to the mast, pressed their hands to their stomachs, and watched the rest of the crew dance. The great ring had broken up into smaller groups; everyone was dancing with the partner of their choice, many of them pressed lip-to-lip. Lizeth frowned. "It's always like this, after a victory. All this kissing."

"I'm not kissing anyone."

"That's only because Cevette went down to the brig with the prisoner. Soon as she came back, you'll run to her like a lost puppy."

Eva's cheeks flushed. But this, she was eager to think of. "Cevette is marvelous. Surely you must understand why I'm drawn to her."

"Oh, yes. She mostly lets us down easy. She's still looking for her missing girl. It's romantic. And sad. She handles sadness well. But I've never seen her smile like she does when she looks at you."

Eva's eyes widened. Her fingers flew to her lips. She hadn't noticed. She couldn't tell one sort of smile from another. *If I can make her smile, truly smile, I can help her.*

"Right, here we go." Donya made her way through the crowd to the mainmast. She had two small glass vials in her hands. Eva and Lizeth each took one and drank. The potion tasted a bit like powdered squid. Donya placed her hands on their chests, right above their sternums, and breathed deep. Blue light bloomed at her fingertips. The pair of them coughed and stuttered. The spinning of the world began to slow. "I checked in on Naeri, too. She's in her sewing nook. She wants to be left alone for a bit."

Eva nodded. "I need to find Cevette."

Donya gave her one more studying look, and nodded. "Go on. Cevette deserves all the good people around her she can get."

I killed two soldiers today. Maybe three; the one she'd thrown over the rail had hit his head hard. He might not wake up from that. *I'm an echo; an echo who wields the power of the Skullrunner.* For a few blissful weeks, she had thought that might matter less than she'd feared. But it marked her profoundly, in ways she could not ignore and did not understand.

But she understood that Cevette needed her. So off she went.

Cevette had taken their newest prisoner deep into the cargo hold. In the dark, damp belly of the ship, where the beams creaked and only a single swinging lantern gave light, a wall of iron bars separated the brig from the pumps. The captain stood inside it when Eva reached the bottom of the ladder, her long white coat swathed in shadows. Lord Merris was the lone prisoner they were holding there, as Tomis had been granted a hammock in the crew's quarters. The Minister for Childhood Welfare sat, trembling, with his pale wrists tied tight to the arms of a chair and his ankles bound together. Bloody drool dripped down his chin and stained the white lace of his shirt. His fearful eyes darted to Eva—and just as quickly looked away.

"I'm sorry I broke your tooth," Eva said. "I . . . I lost my temper."

Cevette looked at her. "You don't have to apologize."

A few moments passed before Eva worked out what she wanted to say. She settled on, "He should know I'm not what he thinks I am."

The captain nodded. "Very well." She looked back to Merris. Her voice dropped an octave, low and dangerous. "You've been most agreeable in answering all my questions so far. You will show the same courtesy to Miss Gavon. I will have none of that *monster* nonsense from back on your ship. Do you hear me?"

Merris nodded.

Cevette unlocked the cell door. Eva ducked inside. The captain locked it up again tight and turned back toward their prisoner. "Now, where were we?" The lantern swung on its creaking chain over her head. Bilge water slopped about her boots. "You were telling me about the navy's search for the Zarcanzi family?"

Merris nodded. "When . . . when they learned a woman named Cevette Zarcanzi was robbing ships in the Five Sisters, they sent messages to all the government ministries asking what we knew of you." His voice trembled. "We searched our records to see if you had been a fosterling, once. Many runaway fosterlings show up on pirate crews."

"I know." A cool contempt filled Cevette's voice. "I have several of them aboard."

"We found nothing to show you had been a fosterling. After that, we searched to see if we had ever sent any fosterlings to a Zarcanzi family. We record the names and ages of blood children in the families we foster to. We found nothing of them, either. Zarcanzi is a common-enough name, both among the poorer citizens of Soladis and the frontier folk of the Five Sisters, but only eight Zarcanzi families have inquired to foster since the ministry was founded, and none of them had a daughter your age. As I told the navy, where our records were concerned, you were all but a ghost."

Cevette frowned. Her lips vanished into a thin line. Eva thought of how she'd looked when they'd burned the memories. So much had been taken from her. "What about the echo fosterlings you oversee? Do you have records of any of them having connections to a woman who might fit my description?"

Merris shook his head. "Only a few families can be trusted to foster echoes. Those allowed to keep them, keep them close. I will admit, we have not been successful in containing all of them. But those under our control would never be allowed near a woman like you."

Eva's nostrils flared. Her cheeks reddened. She stepped forward, water sloshing about her boots. Her eyes went cold as night. "You hear yourself? *Trusted to foster echoes.* You know why my father keeps echoes close. You know what he does."

"You refer to those . . . ridiculous rumors about echo sacrifices?" Sweat ran down the lord's brow. "Commander Gavon would never do anything like that."

"He ripped up an echo's soul to draw me back to him. To punish me for running away. I felt the memories shifting in my mind. I had to fight to keep my grip on them. You can't fool me. Only make me angry."

"Very well." Merris lifted his chin. Some measure of haughtiness crept back into his demeanor. "Yes. On occasion, when necessary, Commander Gavon makes use of his power. He did what was needed to bring your magic back to the Godreaper Corps. You brought that on yourself, girl."

Eva set her teeth. *Was that my fault?* No. Surely, for that, she did not bear all the blame. Tomis Beauchamp had spoken to her of the choice he had made to treat echoes decently. The commander had made a different choice, and she would see that he answered for it. "He steals memories from the citizens of the Republic. Do they all deserve it? Has he raided your memory, too?"

"He may have," Merris allowed. "His magic is great. But I trust him to use it well."

"He uses it to protect his reputation. So he might win elections, maintain his seat on the Assembly, and keep control of the military."

"It is for the good of the Republic that he remain in power. He and I have our differences, but I have always understood that much. I owe my whole place in the world to him."

"And what a place he has given you." Eva narrowed her eyes. Anger coiled in her voice, each word a serpent ready to strike. "You send poor children into forced labor. You sign over echoes to foster families who will keep them close so that my father can more easily exploit them. Every time he rips one of us apart, you must make a note of it in your ledgers. Did you ever wonder how scared we were? How angry?" Eva took a deep breath. Her heart hammered in her ears, a dark drumbeat nothing like the one she'd danced to above. "Tell me the truth. Where is the largest memory archive in the Isles?"

"You truly believe I'll give up my country's secrets to you, girl?"

"Yes, I do. Because you know what I can do to you."

Lord Merris stared into her eyes. Eva clenched her fists and braced herself. She did not look away, though it made her skin crawl to lock his gaze. She hated to think of what he saw in her. She was glad to hate what she saw in him.

"One way or another," Cevette said, her voice low and authoritative, "you will tell us what we want to know. Make it easy on us all. Talk."

His face fell. His hands, where they gripped the arms of the chair, went limp. "There are two archives that matter most to him," he said, quietly. "One is in Soladis, locked away in the catacombs beneath Assembly Hall. It's heavily guarded. You will never be able to take it."

"That's our business," Cevette said. "Tell us about the other."

"It's on an island off the west coast of Soladis. It's very small. The Gray Isle, they call it. There's a Republic fort guarding it, at the foot of a cliff, where nearly a hundred soldiers are stationed. Atop the cliffs sits a ruined chapel. The priests of Iunos hid sacred relics there when the Theocracy fell. When he captured it, the commander decided he would continue to use it for that purpose. Within, he placed the most important memories of all. The *gods'* memories."

"He stole memories from the gods?" Eva said. "Why?"

"He had to. Especially Heraline. He had no other way to stop her." Merris shuddered. "He sent soldiers to find her, after Morghaia fell. But he was never able to catch her. He didn't know where she'd gone. All he could do was reach her through his magic. To confuse and distract her so she wouldn't rise up against him."

Eva frowned. She had never imagined Heraline as a threat. The goddess represented connection, compromise, and peace. She was most widely known for the calamities she had failed to stop. But her father had grown up in the days of the Theocracy. He would be well acquainted with all Heraline could do to bring him down.

"Is it only the memories of the gods?" Cevette said. "Or are there human memories stored there as well?"

"It's everything he wants to keep hidden most." A bead of sweat ran down the captive's forehead. "What more, I cannot say."

"Where were you taking those memories on your ship?" Eva said.

"Night Dragon Isle," he said. "There's a good-sized archive there."

"Right. And how many more do you know of?"

"I . . . give me paper. I'll draw you a map. I promise."

"You'll draw it in the morning," Cevette said, and placed a hand on Eva's wrist. "Enough, Miss Gavon. It's late. Come with me. I want to speak with you directly."

Eva nodded. Cevette unlocked the brig door and held it open for her, then closed and locked it behind them both. They climbed the ladder up to the crew's quarters, then ascended the stairs to the upper deck.

The celebration on the upper deck had quieted. The musicians had put down their instruments; the remaining dancers swayed in each other's arms. With the hold occupied by a prisoner, there would be no taking advantage of the chalk rule. Suspicious sounds rose from behind a number of the larger crates. Cevette looked at them, sighed, and opened her cabin door. "After you," she said, and waved Eva inside. The captain closed the door behind them with a click, set her damp boots on a rack in the entryway, and hung her coat on a hook; Eva followed suit, watching Cevette closely. A strange hope fluttered in her heart. She did not know if she deserved something so sweet to cling to.

The cabin had not been cleaned since the last time Eva had come in here. Clothes, maps, and trinkets were still strewn across the floorboards; maps covered Cevette's desk, a dozen routes drawn and scribbled over. On her desk lay a walrus tusk she had begun to carve with a scrimshaw pattern. A stack of unread books sat on her nightstand, along with an assortment of hats. The captain flopped backwards onto her bed, which was covered in enough down quilts to make a goose weep. They puffed up around her.

"Lie down with me?" she said.

Eva made her way across the floor, trying not to step on loose quill pens or hairbrushes. The quilts billowed up about her as she lay down atop them, the one on the top layer blue and embroidered with shooting stars. From Cevette's small candelabra hung a smiling crocheted octopus.

"Does he have a name?" Eva said, pointing up at it.

"Yim-yim. It means 'little one.'" She turned her head toward Eva. Her brown eyes were wide with concern. "Violent deeds can weigh heavily upon us. I wanted to make certain you were well."

"I'm well enough," Eva said.

"Truly?" Cevette hesitated, then reached out to push a strand of hair off Eva's cheek. Her fingers were callused and warm. They rested near the curve of Eva's ear. "I'm your captain. That means it's my responsibility to look after you."

Eva drew a deep, shaky breath. "I . . . I haven't had anyone look after me in a long time. Not since I was about twelve or so. My father was kind to me before then. But, as I grew aware of the power he held over me, I grew warier of him, and he grew cold to me." A small, bitter laugh escaped her. "It was what it was. My tutors, the servants in the fort—they were decent, some of them, but they all answered to him in the end. I had my brother, but we were the same age, so we could hardly take care of each other. I had Zeke, but he was only two years older than me, and . . ." She hesitated. Her heart twisted. "He chose my father over me. So, you see, caring for me has never been much of a priority to anyone."

"I'm so sorry," Cevette said. "You bring so much joy wherever you go. Only a fool would take that for granted." She leaned in close to Eva. *So close.* Cevette's lashes fluttered. Her lip quivered. The deep bow of it, full and pink, curled like a wave that could pull Eva in. "I am not a fool."

"It felt right," Eva whispered.

Cevette stared at her, brown eyes wide. The ship tossed as it went over a wave. Overheard, the candelabra swung. Yim-yim the octopus fell down onto the bed. "What?"

"The raid. The . . . killing. It felt . . . right. Perhaps that was because I believe your cause is just. Perhaps that was because Lord Merris is an evil man. Or perhaps . . . perhaps I am what the Republic says I am. I felt Death take the souls of the soldiers we killed, and it felt *right*." Her voice broke. "I want you, captain, in any way I can have you. But I fear there is something wicked in my heart. You shouldn't choose me. You should keep looking for your girl."

"You are not the only one of us who fears her own capacity to cause harm. I will not deny that we all have the power to do great evil, should we choose it. But I will not condemn you over a few scattered thoughts in the middle of battle." Cevette smiled, and hesitated. "Please understand. I have no intention to abandon the search for my past. It is about so much more for me than a lost love. It's about my people. My place in the world. But I don't know how long it might take. I only thought we might enjoy each other in the time we have now."

Eva's heart twisted. *Of course.* It made terrible, awful sense.

Cevette only wanted her until she could replace her with a better echo.

"No," Eva whispered. "I would never ask you to abandon your search for your people. But before I could start anything with you, I would need you to promise that, no matter what you learned or remembered of your past, you would choose to stay with me. Anything less would break my heart."

"I'm sorry." Cevette hesitated. Bit her lip. "I can't promise that. Not when I don't know what I might find in my memories."

Cool, prickling tears ran down Eva's cheeks. She wiped them away with her sleeve. "Very well," she said. Her voice trembled. Her will remained firm. "Then it would be for the best for us to start nothing at all."

The Power of the Press

Beginning aboard the ship *Sea Wolf*, six hundred and ten miles southwest of the City of Soladis, and continuing in the City of Soladis itself. 16th Heralmonth, Year Twenty-Two of the Golden Republic.

Truth is so strong / That when Death heard the song / Of the pain that we faced / Ruled by gods and their grace / She wished to step into the fight. // She allied with … / … / … / … / … for the truth is all people have rights. —Archived Draft of the Entry for the letter *T* in A Children's Primer of the Golden Republic, Partially Obscured by Burn Marks, Replaced in Current Edition by a Poem Concerning Taxes.

They sat for a while in silence, Eva and Cevette, a small crochet octopus between them on the bed. Eva wiped her cheeks over and over. Cevette stared at her hands as if she'd forgotten what they looked like. At last, Eva cleared her throat and said, "Well. We have work to do."

"Agreed," Cevette said, and stood.

They had stashed Merris in the brig, but Cevette had permitted Tomis Beauchamp to sleep in the crew quarters, so long as he did not debate Lizeth when others were trying to sleep. Out of the cabin and down the stairs they went. Tomis sat, huddled, in a hammock in the back of the crew's quarters, scribbling in his notebook by the light of a stub candle. His red curls were disheveled; sweat had built up on his brow. When he saw the two of them coming, he looked up with wide, haunted eyes. "Did you find and burn any memories on that ship?"

"What came back to you?" asked Cevette. She kept a voice low—a courtesy to the sleeping sailors about them, though Eva thought it unlikely any would wake up, considering how much they had drunk.

Tomis swallowed. "A . . . a riot in Soladis. Two years ago. An awful terror of a night."

"My sympathies," Cevette said, and Eva said, "We need to burn more."

"Yes," Tomis said, quietly. "I suppose we do."

"Eva will return you to Soladis with Lord Merris," Cevette said. They had discussed this, briefly and businesslike, on the walk down the stairs. *He deserves death for how he treats children,* Cevette had said. *But the commander will simply replace him with another person who will do the same. I can take the gold from his ransom and put it to good use.* "Listen well, Beauchamp. Eva will collect your ransoms and release you both safely to your households. She will also scout the catacombs beneath Assembly Hall to locate the archive Commander Gavon has hidden there. Would you know anything about that?"

"I've heard rumors about that. I believe I could help you locate it." He smiled. "Though, if I'm doing you a favor, I would appreciate you cutting the cost of my ransom."

Cevette raised an eyebrow. "I'll give you half off. Save Eva the trouble of running all that weight home from the city."

"Oh," Tomis said. "Are you not coming with us, captain?"

"I'm staying here." She looked at Eva, who looked away. "To avoid . . . complications."

I'm the complication. Eva glanced at the curtains around Naeri's sewing nook. Tiny, quiet sobs rose from within. The sound of shattered hopes. Well, Eva could do nothing for herself. But she could look after Naeri. "Excuse me," she said, and went to comfort her friend.

ANDREAS GAVON HAD SUFFERED the ten-day sail from Smallfoot Point to Soladis in excruciating silence. He had no wish to converse with common sailors, who had no education and were fairly dull, but his only fellow traveler of any intellectual note was his father, and Andreas preferred to limit the lengths of their conversations, especially as Zeke was always standing guard at his father's shoulder.

There had always been friction between the two young men, ever since Commander Gavon had picked Zeke to claim the Pridebreaker over Andreas. *Because he's all muscle, even where his brains should be.* Of course, Andreas now assumed that decision had been born of his father's more carnal desires, and he almost felt pity for him. He had told Zeke they could talk, if the other man needed someone to talk to. He felt like he owed that to his sister. But Zeke had said, "there's nothing to talk about," with a bit of a growl in his voice, and Andreas remembered why he couldn't stand the man: he lacked the brains to notice that the commander had made a fool of him.

But they had arrived in Soladis at last, on a bright, clear afternoon where the piss scent of the docks carried for miles. They had travelled by carriage to the mansion Commander Gavon rented when he stayed in Soladis. The commander had busied himself ordering servants to run out to the nearest print shop. Zeke had gone to search the grounds for assassins. Andreas had been set free to pursue his own interests.

As evening fell, he set off to the University Quarter, a small and ancient neighborhood, where the streets wound and curled about each other in a labyrinth-like fashion only the brightest could navigate. The oldest buildings here had been erected before the time of the Empire; round stone structures now used to house mules and secret student smoking circles. Andreas whistled as he walked through a maze of alleyways, hopping over garbage and stray cats, his hands in the pockets of his long rose-pink coat. Small carved stars in the white plaster walls of houses marked the way. Several other distinguished, well-dressed people were walking the same path, though, per custom, they pretended not to notice one another. At last, Andreas reached a stack of wine barrels in a back alley.

Without breaking his stride, he stepped *through* them.

A heartbeat later, he stood at the top of a spiral stair made from white wood. Heavy satin curtains lined the walls of the stairwell around him. Andreas smiled. The first time he had done this, his stomach had revolted. But this was easy, now. To walk through the halls of power felt as natural to as striding through a sunlit day.

In the days of the revolution, angry mobs had burned temples and armed soldiers had executed every deity they could find. But it was the writings of the philosophers' guild that had stoked their revolutionary fervor. Their secretive society admitted only the most esteemed thinkers in the Seaward Isles, and the location of their meeting hall was a closely-guarded secret. Andreas was most proud to call himself a member. He was also of the opinion that the guild should be proud of *him.*

In the days of the Theocracy, the Eyesnatcher, god of illusions and trickery, had woven magic to conceal the guild from the uninitiated, and his work remained as powerfully compelling as it had been the day he cast it. It was said he still dwelled here, and would on some nights take on human form to mingle with the guild's best and brightest. Andreas descended the stair and entered a hall carved from white marble, one hundred feet in length. Though buried in a basement, it had high, arched windows down its long sides that looked out on sunlit and green rolling hills. Sheep grazed on the far side of the window-glass, unconcerned by the hall in their midst. From the hall's vaulted ceiling hung three great chandeliers. Countless crystals dangled around the gleaming candles, sending rainbows dancing across the walls and floors. A single table, draped in a cloth of rich indigo cotton, stretched the length of the hall. On the back wall hung the seal of the philosophers' guild, shaped from silver: a pair of crossed quills with a carnelian flame burning above them.

Philosophers stood all about the grand table. Most were clad in Soladisean fashion, in coats and breeches or long gowns and hoopskirts. Some wore different styles: loose-fitting tunics and trousers, high-collared dresses with no hoops or bustles, floor-length ponchos dyed in vivid geometric patterns. One man had no shirt; only tattoos that covered his whole torso in swirling rainbow ink. The air smelled of salt and cinnamon, lively with laughter and friendly conversation. Even with no visible hearth or fire, a palpable warmth hung in the air. Andreas smiled as he walked across the white marble floor. He was back where he belonged.

"Major Kemsworthy!" he said, and met the man's eyes. The Soladisean officer stood with two other Assembly members, Mr. Reitmartin, from a district in the Sapphire Isles, just to the east of Port Dueno, and Lord Kass, the Count of Aurabor, from one of the more rural voting districts on the island of Soladis. Once the vote of impeachment was placed on the Assembly's voting schedule, forty-five members would need to vote yes to strip Commander Gavon of his positions. From the gossip Andreas had gathered, nearly thirty already leaned in favor of impeachment. They would do a good deal of work to convince each other, of course, but he had no desire to leave things up to chance. "How are you? I quite enjoyed your latest publication."

"Mr. Gavon! Good to see you!" Major Kemsworthy smiled. He was a thin, near-sickly man, his coat the rich color of brass, his wig perhaps a bit too large for his head. "Did you hear about Lord Beauchamp?"

"What happened to him?" Andreas crossed the floor to join their little knot of philosophers. His boots clicked strangely on the marble tile. In the back of his mind, he thought it likely that they were all in some dusty basement, walking circles in the dirt while the god of trickery watched and laughed. But even the smartest minds in the Republic could be fooled by something that only looked the part.

"Poor man was kidnapped by pirates. Imagine that!"

"The news just came," said Lord Kass. He was dressed somberly for a Soladisean lord, his coat a blue as deep as the midnight sea. Though a young man still, he wore reading glasses on the tip of his nose. "The crew of his ship were left to drift to the Crest of Soladis after the pirate raid. They sent a letter to his household the moment they made land."

Andreas frowned. He'd always considered Tomis an ally, especially since the nobleman had confided in him about that illegal paper he ran, and, in moments like these, Andreas needed every ally he had. But Tomis was not an Assembly member. He could proceed without him. "Do you know *which* pirates attacked the ship?"

"I've heard a dozen rumors. My money is on the Demon of Dogshead. Did you hear that she burned the fort on Moonwhisper Isle?"

Andreas flinched. *Moonwhisper. I might have been there.* The realization helped him school his features into a look of concern. "Awful. Simply awful." *One more rebellious fucking echo making life harder for the rest of us.* At least it hadn't been Eva. Everyone would associate Eva with him. But the Demon of Dogshead was everything the Republic feared in an echo—violent, broadly visible, and unrepentant of both. "May Heraline resurface from wherever she's been hiding these past twenty years and drag her ship down to the depths."

"That could well happen," Mr. Reitmartin said, with an uneasy laugh. In his fingers, he twisted about a viridian handkerchief. "We live in strange times. As I was about to tell these men, I had the strangest . . . vision, the other day. A mob of angry citizens were marching on Assembly Hall. The price of flour had gone up, and they had heard we were having a banquet. Most had demands. A few had rifles. Commander Gavon sent the army and had them all . . . slaughtered."

"It had to be done," said Kemsworthy. "They attacked the house of the government. Filthy traitors." He paused. "I mean to say, they attacked it in that dream of yours."

Andreas frowned. He had kept his distance from the sailors on *Kembrielle,* but he had heard some whispering about a riot in Soladis. This could not be a vision or a daydream. *These are memories.* When the murmurings had begun, his father had said "Eva," like a curse, and Andreas had pretended that he didn't understand. He had encouraged his sister to do this because it would keep her busy at sea. Her success had been unexpected. But he thought what she had done would be a help to him. Albeit with unexpected drawbacks.

"There was a draft eighteen years ago," Kass said. He folded his arms over his chest. Andreas glimpsed a black ink sun tattoo on his wrist, only just visible beneath the lace of his cuff. *The mark of a proud Soladisean.*

"Commander Gavon recruited all the Republic's youth from eighteen to twenty-five to fight the Kingdom of Serpent Riders in the south. Hundreds died. The people were enraged."

"He did what was necessary," said Kemsworthy. "I mean to say, he did *not* do it. But if he had, it would have been necessary."

Kass sighed. "Oh, must we really keep playing this game? We all know what the commander is capable of. Mr. Gavon, surely *you* know."

They all turned to him. *The echo. Of course they would.* But it was his knowledge they looked to him for, not merely his nature. He had their attention. He should make use of it. "We should take action," he said. "The people of the Isles look to the guild for moral guidance. If my foster father has done as you suspect—"

"He is still an elected member of the Assembly," said Kemsworthy. "It would be immoral for us to undermine the democratic process by removing him from power. The Assembly only rules by the consent of the people."

"What is to be done," Andreas said, "if the consent of the people has been undermined by those who have the power to shape it as they like? What is the purpose of democracy then?"

An uneasy look passed between them all.

All his life, Andreas had been told the revolution had been as much a revolution of words and ideas as it was of bullets and blades. The Seaward Isles had seen their share of violent coups—as Andreas would sometimes point out, only a fraction of those had been Morghaia's doing—but this revolution had begun an new age. An age of democracy, where change came from votes, not violence. But that did not serve echoes. Even if they could vote, there were not enough of them for their votes to matter. The only tool they had was to persuade others to vote in their interest.

"The people sent him to the Assembly," said Reitmartin, "but the people also sent us."

"Agreed," said Kass. "We have the authority to hold him accountable. We must pass the vote of impeachment as soon as it can be held."

Andreas nodded. He did his best to don a solemn expression as his heart swelled with pride. It felt as if he stood ten feet tall.

A crystalline chiming sound filled the hall. Beneath the guild seal, at the head of the great table, a woman held up a small bejeweled bell. All the gathered philosophers turned to face her.

Assemblywoman Onya Thivatan, a professor of philosophy at the esteemed Imperial College of Soladis and the elected leader of the guild, smiled out at the gathered members. She was a short woman, with rich brown skin and black hair trimmed to chin length, clad in pale yellow leggings and a long green tunic. A mantle of gleaming emerald beetle wings draped her shoulders. "Honored members of the philosophers' guild. Please take your seats for this evening's dinner and debate. If anyone has a fresh subject for discussion, come forward and let me know. Something fresh, please. I'll have no more discussion about pushing large men in front of runaway carts."

"Come now, Mr. Gavon," Reitmartin said. "Join us for dinner."

"It would be my pleasure," Andreas said, and off they went.

The four of them went to sit by the head of the table; Andreas and Kass to the left-hand side and Kemsworth and Reitmartin to the other, only two seats down from Thivatan herself. Chairs scraped across the floor as the philosophers took their seats. Even the brightest minds in the Isles were bound by the demands of their stomachs.

A violinist began to play. Servants in starched black coats emerged from the kitchens, which were hidden behind a thick curtain over an archway in the back wall. They carried platters of roasted salmon topped with lemon slices, baskets of pork puff pastries, and tureens of carrots swimming in a sweet-potato glaze, which they laid out all along the length of the great table. Andreas filled his plate as a sommelier poured him a glass of wine darker than old blood. He drank deeply of the wine, and ate the salmon, while only nibbling at the other dishes. He hated the stringy texture of pork, and something about carrots turned his stomach. Rather than force himself to choke them down, he listened.

The philosophers whispered about riots and drafts, plagues and famines, dreams and visions and memories. *Memories.* They whispered *Commander Gavon* with heavy voices, bitter and frightened. *Good,* Andreas told himself. But they whispered *the echo Evazina* or *the Demon of Dogshead* in the next breath, in a tone that sent a shiver down his spine.

I earned my place here, he reminded himself. Philosophers came and went from the head of the table, murmuring topics for debate in Thivatan's ear. *Is the Republic expanding into the frontier too quickly? Did the ancient Sea People live in a utopian state? Is it possible Commander Gavon might ascend to godhood?* A dozen different questions. A dozen different askers. Any sort of person could have a place in the guild, if they earned it.

Andreas licked his lips. If he wanted to encourage Thivatan to vote yes on the vote of impeachment, and to lead her allies on the Assembly to follow, he would need to impress her all over again tonight.

As the servants cleared away the dishes to prepare for dessert course, Assemblywoman Thivatan stood and rang her bell once more. "We have a topic," she announced. All down the length of the table, philosophers set down their forks and wine glasses, quieting to listen. "Here is the hypothetical: say a rebellion was to break out in the Sapphire Isles, and a force of rebel malcontents were to threaten to capture Port Dueno and cut off the trade of the Viridian League with the north." Rietmartin frowned at this; as one of the merchants affiliated with the League, this would be his greatest nightmare. "Would it be more ethical for Commander Gavon to put it down with soldiers, or by modifying the memories of the rebels?"

"Commander Gavon would never stoop so low," said Kemsworthy. He stood, and puffed out his chest like a rooster destined for the stew pot. "We should not legitimize this line of inquiry."

"Keep an open mind," Kass said. "It can't be that hard. There's so much empty space between your ears."

Polite laughter filled the hall. Andreas did not join it. A servant had placed an apple turnover on a small plate before him. He cut the flaky crust off a corner and pressed it through his lips. Clove-spiced apples filled his throat. He waited for his moment.

"Well," Kemsworthy said, "in the scenario proposed by the distinguished Assemblywoman Professor Thivatan, if the commander sends in the army, the rebels will all be slaughtered, and many good and noble Republic soldiers will die beside them. But, if he uses his power, the rebels will forget their grievances and be pacified. Not one life will be lost. Surely, in taking the memories of the rebels, the commander would be doing a great good."

Murmurs sweep the hall. Philosophers exchanged knowing glances. Andreas set his jaw. His cuffs felt suddenly too tight on his wrists. *A great good.* Was that how they saw the destruction of echoes? *Don't make trouble,* he told himself. *You're not Eva.*

"What do you think, Gavon?" said Reitmartin.

Andreas smiled and tightened his grip on his fork. *I think you're a gods-damned bastard.*

"Go on. Take up the gauntlet." Kass said. He met Andreas' eyes and gave him an encouraging nod. "What you have to say?"

Do they truly want to hear my opinion? An echo's opinion?

But he was a member of the guild. He had earned his place here. Why would they not want to hear him?

Andreas lifted his voice. "Surely you haven't forgotten the cost of the commander's magic, Kemsworthy? One echo soul?" *Or more?* There had to be a great cost for memory magic that size. If it was came cheaply, Commander Gavon would have already snatched these newly-freed memories away. "Why do you say *not one life is lost?*"

Kemsworthy seemed unaffected by the bitterness in Andreas' tone. Perhaps Andreas had disguised it too well. Or perhaps it simply did not matter to him. "Think of it logically. To split a soul does not take a life. It creates one."

"By destroying the person that echo was before."

"Well, what's a person? In his treatise *On Existence,* Malone wrote that personhood derives from the independent possession of free will, personality, rationality, and memory. Personhood is what sets us apart from animals and abominations. It is a state of being we share with the gods."

"I'm familiar with the work."

"Now, echoes, your personalities do not form independently. You are all sullen and taciturn; I have met a good number of you and may personally attest to this fact. These similarities prevent you from qualifying as *true* people, in the same way the irrationality and superstition of the Sea People prevent them from achieving personhood, which is a prerequisite for citizenship—"

Andreas made himself nod along as Kemsworthy continued to blather. The philosophical approach to *personhood* had sprung from the study of the atrocities committed by the Theocracy; when the god of charity had made worshippers so giving that they handed off all their worldly possessions in the street, when the goddess of sleep had made whole villages dream for generations. The philosophers had looked at this and said, no, all persons divine or human were entitled to a basic decency of selfhood. They had defined personhood so that they could define the violation of the mind, the seat of personhood, as a great crime.

Of course, non-people received no such protection.

As Kemsworthy finished his tirade, Andreas pushed back his chair, stood straight, and cleared his throat. "Major Kemsworthy, you yourself wrote in your latest published article that all children lack rationality, created as they were from carnal lust. Children who are raised in the good graces of citizen parents achieve the level of rationality required to lives as full citizens at eighteen. Foster children require more seasoning to overcome their defects, and so those who hold citizenship are only awarded their full rights at twenty-five."

"And?"

All eyes had turned to him. Andreas rested his hands on the table and smiled. "Echoes are like the branches of a tree. Each one forked and twisted in its own pattern, stretching back to a common root. Each of us represents what we all could be, were we only given another place on the trunk to grow, and grow we do. Cannot we allow that echoes may too achieve personhood in time? That perhaps some of us already have?"

The words felt like poison on his tongue. *I am a damn person.* He could not speak that truth. They would dismiss him as biased, irrational. *An echo, not a philosopher.* Still, he would point them toward what they had missed. He would let them think that they had discovered that echoes were people on their own. They would like the truth better if it let them think themselves smart.

Whispers spread up and down the table. On the philosophers' plates, the apple turnovers went cold. Professor Thivatan nodded. "We will entertain your point in the discussion, Mr. Gavon. Members of the guild, please do consider the cost of one echo soul in pacifying the rebels, however you weigh it."

I won, Andreas thought. His grin widened. A light glinted in his eye. *And I won like a philosopher.*

Thivatan lowered her voice. "Mr. Gavon, I would like you to meet with me in the guild library tomorrow afternoon. We have much to discuss."

Was that a faint hint of displeasure in the curl of her lip? No. Surely not. He'd earned his place here over and over. He was one of them.

Eva was delighted to make her first journey to the city of Soladis. She had read it described in countless novels and histories: it was often likened to a great spindle, about which all affairs of the Isles turned. The bulk of the city lay around a horseshoe-shaped natural harbor on the island of the same name. At its heart, atop the highest hill, rose the polished dome of Assembly Hall. Its three great hilltops were high and green, the great manors atop them white stucco, roofed in shingles of red clay. Its valleys were brown and densely-built, humans and animals living atop each other in densely-packed squat buildings of stone. Stone walls ringed the city, covered in mosaics of colored glass, and the light of the sun danced off them in a riot of rainbows.

It was a pretty sight, Eva thought, as she surveyed the city through a dozen different windows out of Death. In her hands, she held on to the silvery cocoons of smoke and magic that wrapped around Tomis and Lord Merris, who she dragged behind her, light as feathers. Here, the great hallway of bone, smoke, and drifting souls widened into a great round atrium, the ceiling so high it was shrouded in fog. The windows were not only set into the walls, but rose out of the floor, forming a dozen concentric rings of window archways, broken every few yards where one had crumbled or sunk into the floor of jumbled bones. The currents that carried souls along seemed slower here; they drifted about the gray rings, nodding at Eva as she passed.

Her first destination was the Merris townhouse, in a wealthy neighborhood high atop a hill. She appeared in the salon, where a guest had once dropped dead during after-dinner cigars, and offered Lady Merris her husband's signet ring. The woman burst into tears. Eva rubbed at the back of her neck. Merris deserved to suffer; did she? But there was a young servant girl playing the harp at her feet, a girl with the red outline of a slap on her cheek. Whatever empathy Eva might have otherwise felt withered in her chest.

The Merris servants brought her a chest of unmarked gold ingots. Eva dragged it into Death and back to the dockside locker where she'd stashed her prisoner. She retrieved Merris, his hands spotted with ink from the map he had drawn Cevette (her father might punish him for that, good) and dragged him off into Death behind her. He sobbed at the sight of his own front gate, so drugged and feverish that he vomited the moment Eva shoved him into his guards' arms. It made a good distraction for her to vanish.

Tomis waited for her on the docks, plainly dressed in a borrowed shirt and breeches, his red hair combed back and tied on his nape with a ribbon. He kept a printers' shop in a lower neighborhood of the city; he had hidden away enough gold there to pay the ransom Cevette had negotiated. No one had died near it recently, and so Eva had chosen to walk with him there on foot, the better to see the city. She put the chest from Lord Merris in the locker and joined him.

They strolled up the wooden boards, side by side, toward the thirty-foot-high walls of the city. The air reeked of mud and dead fish; the damp in it clung to their skin. Seagulls flocked at their feet, gray-winged and missing toes, begging for bread. Tomis was hungry for gossip. "I noticed you and the captain came to visit me *together* last night. You were both . . . flushed. Is the notorious Cevette Zarcanzi in love?"

"She is." Eva's heart twisted. "With someone else."

"Ah. I'm sorry.

"It is what it is." She glanced down the docks. A crowd was gathering near the wall. She frowned at the sight. Tomis had promised that the gate they were going to would be unguarded. "When will your article come out?"

"I have a few articles planned. One shall be about you and your crew."

"What? Why?"

"To explain why so many of you took up piracy. Not only from greed, but because the structure of the Republic permitted you nowhere else to go. It will help soften them to the idea of trusting the information you have shared with me—which reminds me, I do have a few more questions to ask you." He pulled a nub of charcoal and a scrap of paper from inside his coat. "They're about your life as an echo."

Eva frowned. "Why do you want to know about that?"

"Because you're asking the citizens of the Republic to trust you, as an echo. They only know you through what father has told them echoes are. I can show them how *you* see yourself. That's the power of the press."

She sighed. It could work. She often found his articles illuminating. The written word could open minds and scrawl some empathy upon them. "Very well. Ask what you will."

"Good. Now, forgive me if this is rude, and you don't have to answer. But do you remember anything about your creation?"

"I was an infant." Eva hesitated. "At least, I remember my father telling me he found me and my brother as infants following the destruction of Morghaia. But I suppose I can't be certain of that."

"That must be quite unnerving," he said.

"It is," she said. But, unexpectedly, she found her heart lightened to speak of it. Back in Halston, echoes were not encouraged to think about their own nature. Only to be ashamed of it "I try not to think of . . . of all the echoes I could have once been part of, between being Morghaia and being me. It's much easier for me to think that she fractured, and now I'm here."

He nodded. "On the topic of Morghaia," he said, and shooed aside a seagull that was biting at the buckle on his shoe, "I'm curious about how you see her. Merely as one of the cruel gods of the Theocracy? Or more like a mother?"

Eva considered the question as they walked on. The closer to the city wall they came, the tighter the crowds drew about them. She had worn a plain dress of maroon wool, practical brown leather gloves, and her hair was tucked up under a bonnet (her knives were hidden deep in her skirts) and so she did not feel as visible as she might. Still, she kept her head low and her voice lower. "Neither. To speak honestly, I would say she is the mark I measure myself against."

"Interesting." He scribbled a note on the page. "Do you consider yourself more of a god, or more a human?"

Eva frowned, and thought it over. "Neither description quite fits perfectly. But we *are* people. I know that much."

The crowds grew tight about them as they approached the gate. Elbows jammed into her side. People murmured and cursed. Whispers of *riots* and *drafts* and *famine* rose on every breath along with the scent of unwashed bodies. At the sight of the guards by the lifted portcullis, she grabbed Tomis by the elbow and whispered, "You promised there were no guards on this gate."

"I've never seen guards here before," he said, pale beneath his red freckles. "I've never seen crowds like this. Why is everyone so upset?"

"It's the memories," she whispered, and they both shared uneasy looks. Of everything she'd expected to achieve by burning them, it wasn't this.

A guard in a golden uniform pushed his way through the crowd. They grumbled, but stepped aside. Eva tried to back away, but the press of bodies would not let her. A heartbeat later, he stood before her, glowering. "Is that an echo?"

Tomis stepped between Eva and the guard. He held out his hand with his signet ring, which Cevette had been good enough to leave him. "I am Tomis Augustis Beauchamp, Marquis of Thistle Bay and Count of Centois. This woman is a guest of mine. You will let her through."

The guard frowned. He waved one of his fellows over, a shorter man, who looked first at Tomis and then at the ring. "It's him," he said. "I'd know that red hair anywhere."

"Apologies, my lord," said the guard who had stopped them. "Commander Gavon's in the city. He sent out orders to be careful, that's all. Welcome home." He bowed, and waved the two of them forward.

The small relief Eva felt still died as they crossed through the city's wide portcullis and joined the great crush of traffic. Carts, horses, carriages, and those travelling afoot shoved and jostled one another. Fishmongers touted heavy baskets of their catches up the way. Sailors carried cargo crates to their ships. Every voice was shouting, and there was even less sea air to blow the reek away. Above it all, posters had been nailed to every dockside building, the crisp new paper flapping in the wind.

Each one bore her face.

The Echo Pirate, Evazina the Skullrunner, is Wanted on Charges of High Treason and Mental Violations of Personhood through Unauthorized Use of Divine Magic. Twenty Thousand Pounds will be Awarded for her Live Capture, as well as the Gratitude of the Golden Republic for the Restoration of Peace. She may be Known by the Godmarks on her Hands.

"They're blaming me for the memories coming back," she whispered to Tomis. She pulled her bonnet forward a bit, shielding what little more she could of her face. She braced herself for the rage she had felt in Halston, when she learned her father sought to have her arrested for running away. Instead, her cheeks burned. Her shoulders slumped. She felt shameful and small. She could only drink in so much of the world's rage before wondering if she deserved the bitter taste. "They think it's some sort of deception. But I only revealed the truth."

"They make it sound as if you've created false memories from magic." Tomis frowned. "A preposterous theory. We will set them straight soon enough. This way," he said, and waved her into a narrow alleyway that smelled of horse manure and straw.

Along they went. They turned left, and left again. At last, they found a small shop that clung to the city wall like a barnacle. It was a dark, dingy, dusty building with only two small windows. A guard tower built into the wall rose high above it, casting the whole thing in shadows. Eva's heart caught in her throat as they approached. It seemed so *small.*

Tomis opened the door and waved her inside.

Inside, the printers' shop was lit by narrow shafts of sunlight that fell on the wooden floor, which was covered in straw, woodshavings, and packing crates. Eva sneezed, then blinked her tears away as she took in the great press. It took up nearly the whole of the one-room shop, though there was a small loft tucked against the ceiling, reachable by a ladder. The press was twelve feet in length and carved from sturdy walnut wood. Galley frames set with rows of metal type were stacked about it, with one mounted directly in the bed of the press beneath the stamping plate. A woman in a printer's apron was directing three apprentices on how to use a leather pad to apply ink to the type when she looked up and met Tomis' eyes.

A heartbeat and a rush of footsteps later, they were surrounded.

"Tomis!" the woman shouted, and hugged him, lifting him off his feet with her ink-spotted hands. "You're alive! Where have you been? I've heard such terrible stories."

"Melody! Never fear. I'm back in Soladis, and all the stories will be good once again." He dropped a bow at the two girls and the one boy who had gathered around them, none of whom could have been older than twelve. "Apprentices! What have you been up to?"

"The big lever broke—"

"John sat on the big lever."

"You told me to sit on it!"

"Tomis!" A man with heavy glasses and an engraver's chisel in one hand leapt down from the loft. He must have been the one who carved the blocks for the illustrations and letterhead. "Thank the gods," he said, as he pulled Tomis into a second embrace and kissed his cheek.

"Thank the pirates," Tomis said. "Thank other people, for the mercy they show to one another." He nodded to Eva. "This is Evazina Gavon. And she's brought us a story that will change the world."

Eva held her breath. She wished she was anywhere but there. This was Tomis' place, where he belonged, even more so than the halls of power which were his birthright as a citizen and a lord. She was not welcome in this city—in this nation. The world looked at her and saw chaos and death.

"Thank you for bringing him home," Melody said, and "A pleasure, Miss Gavon," said the apprentices, as if it were the easiest thing in the world. The woodcutter, still clinging to Tomis, said nothing. But he nodded to her, and there was welcome in his eyes.

"You all truly don't hate me?" she whispered, surprised. "Why?"

"We care about the truth here," Melody said. "Not the Republic propaganda hung on our walls."

"You know that it's false?"

"If it was true, they wouldn't need to say it so loudly."

Tomis folded his fingers together and grinned. "The truth is the greatest power in the vast continuum of reality. And the truth, Miss Gavon, is on our side."

THE POWER OF THE LAW

IN THE CITY OF SOLADIS, IN THE UNCEDED TERRITORY OF THE KETIL YATA NATION, ON THE ISLAND OF SOLADIS. 16TH HERALMONTH, YEAR TWENTY-TWO OF THE GOLDEN REPUBLIC.

In the years since the Republic was founded, our current women have met with its leaders nine times and demanded they cease their incursions onto our lands. They tell us that they have no authority over the frontier settlers; they deny how often and how cruelly these incursions occur. When they do acknowledge them, they say that their conquest will bring great good to us. They say they will make us citizens and allow us to vote on how we wish to be ruled. Once, a current woman told them that we would vote for them to leave us alone. They laughed at her and called her a fool; then, while she slept, stole her money and pistol and ran off into the night. –'Our History of the Golden Republic,' published in *The Dawn Beacon.*

WHAT FOLLOWED WAS A brief discussion on events to come. Tomis, Melody, and the engraver (Stefayne) had a keen interest in the upcoming vote of impeachment. In all the history of the Golden Republic, only two Assembly members had ever been removed from the body, and neither of them had been the chairman. Of course, only Commander Gavon had ever held the rank of chairman.

There was a small wooden table in the back of the shop, with only two chairs. Tomis sat on one, with Stefayne on his lap. Melody tasked the apprentices with sweeping the shop, then sat on the other chain, met Eva's eyes, and patted her thigh. Eva declined the seat on her lap; Melody had already been quite kind to her, and she didn't want to inconvenience her with pins and needles in her legs. Eva dragged up a crate and sat atop it, sweeping out her skirts as she did.

"First, the Assembly will need to place the vote on the schedule," Tomis said. "The session lasts for two months. Commander Gavon will try to push the vote back, to buy himself time, but, so long as twenty members support the measure, he must schedule it at some point in the session."

"How many memories can he steal from us in that time?" Melody said.

"That depends on how many echoes he has at his disposal," Eva said. "There must be a number in this city. But at the present, the only one I know of that he has clear access to is my brother." Her voice quavered with worry. "Andreas believes he must stay close to him to help influence the vote, but he has put himself into a risky position . . ."

"I'll keep an eye on him," Tomis promised. "I'll likely need his help as I write. His input will be most helpful as I tell the world how the echoes aren't our enemies—"

"The Demon of Dogshead is likely your enemy," Eva said. She hated to interrupt, but she wanted them to be precise. "She's an echo. She's the one who burned the fort on Moonwhisper Isle."

"Very well. The echoes are certainly not as dangerous to us as our own government." He sighed. "I only wish we knew what was afoot in the Assembly. I've spoken with a few members about their work, but I cannot trust them fully."

Eva smiled. "We've already planned to scout out the archive under Assembly Hall. Why not slip in afterward and hear what they have to say?"

"A most congenial idea, Miss Gavon."

She grinned. She wanted to be there to see her father humiliated.

Tomis, gentleman that he was, counted the ransom that he had negotiated with Cevette into two good-sized bags of coin. With help from Melody, Eva fastened them both to the inside of her hoopskirt, which was reinforced with iron to hold her weapons. "Are you certain that's not too much weight?" he said, as they stepped out the shop door.

She shook her head. "It's all good training. To strengthen my thighs."

"They seem quite strong as they are," said Melody, leaning out through the door.

"That's only because you haven't seen Cevette Zarcanzi swim," Eva said, and nodded to the printer. The woman looked a bit disappointed as she and Tomis walked away.

WHEN EVA AND TOMIS reached the foot of the high hill topped by Assembly Hall, she paused for a moment and gazed up at it in awe.

The largest building in the city had once been the Temple of Iunos. Though the statues and altars had been hauled out and smashed, what remained was much the same as it had been in the days of the Empire. The circular hall stretched four hundred feet across and stood one hundred feet tall. Gold leaf covered the dome of the roof. Columns with scrolled caps stood every ten feet around the circumference, and, at each one, at least five gold-uniformed soldiers stood at attention. The most modern additions were the brick towers that had been raised at regular intervals along the road leading up the hill, where sharpshooters and cannon crews stood always at the ready to defend democracy.

Eva shuddered as she took them in. "Let's go in through Death."

Back into the city they went. Quickly, they found the alley behind a barber-surgeon's shop, where Eva could sense that a number of unfortunates had died screaming. Posters of her face covered the walls; so did advertisements for tonics and creams that would dispel *false memories* and *hallucinations*. She set her jaw, opened a portal, and pulled Tomis in behind her.

Assembly Hall proved quite easy to locate within Death. The centuries had left the great building pockmarked with portals. Eva gazed out through them, her fingers brushing the bone lintels of the freshest ones. The acrid taste of fear rose in her throat, the horror of citizens and soldiers alike, from the night when the rioters had fought to break into the Hall. Some of the deaths had the flavor of righteous pride, left from those who died believing their sacrifice would force the Assembly to feed the poor. Some tasted like confusion, from those who had just forgotten why they'd come there, who didn't know why their guts were slipping through their fingers. It was all bitter as hemlock.

Rage simmered in her chest. *This is what my father tells the world is my doing. It's him. It's all him. We only have to make them see.*

She stepped out through a portal into a wine cellar. The cool, still chamber was full of barrels and dusty ledgers. The only light came from a door open a crack at the top of the stairs. A lantern hung on the wall; she lit it with a flint from her pocket while Tomis shook out his coat and got his bearing. He crossed the small room, to a door secured with a heavy wooden latch, which he lifted. The hinges creaked. The door yawned open. Beyond lay only darkness.

"The catacombs." Tomis bowed and waved Eva toward it. "Shall we descend, Miss Gavon?"

She nodded, and followed him into the dark.

The lantern cast long shadows on the weathered and half-crumbled walls. The path before them sloped downward; the bricks of the Hall's foundation went down for five feet and then transitioned into walls of packed earth, reinforced by wooden beams. The air grew cooler as they went down. Eva took off her gloves and ran her fingertips along the wall. "Do these run all the way under the city?"

Tomis nodded. "The city is over a thousand years old. It's mostly built on top of itself."

"How did you learn about this place?"

"I happen to be acquainted with a number of young soldiers. Carnally. Stefayne enjoys them as well. They're decent lovers. Overeager at times. Likely two dozen of them down here at least. Soldiers, I mean, not men I've bedded. We'd best be cautious."

The sound of marching footsteps rang up the hallway. Eva squinted. She couldn't see anything that far ahead, but her lantern might give them away. She lowered it down behind her skirts. The tunnel darkened. She squinted. Far up ahead, a light flickered. A sergeant shouted a call. She held her breath until the soldiers marched on. At last, the catacombs quieted.

Eva took a deep breath and lifted her lantern back up high. "We need to follow them."

They hurried down the hall. Their hearts hammered in the shadowy darkness. The air was cool, yet sweat still prickled on the back of Eva's neck. It was another two hundred feet, sloping steeply downward, until the tunnel intersected with a larger one. They followed the path the soldiers had taken along it; their footprints were fresh in the dirt. One hundred feet along, they found a pile of collapsed rubble, blocking the way—but there was a knob in the earthen floor, shaped like a knot of brass tentacles. Eva knelt, grabbed it, and twisted. With a click, a small round trap door lifted up. Tomis helped her pull it open, both of them holding their breath.

Beneath them, a ladder led down into a cavern, to where a dozen torches blazed in the dark. The scent of salt and tallow wafted upward. Eva squinted. *Do I hear waves?* Seawater lapped against the cavern walls. Beside her, Tomis cursed. She shifted her position and glimpsed what lay at the cavern's heart.

On a small, rocky island, soldiers stood guard around what must have been at least fifty stacked crates. The crumbled black-and-white shapes of memories overflowed from the open ones. The soldiers stood at attention, wary eyes watching the shadow for anything that moved.

There must be fifty soldiers down there, Eva thought, and *if I brought him here, Mr. Smoke could simply burn them all to death.*

She pushed the door closed and drew a deep, shaking breath. Tomis looked up at her with wide, worried eyes.

"Thank you for showing me this," Eva said. "I need to . . . speak with Captain Zarcanzi. Make a plan." Her voice quavered.

She wished for any plan besides the one she knew would succeed.

THE LIBRARY OF THE philosophers' guild was a dusty, dingy room that sat off to the side of the great hall. There was illusion; here was truth. The long room had a low ceiling, and every inch of walls were covered in carved stone bookshelves. Lanterns dangled from the ceiling on chains, and a crackling fire filled the room with warmth and light. Andreas sat at one of the small desks that lined the center of the room, shivering as he thumbed through a treatise on the nature of divinity.

The chapter he was reading discussed the shapeshifting abilities of gods, how they could and frequently did take on human form. They were indistinguishable from true humans in these bodies, though they did not age, and their powers, which primarily encompassed their abilities to hear and answer the prayers of their followers, were limited. A philosopher could expose a god's true form with certain rituals; elsewise, only the god themself had the power to show or conceal their divine form. The discussion veered off onto the topic of how the philosophers might experiment on echoes to better understand the lines between gods and humans. Andreas had to fight the urge to rip out the page.

Tomis Beauchamp had once asked him what it meant to be an echo. Andreas had given him the textbook explanation, of Morghaia and her breaking, and thought the other boy grossly ignorant for needing to ask. But what he had meant, Andreas later realized, was what did being an echo mean to *him*? In the life he led, and wished to lead?

His nature was a stumbling block, a curse, a cruel mockery. He faced all the stigma of divine heritage and held none of the power. He had assumed every echo felt that way, right until Eva had thrown the knife he'd given her for her birthday through the Skullrunner's heart. Andreas had been willing to take the magic for the status it would give him. But she had drank it in and smiled.

He had nightmares about that smile. It belonged on a god.

"Mr. Gavon." Professor Thivatan strode into the library. She was clad in the Soladisean fashion today, a long gray gown with a collar of pearls at her throat, her hair tied up at the back of her neck. "Thank you for agreeing to meet me here. What are you reading?"

"Theology." Andreas shut the book and stood. "In preparation for when I next have the chance to assume the duties of an officer of the Godreaper Corps," he added. It would not do for an echo to appear improperly interested in theology.

Thivatan nodded. She approached him, and took a thick, leather-bound book off a shelf as she drew near, which she clutched to her chest like a shield. "So your father's philosophers have seen signs of a god they can catch for you?"

"Not yet," he said. "Has anyone in the guild seen omens of a god's return?" It was said that many gods refused to walk the living world altogether these days; that many of them hid deep within Death, some having snuck into Morghaia's realm by secret byways, some landing there after the godreaper they had been bound to passed away, all of them waiting for a safer and more respectful era to return. But it was also said that gods were arrogant, that they drew strength from worship, that they often acted against their own best interest. In that, they were much like humans.

"There have been no such omens since the shade of Skullrunner was found. Some signs of Heraline have been spotted, but she's enough of a Sea People goddess that our rituals have no power over her." Her eyes narrowed. "Why do you wish to know? So you might claim the god yourself?"

What? Why had she turned so sharp with him? "Only . . . only with my father's blessing, of course. To do elsewise would be treason."

"That did not stop your sister. And now she has unleashed a plague of false memories to stir up trouble in our streets."

Andreas smiled. He fought to keep his tone even. "I am not my sister."

"I am aware of that. There was a robust discussion, when you were nominated for guild membership, if we should admit an echo to our ranks. If you possessed sufficient personhood to contribute to this body. But you were the commander's foster son, and your university mentors spoke quite highly of you. We agreed that we would grant you an opportunity to demonstrate you could speak for yourself." She shook her head. "But you and your sister are branches of the same tree. You said that yourself. And at the root of the tree lies the goddess of death."

That wasn't what I meant. He had argued that echoes were people. Not that he was less of one. *Only a fool would not see that.* He expected better of the leader of the philosophers' guild.

"Why did you ask me to meet you?" he said.

"I hoped to give you the dignity of saying this in private: you are no longer welcome at the philosophers' guild." She shook her head. "I myself have often appreciated your wit and intelligence. Yet it is untenable to keep you among our number at present. The state of things with your sister, and this Demon of Dogshead . . . and, you must admit, your vocal argument last night did nothing to distance you from them."

Bitterness boiled within him. His chest tightened. A sneer crept across his face. *I debased myself for you.* His arguments for preserving the souls of echoes had been soft things, couched in terms so familiar and conciliatory to the philosophers that not one of them could object to what he said. He had thought himself so clever in how he'd framed it, even as he hated that it had to be done. He had won. He had beaten the gentry of the guild at their own game.

I made them lose to an echo. Next to that, nothing else mattered.

Eva found a portal that led into the main hall. A gallery had been erected there; she knew not for what purpose, as meetings of the Assembly were closed to the general public. Perhaps it had been different once; perhaps the change in the rule had something to do with the frightened girl who had once died there. She could not know. She stepped out through it, and pulled Tomis along behind her. They stepped forward and crouched low at the gallery railing, both of them ducking their heads down and out of sight. From the size of the cobwebs and the layer of dust coating the gallery benches, they had not been occupied in some time, and when Eva looked back over her shoulder, the door was boarded shut. No one would even suspect to look for them here.

The chamber below was smaller than she had imagined, though just as grand, a round room two hundred feet across beneath a high domed ceiling. Its walls were papered in bright green and covered with plaster reliefs of nude men and women lifting the symbols of government: the sword, the book, and the scales. A great flag, twenty feet in length, hung from the back wall. The floor was set with marble tiles in an alternating pattern of black and white. The desks, benches, and stools were scattered haphazardly about. The air smelled of ink and the melting beeswax of a hundred candles.

Threescore and ten Assembly members had gathered today, the rest being off on some other business. Some swayed on their feet, passing about a flask, and some donned glasses as they flipped through heavy leather-bound legal texts. Sweat gathered in their powdered wigs. Papers rustled. Politicians murmured in low voices. One drunken Assembly member broke into song.

Commander Gavon sat in a back corner, chin high, dark eyes darting about him, alert and on-edge. He wore his blue sash of office over his plain orange military jacket, medallions of valor shining on the satin. His brow furrowed as he scrawled notes on a scrap of paper. Dimly, Eva remembered her father sweeping her up on his shoulders to march in a parade. The sound of his laughter. The surety of his warm hands. Her heart lurched. She gazed at the man beneath her, willing herself to see that light in him. All she saw was the silver in his hair and the scratch of his pen.

Zeke stood at his back, a silent, watchful shadow, his face unreadable. He was the only non-member of the Assembly present; she did not believe he had been admitted to the chamber in the past. But the commander had brought him in now to make a show of his strength.

"So this is what democracy looks like," Tomis whispered. "I though it would be grander."

Was this democracy? Eva looked through the room, and thought of her history classes. So many members of the Assembly were aristocrats whose families had first come into wealth under the Theocracy. The gods had not been tyrants to the people in this room. There was Lord Akhoran, whose ancestors had claimed their lands after a god turned a neighboring nobleman into a twelve-horned goat, and Marie d'Envissant, whose family fortunes were the result of a god poisoning their rivals in the dye trade. Were these the leaders the citizens of the Republic would choose freely? Or were they simply those who had the resources to aspire to high office?

At last, Commander Gavon stood, and walked to the lectern at the center of the room. Zeke followed behind him. The commander convened the meeting with a tap of his gavel. The gathered Assembly members rose, turned to face the flag, and placed their hands to their hearts, joining in as he recited the Oath of Loyalty: "I pledge my house and my most vaunted honor to serve the Golden Republic. May my blade and dying breath preserve the land I love. And should my peer or kindred turn their coat on liberation, may my hand be the bloody one that strikes them down." Another tap. The members sat.

"Welcome," Commander Gavon said, his voice grave, his face set. The members of the Assembly turned to face him. "I call this year's session to order. Several grave matters await our attention, and so we shall begin forthwith. The first matter at hand is that the Skullrunner raided the *Pleasant Mary* and released the memory of the riot from two years ago, among other things."

Eva stared down at him. Her eyes widened. She had not expected for him to address her first.

"These are not the first memories she's released," the commander continued. "At present, I am planning a naval expedition to track her down—"

A man stood. He was relatively young for an Assembly member, with thick glasses and a coat trimmed in silver thread that spoke to his wealth. As he adjusted his glasses, Eva glimpsed a sun tattoo on his wrist. "How, pray tell, do you plan to track down the Skullrunner? She can move through Death. You'll never catch her.

"I have considered that, Lord Kass. The pirates are protecting her. So I will bring them all to heel, beginning with the so-called Demon of Dogshead. She attacked the fort at Moonwhisper Isle. I will sail to Dogshead Isle and make her pay for her actions in blood."

He plans to target Korinne. Not Cevette. That was not the relief she thought it might be, and she did not know why. Hadn't Korinne brought this on herself?

"I will see to it," her father continued, "that the Skullrunner will find no safe haven at sea. She will have no choice but to submit to the rule of the Golden Republic."

"This plan of yours seems quite tenuous," observed Lord Kass. "Especially where it involves dealing with not one, but two, echoes who have reaped gods."

"They must be dealt with. I am steadfast in my resolve to protect the Republic against the forces of Death."

"You created them." Kass shook his head. He turned to face the rest of the Assembly and opened his arms. "My friends and fellows. My father always said that, when the Empire of Soladis sent colonists north to the Five Sisters, that they surrendered their ties to Soladis for the dark powers of witchcraft and shamanism. Jonathan Gavon was born only miles from the lands where Morghaia held sway—"

"You insinuate I have some link to the gods? I, who did more to defeat them and save humanity from their influence than any other?"

"We have all heard of your heroism in the revolution, though the precise details of those days are scant and clouded as folktales. We are grateful for your service in the past; that does not mean you are the right person to lead us into the future."

Eva frowned. She had always known that echoes were seen as tainted things in the eyes of Soladis. It was strange indeed to hear someone speak of Commander Gavon as if he were tainted as well. *Who is properly Soladisean if not him?*

Her father had gone still. When next he spoke, his voice was as cool as the northern sea. "What do you propose?"

Kass lifted his chin. "A vote of impeachment."

The chamber erupted in shouts and arguments. Some members lifted their fists aloft. Some paled and dropped their quill pens. One man drew his dress saber and shook it aloft. Assembly members turned to their neighbors, arguing, agreeing, and in the cacophony, Commander Gavon held his tongue. Zeke put a steadying hand on his shoulder.

"You've been too soft on the Sea People as well," said an Assemblyman with sunburnt skin. "The Hoca attacked my farms last year. All you did was send a battleship to guard the coast."

Commander Gavon shook his head. "I altered the villagers' memories so they would forget that mess with the fosterlings that had angered them. The cost was significant—"

"That's nothing. We needed their skulls stuck on a palisade. They're filthy murderous cannibals, all of them. You showed them mercy—"

"My district had been plagued by abomination attacks for months!" shouted an Assemblywoman with light brown skin who wore skirts covered in golden ruffles. "I have written to you five times, Commander Gavon, and received no aid. I will not be ignored!"

"I have answered you, Lamunda," said Commander Gavon, voice taut. "You have more than sufficient resources to address the matter. But you lack the will. Abomination are spawned from suffering and violence. You refuse to acknowledge the deviancy practiced in your district. The sloth. The theft—"

"We need the Godreaper Corps. We need Lieutenant Ezekiel Dare and his best fighters. You only use him to guard your cock!"

The chamber stilled. The commander's eyes narrowed. Low, laughing whispers rose from the ranks of the Assembly members. Zeke did not respond, and the commander did not look at him. But both men were sweating now.

"After all I have done for you," Commander Gavon said, "and after all I have sacrificed for my country, you would cast such aspersions on my behavior? Have you forgotten who I am?"

Assemblywoman Lamunda folded her arms across her chest. "You are the only one who knows what we have forgotten."

Up in the gallery, Eva watched, her heart twisting. *They see him for what he truly is. They're moving against him.* But they were not moving for the right reasons. *Does that matter?*

"Very well," the commander said, his voice brittle. "Who moves to schedule the vote? A show of hands—"

Hands shot up across the hall. Eva held her breath and counted. *Twenty. Forty. Forty-two.* Only twenty Assembly members were needed to schedule the vote. Forty-five were needed to pass it. *We're nearly there.* Perhaps they already were, with the absences taken into account.

Commander Gavon brought down his gavel. "The vote shall be held seven weeks hence," Someone in the crowd shouted "coward!" The commander cleared his throat and continued. "Major Kemsworthy will hold the chair in my absence. I will sail to Dogshead and bring the pirates to heel. Perhaps that will remind the members of this body of all I have done for them over these long years."

Seven weeks. Eva drew a deep breath. She looked to Tomis, who gave her a short nod. *Seven weeks.*

That was all the time they needed to set their history free.

THE ECHO COURT

BEGINNING OFFSHORE OF NIGHT DRAGON ISLE, HOME OF THE PEARL DIVER CLAN OF THE TARWIK PEOPLE, ABOARD THE SHIP *SEA WOLF*, AND CONTINUING ON TO DOGSHEAD ISLE, NINE HUNDRED AND TWENTY MILES SOUTHWEST OF THE CITY OF SOLADIS. 18TH HERALMONTH, YEAR TWENTY-TWO OF THE GOLDEN REPUBLIC.

My sister told me there is a sinister rumor spreading about Dogshead Isle. It has always been a haven of pirates; it is too far out of the way of Port Dueno or the city of Soladis to take part in legitimate trade, and it is all rocks and swamp with little to sell. But now the papers allege that a small group of echoes have taken up residence on the island. Neither Ariella nor I can fathom why they would. We would hate to live among other echoes. They would only encourage our worst instincts. –from the diary of Korinne Gavon.

NIGHT DRAGON ISLE HAD been the nearest archive on the map Lord Merris had drawn them. Eva saw how it had earned its name. The island was shaped from dark purple stone, a long, rough shape that resembled a sleeping beast. The violet loops of its stone tail protruded from the sea; white foam splashed up where the waves crashed against them. *Sea Wolf* was aimed dead toward them. The southern current held them fast. The sea that slipped beneath the hull churned and spiraled, gray water mixing with bright blue currents from the south. Cevette leaned out over the bow, spyglass in hand, and grinned.

"Beat to windward!" she shouted. "Miss Gavon, work the drive sail!"

Back on the poop deck, Eva grabbed a rope and pulled on it with all her weight. The small aftmost sail, a triangle of canvas rigged to the mizzenmast, swung sideways, catching the wind. Lizeth smirked. "Ah, Eva. Captain Zarcanzi wants you to work it well."

Eva had been about to explain how the small sail, with its freedom to orient itself in different directions, could turn *Sea Wolf* about much faster and more efficiently than orienting the many large square sails could not. But the way Lizeth had said it caught her attention. "Do you mean to suggest she was hinting at something?" Eva said. "If the captain wants to say something to me, she's perfectly capable of saying it to me directly."

Three days had passed since the Merris raid. They had not spoken about what had passed between them in Cevette's cabin. Cevette had given no sign she regretted what had passed between them.

Down on the upper deck, Lovett spun the helm. The ship turned at a sharp angle. Saltwater sprayed up its flanks, slapping Eva across the face. They shot through a loop of stone. Her neck craned backward to watch it pass by overhead. Her breath caught. The violet stone, shot through with veins of midnight black, had been carved with a pattern of countless overlapping scales.

"That's Sea People work," Lizeth said, and pride swelled in their voice. "Look at that. The Soladiseans could never do something like that."

Sea Wolf bounded across the sea. Crew members raced to adjust the square-rigged mainsails to their new heading. Up on the poop deck, Eva held her head high, her black hair streaming on the wind like a banner, her eyes bright as they leapt through the waves.

"Tack to starboard!" Cevette called.

Eva dragged the drive sail back across the wind. Lovett spun the wheel. Sails snapped. The flag of the weeping skull danced in the breeze. *Sea Wolf* skirted the edge of a coral reef as the nimble barque flew across the warm blue waters of a natural harbor. *So beautiful.* The coral grew in shades from lilac to the deepest maroon. Fish danced through it in shimmering schools of purple and green.

"To the eastern shore," Cevette said. "Be quick about it. We can burn the archive before anyone catches up to us."

The village of the Pearldiver Clan sat on the western shore; they had passed in sight of it, and Cevette had tried to hail them with signal flags, but the Pearldivers had rushed back into their woven-reed homes at the sight of the ship. That had worried Eva, though, as Cevette had said, the Sea People had good reasons to fear unexpected guests. This whole island had been theirs once, but a Republic fort now occupied the center of the island, in the deepest part of its natural harbor, and a small town had grown up around it to trade in pearls.

Eva had offered to run about the small island through Death and scout the ground, but Cevette had dissuaded her from trying. The Pearldivers had lived and died for generations on this land; the spirit waters might flood into Death here and pose a threat to her. Eva had decided to trust her expertise. She was glad Cevette had chosen Night Dragon Isle as their next destination, and not ordered Eva to take Mr. Smoke and burn Assembly Hall. They had discussed the possibility, when Eva had told her about her adventure with Tomis, but they had decided to seek the smaller archives first. Neither of them could stomach doing that to so many people.

The wind shifted. On it, Eva felt the nearness of Death. Murmured curses rose from the upper deck.

Smoke rose from the site of the Republic outpost. Eva pulled out her spyglass, a gift from Lovett, and peered through it.

The Republic colony had been crushed. There was no other way to describe it. The palisades and the wooden walls of buildings had been knocked flat. It was as if the fort and the town around it had been struck by some great wave. *A wave of sound. Korinne's magic.* What remained was charred and black; smoke still drifted off the remnants. The earth had been churned up by footsteps too large and too round to be human.

In the gashes in the soil lay the bodies. Many wore golden uniforms; some wore the drab clothes of sailors and traveling merchants. They had been crushed, clawed at, and cut open. Their blood had pooled around them and dried in the sun. The stillness of them churned her stomach. A six-winged vulture circled high above them. Eva swept her spyglass left and right, looking for motion—weeping mourners, frightened survivors—and saw nothing. Neither the fort nor the town around it had been spared.

She didn't touch the Pearldiver village. The Sea People had been frightened, but their homes and docks had shown no damage. *Did she show them mercy?* No. More likely, they hadn't been in her way.

"Abominations," she whispered, and the word was heavy on her lips. This was the work of the Demon. This was the work of echoes.

Dogshead had always been their next destination, Eva knew. As a pirate, Cevette was obligation-bound to warn the Demon of Dogshead of Commander Gavon's planned attack, which Eva had dutifully told her of when she'd returned from Soladis. Eva had suggested she might run ahead to Dogshead, to bring the warning sooner, but she and Cevette had agreed she was not prepared to address Korinne without the whole of her crew nearby.

The attack on Night Dragon Isle only deepened their resolve to sail south. "She'll be keeping a store of memories on Dogshead to feed her abominations," the captain told Eva and Lovett as they met on the quarterdeck to plot their course. "I dare not let her feed my history to a beast."

Cevette, Tuk, and Nukit had rowed over to the Pearldiver village; Eva had watched through a spyglass as Cevette had called out to the villagers in their own tongue, introduced herself as a current woman, and offered them supplies. They had not left their houses. Cevette had left them a bag of silver coins; she would have left food, she had explained when she'd returned, but colonists had a history of poisoning the food they shared with Sea People in distress. Now, her brow was furrowed with frustration, and she was chewing on her lip. It wore away at her, the distance between her and her people, the not knowing where she fit among them. Eva hoped they could find her memories soon.

Lovett unfurled a long navigational chart covered in his handwritten notes. "I've never seen the Demon go to such desperate lengths. She's always been the violent sort, but this is bloody even for her."

"It's filthy," Eva said, sitting down atop a crate. "Stealing gold is one thing, yes, but memory—it's what makes us who we are. Part of it, at least. I cannot let my father take it from us, and I cannot let Korinne do so either."

"Agreed," Cevette said, taking the chart from Lovett. "But we'll get nowhere near her trove if we offend her. Miss Gavon, I want you to come with me to meet the Demon and her court. She should hear what was discussed at that Assembly meeting directly from the woman who was there. And I must also ask that you treat her with civility."

Eva hesitated. Civility was not a strength of hers. She never quite knew what to say at polite functions. But perhaps a court of pirates would be a different matter. Less formal. And she didn't need to like Korinne, or to make the other woman like her. She only had to answer some questions. "Whatever you say, ma'am. You're the captain."

Dogshead Isle sat between the Sapphire Isles and Soladis on the maps, though it lay further to the west. The island boasted one small town that lay in the shadow of Bitch Mountain, in whose winding caverns generations of pirates had hidden their loot. Criminals and mystics flocked to its shores, losing themself in a place more a boundary of the known world than part of it. For untold generations, it had been the only land all pirates of the sea could call home.

But, as they approached, Eva found herself struck by the island's beauty. The steep black mountain, the twisted peak shaped like the head of a baying hound, rose starkly against the cloudless sky. Down its slopes grew a lush green vale; further down, ramshackle buildings painted every weathered color of the rainbow rose atop stilt foundations and old ship hulls. Cawing flocks of iridescent green parrots filled the sky; distant fiddles played on the shore. The waters were crisp and blue, splashing up on pale white sand. Even the distant scent of sulfur only lent it charm.

A dozen ships were at anchor in the harbor, but one grand vessel dominated them all. She was a fifty-gun ship-of-the-line, twice the length of

Sea Wolf, her masts towering and her pennants flapping in the wind. Her rails were covered in silver leaf, her sails were dyed a deep sable black, and its figurehead—a carved wooden echo—smiled beneath her diamond eyes. The name on its side was *Shadow Queen,* and it was every inch a flagship fit for the goddess of death. Eva shivered at the thought of facing this ship in battle.

But they had come to talk, not fight, and the knowledge made the day a bit lighter.

As *Sea Wolf* neared the dock, one by one, the sailors leapt from the deck for a swim. Donya and Cevette removed their shirts and play-wrestled, grappling, at the rail, until Cevette tossed Donya overboard and she fell laughing into the blue below. Naeri challenged Lizeth to a race; neck-and-neck, they surged toward the harbor. Eva stepped up to the rail, stripped down to her breeches, and took a deep breath.

"Hands over your head, Miss Gavon," Cevette said, and demonstrated. "Jump, and tuck. Reach for the ocean. Don't fear her. She's your friend."

Eva leapt up on the rail. Sweat rolled down her bare skin, both from the heat of the sun overhead and the way she had to force herself not to look at Cevette's bare chest. She lifted her hands above her head, drew a deep breath, and dove. Wind whistled past her. Gravity pulled her down. She set her teeth and imagined stabbing the sea like a knife—

Cold water wrapped her in its embrace. She kicked upward. Her head broke the surface. She breathed deeply once more as the crew cheered above her, her heart hammering with pride, and stretched out to float on her back. Mr. Smoke had taught her that. She lay in the surf, bobbing up and down. Up at the rail, Cevette smiled down at her. Eva waved up at her captain, who waved back, and so she had to raise an eyebrow and wave a second time. Cevette laughed, and Eva laughed, not only because it was funny but because that laugh was so precious to her.

Someone grabbed her from behind and pushed her under. Eva gasped as she popped back up. She twisted around to see Donya, treading water behind her.

"You told Cevette you didn't want to be with her," the healer said. "So you shouldn't keep flirting with her."

Eva's eyes widened. "She told you?"

"We're cousins. I badgered it out of her. What I don't understand is why. It's like there's a sunrise on your face whenever you look at her."

"But I'm not her missing girl. And I can't be with a woman who might replace me." Eva sighed. "Perhaps that's unfair. It's not that Cevette is *only* looking to replace me. I want her to know about her family, her clan, her heritage. But her being Sea People would never stand between us. It's only . . . *her*."

"Right, well, don't set your heart on someone who can't give you what you want. But you should know it would be challenging for you to be with a Sea People woman. Gods, Commander Gavon would sooner have you both hung before letting his daughter marry one of us."

Eva nodded. "Yes, I know. But he has much better reasons to hang us. I'll worry about those." Relationships between Sea People and Soladiseans were common enough; Cevette's lack of finger webbing proved that.

"It'll test you," Donya said, floating on her back, bobbing up and down as gentle waves washed under her. "Most Soladiseans who get close to Sea People end up cheating and robbing us. You'll have chances to profit off hurting us. And you'll have to choose us. Every time. At any risk. Because we don't get the same choices you do."

"I would choose her. Every time." Eva looked out toward Dogshead, toward the black mountainsides and the green slopes. All she could see was Korinne's flagship in her way. "I'm not . . . I'm not like certain echoes I could mention."

"I'm not saying this because you're an echo. I'm saying this because you're Soladisean."

"How Soladisean am I?" Eva said. "You and Cevette being Sea People, that ties you to a culture, a family, a place in this world. Echoes . . . other Soladiseans deny us that. I grew up among them. I came from one of their gods. But can I truly count myself as one of a people who hate what I am?"

"You're connected to them whether they deny it or not. The ties between us and our people aren't always comfortable." She sighed. "As for how Soladisean you are . . . I'd ask other echoes about that. They'll be able to tell you more than I can."

"I would rather not," Eva shivered. "They remind me of what I am. I hate that."

Donya splashed her. Pink webbing flashed between her fingers as she did. "That's what the Republic wants you to think. If you hate echoes, you won't fight for them."

As *Sea Wolf* drew up to the docks, Eva climbed a rope back up on the ship. She went down to dress herself with a fresh white shirt, cream-colored high-waisted breeches with brass buttons, and her dark coat with the embroidered skulls. She then returned to the upper deck, where she fastened half of the ship's six mooring lines herself. Each hempen rope had to be wrapped back through itself and secured with three separate knots; her torn calluses bled sluggishly as she locked them in place. She checked each knot, then climbed down the gangplank to meet Cevette on the pier.

Her captain, who had re-donned her shirt, and donned in addition her long white armored coat and a hat with two bluejay feathers, was signing off with the harbor master, a scrawny man with a thick mustache. The fee, she paid in silver, and, when he stuck out his hand once more, she pulled two gold coins from inside her belt and dropped it in his fist. He smiled as he walked back up the rattling dock, purse swinging.

"He wanted a bribe?" Eva said.

"And I wanted to hand off some counterfeits. So we all prosper." Cevette gazed down the long, rickety dock. A cluster of crew members walked past them, gossiping and laughing, striding off toward the harbor market. "You all have a day's leave. Do feel free to join then after we speak with the Demon. I am grateful for your assistance in this matter."

Together, they walked up the dock. Their boots drummed a rhythmic pattern on the boards. From where they stood, they could see the market to their left. It was built out into the harbor, the stalls and walkways supported by wooden beams sunk into the shallows. Laughter, song, and the calls of merchants filled the air. Ahead, the trail up from the docks led to a palisade wall that enclosed a little town, the thatched rooftops of which could barely be seen above it. To town, they set their course.

As they went, Cevette bit her lip, cleared her throat, and said, "Ah. What were you and Miss Breamtide discussing on your swim?"

Eva's cheeks burned. *Gods. How awkward.* She tucked a loose lock of hair back up behind her ear. "Mostly gossip."

"Gossip? What about?"

You. She couldn't say that. "It was about . . . Lovett. How he's been such a fool."

Cevette nodded. "I've told him, if he and Naeri wed, I would pay them both a handsome bonus as a wedding gift. They could stay aboard *Sea Wolf,* or buy a lift on some island at the edge of the Republic's reach. Instead, he shot himself in the foot and broke her heart. I hate to watch people I care about suffer."

"You aren't the one to blame," Eva said.

"It's my ship. It's my crew."

"It's their lives."

"I suppose." Cevette sighed. "Thank you for saying that. These matters weigh heavily on me."

"Of course. Anything to help you." An idea occurred to her. "Do you think there's a chance that your girl joined Korinne's crew?"

"I've considered it." With her free hand, Cevette rubbed her chin. "If she didn't know how to find me, she might well have placed her trust in her fellow echoes. I've spoken with many of Korinne's crew, though, and never felt a connection with any of them." She looked up at Eva. "Is that what you would have done, in her position? If you hadn't met me? I know you and Korinne have your differences, but—"

"Absolutely not!" Sweat prickled on the back of her neck. Her heart skittered, tapping out an uneven beat. Eva drew a deep breath. "I'm sorry, captain. I don't mean to be rude. But I am more than only an echo. And I would like to be seen as such."

"There's no shame in being an echo, Miss Gavon," Cevette said.

How would you know? You're not one of us. Eva looked away from Cevette, her cheeks burning.

"There's something you should know. About her. About me." Cevette swallowed. "I remembered that, when we last spoke . . . I told her to go to Jonathan Gavon. There was . . . something was wrong. We wanted to fix it. We thought he could help us."

"That's hardly surprising," Eva said. "Everyone thinks well of him until they learn the truth."

"But my girl was an echo. I keep catching glimpses of her face. Didn't she know what he was? Wouldn't she have told me?"

"Not all of us believe he is still willfully sacrificing us. She might have trusted him, too."

"In that case, I sent her to her doom." Cevette stared down at her hands.

To change the subject, Eva said, "I . . . I cannot believe my father has never conquered this place."

"Oh, I'm sure he's tried. But it's expensive to ship soldiers this far. He may have wiped the pirates' memories on occasion, convinced them they were farmers, fisherfolk, model citizens. But the fish are bad here and the farming's worse. They would all go back to piracy in time. Even the Empire of Soladis never managed to build a colony here. There's a queer power in being too troublesome to control."

Eva and Cevette approached the town gate. It was naught but a weathered wooden door, the planks clumsily nailed together and secured with rope; but three abomination guards waited before it. They stood on two feet, round-bodied, hulking figures, their scaled hide skin a bright, venomous blue. Instead of heads, a corona of jagged coral spikes protruded from their neck sockets. The shortest of them was six feet tall; the largest nearly nine. In their scaled fists, they held rusty battle axes, which they lowered before the gate as Eva and Cevette drew near.

Cevette frowned at the sight. "They're strong. They've been feeding."

An echo girl, no older than ten, sat on a stool before the gate. "The Demon saw your flag from the wall," she said. "She bid me to welcome you to her court."

"Thank you," Cevette said. "We are most grateful for the welcome."

Eva looked the girl over. *Did I look like this once?* She, too, had once sat with a slouch in her shoulders; her father had liked to grab her by them and physically correct her posture. Her face also had a tendency to slip into this girl's stony, blank expression; an expression others found petulant; her father had always ordered her to smile. *Did I also play with my cuffs like she does?* The sight of the child made her stomach churn.

The girl undid the rope tying the gate shut. She grabbed a crutch that had been propped against her stool, leaned on it to stand, and pushed the gate open. "Follow me," she said, limping through. "And don't get too close to the abominations."

Eva and Cevette followed. Their boots squelched in the mud. "What happened to your foot?" Eva said. From the fall of the girl's skirt, it was clear her right leg ended at the knee.

The girl looked back at them. Her dark eyes got very wide. "Don't get too close to the abominations."

Eva clenched her fists. *Korinne.*

Through the little town they walked. The roads had been reduced to mud by winter rains. The small buildings clustered about the town square were made from palm wood, painted with stripes of red and orange, the rooftops made from an interwoven thatch of palm leaves. A great fire pit burned in the town's center. Eva shivered as they walked past it, as no fewer than four echoes stood beside it, passing around a pipe. The air smelled of earth and sulfur. A parrot flew by overhead. The gathered echoes shouted obscenities at it; when it cursed them back, they all cheered.

The girl led them to the Blue Whale Inn, the largest building in the small town, where the Demon held court. She opened the door and waved them inside. Eva and Cevette ducked through the doorway, and Eva nearly tripped as she did so. The common room floor tilted at an angle, likely from a flood carrying away parts of the foundation. A curtain of dried bamboo hung over a gap in the wall to their right. Small lanterns lit the room, each one a candle flickering inside a dried, thin-skinned pufferfish. The table-tops were made from turtle shells inlaid with panes of stained glass. Pirates shot billiards and laughed raucously in one corner. The barman served liquor in cups of glistening abalone.

Korinne sat in the center of the great room, atop a chair made from gnarled oak, a skull painted with silver dust carved in the back. The Demon of Dogshead wore a long black skirt, an embroidered violet vest, and a coronet of silver skull beads. Three echoes stood on guard behind her, each with their left hand on their weapons. They watched Eva and Cevette approach with wary eyes. The Demon drummed her remaining fingers on the arm of her chair. Cevette bowed before her, and she lifted her hand for the captain to kiss.

"My lady," Cevette said. She brushed her lips to Korinne's hand, then dabbed them with a handkerchief as she stood.

It seems polite to bow, thought Eva, who stood directly behind Cevette. But her knees did not bend.

"I brought tribute," said Cevette. She drew a sack from her belt and set it at the Demon's feet. Korinne nodded at one of her echo guards. They opened it and held the contents up to the light. Three raw rubies, the longest the length of Eva's little finger, gleamed in the lantern-light.

"Well, I've seen bigger," Korinne said. "But this will do. I see you've also brought the Skullrunner."

The Skullrunner. The Skullrunner. Excited murmurs swept through the room. Eva frowned. Who would be happy to see the Skullrunner?

"Welcome to my court, Evazina," said Korinne. "How do you find Dogshead? I hope you enjoy. It's the safest place for echoes in all the Isles." A note of pride crept into her voice. "Have a drink. Tour the market. Place a bet at the fighting pits. You'll have a good time. I might even convince you to stay."

"Miss Gavon is glad for your hospitality," Cevette said. "We all are. But she brings heavy news from Soladis. I'm afraid our time to exchange pleasantries is quite limited." She looked back over her shoulder and nodded to Eva. "Miss Gavon, if you will?"

Eva cleared her throat. "Commander Gavon is sailing south to strike Dogshead."

A hush fell over the room. Pirates looked up from their dice and billiards. The barman set down the bottle he held. The echo guards tightened their grips on their weapons and whispered to each other in low voices.

"How do you know this?" Korinne leaned forward on her throne and rested her chin on her good hand. Silver marks shone on her skin.

Eva took a deep breath, and let it spill out. She dared not tell Korinne about the archive under Assembly Hall, so she began her story with how she'd snuck into a meeting of the Assembly, and went on to what had happened after. The arguments by the aristocrats. The call for a vote of impeachment. Commander Gavon buying himself just enough time to sail into battle against the pirates in hopes of a victory to restore his fortunes.

"Good." Korinne grinned as Eva finished. "He's desperate. That's right where I want him to be. Thank you, sister, for bringing me this news."

Eva frowned. She folded her arms across her chest. "I didn't do it for you. I did it because one pirate owes another that much courtesy."

Korinne chuckled. "Well, I commend your courtesy." Her smile flattened. She cracked her remaining knuckles against the flesh of her inner elbow. "Though, I will note, you could have run to me and passed this on the moment you learned of it."

Eva froze. Cevette stepped sideways, positioning herself between Eva and the Demon, which was not entirely successful, as the two echoes could still meet each other's eyes over the top of the shorter woman's head. "There are dangers on this island. I would not send her here alone."

"You think I don't look after my sisters?"

Eva scoffed. "What did the abominations do to that girl's leg?"

The worried whispers that filled the common room went up in pitch. Chairs scraped across the ancient floorboards. The door creaked open. More than a few pirates ducked back into the day.

"What do you think it did? It mangled her leg so badly we had to saw it off." Korinne sighed. "Rest assured, I killed the one that did it. Where the other abominations could see, no less, so they'd fear me."

"Did you know that might happen?"

"It's always a risk. How do you think I lost my hand?"

"You may take those risks for yourself, if you choose. But you may not force them on others. It's *wrong*." Eva lifted her chin and folded her arms across her chest. Her heart hammered in her chest. Part of her knew this was foolish, impulsive. But she could not see unfairness and stay quiet. "You raided Night Dragon Isle for memories to feed to your abominations. You killed dozens of people. You're going to destroy memories that should be returned to their rightful owners. You're not fighting for justice or freedom. You fight only for yourself. You disgust me—"

"Miss Gavon." Cevette said. "Enough. That's an order."

Eva flinched. She looked about the room, at the watching echoes, at Korinne's guards and a number of black-clad women seated at the bar. They gazed back at her like she had bird droppings on her face and did not know it. *What's wrong with them?* Couldn't they see Korinne for what she was? Or did they simply not care what horrors she unleashed on the Seaward Isles?

"Let her go on," Korinne said, cool as a knife to the throat. "Keep it up, Eva. Draw more lines of thread between you and me. Make more rope for us all to hang with. Our father is coming for both of us. The ins and outs of right and wrong don't matter now, and they haven't for a very long time. Mark my words, girl. In a storm like this, you live and die by the strength of your sisters."

"You're not my sister." Eva's pulse raced in her neck. "Morghaia's sister, maybe. Not mine. You're just as foul as she was."

Korinne sighed. "Right. Captain Zarcanzi, get her out of here."

Cevette nodded. "Miss Gavon, with me." She pivoted. The tails of her coat snapped out behind her as she walked to the door. Eva turned and followed her, holding her head high. *That was foolish,* part of her said, but the rest of her said *I was right, I was right.*

They stepped out onto the rickety boards of the inn's front porch. The carved whale sign creaked overhead as Cevette closed the door. A few pirates peered out the inn windows at them; another few were watching from the fire-pit. Cevette pressed her fingertips together, then pressed them to her forehead, and gave Eva a hard look.

"I know I wasn't meant to do that," Eva said. "But, ma'am, those abominations of hers took off a girl's leg."

"She's not Morghaia," Cevette said. "You told me how much it upset you to be compared to her. Then you went and did it. To your own sister, no less."

"She's not my sister," Eva said. That came out as a snap. "Don't you understand? We're not people. We're . . . pieces. Broken pieces." She bit at her lip. "We can't do anything right. Not even when we try."

"Do you see your brother that way?" Cevette demanded. "Or that little girl with one leg?"

"No, I don't. But—"

"Is that how you see yourself?"

Eva flinched. With that, the truth slipped out of her.

"You are a person to me, and one I value highly. I wish I could make you see that." She sighed. "Go to the dock market and join the rest of the crew. Take a breath. Eat some food. Meet more echoes, if you can. They may not be your people in the way mine are to me, but it might bring you some solace to learn more of them. Only you must keep your distance from this inn. Is that understood?"

Eva had never felt so small. "I understand, captain," she said, and walked away before Cevette could see her cry.

THE BLACK ISLE

In your last letter, you mentioned that a not insignificant number of fosterlings had run off to Dogshead, including a number of echoes. They are foolish children and they deserve no better than what they will find there: frivolity, sloth, and vice. The echoes insist they have formed their own culture; but this cannot be. Only people have culture. Echoes are not fully capable of independent thought; they are too deeply connected to each other to be people in their own right. —Letter from Commander Jonathan Gavon to Lord Mykil Merris, Minister for Childhood Welfare.

THE DOCK MARKET ON Dogshead was nowhere near as large as the one in Soladis or Halston, though it was three times as crowded and smelled eight times as foul. At market stalls shaded by roofs made from palm fronds or sailcloth, pirates traded stolen goods, and merchants sold mangoes, pineapples, sweet potatoes, and barrels of rice. Children ran up and down the boards, shouting, laughing, picking pockets. A man played the drums, and Eva tossed him a coin even though he was off the beat. He tapped his cap in thanks, and she met his eyes, dark as night.

Echo, she thought, but no, his nose was wide, his lips were full, and he was a short, stocky man. *The son of an echo?* She supposed that was possible. Echoes weren't inclined to lie with men, but there were some women, like

Naeri, who had the capacity to give them a child. Still, it was strange to imagine echoes building families of their own. Echoes whose lives were defined by more than the struggle against the man who had created them.

She strode onwards down one of the wooden walkways connecting the many docking piers, looking all about her. An echo was sweeping out a noodle shop. An echo was writing in a ledger. An echo held an infant to her swollen breast as another woman—her wife, perhaps?—rubbed her shoulders and whispered sweetly in her ear. And everywhere she looked, she glimpsed dark eyes, long faces, and thin lips.

It should have come as a relief. She knew that much. Here, no one would see her as lesser for what she was. But she could not forget what she was, either, and the awareness of that was an ever-present prickle down the back of her neck.

"There you are, Eva!" Donya said as she passed. The healer sat atop a barrel, smoking. She passed Eva her new pipe and let her take a few puffs. "Come on, there's cures to buy."

The healer let her into the crowd, pushing about with her elbows until they reached the front of a line for a fishmonger's stall. Slender red snapper, mottled brown grouper, and silver-bellied tuna filled the wooden bins, their odor mercifully blocking that of the crowd. "Right," Donya said, making eye contact with the fishmonger. "I need—and this is very important, don't get it wrong or my friend here will gut you—I need all the weird, unsettling, disgusting fish you hauled up from the bottom of the ocean. The ones with flat faces and too many teeth and maybe an extra set of jaws. I'll toss in a bonus copper for anything without eyes."

"Miss, are you sure you . . . want to look at those things?"

"Well, it's not like they can look at me."

They got a packet of eyeless fish and a nervous look from the seller. Elbows out, Donya jabbed a path back through the mob. Eva rolled up her sleeves and let anyone who gave them a dirty look see the flash of her daggers, the inky stain of her godmarks. Deeper into the market they went. Donya filled her baskets with powders and potions, the teeth of monsters and the sweat of farmhands— "left pit only, didn't ask me why." She bought a cloth that once draped a widow's bier and a ring sliced off with a counterfeiter's hand, a jar full of preserved octopus pups and another full of pickles.

"Just a quick bite to eat," she said, and Eva nodded. Then she plucked out a small octopus and dangled it over her mouth. Eva yelped. Donya dropped it back in the jar and laughed until she started coughing.

"How can you tell the real cures from the fakes?" Eva asked her as they resumed their walk. The healer's magic relied on amplifying the dormant power within her carefully-mixed cures; she could make them more potent, but she could not work magic without them. "Why can you use lemons to cure scurvy but not apples? Is there a particular logic to it?"

"In the north, we hold off scurvy with fresh whale blubber. There's a power in it. Lemons have it, too. Apples don't. In the Kossi Sea Clan, we're all taught healing from a young age. So I know all of our cures, and Cevette knows a handful, and Lovett can look things up for us in Soladisean books if necessary, though your people have an unhealthy fixation on leeches. There's trial and error, there's keeping good notes, and there's some guesswork. I get the work done."

"You're an excellent healer," Eva said. "I wish I was more skilled at . . . what I do."

"What do you mean? Running?"

"Running the paths Morghaia walked." She drew a deep, shuddering breath. "Of all the echoes, I'm the one with the strongest link to our past. That means something. But I'm not sure what. I'm not even sure of how to go about being an echo."

"Start with trying the food," Donya said. "The best way to learn about people is food. If we were on Kossi now, I'd serve you seal fat porridge. Gods, I would kill for some seal fat porridge."

"You're just hungry," Eva said.

"I am." Donya paused, and pressed a fingertip to her lips. "And . . . homesick. A bit homesick, too."

Eva wrapped an arm around her waist and hugged her. "Here. Does this help?"

"A bit," Donya said. "It would help more if you bought me something to eat."

At a market stall, they obtained two large slices of cornbread topped with roast pork in plum sauce. Steam rose from the carved wooden bowls it was served in. The chef told them it was a traditional Tarwik recipe; the Tarwik people, who lived in the swampy west of Dogshead, had hosted the pirates for centuries, in exchange for a cut of their trade profits and protection from the Kingdom of Serpent Riders to the south. Eva's mouth watered as she and Donya looked about for a place to sit. The stall had several small tables with stools set up before them, but the space was crowded. The only one with two open stools had an echo woman sitting at it. She had short hair and many tattoos; she wore a leather smock over her shirt and breeches; and, when she saw Eva and Donya, waved them over.

"Plenty of room here," she said, and Eva might have run, but Donya had already sat down, so she pulled up a stool at the echo's left. "I'm Barlenn. The pig-keeper."

Eva did not quite know what to say to that. "Do you like pigs?"

"Pigs are cute. And delicious." She lifted a chunk of pork-bearing corn-bread to her lips, then wiped her lips. Donya, her cheeks bulging, nodded along to that. "You're a sailor? I think I'm the only echo I've met who gets seasick." As Eva stuck cornbread in her mouth, Barlenn stared at the marks on her hand. "*Oh*. It's true. We took back the Skullrunner."

We? Eva felt uneasy. The sweet pork and savory bread helped with that, but only a small bit.

"What is Death like?" Barlenn said.

Eva swallowed, and told herself to remember her manners. "Gray. Full of smoke. Plenty of spirits hanging about. It's not as frightening as one might expect."

"Right, right." Barlenn licked her fingers. "Makes sense. Doesn't sound that scary. We're echoes. Suppose we belong there."

Eva flinched. So did Barlenn. Eva felt that the other woman might be afraid she had offended Eva somehow, and decided to put her at ease. "I don't know if I belong there or not. I don't want to belong somewhere only because I'm an echo, though. I don't want being an echo to define me."

Barlenn nodded. "I understand. Being an echo can cause no end of trouble. You want to be like everyone else."

"Because how else can they like you?"

"I don't know," Barlenn said. "I've never been good with people. My pigs like me well enough, though." She jammed her last hunk of cornbread in her mouth and stood. Sauce dripped down her chin. She picked up the plank her food had come on, and swept the crumbs off the table. "I need to clear my pigs out of the fighting pits before the afternoon bouts. You should stop by. It's always fun, and you can meet more of us locals there."

"See?" Donya said as Barlenn walked away. "Echoes aren't all bad."

Eva didn't quite know what to say to that. She took another bite of cornbread.

As they returned their crumb-covered plank dishes to the stall counter, the familiar voice of Lizeth shouted "Donya! Eva!" over the din. Naeri and Lizeth ducked through the crowds and walked towards their shipmates. The short quartermaster carried six rolls of fabric in their pack; the seamstress was dabbing her cheeks with a handkerchief, her shoulders sagging.

Eva rushed over and took her hand. "How are things with Lovett?" she said, gently.

Naeri's chin trembled. "Well, they're done. I've ended it."

"Good," Donya said. "It was the right choice. All that talk of fate and ascension to godhood—"

"He let it poison us. He couldn't let it go." She sniffled. "Can we . . . can we go somewhere a bit more private?"

"Of course," said Eva. The crowds around the food stalls were growing thicker. "Come along. This way."

She led the four of them deeper into the maze of walkways, into a more shaded and less crowded section of the market. It smelled of floral perfume and alchemical compounds. Many of the stalls there had put up screens painted with coiling snakes and leaping toads to hide their wares; burly guards stood at each one to watch over the goods and look menacing. They gave the four pirates careful looks, saw the marks of godreapers on their hands, and found reason to look elsewhere.

"Did I ever tell you of how I grew up, Eva?" Naeri said. "My foster mother was so awful. She made me sew until my fingers bled. I tried to run away, and she caught me, and . . . then she . . . then I . . . and then I had these marks on my arms . . ." She made a little hiccupping sound. Tears rolled down her cheeks.

"She stabbed her with a knitting needle," Donya said. "She was a god in human form. Did you know they could do that? They can stay like that for years."

Naeri cried harder. "I never wanted to be a pirate. I wanted my own dress shop. But with the marks, they would have made me join the Godreaper Corps. Cevette got me out of Soladis, but it was Lovett who was there for me. He sat with me when I cried, helped me braid my hair, read me stories, and taught me magic. I couldn't had known that wasn't enough for forever."

"No. You couldn't have." Lovett's voice was quiet, low. He stepped out of a bookbinder's stall just ahead of them. At the sight of him, Naeri sobbed into her handkerchief. "I've been a fool, and that I cannot blame on anyone but me. I wish you all the happiness in the world." He looked at her, then, awkwardly, looked away. "I'm sorry for how I hurt you." With a tip of his cap, he vanished off into the market. Naeri watched him go. Her sobbing quieted, but tears still poured down her cheeks.

Eva hugged her, and patted her on the back as her shoulders shook. She had done this quite a few times in the days since that awful botched proposal. She was never sure if it helped, but it seemed to be the right thing to do.

"Come on, Naeri," Donya said. "Let's waste some money. It'll help."

Along the boards they went, ducking around the screens into the small private stalls. Eva bought herself three gowns, a new hoopskirt, a lace fan, and ruby evening gloves. To that, she added on a spyglass inlaid with mother-of-pearl, a broach shaped like a black widow spider, and a set of pistols where each barrel protrudes from the teeth of a grinning skull.

A jeweler, ringed by three burly guards, had laid out her wares on tables draped in green velvet. Eva inspected a choker of black lace, while Lizeth studied a walking cane topped by a coiling silver serpent. Naeri took one look at the rings—gold, silver, and obsidian, engraved with scales, feathers, and the bound initials of lovers—and once more broke into tears.

Eva looked about for something to distract her. Her eyes fell upon a small stall, painted with runic symbols she recognized as from the northern frontier. *Fortunes Told,* read the sign above it in swirling script. "Look at that! Come on!"

Together, the four of them approached the stall and ducked behind the painted screens. An old woman smiled up at them from the far side of a small table. She sat slumped in a plush chair, wrapped in countless shawls and scarves, the tattered cloth embroidered with black tentacles and lidless eyes. The lenses of her glasses were half an inch thick. She squinted at them as they approached. "Little gods. Hello. I could read your fates, for a price."

"My friend just cut things off with an unworthy suitor." Eva set on the table what should have been enough silver for a bribe. "She'll find a better man, won't she?"

The fortune teller took Naeri's hand in her weathered one. She tossed a pinch of red powder onto Naeri's palm and studied where it fell. "Ah. A great man will be drawn to you. He will treat you like a queen, and all the pain you feel now will cease to matter."

Naeri dabbed at her eyes with a handkerchief. She took a deep breath and steadied her shoulders. Grateful, Eva set another silver coin down on the table. The fortune teller grabbed it up.

"I'll go." Lizeth slid up to the front of the booth, and stuck their hand in the powder bowl on the table before holding it out to the fortune teller. Eva smelled paprika. "What do you see?"

"You are the spark that will light a great flame. You must take care what you burn."

"That's vague," Lizeth said. "Can you say something more specific?"

"Yes," said the fortune teller. "But if I tell you now what you must do, you will argue."

Lizeth rolled their eyes and stepped away. The fortune teller looked to Donya. "You want a reading?"

"I don't trust Soladisean witchcraft," Donya said. "Bad history."

Eva stepped forward and set her hand on the table. "You can read me. Will I fall in love?"

The fortune teller looked up at her. "You're already in love."

Eva bit her lip. "Aren't you supposed to—the powder? On my palm?"

"Your fate is written on your face. In the marks on your skin. I see an army of the dead rising at your call. I see the great city of Soladis in flames. I see the bodies at your feet, thousands of them, and your own brother cursing you for what you have become. You already know your future. You are running away from it."

Eva shivered. Her fingers trembled. She stepped back from the booth, blinking rapidly, unable to speak.

"Right," Donya put a hand on Eva's shoulder. "Come with me. Let's get out of here."

Grateful for the healer's intervention, Eva turned. The four of them walked out of the fortune teller's stall in silence. Back toward land they went, walking up a pier that led toward a white sand beach. It crunched underfoot as they followed a small trail marked with stones. Eva barely noticed her surroundings. Her feet shuffled as she walked.

The prophecy seemed to spin circles around her head. *Will Andreas curse my name one day?* She did not fear much, but she feared that worst of all. *To think I once believed I could be a godreaper in the same way Zeke is.* From the moment she killed the Skullrunner, she had marked herself as Morghaia's heir. She didn't want that to be her fate, but she didn't know how to escape it. She only knew how to run from these women who reminded her so much of what she was.

They came to the base of a cliff of dark volcanic rock. The maw of a vast cavern opened to the beach. A great crowd stood about the entrance, drinking and laughing. One in every three was an echo. None of them seemed at all surprised to see Eva walking among them. Shouts and hollers rang out from inside the cavern. Then came the crack of a slap, a grunt of pain, and a great cheer. *The fighting pits,* Eva remembered. The echo Barlenn had told her about these.

"Let's see what's going on," she told the others. "Follow me." Eva stuck out her elbows and began to work her way through the crowd about the cavern mouth. The spectators stepped aside for her. Her boots squelched in the sandy mud as the four of them entered the cavern.

It was a warm, dark, humid place inside. Tallow torches burned in iron stands. A sluggish stream flowed along the back wall of the cavern, vanishing in a crack in the rock. A pigpen had been erected beside it, a muddy ring thirty feed across, with a smaller pen beside full of pigs. Barlenn sat on the rail of the small pen. Two muddy echo women were shaking hands in the large one. The air reeked of pigs, sour beer, and the sweat of the crowds. Perhaps two dozen women leaned over the fence of the central pit. Many of them were Korinne's black-clad echo pirates. Almost all of the watchers were echoes. Most were drinking and passing around a pipe of smokeweed; two were kissing fervently. The sight of that made Eva's stomach flip. *I didn't know we could do that. What would Father say if he saw it?*

"What do we have here?" said a familiar voice. "More of Zarcanzi's god-killers. Welcome to the fighting pits."

Korinne had changed her gown for breeches and a loose-fitting shirt. She sat atop the fence, swinging her legs as Eva and her friends approached. At her feet sat an abomination: a panther-like beast, seven feet long, with black fur and reptilian claws. With a hungry, too-smart gaze, it watched the echoes. Drool gathered in the corners of its jaw.

Eva's nostrils flared. Her eyes went cold as death. How could Korinne bring those beasts anywhere near her crew?

"Miss Gavon." Cevette stepped out of the shadows on the far side of the pigpen. She had a cask of wine under each of her strong arms; her boots squelched in the mud as she carried them to the waiting echoes. They applauded as she set the wine down at their feet. One echo tried to put a hand on her shoulder, but Cevette shrugged it off, only looking at Eva. Her face was unreadable. "And the rest of you. Enjoying your day ashore?"

The others nodded. Eva, who was enjoying herself but feeling a dozen other things besides, changed the subject. "Did you come up with a plan about the commander, ma'am?"

"I have a plan," Korinne said. "I will sail out to meet him and negotiate for peace."

Eva looked to Cevette, who gave her a small shrug. That did not seem like the Korinne who had burned two Republic forts since the end of summer. Even the echoes of her crew looked rather disappointed to hear that. "Shouldn't we gut him, ma'am?"

"Be patient, Chaz." Korinne smiled. "That's not *all* of my plan. But I'm not about to share the whole of it with a woman who insults me to my face." She gave Eva a pointed look.

Eva sighed. Heat prickled in her cheeks. "I . . . you have my apologies. I shouldn't have compared you to Morghaia."

"I don't mind that you did that. I mind how it was done. We're all connected to her, Evazina. But I didn't like how you spoke of her. With that venom in your voice."

"She was a tyrant."

"She was a goddess and a queen. I've sailed north. I've seen the ruins of her kingdom. The remnants of great bone monstrosities that litter the land. The gashes in the earth where nothing grows. I've read what her priests and servants wrote of her, too. Of how she offered the northern Sea People diplomacy instead of violence. Of how she ordered schools built on her lands and made them free for all children. Of her love for—and her frustrations with—her goddess wife. I will not tell you she was good. She was a terror, in an age of terrors. But she was a person, too, and she not the worst of her kind. Have you ever wondered why the Golden Republic insists she was?"

Eva hesitated. It was true that the history books recorded all sorts of horrors that the gods had unleashed on the Seaward Isles. Morghaia was not unique among them.

"They hate her so that they can hate us. So they can look the other way when he rips our souls apart. Do not disrespect her memory from a place of ignorance. That only empowers the Republic to disrespect all us."

Eva balled her hands into fists. Her dark eyes went cold and flinty. How dare Korinne speak to her as if she was a child? "You have no right to lecture me on respect. Not when you destroy memories for power." She took a step towards Korinne. Cevette was glaring at her. But even Cevette didn't matter more to her than this: what Korinne was doing was *wrong*. "I'll make you a wager. You and I. In the fighting pit. Right now. I win, you let me free all the memories you have left. You win, and I'll tell you what I know about the remaining archives."

Korinne cracked her remaining knuckles on her collarbone. "Why not?" She smiled. "Always happy to get in the ring with a sister."

"Miss Gavon!" Cevette shouted. "These fights get bloody. You can't—"

"It's my day off, Captain." Eva shrugged. "I can do as I like."

With the aid of her crewmates, Korinne stripped down to her trousers, boots, and shirt. Her tattoos—both her godmarks and the skulls inked on her collarbone—shone in the torchlight. She removed her claw hand, and an echo passed her a leather-covered hook to slide on her stump.

For Eva, setting aside her knives took several minutes. They clattered to the cavern floor, eight, ten, twelve of them. At last, she wrapped them in her coat, along with her pistols, and passed them to Naeri, who had offered to hold them, along with her market purchases, as she fought.

"Be safe," Naeri said. "I'll be cheering for you."

"Five silver pounds on the Skullrunner," Donya said to one of Korinne's echoes. The woman nodded and shook her hand. Eva raised an eyebrow. "What? I'm betting on *you*."

Cevette bustled over to them, leaned in at Eva's side, and lowered her voice. "Why are you doing this?"

"Because I've seen how much losing your memories hurt you," Eva said. It was simple. It was true. "Because it's wrong of Korinne to destroy memories to feed her army. Because I mean to make what she did right." These were true reasons, good reasons. She did not need to say that she wanted to break the nose of the woman who was everything she feared she might become.

Cevette hesitated, then stepped back. "I . . . Best of luck, Miss Gavon. You can do this."

"Fight until one of you yields!" shouted Barlenn in a practiced, ringing voice. She stood atop the rail, balancing on the balls of her feet, her arms folded across her chest, her leather smock dripping mud. "No shivs. No eye-gouging. No magic."

"Captain Gavon," Eva said to Korinne. She grabbed the top of the pit rail and clambered over. Her boots squelched in the mud as she dropped down inside the ring. "Shall we have an honorable bout?"

Korinne grinned at her and lunged.

The Demon of Dogshead struck low, with both hook and fist, three quick boxer's blows to Eva's ribcage. Pain shot through Eva's chest. Her heart raced. She darted backwards to blunt the impact, trying to put some distance between them. Abruptly, she realized she had never trained for a fight like this.

Korinne laughed and strode toward her. The flicker of a torch wrapped her pale frame in a halo of red. She feinted left, then right. The torch blazed behind her. Eva blinked, her hands up, fighting to keep sight of the other echo. Korinne hooked her foot around Eva's and pulled her legs out from underneath her.

The world lurched sideways. Eva slammed down. The breath pounded out of her lungs. Mud splattered up across her side. Cold, gritty, and heavy, it soaked through her shirt and trousers. She winced, slipping and sliding about as she tried to stand. Around the pen, pirates and gamblers alike raised a ragged cheer. Echoes booed her in her own voice.

"Get up!" Cevette shouted. Eva set her teeth. She couldn't fail her. *Fight dirty. Just win.* Without bothering to get her feet underneath her, she pushed herself up on her knees and threw herself at Korinne. Her head slammed into Korinne's thighs. Her arms wrapped around Korinne's legs. A twist of Eva's shoulders, and the other woman flopped down like a fish.

Mud flew. The watchers gasped. Eva wound Korinne's hair around her fist and pulled her head back as hard as she dared.

"Yield!" she shouted.

Korinne flipped over, her hair twisting in Eva's grasp. Their eyes locked. Only for a heartbeat; then, Korinne looked away. *I do that, too,* Eva realized. *I never look anyone in the eye if I can help it—*

Korinne *screamed*. Magic pulsed in her throat. It poured out as a wave of electric pain. Eva collapsed. Korinne pulled away from Eva's grasp as Eva curled in on herself, covering her head in her hands. Blood trickled from her ears through her fingers. Shocks flew up her spine as Korinne kicked her in the small of her back. Once. Twice. *Fight. For the memories. For justice. For Cevette.* Eva cursed, scraping at the mud. She shoved some in her ears and threw a handful at Korinne's face. The Demon of Dogshead recoiled. *Fight her. Fight yourself.*

"You dishonorable cheat!" Cevette shouted. Eva could only just hear her over the ringing in her ears. She glanced back over her shoulder. Three of Korinne's sailors were holding Cevette back from charging into the pen.

Coughing, trembling, Eva grabbed the railing of the pen and pulled herself up. Her feet slipped as she scrabbled for purchase. Her chest burned painfully with every move. She set her jaw. She had to stand. For Cevette—

"I'm teaching my sister a lesson," Korinne said. "Echoes can't expect fairness, justice, or honor. Better she learn it from me than how I learned it at that age."

"So you're beating her because you can't strike the girl you were at twenty-two," said Cevette.

Oh, Eva thought. *Gods. We're the same.*

Korinne lunged once more. Her shoulder slammed into Eva's side, all her weight behind the blow.

Eva flew sideways across the pen, slammed ass-first into another rail, and toppled backward into the smaller pen where they kept the pigs. The hogs grunted and snorted as they gazed down at her. *I hope that's only mud I'm lying in.* Korinne leapt over the rail and strode forward to stand over her. She hoisted a piglet and heaved it at Eva like a brick. It thudded into her stomach, right near her liver. Eva gasped. It was bigger than it looked, and it *kicked.*

From across the pen came a squeal of molten rage. Eva seized her chance. "Fuck you," she gasped, and slammed her foot up between Korinne's legs.

Korinne reeled back into the rail. Her furious black eyes locked on Eva's. "You little—"

She didn't notice the mother pig charging until the beast knocked her flat in the mud.

It took three echo pirates and Barlenn the pigkeeper to pull off the sow. When she stood, Korinne's pale skin was covered in fresh bruises, and she was bleeding from a bite on her cheek. One of her crew offered a hand to help her walk. Korinne ignored it, tried to stand, and collapsed back in the mud. Eva limped out of the pit, battered but breathing, as Donya collected coins from the watchers and Cevette stared with wide eyes, her hands pressed to her mouth. The crowd cheered for her, and warmth flickered in her chest. There was a tie between them; she had spoken, albeit with her fists, and they had answered.

"Right," she said, as Korinne staggered toward the mouth of the cave. "Take me to the memories you stole."

Korinne looked back over her shoulder and nodded to her crew. "Seize the Skullrunner."

What?

Something struck her from behind. Off-balance, unprepared, Eva stumbled forward and fell. The breath flew from her lungs. Mud splashed up around her. Instinctively, she reached out with her magic. Death was close. A bone portal bloomed only a few feet away. But the echoes' hands were on her. Long, nimble fingers wrapped her in rope from knee to ankle. Death was only a sliver out of reach.

"What are you doing?" Barlenn shouted. There came the sound of a punch, and a gasp of pain. "Let her go!"

"Grab Barlenn," Korinne said. "Don't let her interfere."

"No!" Barlenn shouted, and then her voice was muffled, as if she was speaking through a gag.

"Dishonorable bastards." Cevette growled. She marched toward Eva and her captors, sword drawn. "You three! Go find Lovett. He's the first mate; he'll need to know what happened here." Donya, Naeri, and Lizeth shot each other worried looks, then turned and ran toward the exit. Eva knew why Cevette had told them to run. The echoes outnumbered them, and Korinne's panther-like abomination stood on guard in the shadows, a snarl on its fanged face. But what Eva didn't understand was why Cevette hadn't run with the others.

Korinne turned to face Cevette and let out a sharp trill. Waves of energy pushed Cevette backward. She grabbed her hat with one hand to keep it from flying off. Korinne grinned. "You're outnumbered, Zarcanzi."

"I know." Cevette dropped to her knees, and threw her sword away. "I surrender. Take me with her."

THE SHADOW QUEEN

BEGINNING IN THE CITY OF SOLADIS, ON THE ISLAND OF SOLADIS, AND CONTINUING ABOARD *SHADOW QUEEN*, SAILING A NORTHEAST COURSE FROM DOGSHEAD ISLE. 19TH HERALMONTH, YEAR TWENTY-TWO OF THE GOLDEN REPUBLIC.

The students ran me off when I arrived at the library. They threatened to beat me with clubs. One of them chased after me to apologize for his friends. He said one had just lost his father, and another had grown up on land Morghaia once held. As if that was my fault. As if I was still the goddess of death. Some days, I wish I was. At least then, I would understand my own nature. –from the diary of Korinne Gavon.

EVER SINCE HIS EXPULSION from the philosophers' guild, Andreas had spent his days flattering Assembly members and his nights getting drunk. He might have been closer to nudging the vote of impeachment to pass. He was certainly closer to damaging his liver.

In the dark hours after midnight, he walked back towards the house his father had rented, his arms swaying, his coat unbuttoned. He'd lost his hat somewhere; his dark roots were beginning to show. Through the winding streets of the University Quarter he strolled, past the stars carved in the walls and the ancient ruins and entrance to the guild where he was no longer welcome. As he approached the gate that led to his street, set within a tall but narrow arch of white plaster, a guard stepped out from inside the small watchpost booth and opened the latch. Andreas was already inside when he realized this man wasn't the usual evening guard on duty. And the two men stepping out of the watchpost behind him weren't even wearing uniforms.

They strode into the cobblestone road before him, blocking his way. Andreas tried to elbow past them. One grabbed his right arm. He tried to swat them away. His drunk fingers fumbled, and then they had his left arm. He cursed and kicked. His heels drummed on the cobblestones as they slammed him up against the brick wall of a townhouse.

"Is this you?" One man thrust a poster into Andreas' face. Between the darkness and the alcohol, he could barely read, but he would recognize the advertisement for his sister's bounty anywhere. "You're the one changing our memories?"

Andreas only sputtered. His heart pounded. Cold sweat beaded on his forehead. *No,* he wanted to say, but no words came out.

"My wife can't sleep," said another man. "She sees abominations in her dreams. She says she had five brothers before the attack. But the commander made her whole village forget about the two who died. Why would you put that in our heads? It's false. Tell us it's false!"

"Of course it's false!" Andreas gasped. His head spun. He searched for something clever to say that might get him out of this. But his wits slipped away from him like roaches dodging a boot. "It's not me who's doing it. I'm not Evazina. She has dark hair, and black godmarks on her arms. I've been remembering things, too. Terrible things. The riot at Assembly Hall—but it must be false. The commander would never deceive us. He's a good man. A great—"

That was all he got out before they punched him in the stomach.

Andreas doubled over and vomited.

A hail of blows rained down on him. He tried to curl up as best he could, to shield his head and chest. He could do very little. They held him fast. With each punch, with each blow of an elbow, he told himself they were all ignorant fools, easily led by propaganda, embarrassments to the title of citizen. He could do nothing but go limp and seethe in his contempt—for these men, for the guild, for his father. For a world that only saw him as what it would gladly kill him for.

"What are you doing?" shouted a sharp, familiar voice. "Hey! You! Let that man go!"

The attackers cursed. They dropped Andreas and scattered, running off into the night. Andreas rolled over on the cobblestones. He fought to stand—to get his hands underneath him, to push his chest up—and a stabbing pain shot through his side. A cracked rib. He winced.

"I've been looking all over the city for you." Tomis Beauchamp put a hand on his shoulder. "I heard about your dismissal from the guild. A preposterous injustice. The groomsman at the manor said you'd gone out drinking, so I went down the road, and now—what has the Golden Republic come to when its citizens and soldiers conspire to beat an innocent man in the streets?"

"They thought I was my sister." Andreas braced himself, and stood. Red waves of pain shot through his side. A cut stung along his lip. Tomis passed him a handkerchief, and he took it, dabbing at his face. "Thank you very much."

Tomis clucked his tongue. "Awful business. Neither you nor Eva deserve this."

"You know my sister?" He had spoken of her in familiar terms. The commander had never brought her along to Soladis. Only Andreas. He'd met Tomis a number of times at the philosopher's guild, exchanged letters with him concerning ethics and political theory. The other man had even confided in Andreas that he wrote and published *The Silver Sentinel*. But never had Tomis mentioned his sister.

"She was the one who kidnapped me recently, as a matter of fact." Tomis chuckled. "But she and I have a good deal in common, beside that. We became fast friends. She asked me to look after you."

Andreas winced. "That's good of her," he said, gruffly. That would be what he was expected to say. He'd considered Tomis' friendship a point of pride. Surely not just any echo could befriend one of the richest men in Soladis. Now it seemed the man had as much favor to give as he had papers to sell. "Why are you befriending pirates? You truly have no sense of self-preservation, Beauchamp."

"We share that in common, you and I," Tomis said. "Now, you're coming with me. My estate is well-guarded. You'll be safe."

"I don't need your charity." Andreas bowed his head. His chest hitched as he tried to breathe. He swallowed hard. He had use of his father's rented mansion, but his father was not here to protect him, and his father might very well be one more threat to his safety. Clearly, it was known an echo lived in this neighborhood. He should seek lodging elsewhere. But the only money he had was the small allowance his father had given him, and those funds were running low. His pride would not serve him here.

"Not charity. Employment. My paper is always looking for journalists. I have need of an echo's perspective on a special edition I'm preparing. A plea for the Republic to sympathize with your plight. You are a skilled writer and an incredibly intelligent man. I would dearly appreciate your advice."

Andreas hesitated. *He wants me to write about echoes.* He hated being seen as an echo. But he hated feeling weak even more. *He doesn't want just any echo. He wants me. I'm the only one who can do this. And it should be done.* The more sympathetic the echoes were, the more reasons the Assembly had to vote yes on the vote of impeachment. And only Andreas had the power to make them so.

"I'm your man," Andreas said. He and Tomis shook hands.

IN A FURTHER BLOW to Eva's dignity, Korinne's crew carried Cevette and her out of town in potato sacks. They were hauled up aboard the *Shadow Queen,* dragged down into the hold, and dumped in the brig, where they were held at gunpoint as their captors untied them, stepped out of their cells, and locked them in. "Can't have you losing a hand," said one, as Eva and Cevette massaged the blood back into their aching limbs. "We'd confuse you with the Demon then."

Eva gritted her teeth and reached out with her magic. There was no way into Death close by. No one had died in the brig. *Shadow Queen* was a newer ship, perhaps three or four years old, as she judged by the rawness of the wooden planking. Still, that no one had died in the brig came as a surprise to her. She did not associate Korinne with mercy toward her captives. *Then again, perhaps she slaughters them all before bothering to haul them aboard.*

How did she go from the shy, hesitant girl in her diary to . . . this? Eva had previously assumed that all echoes might take this path, if left to their own devices. But on Dogshead, she had seen that was not so. *She walks the path of Morghaia.* Eva only knew what the Republic taught of what that path was and where it led. Still, it was hard to think herself entirely wrong about Korinne and her character when the other echo had kidnapped her.

The *Shadow Queen* was twice as long and twice as wide as *Sea Wolf*, which meant the brig could accommodate multiple cells, and the two of them had been tossed in adjoining ones. Eva did not want to think of how awkward or uncomfortable it might have been if they were both penned up in the same one, with one straw mat of bedding to share. The hold was dry, as well, the ash wood planks clean, and a number of lanterns shone overhead, illuminating stacks of crates, all securely strapped to the walls.

Less ideally, while Cevette occupied the cell to her left, an abomination sat in the cell to her right. It was another panther-lizard, lying on its belly as if dozing. Hunger flashed in its bright green eyes when it looked at her. Eva shuddered. *Vessels for the damned.* How could Korinne carry such creatures on her ship? The abomination saw her staring; it growled and bared its sharp thicket of mismatched fangs. Eva shuddered.

"You get used to them," said one of Korinne's echo pirates, looking up from the net she was mending to meet Eva's eyes. She sat on a stool near the center of the hold, a heavy coil of rope at her feet. She had been there when Korinne had hauled them in, and had showed no interest in moving since. Her shirt and breeches were simple black; a long scar cut down the side of her neck. Eva didn't know her name. "The abominations. If they bother you, think of something cheerful. They can smell pain."

"Thank you," Eva said. "Do you . . . do you enjoy sailing with them?"

The other echo considered. "No," she said, and looked back down to her rope. It was hardly friendly, but Eva might have done the same thing in her position.

Cevette cleared her throat. Eva looked to her. The captain waved for her to come over. Eva scrambled over to the bars between them. Cevette leaned in at her ear and whispered, "Thank the gods Lovett is a good navigator. The moment the others find him, he'll follow us."

"If he's not drunk in a tavern. Naeri ended things."

Cevette sighed. "Well, at least they didn't steal my hat."

The stairs down into the hold creaked. Two echoes stepped out of the shadows. They strode past the crates toward the brig. Each one carried a bubbling bowl of stew. They were both the same age, their dark hair fading to silver. One wore it short, along with breeches, a silver vest, and two sabers on her hips. The other wore her long hair pinned up under a bonnet, a gown, and an apron splattered with what must have been the crew's supper. She gave Eva a nervous smile. The other, with the short hair, wore a visage of sculpted anger.

Eva shivered. Was that how she looked before she killed someone? She didn't know what to say. She started with, "Hello."

"Here's your supper," growled the short-haired echo.

Eva stood, walked to the front of her cell, and reached through the bars. The short-haired woman held out the bowl—and flung the contents at her. The stew was hot enough to sting, and dripped down the front of her already-ruined mud stained shirt. She cursed. In the cell to her right, the abomination sat up, watching with interest.

"What did I do to you?" Eva gasped.

"Got our face on wanted posters all over the Isles!"

"I didn't do that. The Republic did." She wiped broth off her cheek. "What would they think of us if they saw us brawling—"

"I don't care." She spat. It hit Eva's stew-covered side. "They'll hunt us for this. Echoes will die."

"Leave her be," Cevette said. "Or I'll—"

"You'll what?" she said. "You're locked up, Zarcanzi."

"Oh, Chaz, it's not her fault," said the other echo. *Patience.* Eva recognized her from the cavern. Patience passed the bowl she held to Cevette, then folded her arms over her chest. "We're all pirates. The commander could have done the same thing to any one of us. He's making an example of Eva because she has the Skullrunner's magic. Be angry at *him.*"

"Oh, I am, sister. But he's not here right now, is he?"

"Go on," Eva said. Her nostrils flared. She lifted her chin and bared her teeth in a raging grin. Did they think she *wanted* echoes to suffer? She was trying to stop her father. Only Korinne's way wasn't' the only one. *Why do we all have to be exactly what the Republic says we are?* "Do your worst. Throw food on your prisoner. Spit on her. We're cruel people, are we not?" She would even give her a reason. "What does *Chaz* mean? Because I've only ever heard it used as shorthand for *Chastity.* Is that your given name?"

"Shut up!"

"How did you get to be *Chastity?*"

"We were fostered by a noblewoman with the creativity of a dead skunk. Patience and I burned down half her manor on our way out. Because echoes stand together. Whether it's two of us or a whole ship." Her eyes found Eva's, cold as the midnight sea. "You're a child. A reckless, dangerous child. We—*you,* Skullrunner—belong to something older and more powerful than you could possibly imagine. And you're fucking around. Like a—"

"Leave her be." It was the same voice every woman on the ship spoke with, but heavy with authority. A godmarked hand grabbed Chaz by the wrist. Korinne pulled Chaz backward as, to the side, Patience hung her head and sighed. The abomination clawed at the bars of its cage. With her hook hand, Korinne pulled a crumbled memory from a satchel at her hip and flung it to the beast. It swallowed the scrap whole, then stretched out to lay on its black-furred belly. "Chaz. Kitchen duty. Now."

Chaz lowered her head. Patience took her by the arm and led her back toward the stairs. She said a few words to the echo mending nets, who set down her work and swiftly followed after. When all three were out of earshot, Korinne reached through the bars and held out a clean shirt. "Here. For you."

Eva took it. The shirt was cut from the same black fabric most echoes on the ship wore. Of course, it was her exact size. She hesitated, but practicality won out. She pulled off her old shirt, tossed it in the corner, and donned the black one in its place.

"I could bring you a dress if you'd prefer," Korinne said. "I thought you likely leaned towards breeches, though. It's a coin toss which way an echo likes to dress."

"Do you know why that is?" Eva asked, curious despite herself. "Why some parts of us are all the same, and some are different? I know we're all left-handed."

"Thankfully," Korinne said, gesturing with the hook on her right. "With the hands, well, we all have much the same body. With how we dress, well, that's a matter of the soul. When we're split, the parts of our soul that conflict against each other are ripped apart. New echoes form around them, as if they're spindles, each drawing a whole girl together. That's why we're often so different from our twins."

"When Andreas was twelve years old, he told us he was a boy," Eva said. "Doesn't that mean I should be quite feminine?"

"We also build ourselves. In that, we're no different from everyone else. We only start in different places." Korinne knelt, and pulled Eva's ruined shirt out through the bars. "Well, what's done is done. I'll have more stew sent down for you. By someone calmer."

"Thank you," Eva said, mannerly by reflex. Then she hesitated. "You cannot sneak into my good graces by simply answering a few questions. You kidnapped me."

Korinne stood, and shrugged. "It had to be done."

"I know where you're taking me," Eva said. She had pieced it together while being carried in the sac. "You're going to Commander Gavon. You're going to lure him aboard with the promise he can have me if he promises not to attack Dogshead. And then . . . I believe you plan to kill him."

"You're smarter than I thought." Korinne's eyes glinted. Her voice softened. "I know this won't be easy for you. I ran away from him, too. I know how confusing those first months of freedom can be. The joy. The guilt. All your life, you've heard what a great man he is. All your life, you've known it to be a lie. Part of you still wants to believe that you're the one in the wrong. About him. About us. You cling to pieces of what he and the Republic teach us, because it's some comfort in a strange new world that asks so much of you. But understand this, Eva: the echoes will never be safe until our father is dead."

Eva shuddered. She had never imagined a world without her father in it. Not even when she had saved him from that assassin. Not even when Zeke had mentioned another attempt on his life some weeks ago. Commander Gavon was the cornerstone of the world. To imagine his death was to imagine the end of all things.

Did she want him dead?

Yes. But she dared not speak it out loud. She would hear her own voice and know it for the voice of the goddess of death.

"The echoes . . ." Her lips were dry. She licked them and continued on. "What if he simply climbs aboard the ship and starts splitting your crew?"

"He's strategic. The older we get, the more power we can offer him. He wouldn't want to waste us."

"And you're certain this is what you want to do?"

"I'm certain about everything I do. I'm too old to waste my time doubting myself. The work to reach this point has cost me three lovers, two ulcers, and my right hand. I will see this through." Korinne patted her cheek. "Sweet dreams, sister. Welcome to the *Shadow Queen.*"

Korinne pivoted as she walked away. Her boots clicked on the boards as she crossed the hold and climbed up the stairs. When she was out of earshot, Eva turned and looked at Cevette. The captain had lain down on the straw mat near the bars that divided their cells, her hat still snug on her head. Korinne had also let her keep her white armored coat after taking her weapons; a mark of respect, captain to captain. "Should we . . . sleep?"

"Can you open a portal?"

"Not here. I felt the nearness of death on the upper deck. If we can make it there, we can escape. But Korinne won't underestimate me."

"Do you have any hairpins?"

Eva shook her head.

"Very well." Cevette shrugged. "Then we rest and wait."

"Do you think that we can get any rest here?"

"Yes," Cevette said. "We're both in good company."

A small smile crept across Eva's face. "Thank you for coming along."

"But of course."

Why didn't you run with the others? she almost said. But she didn't think she could stomach hearing the most likely answer: *I look after my crew.*

The straw mat laid out in her cell was also close to the bars separating her and Cevette. She lay down on it and lost herself in the rocking of the sea, in the captain's steady breathing. *I should do something,* she thought, but what did you do when there was nothing you could do? *I could pray.* The gods had been tyrants, but people had still worshipped them. Perhaps there was something to it. But what god would hear the prayer of an echo?

She could only think of one: Heraline, missing ever since her wife fell. Perhaps she was still out there, watching over the broken pieces of the goddess she loved. Did she see the echoes plotting to murder the commander? Would she condemn them for that? Or had the violence been the part of Morghaia she'd loved most?

No. Not that. It would be a gross injustice to reduce a goddess of the Sea People to some bloodthirsty monster in her mind. The love between Heraline and Morghaia had been the love of one woman for another. And that meant Eva and all the rest of them had come from a woman who could be loved.

Goddess of the sea, if you can hear me, if it's permissible for me to ask you, being not one of your people, show me the right path.

Cevette reached through the bars and squeezed her hand.

THE *SHADOW QUEEN* RACED northward, aiming its course to intercept Commander Gavon as he sailed south from Soladis. Come morning, Korinne had Eva and Cevette let out for a walk about the hold. She gave them fresh water and chunks of brown bread when she locked them both back in, and gave one of her sailors a warning glare when she looked at Eva with clenched fists. Patience and her friends came down to the hold for long hours each day to work on their mending. They shared some of their rum rations with Eva and Cevette, and even let the prisoners darn some stockings to distract themselves, though they counted the needles they gave them and always took them back before they left

And Eva had nothing to do but study her fellow echoes, what they did and how they spoke when they were all together. They wore breeches and gowns in equal numbers; most wore their hair long, down past their shoulders. They spoke loudly and freely, sometimes flatly, and there was not as much quarreling between them as she might have expected. They seemed to breath easy, amidst their sisters, and shared the work of the ship equally among themselves.

They were decent people, she thought, or at least they were no worse than any other pirates. She could watch them, and she was grateful for their presence as it held off the uncomfortable conversation with Cevette about what all that hand-touching-between-the-prison-bars meant, but she did not know what to say to them. She did not know the proper rules of how to politely converse with strangers she had once been part of a goddess with, and she worried she might unintentionally offend someone.

Cevette had an easier time speaking with them than she did. "How long have you sailed with Korinne?" she would ask. "Does she drive you hard?" They would grumble about their captain a bit—yes, they'd sailed with her for years, yes, she was stubborn and demanding and they got no rest, but they said it warmly, all of them. One told the story of the time Korinne had punched a bull seal in the face; one spoke of how she'd taken a knife through the chest killing an officer of the Godreaper Corps. "Commander Gavon made the rest of the Republic forget, but we held onto it. She taught us how." They spoke of Korinne's dark humor, of her brutality, of her brief and terrible attempt to learn to drum (she had an innate deficiency of rhythm.)

Eva took that all in. She knew very little of what passed outside the brig in those days. But strange noises echoed in the depths, seeping in through the hull, not the songs of whales or the whistles of sea serpents. Darker things. Low rattles like the breath of dying men and screeches like a flock of crows. On the second night, a great roaring noise and the bangs of gunfire woke both of them. She and Cevette held hands as the abomination in the cell beside them sat up and smiled a too-human grin. The next day, Korinne and her sailors brought down a half-dozen small crates of loot and tied them down atop the others. When Patience and her friends came down for their sewing circle, they told their prisoners that Korinne had summoned abominations to guard *Shadow Queen*; they had come across a cargo ship blown off course in a storm and Korinne had ordered the abominations to attack. Not one sailor of the crew had survived, and the damaged ship had quickly sunk beneath the waves.

How can she believe this is the path to free us? Eva thought. It was one thing to kill in battle. People fought and people died. Even the winners of wars paid a terrible price; she had seen countless veterans scarred in body and mind by what they had done. But the abominations killed without consequence. They felt no regret, no pain, no conflict in their choices. They did not only end lives; they insulted the value of each life they ended. Rage at them and rage at her own helplessness churned in her stomach, rendering her mute when she most wanted to scream.

Cevette continued to chatter with Patience and her sewing circles. She asked them where they had grown up, their favorite places they had travelled to, what stories and folklore they could share. Her voice warm and soothing. Her shirt was half unlaced; all the echoes kept stealing glances at her bare collarbones. Eva sat in her cell and listened.

On the evening of the third day, Cevette asked Patience and her friends what they would do if the commander was no more and echoes could be citizens of the Republic, when they were free of him. Most wanted to stay pirates. One girl wanted to be a dancer. Another said she wanted to make fancy hats.

"What do you want, Eva?" Patience said after that. Her knitting needles clicked, a long maroon scarf trailing down from them. All the echoes on their stools in the center of the hold looked up from torn socks and the worn knees of breeches to face her.

Eva, sitting on her sleeping mat, a half-hemmed petticoat on her lap, hesitated. Was she part of this conversation? "I want . . . to be loved." Then she looked away from Cevette. The words had come to her because they were true. She only realized they might put some weight on her captain after they were out. Quickly, she shifted the subject. "Loved by anyone, really. No one in particular. There aren't many women queueing up to love a fragment of death. Is it true that all of us only fancy women?"

All around the sewing circle, echoes nodded. "Tabitha lay with a man a few times," said a younger echo named Cornellia. "But that was only to get pregnant. He's her wife's brother. They're raising the baby on Dogshead, all three of them. It stinks, and screams, and looks like a bald toad—"

"It's a baby," Patience said. "Babies are like that."

"I was never like that," Cornellia insisted.

"No, you weren't. The commander doesn't split us that young. There's not much power in it. When he made me and Chaz, we were about eight years old."

"How do you know?" Eva said, curious despite herself.

"Well," Patience said, as her knitting needles flashed, "before I was eight, my foster mother was quite kind and loving. Afterwards, she was demanding and cruel. When the commander has in mind who he wants to foster a set of echoes, he gives them memories of their foster parents loving them. It's part of how he keeps young echoes compliant; those of us he has raised close to him, anyhow. He wants us to want them to love us again."

Eva's eyes widened. The needle dropped from her fingers and landed on the petticoat in her lap. She pressed her hands to her mouth. *Twelve years old. I was twelve years old.* Her father had been so attentive. So doting. So proud of his little girl. Then he had turned on her. All this time, she had thought it was her failing. *It was all a lie. It was all him.* There was no comfort in that truth. *By the gods, what sort of creature am I?*

"Back to your earlier point," Cornellia said, as if Eva's world had not cracked, "we can be loved, and loved well. I have a girl back on Dogshead. Her name is Nya. She works in the fish market." She went on about Nya's lovely smile and the way the sun shone on her soft brown skin, how her laugh was like a crystal bell, and all Eva could think about was *I've only existed for ten years.* Did that make her a child? No. It meant she never had a childhood. She pressed her knees into her chest and began to rock back and forth. Her father would have chided her for her lack of dignity if he saw her doing that, but the echoes seemed to take it in stride. Cornellia's story about Nya went on and on. From the far side of the bars, Cevette quietly whispered her name. Eva could hear her, but she could not speak.

"Excuse me." Abruptly, Patience put down her knitting needles, rose from her stool, and went to the bars of Eva's cell. She reached through and put a hand on Eva's knee. "You're allowed to struggle," she said, quietly. "It's hard to accept, how very different our lives are from what we've been told a life should be. We can speak about it, you and I."

Eva shook her head. "All you'll tell me is the only place for echoes is by Korinne's side." Even to herself, she sounded terribly weak. Terribly lost.

"I don't have to tell you that. Listen. Korinne . . . she sees herself in you. A young woman, full of righteous anger, escaping the father who abused her so cruelly, full of power and passion to stop him. A young woman who grew up in the Golden Republic and who has a good deal to learn about what it means to be an echo in this world. She wants to look out for you, in much the way Chaz and I looked out for her when she first fled Halston. But you don't always do what she expects. And that frustrates her very much indeed."

"Why do any of you follow her?"

"Because for ten long years, she has risked her life to protect echoes. That matters, Eva. More than any quarrel I have with her. Very few of us approve of destroying the memories. Even fewer agree we should weaponize the abominations. But we follow her. We trust her. You can't simply stand up and lead us against her. You can't even hold a conversation with us."

Eva winced. Her cheeks burned. *What a fool I am.* Back in Halston, hating what she was had been her one protection. It had kept her from standing up to the constant jabs and indignities. It had kept her alive. But the hate was now as much a trap as the cell door.

"Does it get easier?" she whispered.

Patience squeezed her knee. "It does. I promise you." For a moment, Eva wondered if this was how having a mother felt. *No.* That wasn't right. Echoes didn't have mothers. They had each other. "When this matter with the commander is over, you can come and visit us whenever you want. We can talk. We can help you. I'll see to it that Korinne makes you no trouble. If she does, she can cook her own stew."

"Thank you," Eva whispered.

On the morning of the forth day, Korinne brought Eva and Cevette to the upper deck.

She had Eva bound wrist and ankle, first, so she could not run. It took two echoes to lift her up on their shoulders and carry her up the stairs. Korinne led Cevette, unbound but with a pistol pointed at her chest, up to the topdeck. She tied both her prisoners to the mainmast, Eva facing the bow, and Cevette facing the stern.

The deck of *Shadow Queen* was twice as wide and twice long as that of *Sea Wolf.* Her three great masts were as wide about as the greatest pines; the dark sails, their edges stitched with silver, blacked out the sky. She had cabins fore and aft. Her upper deck, its ashwood planks a pale gray in the light of the morning sun, was neatly kept and clear of cargo crates. The silver bands on her well-polished cannons gleamed. There were over a dozen echoes on the upper deck, climbing in the rigging, ducking in and out of the crew's quarters beneath the forecastle, though the grand size of the ship meant it did not feel crowded. Sticks of incense, burning in brass vessels that hung from the masts, filled the air with a lavender scent. Somewhere back toward the bow, a harpist played.

It would have almost been pleasant, was it not for the fact Korinne had also freed the abomination from its cell. Up and down the length of *Shadow Queen* it patrolled, its lizard-like claws clicking on the wood. More abominations swam off the starboard bow: three massive sharks, a pod of dolphins covered in razor-sharp spines, and one massive squid-like kraken. After securing Eva and Cevette, Korinne went to the port rail. She drew crumpled handfuls of memory from inside her long coat—the sturdy dark leather embroidered with silver thread on the outside and reinforced with metal rings on the inside—and threw the black-and-white scraps to her army. They vanished into the maws of beasts. "Calm, calm," she urged them. "Dive deep. Deep, deep down. Don't attack the *Kembrielle.* Don't show them our numbers. Wait until I call you." One by one, the creatures sank below the waves.

Cevette raised her voice. "Do you know what the Sea People say about abominations?"

"I've spoken with a number of them, yes."

"The souls inside them were so cruel and violent that they destroyed their own ability to reason. They exist only to cause suffering. It's the Sea People they hate most, but they will turn against anyone they can feed on."

"I do my damn best to keep them away from the Sea People," Korinne said. "I kept them in check on Night Dragon Isle. The Tarwik shamans know what I'm doing. They don't like it, but they know I'm after Gavon, and so they look the other way. The abominations are the best weapon we've got against him." She grinned, cool as the winter wind that whipped back through her long black hair. "Of course, I never thought the commander would be fool enough to meet me at sea. Tell you what, both of you. When he's dead, I'll kill them all."

"They might turn against you."

"They might," Korinne said. "They could feast a good long while off what I've suffered. But, if today goes well, I'll know the first peace I've known in ten long years."

Ten years. Eva frowned. *Ten years ago, he made us.* Her heart sank. She thought of the Korinne in her diary, young and eager, curious and thoughtful, who had approached abominations with the interest of a natural philosopher. Korinne, who had loved her twin sister Ariella with all her heart.

"By the gods," she said. "He split your sister into Andreas and me."

Korinne stiffened. She gripped the rail tightly in her fists. Her voice went flat, but for echoes, who often struggled to match their tone to their sentiments, that meant nothing save for that she was overwhelmed.

"She was the golden daughter," Korinne said, still gazing out on the sea. Eva had to strain to hear her. "We never dreamed he would split her. We decided I should run off to sea because we were afraid he'd split *me*. But then she challenged him for his seat on the Assembly. She convinced citizens to vote for her. And he tore her apart."

Andreas and I were once Ariella Gavon. He had inherited her charisma. Eva had got the recklessness. And there must have been another echo before them all, a soul in which all three of them had been one. Eva had wished to distance herself from Korinne, but such a thing could never be.

"We were as naïve and foolish as you are now," Korinne said. "We thought she would be safe. Ariella was so good at following their rules. She made the gentry love her. I struggled with that. But that meant nothing in the end. In the Republic, every single echo can be torn up and thrown away."

Eva's head spun. Tears stung the corners of her eyes. A weight grew in the pit of her stomach. "Why didn't you tell me where I came from when we first met? Or on Moonwhisper Isle?"

Korinne turned to face the mainmast. Her nostrils flared. Her good hand trembled on the hilt of her sword. "On Moonwhisper, you looked on me, with my sister's eyes, and asked what had made me the way I am with repellant disgust. It would have broken me to confess I was avenging the violation of your soul and receive only scorn in return."

"Gods, Korinne." The tears slid down Eva's cheek. "I . . . I am sorry for how I spoke to you then. I never thought of the circumstances of my own creation. I failed to see your grief. I only saw in you the parts of me I had been taught to hide away." Her voice trembled as she finished. "If you please . . . I would like the chance to know you. As you are."

Korinne closed her eyes. Tears ran down her cheeks as well, thin lines of silver gleaming in the sun. She wiped them away, then squared her shoulders and walked to the mainmast, where her prisoners were bound. "I hope, soon, that we can have that chance. But *Kembrielle* is drawing near, off to stern. You likely can't see it from there." She leaned in at Eva's ear. The necklace silver skull beads she wore swung forward and brushed, cold, against Eva's neck. "If you so much as hint at my plan to our father, I will throw Captain Zarcanzi to the sharks."

Eva flinched. Her stomach churned. "You—you can't." Of course she could. Of course she would.

Her father would come aboard. Korinne would try to kill him. A word from Eva could save his life.

She would have to choose if her father would live or die.

Korinne grabbed Eva's right hand and pulled it free of the rope bindings, exposing the black godmarks to the sun. She raised her voice. "Run up a white flag! Tell Commander Gavon I brought him the Skullrunner!"

The Ageless Horror

Aboard *Shadow Queen*, three hundred and sixty miles south southwest of the City of Soladis. 25th Heralmonth, Year Twenty-Two of the Golden Republic.

In your last three letters, you have pressed me for more information about the revolution. You have brought up examples of military records that conflict with each other and have confessed that you doubt your own memories of that time. Put your doubts aside, sir; they are not befitting a gentleman. There are details of the revolution I have concealed from the public, yes, in the same fashion a general will hide the movement of his troops from his foe. But this is all necessary, and done with the best interests of the Republic at heart. On this, only a subversive traitor would dare to question me. –Letter from Commander Jonathan Gavon to Lord Mykil Merris, Minister for Childhood Welfare

Rope and rigging creaked as *Kembrielle* pulled into position alongside *Shadow Queen*. Both ships were cleanly matched for size and guns. The gilded rails lined up with the silver ones, the sparkling metal dulled by the clouds that were beginning to knit themselves together across the blue. Sailors tossed ropes across the gap and fastened them securely to iron rings in the deck. The two ships steadied. Soldiers in golden uniforms watched Chaz and Patience with wide and wary eyes as they lowered a plank bridge across the gap.

"I don't like this," Chaz said in a low voice. "Something's off. He should have brought more than one ship with him."

"He's a proud man," Patience said. "He would want to claim all the credit for the victory himself."

"I know he's a proud bastard. But I'd bet my gold tooth there's something more to it. He planned to sail to Dogshead. He'd be facing more than just echoes there, more than people he can just split in a fight." Chaz shook her head. "Why isn't he doing more to guard his own ass?"

Zeke was the first man to cross. Clad in his orange uniform jacket and the violet beret of an officer of the Godreaper Corps, he strode over the plank bridge, his eyes bright and alert. "Thank you," he said, nodding to Chaz and Patience as he hopped down. "Commander Gavon sent me to treat with your captain. Which one of you is she?"

"I'm the captain here." Korinne said. "Tell your commander that I have the Skullrunner. If he grants us peace, she's all his."

"I'll need proof it's her and not some echo girl with charcoal drawings on her hands."

Korinne gestured toward the mainmast. "Check her marks."

Zeke nodded, and stepped forward. The panther abomination stalked toward him. He stiffened as it sniffed at his chest, and paused for a heartbeat to wipe the sweat from his brow. Then he closed the distance between himself and Eva, blinking several times in rapid succession, a tremble in his chin. Briefly, he glanced at her exposed hand. Then he met her eyes. "Miss Gavon," he said, all cool formality. "Are you well?"

"Well enough." The knowledge of what her father was doing to him urged her toward pity. But this coldness was his choice, so she matched it.

"I spoke with Lord Merris. He told me of the soldiers you butchered."

Eva shivered. The memory rose up and clung to her like the faint fog now building on the sea, clinging cold to her skin. The clash of steel. The screams of the dying. The nearness of Death. The power. The rightness. *But I had my justification.* "Lord Merris is a child-seller. Anyone who protects him protects that."

Zeke stiffened. His eyes darted about. To his right, Chaz and Patience watched him with unblinking dark eyes; to his left; Cornellia and her friends polished their pistols. When he spoke, his voice was tight and strained. "The foster system has its cruelties. But . . ." A cloud passed over the sun. The color seemed to fade from his light brown skin. He sighed, and lowered his head. "Were you hurt? By the fighting? By these pirates?"

"I'm well enough," Eva said. The bruises from her brawl with Korinne had started to fade. "How's the arrow wound?"

"Healing cleanly." A small smile tugged at the corners of his lips. "I'll be much better off when you're back in Halston with the Godreaper Corps."

"Zeke . . ."

"He'll pardon you. Your power is far too useful to him." He squeezed her hand. "I'll go get him. You'll see."

With that, he turned his back on Eva and walked away. Back across the plank bridge he went, Chaz and Patience watching with careful eyes. Several minutes passed. Eva felt as if she could barely breathe. Her pulse raced, ragged and uneven. *He's coming.* To face him, now that she had come to terms with so much more of what he had done—would she find the strength to condemn him to his face? Or would he wear her down again with petty cruelties? Whittle away at her sense of self until all she felt she could do was serve him?

A drummer played a military salute. A dozen Republic soldiers marched over the plank bridge. They stepped down and stood at attention to either side of it. As more clouds washed over the sun, their orange jackets turned a dull brown. Sweat beaded at their temples. Their hands gripped tightly to their rifles. Chaz and Patience and a dozen others of the *Shadow Queen* crew watched them with wary eyes. Korinne, the lizard-panther abomination at her heels, stood at the end of the plank bridge. A plume of fog drifted about her like a cloak of gossamer.

Zeke crossed back over and jumped down beside Korinne. He reached up a hand and helped Commander Gavon step down from the plank bridge. The commander wore a coat of austere brown wool with silver fastenings, a felt cap, and a thin set of leather gloves. He adjusted the positioning of his bicorne hat, and gave Korinne a polite nod. The Demon of Dogshead nodded in return.

Behind her, off in the sea, the tall gray dorsal fin of an abomination cut through the surf.

"Where is Evazina?" her father said.

Zeke nodded towards the mainmast.

Slowly, deliberately, the commander crossed the deck. His silver-buckled shoes tapped on the ashwood boards. Echoes stepped back from him as he passed. Fear shone in their eyes. He glared at Eva down the length of his straight patrician nose. She shivered as his dark eyes met hers. Her lip trembled. She dug her nails into her palms.

And her words rushed out like a crashing wave. "*You.* I know what you've done. I remember. How many of us have you torn apart? What gives you the right to destroy us?"

He frowned. "You are shrieking delusions."

"Look at all these echoes. I can count."

"Arrogant girl." His brow furrowed. His fists tightened. "The gods thought they were better than us, too. More intelligent. More virtuous. More fit to rule. When I was your age, I served as an officer in the army of Iunos. We had been sent to defend the Soladisean colonies of the Five Sisters from the forces of Morghaia. I had grown up in those lands; I was an expert on the grounds. But the other officers showed me no respect. I was from the colonies. I was less than them. That was how the gods had taught them to see me. After all these years, I remember it still: that first slap of tyranny." His lips curled. His pale face reddened. The gray clouds overhead grew darker. The fog swirled about him, washing out the rest of the world save him. "It took a revolution to earn their respect. But the world is full of fools who let their envy of a great man turn to hatred. They forget what I did for them. And so I must make them remember who I am."

He admits it. At last. But there was no comfort in that. It was hard to see any victory in the truth of what he did to echoes. "What about democracy? How can the citizens of the Republic choose their own leaders when they cannot form their own opinions of them? Do you believe in it at all?" *Ariella.* "No. You don't. If you did, you would let echoes vote."

"I have considered extending the right to a few of you. Your brother, for one. You, if you serve me. If you prove yourself to be better than the rest of your kind and worthy to claim me as a father."

"How can I trust you?" Eva narrowed her eyes. "I remember you carrying me at the victory parades. I remember you teaching me to fish and shoot. I remember you holding me in the dark after a nightmare. And all of it was a *lie.*"

He folded his arms over his chest. "Would you blame a father for giving his daughter pleasant memories of her childhood?"

"It wasn't a kindness. You hate me."

"Eva—"

She looked him in the eye. "You hate echoes so much. Not because of anything we've done to you. Because you need to hate us. It's the only way you can keep ripping us apart. I will never earn your respect. And I don't want it. I am an echo. I have no father."

Eva smiled. He flinched, as if he saw Morghaia smiling through her. She thought of Tomis and Sebastian Thimmely, how she'd told them the commander should be tried and convicted for his crimes. *This is not justice.* But how could you bring justice to the man who wrote the law?

He would die today.

A shadow passed over her father's face. For a moment, he looked old—not a man of fifty-odd years, but a statue of carved from marble, eroded by the centuries. He frowned. Thunder rumbled in the distance. A drop of rain struck Eva's cheeks, cold as the northern sea.

Patience is at least forty. Something was rising in her mind, a dark leviathan surfacing from the deeps. The waters of her were stirring, though she could not yet see the beast clearly. *He made her as a six-year-old. Over thirty years ago.* But he had killed Morghaia and founded the Republic only twenty-two years ago. What had Sebastian Thimmely said back on God's Garden? *My first tattoos about Commander Gavon were already starting to fade twenty-two years ago.*

"Take her, and begone," Korinne said. A raindrop shone as it slid down her neck. She leaned forward and began to undo the knot in the rope that bound both Eva and Cevette to the mast. "You have what you came for. Turn your ship around and sail for Soladis." The rope fell to the deck. Behind the mast, Cevette gasped in relief.

"Back to the ship!" Commander Gavon shouted to his soldiers. "Lieutenant Dare, bring her."

Zeke nodded. He grabbed Eva, who was still bound hand and foot, about her chest, and flung her up over his shoulder. Her head spun. Her cheek pressed against his back, against the well-worn wool of his uniform coat. Back toward the plank bridge he walked. Eva held her breath.

This was the moment Korinne would want. When the commander's bodyguard had his hands full.

There came a ripple of silver sound—the drawing of two dozen blades at once. A round of shouts, then gunshots, then screams. Three souls dropped into Death. Zeke swore. He knelt and laid Eva down on the deck, then rose, reaching for his sword. Before he could draw, Chaz pressed a pistol to the side of his head.

Eva sat up just in time to see Korinne press a knife to her father's throat.

Commander Gavon froze. His pale face went white as snow. The twelve Republic soldiers left standing had their guns pointed at Korinne. But her crew had guns as well, and they outnumbered the Republic soldiers three to one.

Echoes leaned over the rail of *Shadow Queen*. A few quick swipes of their swords severed the ropes binding the two ships. Shouts rose from *Kembrielle*. Rifles fired. The shots went wild—one struck the mizzenmast, one chipped a railing. A troop of soldiers leapt onto the plank bridge. Cornellia and her friends gave it a shove. The soldiers plummeted. Abominations surfaced from the waves, clicking and snarling as they fell upon the screaming soldiers.

Eva looked wildly about her. Cevette was nowhere to be seen.

Korinne laughed. Her knife traced a thin red line along the commander's throat. "Hello, Father. Remember me?"

"Korinne." His voice was grim. "I remember you. You're making a very grave mistake."

Her fingers trembled. A vein throbbed in her neck. The whites of her eyes shone in the gathering gloom. "You shouldn't have split my sister."

"It should have been you," he said. "Ten years, it took for you to spring this trap. Ariella would have caught me faster."

Korinne set her teeth. The wind picked up, howling and whistling like a lost soul. Tendrils of mist wafted across the upper deck, curling around her. Rivulets of rain rolled down her face. She took a deep breath and steadied her trembling hand. "Godspeed, Father, and may hell take your soul."

She shoved the dagger into his throat.

It vanished from her fist, leaving but a shallow nick behind.

No. Eva blinked over and over, trying to make sense of what she had seen. The dagger had vanished. *Where did it go?* Her head spun. The back of her neck prickled. *He should be dead. Why isn't he dead?*

Cornellia sprinted across the deck, a sword in her fist. "For Theodora!" she shouted, and lunged at the commander. The blade shone. As it pierced his coat, it vanished. Eva blinked. Had she seen a flicker of black smoke? Cornellia screamed and struck him with her fist. The commander only laughed, a deep and terrible sound. *He can't be killed. By all the gods, he can't be killed.*

This was the true Jonathan Gavon. The face he kept hidden from the world. Ageless. Invulnerable.

How can we ever hope to stop him?

Above, the sky had gone dark. Lightning forked across the clouds. All of *Shadow Queen* shuddered in the wake of the thunder boom.

"Miss Gavon!" A warm hand grabbed her shoulder.

Eva looked up. "Captain!" she gasped. Cevette had snuck around the deck and come up behind her.

Cevette grabbed the rope that bound Eva's wrists. "Let's get these off. We need to run."

Eva nodded. She shifted about and sat up. Cevette fumbled with the rope at Eva's wrists. She had no knife, only her fingers, and the rope was already swelling with rainwater. But until it was loose, there was no way for Eva to grab her and flee into Death.

And all was chaos around them. Echoes charged at soldiers. Soldiers ran at echoes. The crack of gunshots and the smell of powder filled the air as the crews of both ships fired at each other. A bullet stung the deck of *Shadow Queen* inches from Eva's leg. She gasped. A piercing scream sounded near the bow as Korinne unleashed her magic on some unlucky foe.

A thirty-foot kraken tentacle lashed up from the sea. Another followed. Another. They were a pale pink, covered in suckers like dinner plates, and they lashed across the breadth of *Shadow Queen*'s deck. The ship shook and tilted sideways. Soldiers and echoes staggered and cursed, slamming into one another, slipping about on the rain-slick deck. Eva and Cevette held each other tight.

Zeke, bleeding from a half-dozen cuts and clinging to the mainmast as the ship lurched, flung out his hand. A white bolt of magic struck the nearest tentacles. They dissolved into sea foam. The *Shadow Queen* twisted. Its stern lurched across the sea and struck *Kembrielle*. Wood cracked. Ropes snapped. Zeke bent down and grabbed Commander Gavon, who was cowering for shelter near his feet. He ran toward the stern, shielding his commander with his body, and took the steps to the quarterdeck two at a time. Gold-uniformed soldiers stood just across the gap where the ships had collided. Zeke shoved the rain-soaked commander into their arms. They closed ranks about him.

Zeke hesitated. He looked back over his shoulder. An abomination like a bright red snake with five spear-tipped tails was slithering along the deck toward *Shadow Queen*'s starboard bow. Cornellia and her friends faced it with bayonets, eyes wide, hands trembling. He threw a second bolt of power. The creature collapsed, trembling, and the echoes rushed in to finish it off.

Then he looked back to Eva, tipped his cap, and leapt nimbly back onto *Kembrielle*.

"Honorable bastard," Eva grunted as the commander's ship turned toward open sea.

The air rang with the ringing blades, gasps of pain, and screeching monsters. Lightning flashed. Thunder boomed. In the blaze of light,

Korinne dueled two soldiers on the stairs to the forecastle. Patience chopped through kraken tentacles with an axe. Gunshots echoed. A cannon boomed. The howling of abominations blended with the howl of the wind. Spars cracked in the rigging. Loose rope and heavy winches flew through the darkness.

"How did this storm come up so fast?" Eva said.

"This is no natural storm." Cevette frowned. "Look to starboard."

Eva turned her head and *saw*.

A nimble barque sailed through the concealing mist, a leaping orca as her figurehead. The seas tossed against her flanks. She leapt over the waves, aimed at *Shadow Queen* like a dart. Pirates darted across the deck, racing to find their footing in the storm, trimming sails and tacking fresh rope to the ones they left up. In the rigging of the mainmast stood a small figure with threads of lightning running down their back like a cloak. A wild delight glowed in their eyes.

Eva gasped. *Lizeth.* The quartermaster had summoned a storm to drive them here.

"Captain!" Lovett shouted, his voice barely audible over the wind. The first mate of *Sea Wolf* stood atop the forecastle, his shirt soaked and clinging to his skin, a grappling hook in his hand. He threw. It latched onto the rail of *Shadow Queen* near the stern. Naeri stood beside him. She threw a second hook onto the rail. The ropes strained, but Eva knew Naeri had worked magic into them. They would hold.

Tuk and Nukit stepped out from behind Lovett and Naeri. They held a long wooden gangplank in their hands. As Lovett and Naeri tied their ropes to the iron rings mounted in the forecastle, the two Upailitian men lowered the gangplank, bracing it with their shoulders. It hit the rail of *Shadow Queen,* resting precariously. "Come on!" Tuk shouted.

"You'll kill us all!" said Cevette. "I need a knife—to get Eva free—"

Nukit shouted, "Look! Up the deck!"

Both Eva and Cevette turned to look. Korinne's panther-like abomination stalked down the length of the deck, its gait like that of a cat, its claws like that of a great lizard, its grin all too human. In the fog and darkness and chaos, it moved as lightly as a spirit drifting through Death. Blood covered its chin. It had grown another foot, eight now in length, four at the shoulder.

And it had Cevette and Eva in its sight.

Cevette cursed. She scooped Eva into her arms, stood with a deep grunt of effort, and ran for the gangplank. Her long white coat billowed on the wind. The deck lurched beneath them. Cevette stumbled, but kept her feet. A vein pulsed in her neck. Eva wrapped her bound hands around Cevette's shoulder and did her best to hold on.

Cevette clambered up onto the plank bridge. Tuk grunted; Nukit murmured a prayed as he fought to hold it still. It rattled and bounced as the captain ran. Rain washed down her face. Her arms shook as she squeezed Eva against her chest. The gangplank lurched. *She'd be safer if she dropped me,* Eva realized, but Cevette did not let go.

"It's coming!" Naeri screamed, and Cevette *jumped*.

Eva gasped as they slammed into Tuk and Nukit, all the air forced out of her lungs on impact. The men grabbed them tight. The gangplank fell down into the waves.

The abomination leapt across the gap between ships.

"Naeri!" Lovett said. He barreled into her, knocking her sideways, out of the abomination's path. The beast slammed down atop him. There was a terrible crack, wood and bone. Splinters of a shattered rail flew through the air. The ropes binding *Sea Wolf* to *Shadow Queen* snapped as the ship lurched. Lovett's glasses flew across the forecastle and vanished into the sea. Naeri screamed.

And Eva felt one more soul slip into Death.

"Over here!" Cevette grabbed a length of broken rail with a jagged edge and jumped to her feet. "Over here, you monster!" The abomination raised its head and looked at her. Cevette lunged. The abomination reared up, its claws outstretched. With a twist of her shoulders, Cevette drove the spar through its throat like a spear. Flesh parted. Steaming blood sprayed from the gap and melted into sea foam. Cevette side-stepped as it crashed down to the deck. As it melted into sludge, Cevette ran to Naeri's side.

"Stay still, Eva," Tuk said. His fingers were trembling. A spray of blood covered his cheek. The knife in his hand was steady as he sliced the bonds at her wrists and ankles.

"No," Naeri sobbed, holding Lovett's body. "Please, please, no!"

The only reply was the howl of the storm.

ORANGES

ON AN UNKNOWN SANDBAR AND IN UNMAPPED WATERS. 26TH HERAL-MONTH, YEAR TWENTY-TWO OF THE GOLDEN REPUBLIC.

My grandmother told me that when it rains, we all get wet. There is no bad thing that only affects one person, or one group of people. She told me that some people have great houses to shelter in and others only have the clothes on their backs, but we all must dwell beneath the gray skies until the clouds part. –'Our History of the Golden Republic,' published in *The Dawn Beacon*.

LIGHTNING STABBED INTO THE sea like falling swords. Thunder boomed. Rain and hail fell in driving sheets. The survivors from the boarding party ran for cover. Cevette held Naeri close, but she was not moving. "Captain!" Eva shouted. Cevette only trembled.

Eva cursed. "Hold on tight!" she shouted to Tuk and Nukit, and ran to the other women. She grabbed one with each hand and dragged them both to the foremast. The wind howled and dragged at their coats. Cold wet needles struck her face. She grabbed the mast with one hand and caught a flying rope with the other. She looped the cord around their waists, knotting it tight. "All secure! I've got you!" Her words were lost on the howling wind.

Eva, Cevette, and Naeri clung to each other as the storm sent *Sea Wolf* racing through the gray-black sea. The ship tossed like an enraged bull. Wood cracked. Canvass ripped. Lizeth screamed and cursed up in the rigging; Eva dimly recalled them telling her once they could not stop a storm once they had started it. Naeri buried her face in Eva's shoulder. And Eva could only hold on and hope.

The dark hours bled together. At last, the clouds parted. The tossing ship stilled.

Sea Wolf floated in a pale azure ocean, its glistening surface smooth, untouched by any wind or tide. A blue sky hung over the sea, free of even a wisp of cloud. Low, flat sand bars stretched out as far as the eye could see, white as cream and bare of life. Eva didn't know where they were, but it reminded her of Death, another place between places.

Cevette unwound the rope wrapped tight around the three of them. Her head lowered, she murmured "I'm so sorry."

"That wasn't your fault," Eva said.

"I'm so sorry. *I'm so sorry.*"

Naeri looked up at Eva. Lines of dried sea-salt from slapping waves covered her dark cheeks. A gash bled sluggishly on her forehead, but the worst pain was in her eyes. It was as if a shroud had covered them.

"Is he truly gone?" she whispered.

"What do you mean?"

Naeri reached out. Her trembling fingers traced the dark lines of Eva's godmarks. "Skullrunner. Please."

Oh. Naeri wasn't speaking to her as a friend, but as the goddess of death. Perhaps she should have been upset at that. But she wasn't. She was the closest to the goddess they had.

"I . . ." Eva swallowed. A hard lump filled her throat. "He's dead. I'm so, so sorry."

Naeri fell to her knees. She buried her face in her hands and wept. Eva wrapped her arms around her and held her close once more.

Time faded into a blur. There was little to mark its passage with. The wind was still. The water was still. With dull eyes and slumped shoulders, Lizeth informed them that what they did would have rippling effects on local weather for days to come. Donya came to sit with Naeri, and Eva went to inspect the ship. She found that the cargo hold was flooded and that a rail was broken on the port side of the poop deck. Two of the masts had deep cracks in the top and would need to be taken apart and repaired. They had run aground beside a slender sandbar island, an exposed position, visible from miles around. But she could see no other harbor and no other ships, only water that turned pale pink as the sun set.

As night fell and the moon rose high, the crew of *Sea Wolf* gathered on the shore. For once, they kept to silence. Tuk and Nukit had secured Lovett's body in the storm so all might say a proper farewell. The crew gathered the pieces of a broken rail and stacked them in a heap, then set the first mate atop it and gathered in a solemn circle around the pyre. Mr. Smoke opened a cask of rum and passed around cups. "To Lovett," he said, lifting his.

"To Lovett," Eva said. She tapped her cup against the one Lizeth held. The quartermaster was worn from the effort of their magic; they shivered, despite their long violet coat. Still, they had come, and they stood by the pyre with their head held high.

"To Lovett," Lizeth said, and they drank.

The circle opened. A drummer beat a formal rhythm on his drum. Naeri and Cevette walked through side-by-side, carrying a lit torch. They stopped before the pyre. Naeri took a breath, and lowered the torch. A moment passed before the wet wood caught. Mr. Smoke knelt and added his own fire to the blaze. Sparks flew. Pale yellow flames danced through the pyre. The smoke drifted up past the face of the rising moon. A green light shivered across its surface. *Demon-fire.* Heraline's curse, the legends called it. Eva wondered if Lovett had known any stories about it.

Eva wrapped her arms tight around her chest. Lizeth placed a comforting hand on her shoulder. "You'll get used to missing him," they said, quietly stepping up beside her. "That's how it goes. It's hardest now, when the loss is fresh. But we're only sad when we've lost something worthwhile."

"Thank you," Eva said. "That's quite wise."

"That's what my father told me when my mother died." They swallowed. "I barely remember her. But I remember that."

"Would anyone like to say a few words?" Cevette asked. Naeri only stared down at her hands.

Eva lifted her chin. "I . . . I . . ." The only funerals she had attended had been for Assembly members she'd neither known well or liked. "Lovett was a . . . dedicated member of this crew," she said. "A good fighter, teacher, and friend. We'll all miss him." The words felt thin. False. Anyone could have said as much. What could *she* say, in tribute? "I have walked through Death, and it is a peaceful place. I'm not quite sure how it all works, but I know that he is safe and in no pain. I can promise you all that much."

She stepped back, then, and wondered if Morghaia had ever spoken at the funeral of a friend. Then she wondered what the goddess of death might have known about the magic that made Commander Gavon immortal. *Is this all her fault?* Eva did not know.

A few more pirates stepped forward to speak. Tuk told the story of a fishing contest he and Lovett had once won on Broken Hook Island. Donya told of the time Lovett had stopped two boys from beating a stray dog. Naeri wept harder and fiercer as the flames died down. Cevette helped her back aboard the ship, and most of the crew followed after. Eva watched them go. Some touched their caps in silent respect as they met her eyes. Past all the weight of loss, she felt a certain confusion. *I am not what they are.* She wore the face of death, and tonight, they all saw it. But they were not pushing her away.

She and Lizeth were among the last of the crew left down by the glowing coals. They both stepped forward and warmed their hands over the crackling embers.

"Why did you come after us?" Eva asked Lizeth in a low voice. "I'm the Skullrunner. You could have trusted I would have found a way to get Cevette and me out."

"You're still new to being the Skullrunner," Lizeth said. "We didn't know what to do. Lovett put it to a vote—would we chase *Shadow Queen*, or trust you and Cevette to break free? We all voted to go after you."

"I see," Eva said. "You came for Cevette."

"We came for both of you."

They voted to save an echo. She bit her lip. Drew a quivering breath. One more tear ran down her cheek.

That was what the echoes would have to rely on now. Korinne couldn't kill the commander, not unless she could counteract the magic that kept him alive. Andreas' vote of impeachment would have to suffice. The echoes needed his cleverness, the writings of Tomis Beauchamp, and speed and stealth of the Skullrunner to reveal the truth to the world. They needed the Assembly to remove Commander Gavon from power—not only for the echoes, but for the sake of them all.

"Thank you for coming for me," Eva said. "That was quite the storm you summoned."

"Honestly, I'm always surprised by how strong the storms become when I let them go. I tell myself, the god Toponomitl, his magic is part of my heritage. The Sea People part, the part my family hides away. I want to show them—to show the world—we can be proud of what we are and where we come from. But this power is damned dangerous."

"What you did was nothing short of amazing," Eva said. "But I suppose the opinion of an echo won't encourage you. We can also be quite dangerous." She thought of Korinne and her crew. "And we are at our most dangerous when we are the most proud of what we are."

"You're right." Lizeth squatted by the fire. They pulled out a scrap of charred wood and crumbled it to ashes in their fist. A smile tugged at the corners of their lips. "I won't ever choose shame."

Eva thought that over. Andreas took pride in his scholarship. Korinne took pride in her ship and her strength. And she was proud of her skills in battle, of the strength of her convictions, but what she had always been most proud of were moments where she had conducted herself in such a manner that she could tell herself she'd opened some distance between herself and other echoes. That pride was a brittle thing, easily shaken, that made her look like quite the fool. She had not realized the crew thought highly enough of her, an echo, that they would come to her rescue. She had not realized she could be seen as both an echo and a person who could be loved.

They came for me. They voted to come for me.
She had to find a moment to speak with Cevette.

Donya kept her medicines in a small closet off the small crew's galley. It was a cramped space; cabinets with dozens of small drawers lined all three walls, their brass handles poking Cevette in the back as she held a candle up for the healer. The light danced over the small table in the center of the room as Donya ground herbs and dried minnows in a stone mortar; a sleeping potion for Naeri.

"You can send someone else to hold the candle," Donya said as she worked the pestle. The faint scent of salt filled the room. "You need sleep, too. I doubt they let you get much on *Shadow Queen.*"

"I need to talk to you," Cevette murmured. Both women spoke in Kossket, as they always did when alone together. "When the abomination killed Lovett, I felt this . . . memory . . . stirring inside me. This had happened before. I had watched an abomination kill someone I loved."

"I'm so sorry," Donya said.

"No. Don't be sorry for me. I remembered—it was my fault."

"What?" Donya shook her head. "Cousin, those creatures have hunted our people for centuries. How could it be your fault?"

"I could have stopped it. The elders of the Hoca people carve sacred patterns into stone pillars, then sink them in their harbors to keep abominations from their shores. The shamans of Crab Island can bind abominations using prayers and pots of seawater." Her voice broke. The candle trembled in her grasp. "I knew how to, or I had the ability to . . . I don't know what. But I failed. What if my home village is gone because of me? What if I walked away from my heritage because I couldn't face the loss?"

"Until you get your memories back, you can't know the truth. You can only worry." Donya crushed a dried minnow to bits. "I didn't know that bit about the Hoca and their pillars. Small wonder they keep that quiet. Commander Gavon would fuck a whale to get his hands on those."

"I wish I knew *how* I knew it."

"You're a current woman. I bet you were a good one, for your people, whoever they are. Folk trust you with sacred things. You're good with them, more so than me, or Tuk and Nukit—"

"You're a healer, cousin. You drank the life of a god. That's sacred."

"Yes. But you . . . you hold yourself like an elder. You'll be a great leader one day. If you don't find your people, you can always go to Kossi. We'll adopt you."

"Should you?" Cevette pushed a hand back through her short hair. "I have knowledge, but perhaps I know it only because I made terrible mistakes. I care for the Three Currents, but perhaps I only value my ties to my people because I once abandoned them. I can defend a village, but perhaps I only learned how to do that because I once let people I love die."

"You would never let that happen." Donya shook her head. "You've pushed yourself too hard. You need to rest."

IN THE STORM, *KEMBRIELLE* had lost two masts and three sailors. Ezekiel Dare had lost much of his hope.

While the winds had blown, Commander Gavon had locked himself in his cabin, and Zeke had joined the sailors in hauling rope. They had cursed their absent leader, called him a coward, said he cared not for their lives. Zeke's shoulders had burned and his back had ached by the time the storm subsided. He had welcomed the pain. It had proved a fitting distraction from the truth.

My commander is a monstrous thing. He could not be killed. Every blade turned against him on *Shadow Queen* had disappeared before striking home. *Even gods can die.* This was the man he loved, the man he planned to build a life with. *How many lies has he told me?* Zeke had first laid eyes on him nearly a decade ago. He could not say for certain if the man had aged a day. *How old is he? How many boys has he taken into his bed?* The commander was so reticent to speak of his past. Zeke had always thought that was modesty. But he knew nothing about the man. Nothing at all.

Who is he?

When the storm calmed, *Kembrielle* found itself in a calm, glassy, gray sea. There were no islands in sight; even the great fish and whales seemed to be keeping to the deeps. The navigators determined that the storm had blown them northwest, nearly off the edge of the known maps. There was a chill in the air, but no wind. It was as if the world held its breath.

Kembrielle was well-equipped to make repairs, but the sailors quarreled about the best way for it to be done. Zeke was no shipwright, but he consulted with the one aboard and drew up a plan. He divided the sailors into groups, splitting the arguers and the disorderly drunkards apart, and gave each one a task. He took care not to merely oversee their labor, but to do his share of hauling wood up from the cargo hold and mending rips in the sails. Many of the sailors were fosterlings, or older non-citizens seeking to earn enough to buy papers. He meant to show them that, with discipline and loyalty, they could rise high.

As he worked, he thought of what would come next, and he worried. The storm winds had carried *Shadow Queen* north; *Sea Wolf* had been blown south, closer to their path, though they'd lost sight of it, too. Would the commander continue his search for the echo pirates? The vote of impeachment was scheduled for little less than a month hence; if they did not turn for Soladis once the ship was repaired, he would lose what little time he had left to campaign against it. *What will he do if he loses?* He had not spoken to him of it. The man remained locked in his cabin. Zeke had not gone to him, and he had not been sent for. Part of him was horribly glad he was the only soldier who had survived the chaos on *Shadow Queen*. He did not want to think what would happen to anyone else who knew the truth.

One afternoon, after many hard hours of labor, he went below deck to check on the old woman in the brig. He descended two levels of stairs before he reached the ship's prison. Four sailors had been locked away for brawling; three more for stealing food, as they were on strict rations. As

Zeke walked the length of the row of cells, they gazed at him with hungry, angry, accusing eyes. Their faces were thin; the light cast by the lantern in his fist only deepened the shadows in their cheeks. The scent of rot and refuse washed over him. He shivered, chilled even through the warm wool of his uniform coat.

"Madam Bly?" Zeke said as he reached the cell set the furthest back against the ship wall. "I trust you are well?"

The imprisoned echo sat on a bed of straw. She was wrapped in a heavy quilt that Zeke had brought for her; still, she trembled. "No, I'm not," she snapped. "How can I be *well*? He's waiting for the right moment to split me. At my age, there's great power in my breaking."

She sounded like Eva. But sure of herself, in a way that left the hair on the back of his neck prickling. His stomach churned. He pressed his fist to his mouth, puffed his cheeks out with air. *Split*. He had heard Commander Gavon admit to it. *I must make them remember who I am.*

"If you came down here to beat me, I wouldn't, if I were you," said Dorothea. "You might kill me by accident. Gavon would flog you if you cost him an echo."

"I am an officer and a gentleman." Or he would be, once his foster bond expired. Twenty thousand acres, he'd been promised, and every honor due a hero of the Golden Republic. "You are deeply mistaken in your assessment of my character. I would never hurt an old woman."

"When you serve that man, you hurt every old woman in the Seaward Isles." She looked him over. "You grew up in the southern parts of New Soladis, didn't you?"

Zeke hesitated, then nodded. A god had placed a blessing on the waters that flowed from the springs of New Soladis that those who drank from them as children would grow into peerless soldiers. The details of the story were lost to history, but the magic still seeped into the local waters, affecting one in every twenty or so children in the frontier towns on that land. His height and the strength of his shoulders would always reveal where he'd come from. "Why do you ask?"

"There's many like you among the rebels. They tell stories. Tattoo them on their skin. There was a flourishing whiskey trade on New Soladis once. Hundreds of frontier folk got the money to move back to the Republic and build lives there. The commander had their assets seized and erased all their memory."

"He would never . . ."

"There's only one man on this ship who knows what Commander Gavon would and wouldn't do." Her dark eyes narrowed. "Why are you speaking with me instead of him?"

Zeke sighed. "I . . . my closest friend is an echo. And I miss her."

Dorothea shook her head. "You're no friend to echoes as long as you serve him."

Eva woke up twice that night, cold and sweating from a dream she could not remember. Both times, she looked about the crew's quarters, and thought how upset Lovett would be that they had moved his things. The next morning, threads of light danced in the turquoise sea, the sun rose high and hot through the cloudless blue, and Lovett was still dead.

Clad in a loose shirt and breeches, Eva stood on the upper deck, leaning against the rail as she surveyed the damage to their masts. The mizzenmast had cracked just below the topsail; the main mast, at the topgallant. Broken yards, the spars from which the sails hung, trailed from all three. The mail topsail had a three-foot rip through the canvass. She was most glad she had purchased repair supplies while training her power; only as she thought of that, she remembered training with Lovett, and the memory jabbed like loose wooden splinters.

"Could you haul a ship through Death?" Lizeth asked Eva. They strode up and leaned against the rail beside her. Their eyes were worn and red.

"The ship is my entry point," Eva said. "I don't know what would happen if I pulled a portal into Death inside itself. It might all explode. Like turning a bomb inside-out." She wondered if Lovett would have known if it was possible. *Oh, gods.*

The repair could only begin once they had removed the damaged sections of the mast. Eva and Lizeth fastened themselves into rope harnesses and climbed into the rigging. Tied to the stable section of the mast below, they held on to broken spars and pieces of the mast while Mr. Smoke threw lines of focused fire aloft to chop off the damaged parts. Clutching tight to the damaged pieces of wood, Eva and Lizeth lowered themselves to the deck, and set the scrap on a pile Cevette was chopping up for firewood. So it went. Eva lost herself in the work. The captain brought her hand-axe down over and over, like the beat of a drum.

Perhaps the fifth or the twelfth time Eva set a cracked spar down beside her and turned back toward the mainmast, she heard Cevette curse. When she looked back over her shoulder, Eva saw that a flying splinter had cut a red line down the captain's cheek.

"You're hurt," Eva said.

"It's fine," Cevette said, wiping the blood away with a handkerchief. "Back to work we go, Miss Gavon."

Traditional masts were each made from the trunk of a single great pine, but *Sea Wolf*'s were all composite. Some said it made for weaker masts, but, in Eva's view, there was nothing weaker than a mast that couldn't be replaced once damaged. They sawed and hewed, shaping the new mizzen topgallant from eight round timbers, then hoisted each one into position with ropes and winches, and locked iron rings about them to hold them in place. For hours, they strained in the hot sun. Sweat built on Eva's brow and palms. Once, the rope nearly slipped through her fingers as she tugged it to lift a timber aloft. Cevette stepped in beside her and grabbed the rope. Together, they gave it one great heave. The sailors atop the mizzenmast grabbed the timber and hoisted it into position.

"Easy now," Cevette said, her voice rough from tears. "Well done."

The air cooled as evening fell, but not a single breeze stirred the night. The exhausted crew gathered by the base of the mizzenmast. Some sat on woven grass mats; Eva leaned against the wall of the captain's cabin. As

Lizeth carved a quote from one of Lovett's favorite books into a section of the rail, Nukit dragged a crate into the center of their impromptu circle. "We got these on Dogshead," he said, and pried off the lid with a sword. "Best to eat them now, while they're still fresh."

Plump round oranges glowed in the light of the rising moon. "Thank you," Cevette said. She took one, parted the peel with her belt knife, and bit in. Juice ran down her chin.

Lovett never got to taste an orange. Eva drew a deep breath. One had to take one's pleasures when they could.

"Captain?" she said. "Will you come for a walk with me?"

Cevette nodded. For the first time all day, she smiled.

They descended the gangplank down into ankle-deep, low tide water. It lapped at their boots as, side by side, they slogged through the shallows to the beach. The white sand gleamed like bone. Stars spread above them in a shimmering veil. Eva looked up and traced familiar constellations, the same ones she had seen from her bedroom in Halston. The thief with a blood-red mouth, the swan maid and the snow queen, the broken crown. Old sailors' tales she had read of in books, dreaming of a life at sea. No matter what, she was glad that life was now hers.

"I'm sorry," Cevette said. "I wish I could do more to help."

"Lizeth said grief takes time."

"You shouldn't need to grieve." Cevette paused, and lowered her head. "I . . . I remembered that I had faced a moment like that before. That I had let a friend die. Donya says it isn't my fault, what happened to Lovett, what happened back then. But I feel as if there's something more I might have done. I only don't remember what it is." She chuckled, a sad sound. "Perhaps that's what's wrong with me. I blame myself for everything. Perhaps that's why my girl told me to leave."

"That's not it," Eva said. "I have always had a sense that you are capable of a great deal, even more than you know. You have your failings, but you also saved my life on *Shadow Queen*. We cannot always be at our best."

"I cannot always keep you safe."

"I don't expect you to," Eva said. "My faith is not in your strength, but in your deep integrity. You are profoundly deserving of my trust. I am honored to sail with a woman of your character."

As they stepped up onto the sand of the beach, their eyes met. A blush spreads over the captain's cheeks. She was such a beauty in the moonlight, her hair like shorn silver, her ruddy cheeks as copper as a coin. Beneath her white coat, her thin shirt clung to her skin, outlining every soft curve and taut line of her; she wore neither stays nor a bodice. Scrapes dotted her fingers from handling raw wood. From the shore, *Sea Wolf* could only be seen by the light of its lanterns. The two of them would be all but invisible to the ship. Cevette was the one real thing in the flat, endless darkness of the sandbar at night. Eva felt an overwhelming urge to cling to her.

"May I try some of the orange?" she said. Cevette passed it to her. She bit in and got a mouthful of dry rind.

Cevette sputtered. "No! You need to peel it first. Here, let me."

"I can do it!"

Cevette reached for the orange. Eva lifted it up high. Cevette jumped for it, and knocked into her. They tumbled backward into the sand. It puffed up around them in a ghostly cloud. Cevette did not hesitate. She straddled Eva's waist with her muscular thighs and smiled down at her. "Come now. Give me the orange."

Eva stretched out her arm, keeping the fruit from Cevette's grasp. "Not until you answer me this. Why did you come along with Korinne when she captured me? Was it because I'm part of your crew? Or was there something . . . more?"

"I would have done it for any member of the crew," Cevette said. "But I am glad I had the chance to do it for you." She rolled off Eva, and sat cross-legged in the sand. Eva sat up, pulling her knees up to her chest, and kept the orange out of reach. "Since that night in my cabin, after the *Pleasant Mary* raid, I have regretted how I conducted myself toward you. I was glad of the opportunity to speak with other echoes on *Shadow Queen*; I cannot claim to fully understand, but I know it was a grave insult for me to imply I could so easily change one echo for another."

She drew a deep breath, and continued. "The truth is, I loved a woman long ago: deeply, profoundly, and truly loved her. I do not wish to replace her. But since I met you, I have dreamed less of my losses and more of what you and I could have together. It would be different. It would be unique. And—I can promise you this—it would matter a great deal to me."

Eva nodded. A lump swelled up in her throat. She could barely speak. She had been so painfully wrong. About herself. About her captain. "I asked for too much, that night in your cabin. We've only known each other a short while. I have no right to expect a pledge of *forever,* I thought you saw me as only an echo to replace another echo, and I thought such a promise would ensure you would not discard me without care. But you would never. Even if things ended between us, you would treat me with respect. I did not realize I was both an echo and a person in your eyes. I thought less of myself, and I let myself think less of you. But I am certain now, whatever the future holds, whatever lies in your past, I do not need to protect my heart from you."

Their eyes met. The captain slid closer to her. Eva hoped she was reading this moment correctly. "Do you want the orange back?" she whispered.

"Fuck the orange." Cevette's fingers slid through her hair and wrapped around the back of her head. The space between their lips was a hair's breath, infinite—and then it closed like a wave rushing across the sand. Cevette's kiss was the slightest brush, light as a downy feather, tasting of oranges and tears. "Did you like that?"

In answer, Eva slid her fingers through that short, sandy hair and pulled Cevette's mouth firmly against hers. Their tongues tangled together. Eva breathed in her scent of salt and smoke. As they came apart, Cevette laughed, and it seemed like a secret treasure shared only between two.

"Help me get this off," Cevette said. Eva undid the ties on Cevette's coat, the white leather smooth beneath her fingertips. It dropped from her shoulders and spread out beneath them in the sand. "Gods, Eva, you awaken me. My body sings at your touch." Eva pulled her shirt up over her head and tossed it away. Firmly and decisively, Cevette unlaced her quilted jump stays. Her bare skin pricked in the night as they came away. Cevette set the stays down neatly on her coat. She reached out to caress Eva's breast, then bent low to kiss the pale flesh.

Electric shivers ran up Eva's spine. Her lips parted in a gasp of pleasure. She reached out and undid the lace of Cevette's shirt. It fell off her broad, well-muscled shoulders, baring her to the moonlight. Faint tan lines stretched across her collarbone; her breasts hung full and ample. Eva ran her fingers over Cevette's many scars, drinking the heat of her skin, making every inch of her a memory.

"Lower," Cevette gasped. "Will you go lower?" Eva nodded. Her fingers plunged down Cevette's breeches, through a thicket of hair, to the heart of her. The *heat* of her. The captain groaned, and ground down against her. Eva stroked, rolled, pinched, and kissed all other words from her lips. Cevette shuddered. Her gasps rose higher and higher. Mere heartbeats passed, each one a straining eternity, until at last Cevette came undone. Her head tilted back. Her lips gasped, "Evazina!" She trembled, and Eva shook with her. "Gods. Divine mercy."

As her last small quakes died away, she laid a hand on the buckle of Eva's breeches. "May I?"

"Yes," Eva whispered. "*Please.*"

"Lie back on my coat."

Eva obeyed. They shifted around so that Cevette knelt before her. The captain opened the buckle and rolled down Eva's breeches and underclothes; then she pulled Eva's legs up on her shoulders, gripping her firmly by the thighs. The slope of the beach made the angles work. The captain's tongue slid up through her lower lips and curled around the heart of her pleasure. Each strode sent waves of warm lighting up through her stomach. She tipped her head back and let them roll through her. "Cevette, oh Cevette, oh—" Pleasure leapt within her, washing all else away.

At last, the storm within them quieted. Cevette lay down with Eva atop her coat. Eva held her captain against her and stroked her short hair. The pound of their heartbeats slowed, but they still beat in unison.

A cold shock slammed through them both as a wave ran up the beach and doused them.

Cevette swore and jumped to her feet. Eva sat up, fumbling to pull her breeches back on. "Where did that come from?" she said.

"The sea," said Cevette, and smiled.

Commander Gavon's cabin on *Kembrielle* was sparsely decorated and orderly to a fault. The four-poster bed was made with a single thin mattress. Two sea-chests sat at its foot. Books and naval charts lay in neat stacks on the desk. A great window at the back looked out on the sea; the commander stood before it, gazing out on waves without end, rubbing his chin. Instead of his suit and sash of office, he wore only a weathered shirt and breeches. Silver threaded through his hair. He looked small, and rather lost. Almost vulnerable.

Please, Zeke prayed to whatever god might be listening as he shut the cabin door and stood at attention in the entryway. *Let him be something I can understand.*

The commander gave him a cursory glance, then gazed back out the window. "What would you have of me, Ezekiel?"

"Honesty. I chose you over my closest friend. And I don't even know who you are. If our love is to be worth that cost, I need you to tell me the truth. Now."

The commander shrugged. "Very well. I assume you must have questions, after what you witnessed on *Shadow Queen.* I owe you this much at least. Ask, and I will do my best to answer."

"How . . . how old are you?" Zeke blurted out.

"Older than I look. I confess, I've lost track of my exact age."

"Did you truly lead a revolution against the gods?"

"Do you think I could make up a story like that? It's as you've learned. The Theocracy was real. The revolution was real. All I have done is shift about our memory of that time, concealing certain details and emphasizing others. But that's what every telling of history does."

Zeke took one step toward him. Then another. Each click of boots on the wooden floor sounded a bit too loud. The pounding of his heartbeat filled his ears. "How many times have you founded—or *recreated*—the Golden Republic?"

"Seven or eight times." He sighed. "It's a good deal of work, making everyone remember that I only just defeated the gods a few weeks ago. It takes dozens of echoes. And the army needs to confiscate so many books. I try to line it up with a purge of the universities and the philosophers' guild, but . . . oh, gods, Ezekiel. Don't look at me like that. The citizens of the Republic have elected me to make these difficult decisions. My hand may do the deed, but we have all determined together that we are willing to pay the price of civilization."

"No one votes for *this*." Zeke's stomach churned. For a moment, he was glad that his foster bond prevented him from casting a ballot.

"On the contrary. Many citizens are happy to accept this state of affairs. I would not have soldiers to guard my archives if that was not true."

"That's a small handful of us. Every other soldier in the army—everyone sworn to die in your service—has been convinced to trust you out of lies."

"Every general has his secrets. I cannot lead an army without them. It's the only way."

"The only way for you to stay in power." Zeke came a few steps closer. He grabbed one of the posts at the foot of the bed to steady himself.

"Gods, I wish you were old enough to remember the years directly following the revolution. I suppose that, if I need to start over again, you will be. I'll make you known as a revolutionary hero the next time around." Zeke shuddered at that. The commander moved toward him. He reached out and put a hand on Zeke's shoulder. "Listen to me. It's not about my power. It's about *our* power. A power that stretches back to the great Empire of Soladis. When the world believes the revolution has only just ended, all the Soladisean people, whether we live in Soladis itself or the far-flung reaches of its ancient colonies, can put aside their differences and come together as one nation. We can establish a new government. We can expand our borders. We can prosper. But, with time, the gentry of Soladis remember their pride and the Terraloro of the south remember their Sea People heritage. It drives us apart. There is no Republic without the sacrifices. It cannot be. We must only remember what holds us together."

"You," Zeke said. His heart hammered against his ribs. His head spun. *The truth. I have the truth now.* It should have been enough. *This is the man I love.* "You've taught us that the Republic is good and fair. You've taught us that, as citizens, we are entitled to rights and freedoms within its lands. But you treat us as puppets and as pawns—"

"Ezekiel." The commander pulled him in closer. Pressed his lips to Zeke's neck.

"No!" Zeke wrenched free of his grip and stepped backward. "Sir, I beg of you. Be the leader I know you can be. The one who saved us from the gods. The one who cares about democracy and justice. That's the man we need to make the Republic everything that it can be. I'm only a soldier, I have no experience with such things, but . . . it must be possible. If we try."

Commander Gavon fell quiet. His gray eyes went cold. A vein pulsed in his neck. His voice deepened as he spoke. "What would you have me do?"

"Don't split the prisoner. Return to Soladis. Face the vote of impeachment. Accept what the Assembly chooses. Show us—show me—that the democracy you fought to build truly matters to you."

The commander took another step toward Zeke. He tilted up his head and looked the younger man over, studying him with eyes as dark as night. "Very well," he said at last "I will return to Soladis, speak with my allies, and face the vote of the Assembly. For now, I will leave Madam Bly unbroken. But I will need your help. Can I rely on you, Ezekiel?"

Zeke drew a deep breath and squared his shoulders. He could not smile, not yet. But he could accept this. If he did not, his soul would shatter. "I'm with you, sir. For the Republic. For us all."

BREAKING THE NEWS

BEGINNING ABOARD *SEA WOLF*, ON AN UNKNOWN SANDBAR, CONTIN-UING ON TO THE CITY OF SOLADIS, AND FROM THERE ONTO VARIOUS PLACES BEYOND. 15TH MORGHASMONTH, YEAR TWENTY-TWO OF THE GOLDEN REPUBLIC.

Doubtless there are some readers among you who believe I am overly sympathetic toward the pirates, that I should speak more critically of them, present them as amoral beasts lest I romanticize their way of life. Do we not all desire some romance from our lives? Do we not all hear the call of the far horizon? It is a deeply-rooted part of human nature to yearn to be part of some great story, though the reality of adventure can be somewhat more grim. So I will indulge this foolish desire of mine, and say this: the pirates provided me with assistance when I was in dire need of it, and in this, I found them greater exemplars of citizenship than many of the most upstanding gentlemen of Soladis. –'A Pirate's Life,' published in *The Silver Sentinel*.

IN THE WEEKS SHE spent on the sandbar island, Eva made three fond memories. The first was of the moment Cevette pulled her legs atop her shoulders; the second was of the whole crew looking on and smiling as she carried the chest of her belongings across the deck and stashed it inside the captain's cabin; and the third was of hammering in the last peg to lock the new main royal yard in position. She had always dreamed that she might one day help to build a ship with her own two hands.

Replacing the damaged rigging lines and sails was the work of several days. Then, they waited. From the position of the stars and the information on Lord Merris' map, Cevette and Eva worked out there was another small archive a few day's sail away. Cevette briefly consulted with Lizeth about using their magic to bolster the wind, which they said they could do, but the use of such force might damage the current carrying fish south to the Sapphire Isles, and so the captain chose to wait for the winds to recover of their own accord.

With little else to do, Eva and Cevette found themselves tangled up in bed more, their fingers and their tongues and an intriguing Soladisean instrument flinging them over the brink again and again. When they tired, they would lie together, and Cevette would listen as Eva talked at length about ship construction and naval warfare. At times, a distant look would cross the captain's face, and she would gaze out her window at the sea. Eva would tug her back into the bed, then, and, with a passion that made up a fair amount for her lack of practice, show Cevette how deeply she adored her. The captain began to smile more frequently, but Eva knew the sadness still lay within her, and that they would have to face it in time.

The currents picked up, and with them, a day later, came the wind. On the morning when the ship's flag at last began to stir, all hands gathered on the upper deck. The thin trickle of breeze played with Eva's hair as they gathered in groups of four or five at the starboard rail. Each group took up a clumsily-constructed wooden pole, nailed together from debris and leftover spars from the repairs, and drove it down into the sand where the stuck ship tilted. Eva was assigned to a pole with Cevette, Mr. Smoke, and Tuk. She stood in a line with them both, directly behind her captain, consciously aware that she had much less physical strength to lend to the effort, and that passion mattered very little here.

The tide began to rise. The pale blue waters deepened in color and swirled about the hull of *Sea Wolf.* The ship creaked. Groaned. Slowly, it began to shift on the sand.

"Now!" Cevette shouted. All the crew flung their weight behind the makeshift poles. The wood sank deep into the loose sand. It seemed as if nothing was happening. One pole cracked. Splinters fell down into the sea. "All of you, push!"

Eva set her jaw and threw her whole weight behind the pole. Sweat trickled down the back of her neck. Her palms slipped. Splinters stung at her hands. "Push!" Cevette shouted, lowering her shoulder. Eva followed suit. Pain shot through her back. She ground her teeth together. "Push!" Her boots slipped on the deck. She nearly slammed into Tuk. A callus tore on her palm. Blood dripped on the wood.

And *Sea Wolf* slid free. The poles dropped from the sailors' hands and splashed down in the high tide as she leapt forward into the sapphire sea. A great cheer rose up from the crew. They tossed their hats aloft and thrust their fists in the air. Cevette smiled up at Eva, who leaned down for a well-earned salty kiss.

"No more vanishing in your cabin, you two." Donya said, striding over to them. The scarf that held back her curls had come undone as she'd pushed. Cevette gestured toward it with a tilt of her head; Donya nodded, and Cevette went to tie it back up. "There's work to be done. Eva, give me your hand."

She held it out. As Donya cleaned the cut, Eva looked to Cevette and said, "Now that we're away, I should run to Soladis. I want to check in on Tomis Beauchamp, and I would like to make certain my brother is well."

"Go," Cevette said. "Give my best wishes to Tomis. And my most middling wishes to that brother of yours."

Eva laughed. "You only met him the once."

"True," said Cevette, "because he lacked the courage to claim the Skull-runner and run off with me."

A welcome heat prickled in Eva's cheeks. *She thinks me brave. And she likes me better than Andreas.*

"Gods, cousin," Donya said. "I thought you cared about family."

"I care about Eva. And if she tells me not to mock her egotistical ass of a brother, I'll hold off."

"You have my permission to mock him," Eva said. "He thinks too highly of himself. Some humbling might be good for him."

"I heartily recommend that you call him a pompous ass for the benefit of his health, then." Cevette smiled. "Travel safely. I will be missing you."

"Good," Eva said, and winked at her. "That means I'm hard to forget."

As Eva arrived in Soladis, she took care to enter the city somewhere inside the gates, in an alley behind a butcher's shop where an apprentice had died slipping on ice. It was a bit of a long walk to the printers' shop from there. A damp haze hung in the air; muffling the city sounds of arguing voices and horses' hooves, clinging to her skin most uncomfortably, but it provided her with a good excuse to wear a heavy cloak and keep her hood up. Through the cobblestone alleyways of the lower city she went, wind whistling in her ears, stirring the posters with her face. Passerbys knocked elbows with her as they went. Soldiers marched past in orderly ranks. She kept her head low.

At last, she reached the printers' shop. The narrow alley out front was all but deserted. The guard tower and the wall behind it cast it in shadow. Eva did not see the figure in the dark cloak on the doorstep until the two of them all but collided. There was a shout; she drew daggers from her sleeves as a rapier flashed at his waist. Then the figure pulled back his hood.

"Andreas!" Eva dropped her knives and threw her arms around him. His eyes widened. A heartbeat later, he hugged her back, his bony arms filled with a desperate clutching strength.

"Eva," he whispered. "*Gods.*"

They had spent long stretches of time separated before. Andreas always traveled south to Soladis with the commander when he went for Assembly meetings. She did not know where this sudden surge of affection came from, but she was glad of it all the same.

Eva pulled back a few inches. "What happened to your face?" A healing scar snaked through his left eyebrow. "Were you in a fight?"

"I wouldn't call it a fight. I didn't do any fighting. No. I was jumped in the streets. Someone fools thought I was you, and wanted your bounty." He sighed, a bit theatrically, and leaned back against the whitewashed brick wall of the printers' shop, as if such attacks befell him every day. He spun a wooden pipe in his fingers, then tapped out ashes; he must have stepped outside for a touch of smokeweed. "Ever since, I've been staying with Beauchamp. He's a good man to know."

"He is," Eva said. "I'm sorry you've faced such troubles." She wondered how many echoes had suffered similar violence or worse because of her. *I'm sorry,* she thought. *I'm trying to help you all.* "If Tomis' household isn't safe enough, you may come back to *Sea Wolf* with me. You'll be safe there."

"Safe on that ship? With that captain who shot me? She's a dreadful woman. I don't see how you can stand her."

"Captain Zarcanzi is a good woman. Honorable, dedicated, brave—"

"Ah, I see. You don't stand her. You take her lying down."

Blood rushed into Eva's cheeks. "Well. Yes. But I would still speak in her favor if she didn't."

"And I shall politely decline to join you and your lady-love on her boat." Andreas laughed. "I can protect myself. I've survived the Republic well enough for twenty-two years."

Her voice took on a heavier, more sober tone as she remembered what she had to tell him. *Ten years.* "There's something you must know."

She explained it all to him. Ariella, the echo they had come from. Korinne, the twin she had left behind. The magical protection that kept their father from being killed. The true age of the Golden Republic. The fraudulent nature of their childhood. "So, as you see," she finished, "you were the favorite child from the start."

Andreas had gone very pale. He bit his lip, rocking back and forth on the balls of his feet. Reaching inside his cloak, he drew out a small packet of smokeweed, added it to his pipe, and lit it with a flint striker. He took a puff, and then, in a voice somewhat higher than his usual pitch, said, "I'm the favorite because I'm more like him, you know? That is the only way he knows to measure worthiness."

"Oh," Eva said. "I never thought of that. I suppose . . . I suppose it must be difficult to take pride in your own achievements, if everything you value most in yourself is tainted by his regard."

"He can take a good deal from me, but I refuse to let him take my pride." Andreas took a deep breath of pipe smoke. "How do you feel? You said you confronted him about what he had done. That you told him he was not your father."

"I can accept the truth," Eva said, quietly. "I always wanted him to be a better father to us. But we're echoes. We have each other. And I have no more desire to chase the love of a man who rips us apart." Then, so she could speak of anything that wasn't terrifying, she said, "What else have you been about since you arrived in the city? Did your girl from Halston come with you?"

"Mary? No. In truth, I decided she was tiring."

Eva allowed herself a small moment of petty joy at the fact she had a girl and Andreas didn't. "And how is the philosophers' guild? Have you spent much time there?"

Andreas sighed. "They cast me out. For speaking out in the defense of echoes." He laughed, a small, bitter laugh. "To be precise, it was for speaking out in defense of echoes while having the nerve to be an echo myself."

"Oh. I'm so sorry." Her brother wanted so dearly to be one of the great intellectuals of the Republic. Part of her had always envied that there was a place in the Republic he could aspire to. Eva, lacking his social graces, would never have the same. She had never realized that place might be taken from Andreas on the basis of what he was; that an echo who exemplified every virtue the Soladisean people valued was still an echo.

A wind billowed down the narrow alleyway that led to the printers' shop. Straw and twigs danced on the breeze. The posters waved like banners. Andreas pulled the hood of his cloak back up; Eva checked that hers concealed her face. *We're in this together, the two of us.* Their differences seemed so small now. They were echoes; they were family.

"I'm sorry about the guild," she said. "That must have taken a good deal of courage, to stand up for us. I don't believe I could have done the same."

Andreas chuckled. He took another hit of his pipe and passed it to her. "If you'd been there, you would have stabbed several philosophers."

"I would never," Eva said. It was more a habit than anything. Belatedly, she remembered punching Lord Merris in the teeth. "Right, well, I might have some rough words with them, but I know I shouldn't." She took a deep breath of smokeweed, letting the pungent scent fill her lungs, and passed it back to him.

"Is there such a thing as should or shouldn't for echoes? No matter what we do, the world treats us with equal disdain."

"That doesn't give us license to do whatever we want. It only means we must find our own way."

"Very philosophical. Are you truly my sister? Show me your godmarks."

"Here they are," she said, and pulled back her right glove. Andreas raised an eyebrow. Oh. That had been a joke. "I've been more thoughtful as of late. I want there to be more of me in my head, and less of the commander."

"*Less of the commander* is urgently needed." With a sigh, Andreas took one more hit from his pipe, and tapped the ashes out in the road. "Come now. Tomis needs your help."

Together, they ducked into the printers' shop, shut the door tight, and pulled off their hoods. The shop was much the same as when Eva had first visited a month before. The day was dark, and the apprentices had lit a half-dozen lanterns; they were hanging them from hooks along the wall as the twins walked in. The scent of dust and woodshavings still made Eva's nose itch. Melody worked the heavy lever on the press; her arms bare to the shoulder. The heavy stamping plate went up and down. Stefayne turned the rounce handle; freshly-inked papers slid out from under the platen, and blank pages slid in. Both gave cursory nods to the echoes in the doorway.

"Miss Gavon!" Tomis made his way toward Eva and Andreas, pushing his way through the stacked-up crates of printed papers that filled the shop nearly from wall to wall, clad in a sky-blue suit with a diamond broach on his lapel. "Good day!" He reached into one crate, pulled out a newspaper, and handed it to her. Beneath the masthead of trumpeting cherubs was the headline, 'Citizens Beware – Secret Sacrifice of Innocent Echoes – Commander Gavon Engages in Occult Manipulations.'

The article detailed, in neat, clear language, how Commander Gavon used echoes and the magic of Iunos to ensure his rule went unquestioned, stealing the history of the Isles and altering the minds of his own people. Eva had known this all to be true for a good while, yet rage rose in her as she read, which, she thought, proved the quality of the work. Tomis also assured his readers that the Skullrunner was *freeing* their memories, not forcing false ones upon them. 'Evazina Gavon seeks justice for us all.' His earnest defense of her warmed her heart.

There was a second article beneath it. The headline read 'An Echo's Story – A Patriotic Account – by Andreas Jonathan Gavon.' It was a brief biographical sketch of her brother, detailing his scholarship, his admission to the philosophers' guild, his father's praise, and his friendships among the Republic's elite. It described the indignities foisted upon him, the insults, the lack of citizenship, the cruel beating he'd suffered. It ended with a plea for the Republic to sympathize with the echoes who lived among them, to acknowledge their personhood, and to accept they too deserved the rights of citizens.

Eva liked it, though she could not help but feel a slight sting at how Andreas had rooted his arguments for the echoes in his own achievements. She could not fit into the Republic in the same way he did; and it was hard to imagine the echoes she had met on Dogshead or on *Shadow Queen* could either. As she finished reading, she looked to Andreas and said, "You ask the Republic to have mercy upon us; there is an implicit promise that they should do so because we are or can be like you. But many of us cannot. Many of us *will* not."

"I couldn't write this story about you," Andreas said. "You are not someone with whom the public sympathizes."

"The echoes of *Shadow Queen* and Dogshead . . . none of them live as you do. This will not give the Republic an accurate view of our position." She hesitated. "How many echoes did you speak with as you wrote this?"

"I only associate with the echoes it is fitting to know. There aren't many of those."

Along the back of the shop, the apprentices had begun to argue with Melody, all three children vociferously insisting they had finished all their chores. One of them kicked over a box of type. Small lead blocks scattered across the wooden floor. A furious Melody gave them all a warning look; they dropped to their knees and began picking up type.

Tomis cleared his throat. "We're glad you came, Miss Gavon. We have need of your gifts. I anticipate the army may try to censor this paper."

"I assume they will," she said. "I believe they do it quite frequently."

Tomis nodded. "They can't hope to stop everything—in truth, they wouldn't, for the illegal papers are far more entertaining and informational, but they move fiercely against papers that go too far. I'm not afraid of the risk, mind you. But there's no good in writing the story if every copy is burned on its way to its destination."

"You need the Skullrunner to distribute them."

"If you would be so kind," Tomis said. "I would have brought this up when we last spoke, but I assumed you would be back to visit in a more timely manner."

She blushed. "My apologies. I was distracted."

"I hope all is well aboard your ship."

"The last few weeks have been rather overwhelming. But I'm pleased to say that Captain Zarcanzi and I have . . . made progress . . ."

"Congratulations! That's quite an accomplishment."

Andreas sighed. "It's a love affair, not some great discovery. Speak more of the paper delivery."

"Of course," Tomis said. "It will be a good deal easier with Miss Gavon to help." Eva grinned at that. Andreas folded his arms across his chest. "She'll get them out before they can stop us. Even if the army tries to seize the papers, even if the commander tries to erase these words from memory, the print copies will be everywhere. The people will have undeniable proof the commander is manipulating them."

"Then," Andreas said, "on the morning of the vote of impeachment, we will reveal the greatest truths. We will burn the memories locked away in the archive beneath Assembly Hall."

Eva stared at him. She pressed her fingers to her lips. "Tomis told you of our excursion?" Her brother nodded. "I do want to burn them. But how do you propose we deal with the soldiers?"

"I have a plan," Andreas said. "I can get the soldiers out of there. All I'll need is someone with convincing mannerisms to impersonate an officer of the Republic. Trust me."

Eva nodded. "Cevette—Captain Zarcanzi—she can do that."

"Of course," Andreas said. "I'm certain Captain Zarcanzi could put out the demon fires on the moon if she put her mind to it."

Quickly, Tomis explained how he distributed his papers. He had an agreement with several rings of smugglers who would purchase papers from him when they sailed near Soladis. The smugglers would then sell the papers to news dealers when they reached port. Tomis had travelled extensively through the Isles and had met most of his dealers himself; he had established passcodes with them so they might know a message—or a messenger—came directly from him.

Two days later, all the papers were printed and ready to sell. Eva returned to the shop in the early morning and filled a satchel with papers. Tomis gave her a long, rolled-up piece of parchment covered in notes. "This has everything you need to know. Don't let anyone take that from you. Swallow it if you must."

Her first destination was a harbor town on the Five Sisters island of New Soladis. She stepped out of Death beneath a dockside gallows. A gust of cold wind nearly knocked her flat as she stepped out into the snow-swept day, loose flurries of snow stinging her cheeks like needles. She pulled her long cloak tight about her, and was very glad of the sturdy leather gloves she wore. Down the dock, the small wooden buildings of the town were covered in deep drifts, only visible by the smoke rising from their chimnies. Slabs of floating ice drifted along the deep black waters of the northern sea. Fishing vessels and trading kayaks bobbed in the surf; merchants dressed in heavy furs bartered and shivered in the wind.

As Tomis had told her, the news dealer sat atop a stack of barrels near where the dock met the land. He was a boy of fifteen with a long scarf and a spotty face; he also sold fresh cod. Eva rushed toward him, nearly slipping on ice as she did. She leaned on one of his barrels for balance. Her teeth chattered as she said the password. "Endless river."

"You come from Beauchamp?" The boy dug in his pocket and pulled out a small, knitted purse. It jingled with coin. Eva nodded. She slung the satchel down from her shoulder, opened it, and pulled out one hundred copies, tied in a neat bundle. As she held it out to the boy, their eyes met. He gave her a thorough look-over. "*Echo,*" he whispered, as if the word was a curse.

Eva stiffened. Andreas would have pretended not to hear. Korinne would have thrown him and his fish into the sea. She only wanted to run and hide. Well, she could run and hide, but it would make her no less an echo, and it would not change that this needed to be done. "I'm the echo who has your papers," she said. "Hand over the money and I'll go."

He handed her the purse. She counted the coins, tucked them in the bag at her waist, and all but shoved her papers in his hands before re-shoulder- ing the satchel and walking away.

Eva had lived her whole life in the Five Sisters, but only now did she have the freedom to explore them. Winter held the northern islands in a tight grasp, and stinging cold seeped through her coat whenever she stepped out of Death. Thankfully, the news dealers were easy to find. They sulked around ports and markets, bundles of paper tucked under their arms, darting into shadows whenever soldiers passed. She murmured passcodes, traded copies of *The Silver Sentinel* for tiny sacks of silver, and watched the dealers rush off to wave the papers about as eager readers queued up to buy. Wherever she went, she was greeted with fearful looks and cutting words.

She knew these lands had been devastated by Morghaia and her legions of the dead. She had glimpsed as much eating pears in the orchard of Iunos. As she ran through the northern lands, she could feel the marks Morghaia's battles had left on the halls of Death. The watchtowers of dark brick she had raised on the hilltops still stood across much of New Soladis. Both within the Republic's borders and out in the frontier towns, doors and walls were painted with the symbols of philosophers and hedgewitches to ward off the dead. She felt some sympathy for their fears. She only hoped they would also feel sympathy for the real and present fears of the echoes.

Within the city of Soladis, Tomis had his own courier network; the apprentices would run the papers to the distributors behind its walls. But the rest of that great isle was hers to cover. Eva stopped by the printers' shop to drop off the coin and pick up more copies. Then she set her course to the south. She ran to villages up and down the great cliffs of its western coast; one where twisted black windmills sprouted like mushrooms from the rock, another where buildings built on bridges spanned a vast chasm. The inland towns were trickier to slip in and out of; the sprawling hamlets with their famed wineries and bustling shops were also thick with soldiers. Twice, she was spotted and chased off; once, she had to throw a knife through a soldier's thigh to get away. Her marks were still hidden with gloves, and she'd made certain to step through portals only when there was no one about to see. It was the echo they hated, not the Skullrunner. She did not know what to do about that.

In the mid-afternoon, she reached a town in the south of Soladis. She stepped out of Death behind a tall chapel of white brick and quickly crossed the bustling town square. Dust flew up under her boots as she darted into the shop Tomis had told her of. *White Swallow News and Books.* Only when the door shut behind her could she take a breath.

It was the largest of all the shops she had entered that day, perhaps a thousand feet square, warmed by three crackling hearths along the wall, The air smelled of paper and the ceder wood of the bookshelves stretching out in their long rows. All was quiet, save for the patrons walking up and down the shelves murmuring to one another as they perused rare volumes from all over the Isles.

She walked down the central aisle to the clerk's desk. The woman behind it smiled as she approached. Eva nearly glanced back over her shoulder to see if someone else, unheard, had come in behind her.

"By the sweet water," she said, giving the password. The clerk nodded. Eva opened her satchel and pulled out a bundle of two hundred and fifty copies. She set it on the desk. The clerk gave her a bag of coins. As Eva counted them out and slid them in her own purse, the clerk reached across the desk and pressed her hand to Eva's cheek. "A blessing," she said.

Oh. Eva smiled. "Thank you," she said. A sweet lightness bubbled up in her chest as she turned and walked down the aisle. Perhaps she was welcome here.

Two men were entering through the door as she reached it. Both glimpsed her face under her hood and tapped their fingers on her shoulder as they passed. "A blessing," they murmured, and went about their business. Her skin crawled. Her smile lessened.

As she stepped back out into the square, she saw the white brick chapel from the front. The arched doorway was carved in the shape of a portal into Death.

Her stomach churned. *They still pray to Morghaia here.* It was not *her* they welcomed, not at all.

She turned her back on the town and ran into Death.

Back to Tomis she went, one last time, to refill her satchel. Then she set her course farther south, to the Sapphire Isles. Her legs burned as she ran. Her shoulders ached. She pushed herself onward. Every twine-tied bundle of papers she passed on gave her strength. Thousands would make their way into the world. Try as the army might, they would never be able to confiscate so many.

She reached the Sapphire Isles by the early evening. There were three separate dealers in Port Dueno alone, and two more in the highlands beyond the city. She ran through the coastal farmlands, where the flags of the Viridian League flew alongside that of the Republic over their vast fields and the small houses where their fosterling laborers dwelled, and into the highlands, where Terraloro families grew root vegetables and raised goats. In towns and villages, the buildings painted with murals and alive with evening conversation, some news dealers leapt in fear at the sight of her, but all were eager to receive papers decrying the Republic.

She ran southeast, carrying the news to the smallest and most remote of the Sapphire Isles. One was little more than a great slab of volcanic glass and black stone. It boasted a single small fishing village, the buildings of which rose on stilts over the waves. Eva arrived there near midnight. She ducked out of her portal behind the village healer's and made her way along the boardwalk that connected the houses of the sleeping villagers. Coughs and snores filled the night as she made her way to the home of the news dealer.

It was a round structure, the walls and roof made from lightweight bamboo. A lantern made from a coconut carved with lacelike patterns still shone in the open, glassless window. A painted sign leaned against the wall, advertising the sale of news, books, thread, fine cloth, fish traps, and medicines. Glass bottles hung on strings along the underside of the roof, clanking against each other in the cool night wind. Eva walked up to the window, her footsteps light on the boards. She knocked on the side of the window and said, "Beans and starlight."

"Mmm?" The voice was familiar. There came a shuffling sound as the village news dealer stood. "You come from Beauchamp? Oh!" An echo stepped into view. She wore a loose white tunic and billowing trousers. Her hair was trimmed short. She was about Korinne's age, perhaps a decade Eva's senior. A smile crept across her face. "Sister. It's good to see one of us. It's been a very long time since I have." With that, she reached both her arms out through the window.

Eva hesitated. *She's an echo.* It had been a hard day. She had seen a good deal of the world, and had felt very alone in it. Everything she had been told about echoes felt very small and distant. What was real and close was this woman. An echo. Someone like her. Who would understand.

Eva pulled the other echo into a tight hug. "It's good to see you, too," she whispered. "It's very good to see you."

In Soladis, the night was alive with the sound of rustling papers.

The apprentices and the distributors had done their work. As Andreas stepped out into a market square, Tomis and Stefayne strolling along hand-in-hand behind him, he saw that every soul, from the oldest grey-beard to merest pageboys, was reading by the light of the lampposts that gleamed every few feet. Up in the tall townhouses with ornate facades that lined the square, lights went dark and maids threw shutters across the windows The stalls were shuttered, all but one that was selling roast sausage on sticks. Andreas bought one and listened to the cityfolk whisper.

Commander Gavon. Echoes. Sacrifices. Our history. Our memories.

A smirk spread across Andreas' face. Then he noticed a man giving him a dangerous look; so he bit it down.

A large group had gathered around the market well; a crowd of nearly a hundred, passing about copies of the paper and murmuring in low voices. Most wore solid homespun suits and gowns; some wore the orange wool coats and insignia of Republic officers, and a select few wore the formal wigs of the gentry. Their brows were furrowed in fury. Their hands were shaking in fear. A man shouted a curse.

Andreas ate his sausage as he strolled toward them. Juice ran down his chin. He licked it off his lips. dabbed it with a handkerchief. *I did this,* he told himself. *After countless years of futile struggle, I am the echo who discovered how to bring Commander Gavon down.*

"We did it," Tomis said, coming up behind him. He had an arm around Stefayne's waist; with his free hand, he slapped Andreas on the shoulder. "A noble effort. All of us, working together—look at all we've accomplished here!" He looked to the gathered crowd. "Say something. Urge them to action."

Andreas nodded. Yes. That would be wise. The paper had gripped their attention; now he had to put it to use. He squared his shoulders, stepped forward, and cleared his throat. The crowd turned to look at him. Their eyes were wide; he could see that much. He could not read their expressions very well elsewise.

"My friends," he said, and licked his lips again. A bit of grease had distracted him. "I am most grateful for the honor you have done my people by taking the time out of your evening to read of our struggle . . ."

A few of the citizens in the crowd pulled their papers closer to their chests. *By the gods.* That was fear. He knew that much.

Andreas glanced back over his shoulder and quietly said to Tomis, "You do it."

"Are you certain? This moment is about your people."

"It's about all of us," Andreas said. *If it was only about echoes, it would not matter.*

"Very well." Tomis rubbed his hands together. Shoulders back, chest puffed out, he took three long strides toward the crowd at the well and clapped his hands. "People of Soladis!" The cool night wind stirred his red curls. His voice rang through the night. "By now, we have all read the article in *The Silver Sentinel* concerning the abuses of echoes by Commander Gavon. I call on you now to write to your representatives in the Assembly and demand they pass the vote of impeachment to remove Commander Gavon from office."

For a moment, no one spoke. Then a wave of nods swept through the crowd. One man thrust his fist aloft. Even the army officers seemed grimly resigned. "Time we got rid of him," said one woman. "The taxes are too high anyhow." Another woman said, "It's not fitting for a man of the Five Sisters to rule us. He had no respect for the traditions of Soladis." A man said "I heard he's fucking a boy from the northern frontier. Bet that's why he sends our taxes to build forts in the north."

Tomis stepped back and looked to Andreas and Stefayne. "That went well enough," he said. "I only wish we'd had time to add everything Eva told us about his immortality and whatnot. A pity the paper had already gone to press."

Stefayne shuddered. "It's a good deal of *whatnot*. I can't believe you didn't run screaming when Andreas told us what he's done."

Tomis laughed. "Ah, my sweet, what's fearful about knowledge?"

"I believe what we told them will be enough," Andreas said. "My father has outlived his use as their hero." Yet it struck him that no one was speaking about *his* article, only the one Tomis had written. They were not speaking about the echoes at all.

They want to hate him more than they want to help us.

For the first time in his life, Andreas hoped he was wrong .

MUHLEMLO

ON MUHLEMLO, WHICH THE SOLADISEANS ALSO CALL MAZE POINT, THE HOME OF THE MUHLEMLI PEOPLE, THREE HUNDRED AND SEVENTY MILES SOUTH OF THE CITY OF SOLADIS. 19TH MORGHASMONTH, YEAR TWENTY-TWO OF THE GOLDEN REPUBLIC.

When my father studied with the Soladiseans, they told him we had no history. When he told them of our history, they said it was not real history if it did not come from a book. I have written these words and printed them in ink so that they cannot say we are incapable of such things. But I have always known the Sea People have much to be proud of. There is secret knowledge we will never give the Soladiseans and hidden books that we will never let them read. In this way, we protect our history for generations to come. –'Our History of the Golden Republic,' published in *The Dawn Beacon*.

CEVETTE ZARCANZI DREAMED OF Eva on the sandbar shore.

She lay on a beach of pale sand, gazing up at the night stars, her long black hair swirling out about her head. Moonlight turned her naked skin to alabaster, and her godmarks of bone and swirling smoke were as dark as her eyes. A hunger pooled in Cevette's stomach. She wanted to kiss the curve of her neck, the smooth lines of her thighs, even the delicate arch of her foot. She was a huntress with the face of death, and yet Cevette knew no fear, for her arrows were all aimed at their enemies.

Cevette walked out of the sea and strode toward her. The waves followed her, lapping at her heels. She slid between Eva's legs, the sand cool on her belly, her nerves singing with desire. She tasted her, woodsmoke and honey, then brought her lips up to curl about Eva's pleasure. She sucked, and licked, and worked her gently, around and around. Eva moaned, tilting back her head, and shuddered. Waves lapped up the beach and washed over them. Cevette felt no need to come up for air.

"Did you like that?" she murmured to the inside of Eva's sea-drenched thigh. "I liked that."

"I liked it very much." Eva reached under Cevette's chin and tipped her face up to the light. Their eyes met. Both women smiled.

Then a curtain of ripples danced over Eva's face. She vanished, or the image of her did. Cevette blinked, and realized she knelt before a pool of water in the sand. Another woman's reflection smiled up at her from the depths. She wore an old-fashioned gown made from cascading black smoke; a ruff of human finger bones wrapped like lace at her throat. Her black hair fell unbound behind her. Her eyes were like the deepest void of night, and the diamonds of the coronet on her brow glowed bright as stars.

"It's your fault," said the goddess of death. "Everything. All of it. It's your fault."

Then Cevette woke up

She lay in her bed, in her cabin on *Sea Wolf.* From her small candelabra, a smiling crocheted octopus swung, just out of reach. It was early morning. The first lines of sunlight crept through the cabin window and spilled onto her deep blue quilt. Eva lay beside her, her arm across Cevette's chest, her face curled into Cevette's shoulder. She smiled in her sleep. Cevette only wished she could smile back at her.

Her heart still hammered in her chest. *Only a nightmare.* She had good reason to dream of Morghaia. The goddess had terrorized the Five Sisters during the time of the Theocracy; the Sea People and the Soladisean colonists had both feared her. Some had said that Heraline had kept her from encroaching on Sea People territory; Morghaia had kept to the territories ceded to the Empire of Soladis, but no one of the Sea People could fully trust their safety to that. Even after the fall of the Theocracy, children had swapped stories of the broken goddess to scare each other in the night.

Perhaps me dreaming of her means I grew up in the Five Sisters, she thought. If she was truly from Upailit, an island that was the center of so much trade between peoples, it would explain her mixed heritage and her Soladisean name. *Though my name might have come from anywhere. I might have a dozen other names I've forgotten.* It could not be a coincidence she had lost her memory so soon after the successful raid of the shipyard of Upailit. *He took my memories to punish me for fighting for our freedom.* Well, Cevette was happy to tell herself she was a freedom fighter. But it was only a story. Even if it was true, it would not capture the whole of who she had been.

Would I even want to be that her *again?*

THE ACHE OF RUNNING papers to all corners of the Seaward Isles had faded from Eva's back and thighs, but not the pride of what she had accomplished. She had spent a good few hours talking with Paige, the echo in the fishing village, who had told Eva of how she'd sought out the furthest point south she could, to distance herself from the commander and her fear of being split. Paige enjoyed life in the village; all knew she was an outsider there, but she was tolerated, as the local people had no love for the Republic and its soldiers. Eva had promised to come back and visit again when she could. "Sell the papers," she had urged Paige. "Show all the people of the Isles what he's done."

When she returned to *Sea Wolf,* she found her friends most eager to hear of her journey. Naeri, in particular, wanted to hear of Soladis, the city she had lived in all her life before joining up with Cevette's crew. "I would so love to return to Soladis one day. To open a dressmaker's shop. But I would need some wealthy patrons. Ones who can make certain there's no longer a warrant out for my arrest."

"When you're ready, I'll introduce you to Lord Beauchamp," Eva promised. "We will miss you dearly, but if a dress shop is your dream, we'll all be happy for you."

"Especially," Donya added, "if we can smuggle luxury goods to the black-market dealers through your storefront."

Sea Wolf set a northward course. Eva and Cevette had checked the position of the stars against the map Lord Merris had drawn them. The nearest archive was on a small island, just south of the great island of Soladis, known as Muhlemlo to those who lived there, or as Maze Point to Soladiseans. They would stop in and burn the memories; after that, they would need to trust the plan Andreas had proposed to burn ones under Assembly Hall. The vote of impeachment was scheduled within days. If all went well, Commander Gavon would be ousted from power.

Eva threw herself into the business of preparing *Sea Wolf* for whatever might come next. She ran across the Isles to purchase guns, bullets, and blades; robbed a Republic fort of two cannons and dragged them, rolling on their wheels, back to *Sea Wolf* through Death. She and Cevette began a ritual of morning strength training in the cargo hold: lifting weights, dragging chains, and throwing cannon balls as far as they could. She made it a point to study the captain as well; how she led the crew by keeping them to routines and schedules, how she worked to promote discipline and calm, and Cevette was happy to answer any question Eva asked her.

She also found the time to enjoy herself. She played cards with Mr. Smoke, learned bird-calls from Lizeth, and sat with Naeri to monogram a pair of handkerchiefs. In great detail, she explained to her friends how warships were categorized by size and number of cannons, then drew up a chart she nailed up in the crew's quarters for their reference. For Donya's birthday, she ran with Cevette to the island of Kossi. The captain purchased fresh seal fat and helped Mr. Smoke work it into a porridge. The healer nearly wept at the taste. Later, down in the small nook where she mixed her medicines, Eva offered to help with her chores in exchange for lessons in Kossket. Donya agreed.

"I will warn you, it's very different from Soladisean," Donya had said as Eva crushed dried garlic in her mortar. "It might take months before you can eavesdrop on Cevette and me."

"So it takes months." Eva had shrugged at that. "I hope to still be with Cevette months from now. When she finds her people, I want to be able to speak with them too. I want to be part of her life, in whatever way she will have me."

"We'll start with 'mohyenosh ulalit.' Can you say that?"

Eva tried, and tripped over the L. "What does that mean?"

"That you're so in love, you look like a fool." Donya chuckled. "Well, we have time. The language will still be here once Commander Gavon falls."

Eva tapped her lip thoughtfully. *I will still be here when he falls.* She had told herself once that she was sailing with these pirates to escape Commander Gavon, to help put an end to his regime. But she had to admit to herself that she enjoyed the life of a pirate. She did not wish to give it up.

What did that say about her?

As THEY DREW NEAR the stony island of Muhlemlo, the deep blue sea turned to a dark gray, and a chill crept through the salty air. Great shoals of herring swam along the ship's flanks in rivers of flashing silver, and leaping sharks ripped into them with serrated fangs. A thin veil of gray clouds filled the sky. The hull creaked like the bones of an old woman, reluctant to rise from her chair. Cevette sympathized. She, too, was uneager to face what lay ahead.

When Muhlemlo first appeared on the horizon, it resembled nothing more than a pale dot on the horizon. As they drew closer, its three small hills could be seen, as could the greenery clinging to their peaks. The island was best known for the narrow gorges that ran through its valley like a tangled maze. Cevette had heard the stories of how the Muhlemli people had once dwelled in the sky. The seas had called to them to come down and dwell upon it, but, before they had left, they had reached down and carved the gorges into Muhlemlo so that their children and their children's children would have somewhere safe to shelter should they need it. It was a symbol of love so ancient that the rocks it had been carved into were crumbling now. The sight of it warmed her heart.

She wished she could remember how she'd first heard the tale.

Cevette stood atop the bowsprit as they drew near, steadying her balance with a tight grip on a jibe line, her white coat fastened tight against the cold bite of the wind. Soon, it became clear that 'valley' was a misnomer to describe the geography of Muhlemlo. The island was instead a flat-topped mesa of white stone; its hills, three steep cliffs of white stone, rising up from the sea to surround it like the fingers of a cradling hand. Its steep flanks left no ground for a beach to form; however, as they sailed about one hill, with seabird nests and barnacles clinging to its sides, they caught sight of a half-dozen wooden platforms floating on the waves, tied together with sinews and lashed to a pole driven into the side of the mesa.

Three Muhlemli women stood on one platform, pulling up crab traps and emptying their catches into seagrass baskets. They were clad for cool weather in robes of brightly painted fish skin Behind them, a group of Muhlemli children were gleefully tossing one another into the deeps. Some wore fish skin trousers and some wore naught at all. They stared at *Sea Wolf* as she approached; both at the guns and the carved orca of the figurehead.

"We're friends!" Cevette shouted, leaning out from atop the bowsprit. She addressed the women in Aleki, the language spoken by the Sea People who has once dwelled along the entire southern coast of Soladis. "We've brought you gifts!"

"Who are you?" shouted one of the women. Her long, dark braid fell nearly to the small of her back.

"I am Cevette Zarcanzi, a current woman." She pulled off her hat so they could see her short hair. "With me, of the Sea People, is Donya Breamtide of the Kossi Sea Nation, and Tuk By-Water and Nukit, son of Nowi, warriors of the Six Brother Clans of Upailit. We have a message for your elders. May we come ashore?"

The women lowered their heads and spoke among themselves. One made a shooing gesture at the children. They darted back along the platforms to the side of the mesa, clambered up the rock, and vanished through a near-invisible gap in the stone. The women looked up to face the ship.

"Come ashore and bring your gifts," said the woman with the long braid. "My name is Nachewa. We will take you to the elders."

Cevette nodded, and gave her crew the order to drop the anchor. It splashed down in the sea. She decided to take only women ashore with her; to the Muhlemli, it would be a sign they meant peace, and to make her intentions clear, she instructed her chosen women to remove their weapons. Eva began the long work of unstrapping her knives, a process Cevette was intimately familiar with now. The rest of the landing party filled a long crate with hunting rifles and three more with ammunition (the Republic restricted arms sales to the Sea People, so the Muhlemli would be most glad to receive those) and Cevette filled another small chest with gold bars from her personal store. She told Mr. Smoke to take charge of the ship in her absence—she would need to appoint a new first mate soon—then ordered her women into the dinghies and had the crew winch them down.

Cevette and the rest of the landing party rowed ashore and tied their dinghies to the pole where the floating platforms were anchored. They clambered up onto the steep side of the mesa. The captain carried the heavy chest of the gold on her shoulders, made sure Naeri and Donya didn't drop the rifles, smiled in pride as Eva managed to hoist a crate of ammunition on her own, and nodded to Nachewa and her friends. "We're ready."

Nachewa nodded. The Muhlemli women led them into through the cleft in the rocks. Beyond was a steep, narrow trail cut into the white stone of the mesa itself. The rock walls had crumbled slightly with time, but in places they were cut as cleanly as if they were hard cheese sliced through by some great knife. The air was crisp, cool, and smelled faintly of fish. Shale crunched underfoot as they advanced, turning around the narrow switchbacks in the trail. High above, a seabird circled. It dove, aiming for the crab basket one woman carried. She caught it in her fist, broke its neck, and added it to the basket. Eva made a little gasp at that, her eyes wide and impressed. Cevette decided she wanted to learn that trick, too.

The din of chatter and the bleating of goats rose from beyond the last turn in the trail. They stepped about it. Cevette smiled. Her crew froze.

A great square pit opened before them, cut into the very heart of the mesa. It stretched hundreds of feet to either side of them; ladders made from whalebone and a rickety pulley lift led downward. The buildings of Muhlemlo rose five to six stories tall, high square towers and wide squat storehouses, all carved of shining white stone. Wide roads stretched between them, connecting wells and community fire-pits, and the Muhlemli people strolled along them, herding goats and chasing toddlers. Near the base of the ladders, a group had gathered about a spear-throwing contest. Every time a warrior's spear struck the target, an old sack filled with broken seashells, the onlookers shouted with pride.

The pride stirred in Cevette as well, pride and a great sense of relief. She pressed a trembling hand to her lips. Tears prickled in her eyes. It was so good to see Sea People be happy and safe.

"Put your gifts on the lift," Nachewa said. "Follow us down the ladders. We'll take you to the meeting pit. The children will have let the elders know you arrived."

Cevette nodded. She led her party down the ladders. They picked up their gifts and followed Nachewa and her friends down the broad central road of the town. Cevette waved Eva forward to walk beside her. She wanted to show her everything. "Those are diver berries," she said, in Soladisean, nodding to a woman pulling a handcart laden with pink, violet, and pale yellow fruit. "In these waters, they bloom so deep that only we can hold our breath long enough to harvest them." They passed a round court where a group of young men and women were tossing two balls—both made from heavy fish leather, one white and one dark—at a high central hoop. "Tossball. Do you play in the Five Sisters?" Eva shook her head. "Right. The land folk say they invented it. That's a lie. We did, and we know we did because we're the best at it. You should watch me play."

"I would love that," Eva said. Then she smiled that wide, true smile that would never hide anything from Cevette at all. The captain felt her heart melt like fat in a frying pan.

Into the heart of the town they went, past a well where women gathered to draw up water for their homes and a firepit where Muhlemli of all genders worked at carving pots and cups from stone. Cevette knew they still possessed the great sun-cutters that had carved the town, and maintained much of the memory of how to build them anew, but they had lacked the resources to do so since the ancestors of the Soladiseans invaded. To the left, drummers in long fish skin coats were practicing pounding out beats on great ceremonial drums. To the right, dye-makers were crushing diver fruit and seaweed in stone basins, and the sweet scent filled the air. She could have breathed it in for hours.

This felt *right*. Not in the sense that she was *from* here, but in the sense of a current woman. She was meant to do this, to travel and speak with the different clans, to bring gifts and news, to listen to their needs and stories, and to look after the seas that connected them all.

In the center of the town, a three-foot-deep pit had been cut into the earth. Veins of golden ore shimmered across the floor. Cold seawater filled the great stone basin at its heart; the pattern of dual-pronged spears and darting fish carved in its side said it was dedicated to Heraline, so she might reach her people and answer their prayers. *If she cared to do so.* A canopy of sea serpent skin, pale green and patterned with scales, stretched across overhead, suspended from great stone pillars. "Wait here," Nachewa said, as Cevette and her sailors set their gifts down near the basin and sat atop the wall on the east side of the pit.

The elders came over the course of the next hour, and gathered on the side of the pit across from Cevette and her crew. There were three old women, one who came carried on a litter by her grandsons, all who wore fish skin gowns covered in intricate beadwork and bore the tattoos of elders on their cheeks. A younger woman joined them, perhaps forty—a current woman, by her short hair. They exchanged wary looks with Cevette and her party as they sat along the west side of the pit, but none of them spoke. A crowd gathered about them, mostly youths, keeping a respectful distance but watching intently. Cevette's heart cheered to see them, even though they were all gossiping about her crew in Aleki and making lists of which ones they could take in the wrestling ring. Most of them thought they could beat Eva. They all agreed Donya would be the hardest to bring down.

A drum pounded. To the north, twelve warriors strode out of a great stone hall and proceeded down the avenue toward the meeting square. They were men between sixteen and forty, clad in hauberks strung together from plates of thin stone, carved with patterns of fish scales and spearheads. Their leader was a man of near forty, strongly built, with warm brown skin and twin braids falling down his back. His leggings and breechclout were studded with the silver insignias of Republic officers. Six of them, he had killed personally. Cevette remembered killing four herself—she did not wear their trophies, as a current woman counted her victories in connections made—but clearly, this was a warrior to respect.

The war leader sat in the center of the women of the council, swung his legs down into the pit, and met Cevette's eyes. *Oh,* she realized. He had come because they were seen as a threat.

"Honored elders," Cevette said, and smiled. She spoke in her most formal Aleki. "I am Cevette Zarcanzi. A current woman, and captain of the ship called *Sea Wolf.* These women are sailors on my ship, and my friends and advisors, but they do not speak your language, and so I as their leader speak for them. We have brought you these gifts. How may I address you?"

The council members shared cautious looks between themselves. "I am Hinuri," the war leader said. It meant 'three axes' and likely spoke to how he'd killed those Republic officers. The current woman was called Tomilshamhi, for 'she advises the ceremonies.' The elders were Tekkehak, Tokhuch, and the oldest of them was Nomyit. She smiled at Cevette as she introduced herself. The others kept their features as still as the stone that surrounded them.

"I speak for my island today," Hinuri said, and folded his arms across his chest. "We are grateful for your gifts. But we cannot trust in your friendship just yet. You will surely understand why we do not trust strangers on ships—if you are the current woman you claim to be."

Cevette did not flinch at the barb. "I would not have come here to do you harm. A captive of mine, a lord of the Republic—" a current woman could brag about taking a captive, even if she wouldn't wear a trophy "—told me that his people had buried relics of evil magic on your land. I have come to destroy them."

"The ones that look like old paper?" Hinuri said.

Cevette raised an eyebrow. "So you've seen them."

"The soldiers threw them down a pit in the northeast, in the ruins of a collapsed tower. They thought we would do nothing about their pollution. We tunneled beneath the tower using a sun-cutter and retrieved the foul things."

"Did you destroy them?"

"We did not know the safest way to do so. Such Republic magic is unknown to us. We put them back in the chest they had come in, threw them down a cistern in an abandoned building, and flooded it with seawater. Those of us who had touched them washed with water in the great basin to cleanse ourselves."

Center stood, and took a step toward them. She rested her hand on lip of the stone basin, which rose as high as her hip. "Lead me there and let me burn them. I have destroyed dozens of the things. They are memories trapped in physical form, stolen from us by Jonathan Gavon. Burning them will free them from his power."

Tomilshamhi, the current woman, hopped down into the pit and took a step toward Cevette. Polished mother-of-pearl earrings framed her petit face. She wore a men's tunic and leggings, and the webbing between her fingers was madder root red. "Are you the reason we remembered how our old treaty with the Republic allowed a hundred miles of fishing rights that those cheats made us think we'd given up to them?"

"That was our work, unless someone else is burning them as well."

Tomilshamhi nodded. "Who are your people, Cevette Zarcanzi?"

Cevette took a deep breath. She gazed down into the basin, at the water carried up from the sea. She wished she knew the names of her ancestors to call on. But the ancestors of the Muhlemli would be watching. Perhaps they would help her tell their family what she had to say. "Commander Gavon stole my memory of my family and my people. I am searching to reclaim it from him."

The members of the council, and the young folk gathered off to the edges of the meeting pit, recoiled in horror and shock. The council bent their heads low and whispered amongst themselves. *How could such a thing be?* Cevette heard, and *Could he do that to us?* Some of the children darted away. An elder murmured a prayer of protection.

Tomilshamhi took another step toward Cevette. She, too, rested a hand on the basin. "I am sorry for your loss. We are no strangers to the cruelty of the Republic. But, for the sake of the Three Currents and the peace between the clans, I must ask: can you prove that you are a current woman? Not just any woman can cut her hair and claim that station."

"I can prove it," Cevette said. She addressed Tomilshamhi in Mecha, the language of the Kingdom of Serpent Riders to the far south. "I can speak with the people of every nation."

"Do you speak Lohsonni?" Tomilshamhi asked in that language. A wind blew over the top of the mesa; a distant whistling noise picked up overhead. The air in the town itself was calm. "The tongue of Broken Hook and High Hill Island?"

"I know it," Cevette answered in the same tongue. "I have sailed those coasts, and shared game and fish with the Wichil."

"What of Kossket?" she said, switching again. "Do you know the tongue of the poets of Ya Raug and the shamans of Crab Island?"

"Very well," Cevette said, following her. "This is the language of my dear cousin, Donya Breamtide, the healer on my ship." She looked back over her shoulder and nodded to Donya, who was shifting about uneasily where she sat on the side of the pit, and had the look of someone who wished she'd brought a weapon.

Tomilshamhi returned to Aleki. "You know the tongues. Do you know the first prayer to Memawo? Say it now."

Cevette stiffened. "Memawo? Call her Heraline. That was the name she chose. She *betrayed* us. She chose her land goddess wife over us. She raised a son who attacked our people. I will not pray to her."

"Memawo is a current woman. Our student and our teacher. The keeper of our knowledge. Do you not know this?"

"I know. But she failed us. Such things cannot be forgiven."

"So you would turn your back on one of us?"

Cevette winced. *No.* "Is she still one of us? Where has she been since the Republic rose? Where has she been since the ancestors of the Soladiseans arrived in the Seaward Isles?" Something broke in her voice. Heraline had adopted a Soladisean name, a Soladisean appearance, a Soladisean family. She had chosen that of her own free will. Cevette could have nothing but contempt for her. Not when she had fought for years to find her way back to the place Heraline had left behind.

"The pirate speaks the truth," Hinuri said. "Heraline turned her back on us. We deserve gods who will fight for our people."

"We cannot simply choose to abandon her," Tomishami said. "No matter where she has gone, the waters still connect us all." She eyed Cevette. "A current woman should know that."

Cevette flinched. Her cheeks burned. Her shoulders slumped. She looked away from Tomilshamhi's eyes and gazed down into the basin. The cool, still water covered a carving of a goddess with three long snake tails instead of legs, a fishing spear, and a basket of oysters. *Memawo. Heraline. I cannot escape her.* The truth of the Three Currents was clear; all the people of the Seaward Isles were connected, gods and humans, Sea People and Soladiseans, those she loved and those she hated. She did not think she could ever forgive Heraline for what she had done. But she could not pretend there was no link between the goddess and herself.

"Mighty Parha," she whispered, in the old classical Kossket, only now used in ceremony and song, "mother and daughter of the current without end, teach my tongue to speak for the needs of the water." Her head seemed to lighten with relief as she spoke. "Teach my ship the path between islands and teach my flesh to swim the spirit waters as I do the sea, for I and my ancestors are one and the water is the cord between us."

"The water is the cord between us," Donya said.

Light pulsed through the waters of the basin. Cevette's eyes widened. Tomilshamhi and the council gasped and stared. Donya swore.

Then the shining water leapt free of the basin. It took on the shape of a young sea serpent, a glimmering and undulating creature, the cylinder of its body only eight inches across. Swimming through the air, it wrapped around Cevette and Tomilshamhi in three great loops. Then it coiled around Donya, then Hinuri, then the elders, growing longer and longer as it went. It embraced the grandsons who had carried old Nomyit to the meeting, then raced out to wrap around each youth and each warrior watching the council. Murmurs of joy and awe rose from the gathered Sea People. *The Three Currents still flow. The ancestors and gods are here with us.* Cevette tipped her head back and drank it in.

"Where does this come from?" old Nomyit whispered.

"From us," said Tomilshamhi. Tears shone in her eyes. "But this current woman and her godmarked cousin have made it visible."

The serpent wove one more loop about the pavilion and dove back into the basin. The light faded from the water. But Cevette could still sense the Three Currents flowing around and through her; the sea flowing beneath the mesa and glistening in every tear. *It has always been close to me,* she realized. She'd grown used to it like the slap of waves against the hull of *Sea Wolf.* But, even with her memories missing, she had never been cut off from her people.

Tomilshamhi looked back over her shoulder at the council. The elders murmured amongst themselves, then spoke to Hinuri in a lowered voice. The war leader nodded, and stood, the medallions shining on his breech-clout. "We will take you to the relics. You will need to dive for them."

"Thank you," Cevette said. "For your aid and . . . for helping me remember what matters."

She thought of the women on Upailit who had given her a ship when she'd needed one. There had been no expectation of repayment; to give generously to others kept the Three Currents strong. The council was giving her trust.

What did Cevette have to give the Sea People? Her ship. Her strength. Her service. *And I could give it right now. As I am.* She could have a real future ahead of her, a future that would matter far more than her past. Her girl would be Eva, and her family would be her crew, and her clan would be whatever clan needed a current woman. She had always thought such a surrender would be nothing less than the ultimate betrayal. But she would be doing what she was born to do once more. And perhaps her past was best left buried.

Eva had understood very little of what had passed in the conversation of the council. But she could tell Cevette was tired, and overwrought, though she was glad her fellow current woman seemed to have accepted her. She had known it was significant when the water came to life; the Sea People did not often speak of their magic to outsiders, but the shock on the faces of the Muhlemli had been so clear that even she could see it.

Now they walked through the town with its tall stone buildings, taller than any she had ever seen in her life. She had to stop herself from staring up at them; that seemed rude. The sound of their footsteps and the voices of the townsfolk rang off the high walls about them. The warriors with their stone armor walked to either side of the group of pirates, watching them with wary eyes. Hinuri led from the front of the procession, his chin high and eyes alert. Cevette walked just behind him.

Eva went up to her and took her hand. As Cevette turned to face her, she murmured, "A nin wope pu."

"What?" Cevette stared at her. "I am a . . . shining giant?"

"Donya said it means 'you are a beautiful woman' in Kossket."

"Oh. You mean 'a nin wopi pu,'" Cevette said, gently correcting her pronunciation of *nin* as well. "Did she mention 'hehu yap?'"

"If I ask a festival piper to play a song, I have to be careful how I pronounce it, or I might ask them to suck my cock." Eva nodded. "I'll work on that. I want to be ready. For whatever lies ahead."

"For whatever lies ahead." Cevette nodded. "I . . . I'm a current woman. My life is on the sea. But I need to sail for more than just my own desires. To find some way to pick up the duties I have let lapse. And, at some point, I may need to admit that I will never find my memories. That they are lost to me, and I must move forward without them."

Once, Eva would have been glad to hear that. But she saw more now of what Cevette would be giving up on—not only the echo she had loved, but a portion of who she was—and she could take no joy in it. "I'm so sorry. That will be quite very hard."

"Yes," Cevette said. "But it will be much easier with you around."

"I'll be there," Eva said. The answer was a simple thing to give. "It will not be a great credit to my virtue, should I continue with piracy after the commander is expelled from the Assembly and the echoes are saved, but one more echo without proper virtues will hardly destroy the world." She looked about her. "The world is a good deal larger and more different than the Republic let me imagine it was."

"And I look forward to seeing it all with you." Cevette squeezed her hand. Eva leaned down and kissed her cheek.

The warriors led them to the western edge of the town. There were no lights burning in the windows here; Eva sensed, from the distance of Death, that the Muhlemli had lacked the numbers to fully occupy their town for quite some time. They approached a small stone building, a cube ten feet on all sides, the rounded archway of the door closed off by a curtain painted with intricate curved and interlocking symbols.

Hinuri gave a command in his own language; one of his warriors offered Cevette a torch. She took it, and nodded to Eva. "Stay here."

Cevette walked up to the doorway. Before the curtain, she murmured a prayer in a language Eva did not know. "For protection," Donya said quietly. She and Naeri came up to stand to either side of Eva, whose heart hammered as Cevette pulled the curtain aside.

The stone building was empty, save for the cistern. The stone basin rose four feet above the floor; Eva assumed it went down much deeper on the inside. Cevette set the torch in a stone ring carved to the side of the basin. In a quick and practiced manner, she removed her clothes, folded them neatly, and set them aside. Then she climbed atop the lip of the cistern and dove down into the dark. Eva watched and murmured her own prayer. *Heraline, if you can hear me, keep her safe. Please.*

Then she held her breath. Seconds slipped by, each one an agony. *She's a good swimmer,* Eva knew, and *she can hold her breath a long time.* But she hated to think of Cevette alone in the dark.

Then Cevette's head popped out of the water. She drew a deep breath, and hoisted a small wooden chest, made in the style of the Republic, up over her head. Donya sighed in relief. Eva and Naeri clapped as Cevette pulled herself from the cistern. The captain re-donned her clothes, then opened the chest and poured the contents out. Memories tumbled free, crumbled fragments of almost-paper rattling along the stone. Cevette took up the torch, lowered it to them, and set them ablaze. They went up in a flash of white light. Eva smiled.

Then she took a step backward. Pressed a hand to her chest, as if a crack had just run through her heart. *No. Not now.* Cevette was prepared to put the past behind her. *I could keep it secret.* No. That would make her complicit in what Commander Gavon had done.

"What's wrong?" Cevette asked. She raced out of the building and pulled Eva into her arms. The captain pushed her hair up behind her ear, brushed a kiss across her cheek. "Eva, what's wrong?"

Eva took a deep breath and whispered, "I know where we can find your memories."

Cevette's eyes got very wide. "What?"

Eva nodded. Her head spun. She told Cevette what she remembered.

It had been just after the Ya Tonim raid on Upailit. Her father had been furious. For days, he'd spoken of nothing save the brutality and stupidity of the attackers, how the fort had only been placed where it was to protect Upailit from abomination attacks, how he had planned to make that territory part of the Republic and grant citizenship to its people, about how the whole island had rejected his charity and it could burn for all he cared. Nowhere in his anger had he mentioned that his soldiers had been holding women in bondage. Eva had been keeping well clear of him. She dared not tempt his rage by offering him an echo close to hand.

She had been in a hallway on the upper floor of the fortress keep, the walls covered in fading and torn floral print paper, practicing knifework by throwing her hairbrush at a stair post. The sound of his enraged voice had drifted up from below. She'd ducked into a closet to hide, nearly tripping over the rug as she scrambled for shelter. The smell of dust and old coats had washed over her as her father had walked down the hall.

"Why didn't you erase the memory of the raid yet?" another man had said. Eva knew that voice now—Lord Merris. "That echo you split was nearly seventy."

"I had to target *her* first," her father had said. His voice had trembled with anger. "She's too dangerous."

"Can we not simply have her killed?"

"I must have sent a hundred soldiers to find her. Most of them have never found so much as a single clue. The ones who get close to her wind up dead."

"You mean, you don't even know where she is?"

"I don't need to know where she is. I know who she is. I take away everything but the knowledge I have robbed her of her identity. Then, instead of attacking the Republic, she runs off to chase Sea People and echoes. All I must do is simply erase her memory whenever she starts causing trouble."

"Sir, if she recovers it, she'll destroy us."

"Then we best make sure she stays away from the Gray Isle."

The conversation had shifted there, to other matters, but Eva had heard enough. She relayed this conversation to Cevette the best she could. "It must be about you," she said. "Only a powerful sacrifice could take that much of your memory."

"The Gray Isle." Cevette's voice shook. "Lord Merris told us about it. Where he put the memories of the . . ." Her voice faltered.

"It's off the coast of Soladis," Eva said. "Not too far from the city. We can sail there directly from here. It's so close."

"But why use such power against one current woman?" Cevette's voice trembled as she spoke. "Why would he go to such lengths to keep my memory hidden?"

"You must have organized the raid," Eva said. "The thought of Sea People organizing against him must be one of his greatest fears."

Cevette lowered her head. "If he's so scared of me, then why am I the one terrified?"

Donya and Naeri exchanged worried looks. Eva pulled Cevette tighter. Held her closer. "Whatever we find there, we'll face it together." *Even if it splits us apart.*

THE VOTE

In the City of Soladis, in the unceded territory of the Ketil Yata Nation, on the Island of Soladis. 21st Morghasmonth, Year Twenty-Two of the Golden Republic.

In my time with the pirates, I learned a good deal about democracy. In the Golden Republic, we pride ourselves on the establishment of a democracy that allows for the election of leaders of merit. If only the best and most virtuous among us hold power, we say, then we shall never again face tyranny or malfeasance. And yet the reality is that to campaign for office requires vast wealth; and many of those with vast wealth are those who have vast inheritances. Pirates, in contrast, judge the merit of a captain by what the captain does for them. This produces captains who, though they cannot be called gentle, are leaders of more merit than any number of Assembly members. They care for merit not as an abstraction, but as a matter of life and death. In this, they put us to shame. –'A Pirate's Life,' published in *The Silver Sentinel.*

THE MORNING OF THE vote of impeachment, Eva took Cevette and ran to Soladis. They had agreed to meet with Tomis and Andreas to burn the memories under Assembly Hall and deliver the final blow to Commander Gavon's hopes of political survival. Eva also dearly hoped all would go well when Cevette met her brother properly, without cell bars or a pistol drawn between them. She wanted nothing more than peace between them both.

The Beauchamp family home, a grand estate called the Nautileum, was built atop the high hill on the city's eastern edge. Eva and Cevette stepped out of Death through a portal in the shadows behind the gatehouse, where a thief attempting to burgle the estate had fallen and broken his neck. Both were informally dressed, in plain shirts and breeches; Cevette had a heavy satchel on her shoulder and Eva wore a long cloak and gloves. Hand in hand, they walked down the pale cobblestones of the promenade that wound through the estate lawns. The sight that struck Eva most was the spire: one hundred and fifty feet of white quartz, twisted as a goat's horn, jutting up from the earth at the estate's heart. The foundations of a crumbling stone ruin, from the days of the Empire, could still be seen at its base.

"I've heard of this place," Cevette frowned. "Once, this was the palace of Kasperos, the Crownbearer."

Eva shivered at the mention of that name. *Kasperos. The son of Morghaia and Heraline.*

In the shadow of the spire sat a two-story manor of whitewashed brick. Its tall, arched windows were framed with delicate white wooden lattices. A colonnade lined the front of the house, pillars spaced at regular intervals holding up a clay-tiled roof over a stone patio. Between the pillars stood sculptures of mice and dancing maidens, and planters where the flowers had gone brown for winter. Servants bustled up and down the length of the colonnade, hauling crates, chairs, tables, and piles of folded formal linens. *That's right. Tomis is hosting a ball this evening.* It was meant to be a celebration of the commander's downfall. He had invited her, and she had accepted the invitation to be polite, but she privately hoped she would be able to slip away before needing to fulfill that obligation.

A strange flash of color caught her eye. The servants wore neat uniforms, consisting of pale blue skirts and jackets. Yet several among them had brightly colored tattoos just visible where they protruded from their cuffs and collars. Eva frowned. *That man. The tattoo at his collarbone. The archway, with the star inside it.* She knew that mark. It had grabbed her attention the first time she'd seen it, though she did not know why. But she knew it marked the rebels of the True Ink Movement.

And, alongside the rebels, Eva saw echoes. One, two, three—no, ten or twelve of them, carrying furniture and sweeping the walk. She supposed it was decent of Tomis to hire echoes; few in Soladis would give them a chance. But not all of them were servants. Eva recognized one girl clutching a box of silverware with a focused, furious gaze. *Cornellia.* What would a member of Korinne's crew be doing in Soladis? Whatever had brought her here, Eva was glad to see her alive.

She and Cevette had often, in the last few weeks, wondered where the storm had blown *Shadow Queen.* How close might her older sister be?

"Miss Gavon!" Tomis strode across the lawn to meet them. He was also dressed simply; though his shirt was trimmed with a good deal of lace, and gold and silver rings shone on his fingers. "Captain Zarcanzi!" He gave Cevette a firm handshake, then opened his arms to Eva, who hugged him. "A pleasure to see you both."

"A pleasure to see you as well," Cevette said. "I do hope there's no hard feelings between us."

"What, that you boarded my ship, killed a man, and held me for ransom? I won't lie. I found my arrival on *Sea Wolf* quite upsetting at first." Tomis shrugged. "But I am not a fool. I will not pretend the Beauchamp family fortune was founded on anything less than an absurd amount of violence and depravity. How can I judge you to be my moral inferior when I own all of this? You are an interesting woman, Captain Zarcanzi, and I have no desire to dislike interesting people."

"And I in turn must express my gratitude for the assistance you have provided Miss Gavon and her fellow echoes by publishing this article. How has that gone? Has the revelation of the truth had the effect you desired on the city?"

Tomis hesitated. He bit at his lip. But then he lifted his chin and smiled, ever so slightly. "Well. Perhaps not as much as I would have wished for. The city discussed it for the past few days, but the talk has died down. There is anger in the streets, yes, and many rightfully attribute it to the commander's actions, but many are also happy to blame . . . echoes. You, specifically, Miss Gavon, but echoes in general, as you are a rather hard woman to find."

Eva frowned. Her hands curled into fists.

"Come now," Tomis said. "Your brother is waiting for us."

He led them both down the length of the colonnade, past the bustling servants, toward the great stone spire. A cool wind tugged at Eva's hood; she pulled it up to shield her face and nearly bumped into a chambermaid carrying a basket of napkins. The chatter of the servants rose around them, then faded into a hush as they approached the stone spire. The tall quartz monolith, nearly fifty feet in diameter, sparkled faintly in the morning sun. A small kitchen garden, smelling richly of basil and rosemary, grew at its foot. Tomis led them around the sprouting herbs and into the shadow of a birch tree.

Andreas leaned against the mossy lip of a well. His freshly-bleached hair cascaded back over his shoulders in a pale river. His long coat was midnight black; silver cufflinks flashed at his wrists. His thin lips curled into a smile when he saw Eva. "Sister!"

She rushed toward him. They hugged each other tightly. For both of them, there was a new relief in seeing the other one safe. "I brought Cevette," she whispered in his ear. "Be polite."

"I have never in my life been anything less than polite," he said. Eva nodded, and stepped back from him. Cevette walked up and put a hand on Eva's shoulder. Andreas smiled at her. "Captain Zarcanzi. I'm pleased to see you're not in jail."

"Mr. Gavon," said Cevette. "I sincerely apologize for the wound I dealt you in Halston. My aim was solely to intimidate your father. I'll have you know I did not shoot to kill."

"I'll have you know that you could have aimed higher." Andreas nodded at his sister. "In more ways than one."

Eva kicked him in the shins. Not hard, but hard enough that he jumped and yelped.

"You make my sister quite happy," Andreas said, grudgingly. "I . . . perhaps we should start over, captain. I do hope you and Eva will stay for tonight's ball; Tomis told me he extended an invitation to you. The gentry of the Republic should be made accustomed to the sight of echoes walking among them as equals. It will be a most useful symbol of our personhood."

A symbol. It felt like such a small thing. How much could it truly help echoes, to position them as players in the political games of Soladis? *Korinne would laugh at us for that.* But what choice did they have? Korinne's plan to free them had failed disastrously.

"We'll stay for the ball," Cevette said. "I would dearly like us to be friends, Mr. Gavon."

"We'll stay," Eva said. She would do it, if for no other reason than to encourage Cevette and her brother to make peace. "Now, then. To Assembly Hall."

ZEKE FOUND HIMSELF MOST encouraged by the change he saw in Commander Gavon after their conversation in his cabin. For the entirety of their journey back to Soladis, he had been in a quiet, reflective state. Zeke spent much of the journey keeping order among the soldiers and sailors aboard. He had to stop them from fighting each other for rations; the journey had pushed many to the edge of civility or beyond. He also organized a ship-wide chess tournament, and all aboard were quite cheered by it, which gladdened him. The demands of his duty meant he often lacked the time to enjoy companionship.

Kembrielle had arrived in Soladis five days before the vote of impeachment was scheduled to occur. The commander had returned to the manor house he had rented. He had been mildly annoyed to find Andreas had left for the Nautileum, but took no action to retrieve his wayward foster son. He had old Madam Bly brought ashore as well, and given a comfortable room, albeit under heavy guard. Zeke decided he would speak with him about scheduling her trial when the matter of the vote was settled; though, if the vote passed, it would be out of the commander's hands.

And the odds did not favor him. The members of the Assembly were close-lipped about how they planned to vote, but Zeke knew a number had been invited to meet with the commander at the manor house, and only a handful of those invited had come. He read newspapers, both legal and illegal publications, all of which indicated the Assembly was most displeased with his leadership. After all, its members were receiving hundreds of letters concerning the memories returned to them.

The ones Zeke had recovered weighed heavily on his thoughts. *His anger at the Sea People after the raid on Upailit . . .* It made the hair on the back of his neck prickle to think of it. But that had been five years ago. A man could change in five years. *He has not split the old woman. He is not that much of a monster.*

Part of Zeke hoped the commander would lose the vote. If he could accept it with grace, it would show he could still be the man Zeke wanted so desperately for him to be.

Tomis held a lantern out over the mouth of the well. The flickering flame revealed a narrow staircase had been carved into the stone wall, curling down into the dark. "Follow me," he said, and clambered over the wall. With his feet resting on the first stone, he said, "We can reach Assembly Hall through the tunnels. They won't be guarded. Andreas went through the old maps in my grandfather's collection and discovered there was one route that led to the archive directly."

Andreas nodded. "Old Augustis Beauchamp was obsessed with the search for the Crownbearer. In his diaries, he theorized the god might have been imprisoned beneath the great Temple of Iunos, which is now Assembly Hall."

"Did he find the god?" asked Eva.

"Not to my knowledge," said Tomis. "But many of his diaries are missing. The Republic has at times sent soldiers to demand all books over a certain age from our property. My father always complied, god-fearing patriot he was. But, before he died, my grandfather told me that the Nautileum was full of secrets, if you knew where to search for them."

Andreas looked to his sister. "Did you bring what I asked you for?"

Eva nodded. "The uniform of a Republic officer. Captain Zarcanzi has it in her satchel."

"Along with our eveningwear," Cevette said. As Tomis vanished from sight, she stuck a leg over the edge of the well. "For afterwards."

Eva raised an eyebrow. "You *hoped* they'd talk us into the ball. You know, if you want to see me in a ballgown, you only have to ask."

"I know. But perhaps I want everyone else to see how lovely you are in a ballgown." Cevette winked at her, then turned and followed Tomis down into the dark. Eva clambered over the well wall to follow her. Andreas took up the rear.

Their footsteps rang out on the stone stair as they followed the spiral of the staircase down, around and around. As the darkness rose up to cloak them, the lantern cast long shadows on the well walls. The rich scent of earth rose up about them; and so too came the distant crashing of waves.

Tomis cursed. "Gods, that's a big spider!"

"Are you scared of them?" Eva said.

"I must confess," he said, his voice drifting up the well from the one bobbing point of light ahead of them, "I've never been fond of spiders. Or the dark. I suppose everyone is much the same."

"There are worst things to fear than the dark," Cevette said.

"I don't mind the dark," Eva said. "I find it peaceful." The darkness could not judge her. It could be dangerous, but it was never cruel.

"I enjoy the darkness as well," Andreas said.

Eva looked back at him, his pale hair shining like a beacon in the lantern light. "Perhaps all echoes share that?"

He shrugged. "Perhaps we do."

"Korinne had a theory about that. About how we're similar in body, but quite different in soul."

"Korinne?"

"The Demon of Dogshead. You would like her, I think, if you met under peaceful circumstances. She studies abominations."

"She sounds intriguing. Though I would not risk an abomination's jaws to meet her." Andreas reached into his coat pocket and pulled out a sealed letter. "These papers are signed with the commander's seal. I forged orders for the archive guards to be re-assigned to the harbor and signed them with Father's signature. All you must do is give them the papers, captain, and they'll walk away. There was a kraken spotted off the shore of the city last night, so they shouldn't find the reassignment suspicious."

Cevette frowned. "A kraken? The navy should have driven it off."

"There have been a number spotted off the coast," Tomis said. "The navy is occupied. It falls to the army to defend the docks from the creatures who come to feed on the suffering of the poor."

Abominations. Korinne's work. Eva shivered. "I thought I saw one of Korinne's echoes with the serving staff. Cornellia."

"Are you certain?" Tomis said. "My housekeeper, Mrs. Lasalle, is an echo. I gave her leave to hire some of her sisters in the city; they couldn't find work elsewhere."

"This was Cornellia. I know it. We share a face, but not always how we use it. It was her." Eva sighed. "We had best move quickly. We may not have much time."

At last, they came to the bottom of the well. A shallow spring bubbled up by their feet, smelling of dead leaves and rot. A tunnel stretched out to the west, a narrow passage with an entryway only seven feet tall. A crude arrow was carved in the wall, with directions beneath it written in Classic Soladisean. Andreas ran his fingers over the inscription. "This route was used by priests to move between the Temple of Iunos and the palace of the Nautileum. They carried messages between Iunos and the Crownbearer. It's said that the roof was deliberately carved low so that the gods could not enter and eavesdrop on the conversations of their worshippers. A ridiculous legend. Gods don't *have* to be ten feet tall. The books say they can take on human form and walk among us."

"Why would they do that?" Eva said.

"To spy, perhaps?" Andreas said.

Cevette frowned. A grim expression had washed across her face. *Did my brother do something to upset her?* Eva wondered. She would need to have words with him.

Tomis hoisted the lantern high, and waved them forward. Into the tunnel they walked. Swirling patterns of quartz shone in the dark stone of the walls. The still, damp air clung to her skin. Eva shivered. The four of them had fallen silent. Cevette stood particularly still, the set of her shoulders stiff. She had been so frightened these past few days. Part of Eva wished she could rush along to the Gray Isle, slip past the soldiers guarding the archive, and free Cevette from the shadows of her unknown past. But the archive under Assembly Hall was also rich with memory, and this was the best chance they'd had yet to strike it. To do one final blow to the commander's cause ahead of the vote of impeachment.

The tunnel sloped gently downward as they went. The crashing of waves grew louder. At last, the narrow tunnel widened. "We're close," Andreas said, and they all paused. "I believe it would be best for Captain Zarcanzi to go on alone. If she pleases."

"I will," Cevette said. She slid the satchel from her shoulders, rooted around inside it, and took out an orange uniform jacket. She pulled it on and squared her shoulders. "How do I look?"

Eva shivered. "Like an officer of the Republic." There was a harshness to her face that Eva could only hope was a trick of the light.

"Good." Cevette put the satchel in Eva's arms. Cloth threatened to spill out of it. She took the lantern from Tomis. "Stay here. When the soldiers clear out, I'll whistle for you."

The three of them held their breath as Cevette marched forward. Her footsteps rang off the stone. The light of the lantern dwindled. Darkness wrapped around them. Tomis shivered. Eva took his hand with her left, and grabbed her brother's with her right. She could hear Andreas breathing, calmly and evenly, and she told herself to think about that, and not her fear for Cevette. A handful of minutes passed. A faint breeze wafted down the tunnel and brushed against her cheek.

Death. Only death lay ahead.

Further up the tunnel, Cevette swore.

"Cevette!" Eva gasped. She pulled forward, breaking free of Andreas and Tomis. Her foot caught on a snag. She plunged forward and slammed down on the stone. Pain shot through her knees and her gloved palms as she broke her fall.

Cevette raced back down the tunnel, the lantern swinging in her hands. Her face was pale white. Her hands were trembling. She shuddered, drew a deep breath, and straightened her back.

"The soldiers are dead. All of them. They numbered at least twenty. And the memories are gone." Cevette swallowed hard. "The Demon of Dogshead got here first."

EVA REMEMBERED NOTHING OF the walk back through the tunnels. Her head had spun the whole way. *Korinne. She beat us to the prize.* The storm must have blown *Shadow Queen* north. *How did she know of the archive here?* Had she also spoken to Lord Merris? *What did she do to him?* She didn't know. All she knew was that Korinne had ambushed and killed twenty soldiers. The thought turned her stomach. Only a few minutes before, she had been thinking of Korinne in familiar terms. Worrying about her. What did it say about Eva that she could worry over someone like that?

"The work we've done here should be sufficient," Andreas said as they climbed up from the well. "The citizens of the Republic have all the proof they need of the commander's crimes. They have spoken to their Assembly members on the matter. And the distaste toward the commander in the Assembly has been building for years. They gain nothing from keeping him in office."

"The Assembly will be enraged when they discover this," Cevette said. "The vote may be delayed."

Andreas shook his head. "The guards only change shift every eight hours. The Demon timed her strike for when they first arrived. With luck, they will not find the bodies until later tonight."

Eva frowned. "Whatever she's planning, it doesn't stop at Assembly Hall." She had to speak with Cornellia and the tattooed revolutionaries directly.

Zeke and Commander Gavon arrived at Assembly Hall in the late afternoon. The commander preceded him into the grand circular central chamber. In the light of the setting sun, the green wallpaper was the same color as a stormy sea. The plaster reliefs and even the great flag hung in shadows. The chairs and desks had been organized in a more orderly pattern about the central podium since the commander's last venture to Assembly Hall. The candles were burning low, and the air smelled less of wax than of dust.

All members of the Assembly stood to watch as Commander Gavon entered the chamber. Not as a mark of respect, Zeke thought, but with an air of shock, as if they'd just seen a ghost. The commander seemed somehow thinner; his blue satin sash of office hung loose on his shoulder. He wore his military uniform, but the dye in the orange coat had faded with time. His footsteps clicked on the marble tile of the floor as he approached the podium. Major Kemsworthy passed him the gavel with a nod of respect. Zeke, keenly aware he was the only non-member to be invited into the hall, took up the position of a bodyguard, standing just behind the commander's shoulder, his hands resting on his weapons belt.

Lord Merris was nowhere to be seen. Zeke frowned. The Minister for Childhood Welfare was one of the commander's closest allies.

Commander Gavon looked back at him. "Ezekiel," he said quietly. "Trust me here. Listen, and say nothing."

Zeke nodded.

The commander tapped his gavel on the podium. He raised his voice and spoke. "I call today's session to order. Join me in reciting the Oath of Loyalty." The gathered Assembly members rose, turned to face the flag, and mumbled the words. More than a few remained seated. "I pledge my house and my most vaunted honor to serve the Golden Republic. May my blade and dying breath preserve the land I love. And should my peer or kindred turn their coat on liberation, may my hand be the bloody one that strikes them down." Gavon tapped his gavel on the podium once more. He lowered his brow and said, "Let us begin."

"This should have begun days ago, Jonathan," said Lord Kass. The Soladisean aristocrat rose from his seat and strode out to stand in front of the podium, his arms folded across his chest. His coat was violet velvet with gold accents at the cuffs. "Ever since you returned to Soladis, you have been ignoring the work of the Assembly."

The commander glowered at him. "I have been doing the work of the Republic."

"What does the Republic have to show for your work? For the hasty folly of your journey south? I heard the pirates double-crossed you. Lured you in with a peace banner and slaughtered your soldiers. Whatever happened to the Jonathan Gavon who slew Iunos in single combat?" He scoffed. "If indeed that's how you did it. I've never met a soldier who could convincingly prove they had witnessed the fight."

"You know nothing of war," the commander said. "Not all battles are easily won. We faced abominations, pirates, and a rogue godreaper who can summon storms. You've faced no foe more formidable than your own mirror. But what I brought back from the southern seas is priceless: information. I have uncovered a plot against the Republic. A plot directed by the echoes."

The gathered Assembly members bent their heads together and murmured in a nervous fashion. Zeke raised an eyebrow. *A plot of echoes.* There were echoes, and they were most likely plotting, but Zeke would not have said it that way himself. It was far too simple a way to address the tangled cord of truth.

"After the breaking of Morghaia, I showed the echoes mercy," said Commander Gavon. "I allowed them to live in the Republic. I offered them the chance to prove they are better than the tyrant they were spawned from. What did they do? They've raided our forts. They've killed our soldiers. They've exposed our secrets. And, when I faced them on their warship, I learned that each and every one of them has united to bring the Republic down!"

Worried whispers swept through the gathered Assembly members. Zeke frowned. *It isn't like that.* The Demon of Dogshead and her crew had sought to kill the commander in vengeance for their slain sisters. He had lost his own sister ten years ago. He understood. He disagreed with them, but he understood.

"Do you have proof of this, Jonathan?" said Lord Kass.

"The Republic is in grave danger indeed, if one gentleman will not take another at his word." The commander shook his head. Then he paused. Turned a half-step. Looked back to Zeke. "You would do well to learn from the example of Lieutenant Dare."

Zeke frowned. A wave of dizziness swept through him. *What are you doing?* All across the hall, Assembly members looked to him, in the same way they would sight down the barrels of their guns at a stag.

Commander Gavon smiled. "Lieutenant Dare has been a close personal friend to my fosterling Evazina for years. And yet, when she turned against us, not for one moment did his loyalty falter. Through his discipline, dedication, and heroism, we have uncovered the echoes' plot." Commander Gavon placed his hand on Zeke's shoulder. "He has shown himself to be every inch as worthy as a great gentleman of Soladis."

It took all of Zeke's training not to flinch away. His stomach flipped. His skin crawled. *Is this what my friendship with Eva is to him? Something he can use? Something he can lie about?* It struck him then that the commander had never once asked if Eva's departure from Halston pained him.

Lord Kass laughed. "Neither of you know anything of what it means to be a gentleman of Soladis."

Whispers swept through the chamber. Assemblywoman Lamunda stood and folded her arms across her chest. She was dressed in a style from the Sapphire Isles, her dress embroidered with a hundred bright flowers along the hem. "We are all of Soladisean blood," she said. "Watch yourself."

"We are all Soladisean," said an older Assemblyman. "We are the descendants of the greatest empire this world has ever seen. And it is our brave soldiers who carry that legacy forward. Not men like you, Lord Kass."

"Really, I—"

"Thank you," Commander Gavon said, cutting Kass off. He squared his shoulders, then rested his hands on the podium, spread his fingers wide, and leaned forward. "We are the citizens of the Golden Republic. The greatest, most moral, and most prosperous nation in the history of the world. We must stand united now. As one people. Behind one leader. And I will never let us be the slaves of gods or echoes."

At his last word, the great chamber fell silent.

Zeke held his breath.

EVA WAS IN NO mood for a ball. None of them were. But the guests had already begun to gather at the Nautileum, and so she would need to outfit herself properly to move about the grounds. Andreas let them into his rooms in the guests' quarters so that they might change for the evening.

Naeri had fashioned Eva a gown as scarlet as a snake's eye, the mask a night-dark pair of crow's wings. Silver embroidery along her hems and bust mimicked the shapes of bones and clouds of wavering smoke. Her evening gloves, to conceal her godmarks, were made of satin covered in black lace. Her hoopskirt, the frame of which collapsed small enough to fit in a purse small bag, had two weapon racks hidden within the wide panniers.

Cevette, meanwhile, dressed herself in a suit with a gold jacket and breeches, a white lace cravat, and a waistcoat of rich cream. Golden droplets sparkled in her earlobes. White lace epaulets sat on her shoulders, and she wore a mask of gold foil shaped like the flukes of an orca. With firm and steady fingers, she braided Eva's hair and pinned it up around her head like a crown. She suggested a pot of red lip paint to Eva, who thought it would look striking with her dress, but turned it down knowing it would rub off all over Cevette at some point in the evening and cause a scandal.

Properly attired, they followed the directions Andreas had given them to the ballroom, Eva's brother having gone on ahead of them when Eva began talking about how often she planned to kiss Cevette. The main ballroom entrance was through a door that led onto a balcony, from which a grand staircase cascaded down to the ballroom floor. Hand in hand, they descended, their shoes clicking on the white marble floor. The room was several hundred feet across, its pale white plaster walls covered with golden embellishments. Crystal chandeliers scattered rainbows across every surface, even Cevette's cheeks, and murals covered the ceiling, depicting pretty young men and women cavorting in a field. Servants in blue livery poured wine and passed about trays of strawberry cake. As Cevette and Eva descended into the ballroom, a twenty-person orchestra tuned their instruments, and the hum of music rose to greet them. Unlike at her father's affairs, where guests displayed loyalty by wearing the colors of the Republic, Tomis' guests were clad in a rainbow of shimmering silks and satin. Perhaps that meant something; perhaps it was only the custom of the city of Soladis.

Eva and Cevette reached the foot of the stair and set off across the ballroom. All eyes flickered to watch them. The guests' warm laughter paused. *Echo,* someone whispered, and the sound seemed to ricochet off the walls. *Another echo.* Cevette shot a warning glance around the ballroom, her eyes stern behind her mask. The guests looked away from them, a bit abashed. The conversation resumed.

"I would expect better of Tomis' friends," Cevette said.

"This is the warmest reception I've ever had at this sort of party," Eva told her.

They took their seats, marked by two place cards reading *Captain Bluebonnet & Her Wife,* at the long teak dining table that stretched down the east side of the ballroom. Andreas sat to Eva's left. He had exchanged his practical black cotton coat for a similar one of rich velvet, with diamonds in his cufflinks and fasteners. His mask was pale pink satin. "Tomis is a generous friend," he said, gesturing at his clothing as he sat. "But I simply must meet your new seamstress, sister. Her work is divine."

Servants walked down the length of the table, setting small plates of food out before each guest. First came a salad of fresh greens dressed in vinegar, accompanied by rose-pink wine and pine nuts. A wheel of cheese with a red rind was rolled down the table; the servants sliced it with circle-bladed knives said to be Tomis' own design. Then came rosemary-dusted lamb ribs, served alongside glasses of a tannin-rich red wine, roasted until meat was falling off the bone. Eva peeled them apart with a small fork to spare her gloves.

Up and down the table the servants went. She watched them all closely. *That one. With the tattoo near his neck.* As he walked past her, carrying a silver ewer of water, she put a hand on his wrist. He paused. She pushed back his sleeve, revealing the tattooed coordinates of a navigational map.

"I knew I recognized you," she said, keeping her voice low. "What are members of the True Ink Movement doing here?"

He leaned over and refilled her water glass. "The same thing you are," he said quietly. Saving echoes." He pulled his arm free and continued down the table.

"Are those the revolutionaries you told me about?" Andreas murmured when the man was out of earshot. Eva nodded. He frowned. He had barely touched his food, but he had emptied his wine glass twice. "Something's wrong. I don't like this."

"I find myself agreeing with your brother," said Cevette.

An echo in a blue servant's dress stepped up behind them, a tray of dishes balanced on one arm. Her pale skin was worn by the sun, and her hands had heavy calluses from pulling rope. Andreas stared into his wine glass and pretended not to see her.

"Hello, Cornellia," Eva said quietly as she cleared their dishes away.

Cornellia smiled. "Hello, Skullrunner."

"What are you doing here?"

"Looking out for my sisters." She winked. "Keep safe. Both of you."

Something is most certainly afoot, Eva knew. But she could not tell what.

The dinner concluded with cups of coconut ice-cream sprinkled with almond shavings, served in porcelain cups covered in gold leaf. Eva savored every sweet drop and licked clean her spoon. As she did, Tomis, who sat at the head of the long table, stood and clapped his hands.

"My guests!" he said. His voice shook a bit as he spoke, but his smile did not slip. His dinner suit was also of the Beauchamp pale blue, his mask like a puff of cloud. His oiled-down red curls were tied back with a ribbon. "I know that many of you, as do I myself, wait impatiently for news of the vote of impeachment to arrive from Assembly Hall. We have done what we can. We have spoken to our representatives on the Assembly. We have urged them to take action. Our part in this is over. Now, I invite you all to join in the dancing. Dark days may lie ahead of us, but in here, together, the night is as bright as we make it."

The guests nodded in agreement. Eva joined in. *I have done everything I can to make this right,* she told herself.

What would her sisters do? What would Commander Gavon do?

THERE WAS SOMETHING FOUL in the air of Soladis that evening. Danger of a rank and poison sort. Deep in her bones, Cevette remembered she had felt this before.

In a great clatter of porcelain and silverware, the servants cleared the table. The diners stood and made their way to the center of the room. The orchestra played the first gentle notes of a minuet. In a rustle of skirts, couples took to the open floor. They spun graceful circles across the pale white marble.

Cevette took Eva's hands and led her out onto the floor. It would be best to follow the crowd, to avoid drawing undue attention, and Cevette did like to dance. *When did I learn the Soladisean dances? And for what purpose?* They turned to face one another. Cevette pulled Eva up against her chest and placed a firm, guiding hand on her lower back. Her crimson skirts whispered about them as Cevette swept her into the opening foot-work of the minuet.

Beneath the glistening crystal chandeliers, they slid through the neat, measured steps. Violin, flute, and harpsichord played with a tempo smooth as a cascading waterfall. The scent of perfume and candlewax rose through the air. Sweat prickled where her fingertips entwined with Eva's. The world narrowed to her hand on Eva's back, the arch of Eva's narrow lips as they parted slightly. Cevette's throat flushed beneath her lace cravat. *I want those lips all over me.*

They stepped apart, clapped, and came back together. Eva's left hand settled back on Cevette's shoulder, on the gold thread of her epaulet. Cevette shivered. They spun in tighter, ever tighter circles. The cellos took up the harmony, and the music shifted to something almost mournful. Eva twirled Cevette under one arm and pulled her in close to her chest. A shudder ran through Cevette's frame. Eva grinned, a flash of pride in her dark black eyes.

"Do you know what they're up to?" Cevette said, her voice lowered, nodding toward Cornellia and the disguised revolutionaries. They had taken up posts around the side doors to the great ballroom; the ones that led out onto the lawn.

Eva frowned and shook her head. "No. I don't like it, though. If Korinne has what she wants, why are they still here?"

"I don't know. But I don't like it." Cevette shuddered.

It stirred *memories.*

She had walked the grounds of the Nautileum before. She had swum in the waters of the small harbor on the edge of the estate. She had lain in the shadows of the great crystal spire. A woman with long, dark hair had lain besides her.

She had been happy here.

"I am reminded," Cevette whispered, "of how easy it would be for me to slip into the life of a Soladisean. To give up everything I am for a place of wealth and comfort. Part of me fears I already did."

They stood in the middle of the dance floor, where all could see. Eva pulled her in close and kissed her. As their lips met, the violins reached a resonant crescendo. The kiss was firm and strong, tasting of coconut ice-cream and woodsmoke. The ballroom spun around them, rainbows dancing off the crystal chandeliers, and the kiss went on and on.

"I cannot speak for the Sea People," Eva whispered as she pulled back, "But whatever lies in your past, and whatever lies ahead of us, I love you."

"Oh, Eva," she whispered. A great warmth filled Cevette, from head to toe. A great peace, a great calm, as if the dark of Eva's eyes was the sea at midnight. It was a precious gift Eva offered her. She had to find the perfect words to reply.

Before she could, the doors at the top of the grand staircase flew open and banged against the walls. All the guests paused and looked up as a messenger ran in, a boy no older than fourteen, panting and out of breath.

"Word from Assembly Hill!" he wheezed, bent double. "The vote of impeachment has failed! Jonathan Gavon remains the chairman of the Assembly and the commander-in-chief of the military! Long live the Golden Republic! Long live Commander Gavon!"

SOLIDARITY

In the City of Soladis, in the unceded territory of the Ketil Yata Nation, on the Island of Soladis. 21ˢᵗ Morghasmonth, Year Twenty-Two of the Golden Republic.

Ariella asked why I hadn't left my room in two days. She feared I was ill, and so I told her nothing was wrong, only that some boys had said unkind things at the library and my room was where I could avoid them. Within a day, I had a formal written apology from all of them, and Father posted new guards to ensure I could read and study unbothered. I know it was all her doing. He wouldn't care unless she cared. He's the one who never lets me leave the fortress. I don't mind. I have my research, and I have my sister, and so I want for very little indeed. My sentiments are those of profound gratitude. Every echo deserves a protector like Ariella. While my dear sister is close, I fear nothing. –from the diary of Korinne Gavon.

Andreas laughed.

It was a terrible sound, high and hacking and desperate, the cry of some creature and not a gentleman of intellect at all. One moment he had been leaning against the north wall of the ballroom, thinking of the corpses under Assembly Hall, the fact his sister had a lover when he did not, and his own imminent victory, and then the truth had come in and struck him in the chest. He sunk to his knees on the polished marble floor and trembled.

"Andreas?" Eva rushed through the crowds and knelt beside him. Her hoopskirt telescoped inward; her skirts pooled out around her. She put a hand on his shoulder. "I'm here. All's well. I'll look after you."

The orchestra remained silent. The guests spoke amongst themselves in hushed, lowered voices. *But the riot,* they whispered. *But our minds.*

Tomis pushed his way through the shocked crowd and rushed to Andreas' side. "Are you well?" he said. Andreas could only nod. "Good. Gods, I'm sorry. The Assembly will live to regret this."

"I must have released too many memories," Eva said. She looked distraught. Cevette knelt beside her and took her hand. "I gave them a reason to hate us. It would have worked if I hadn't—"

"We had no chance," Andreas said. His fists tightened. His nails dug into his palms. The rank unfairness of it burned away inside him. "This was my fault, not yours. I was fool enough to think I could play their game and win a place among them. But the first rule of the Republic is that the echoes always lose." They would always see him as an echo first. An echo *only*. He had no place among the gentry of the Republic. He was better than all of them at everything they valued most, and yet he would never be their equal. Only a fragment. A living trophy from a vanquished foe. *An echo. Echo. Echo.*

"Come with us," Captain Zarcanzi said. "You'll have a place on my ship, Mr. Gavon. Far away from your foster father and his magic."

"Please," Eva said. "Come with us. We'll find a new way to stop him. Somehow."

"You don't understand," Andreas whispered. "You have your ship and the halls of Death. But I am Soladisean—at least, I've always been Soladisean—and the skills I have are the ones Soladiseans value. I belong in this city. In this country. And it wants to kill me."

EVA PRESSED HER FINGERS to her lips. *Oh.* A thousand thoughts raced through her head. She had never seen her brother like this. She had always envied his ability to navigate society. She had never realized how heavily it weighed on him.

The crack of a gunshot echoed through the ballroom. Guests screamed. Plaster rained down from a crack in the ceiling where the painted face of a dark-haired maiden had exploded. Eva looked up to see a dozen soldiers in orange wool jackets standing at the top of the ballroom stairs.

"The City of Soladis has been attacked," said the lead officer, a short woman with a dozen medallions on her chest. "The echoes known as Korinne, Demon of Dogshead, and Evazina, the Skullrunner, have slaughtered twenty of our bravest defenders in a brazen ambush."

Eva's stomach dropped. She blinked in disbelief. *It wasn't me.* Were they confused? Or did they simply not care?

"The Assembly has passed a declaration of emergency. All echoes in Republic territory have now been designated as enemies of the state. The echoes in the city are hereby commanded to report to the city armory. They will be safely sequestered from the citizens of Soladis until their loyalty can be proven. Those who refuse to come willingly will be arrested on charges of treason."

No, Eva thought. *It's not fair. They can't punish all of us.*

A long-fingered hand closed on Eva's shoulder. "Can you open a portal here?" said a familiar voice.

Cornellia. Eva stood, and turned to face her. She met the eyes of her fellow echo. "Not here," she said. "Up near the gate, yes. But if the soldiers came from the main road, they may well be looking for us there." *Us, or whatever echoes they can find.*

"We'll go out the side, then." She nodded toward the doors at the northeast side of the ballroom, which hung open. The revolutionaries stood guard about it, sleeves pushed back to reveal their tattooed star charts and codes. Eva stared at them. All seemed hazy, as if she floated in a dream. She could hardly believe this was real. It wasn't fair. Commander Gavon deserved to lose everything. Not the echoes.

"Go," Tomis said, his voice low and urgent, as Cevette helped Andreas to his feet. "I'll deal with them and buy you some time."

"Will you be safe?" Eva said.

"I don't know. But it will be the least risk for me to confront them." He winked at her. "And it will make a good story."

Then he turned and strode toward the grand staircase. The guests parted in a ripple of skirts and shining coats to let him through. The rainbow reflections of the crystal chandeliers danced off his coat as he climbed. The soldiers looked toward him, their hands on their weapons with wary eyes. The footmen on the main door, who had backed away from the soldiers, shot him wary looks as he marched up to the lead officer and put his hands on his hips.

"What is the meaning of this?" Tomis asked. "I am the master of this house. You have no right to come onto my property and arrest my guests."

"In times of emergency, Lord Beauchamp, even the rights of citizens must bow before the good of the state."

"I am a free man. I bow to no one."

"Eva," Cevette whispered. "He made his choice. Don't waste it. We need to go."

Gritting her teeth, Eva looked away from Tomis. She grabbed Andreas by the hand and tugged him forward; Cevette and Cornellia followed her. They were already close to the north wall of the ballroom, thank the gods, with all the guests between them and the stairs. The doors were barely a hundred feet away. The cool night air brushed against her cheeks. The tattooed revolutionaries closed protectively around them as they stepped out onto the gravel path outside.

As the revolutionaries closed the door, there came a sound like the thudding of a fist, and Tomis cried out in pain.

"We need to hurry," said a revolutionary. "To the harbor. Come with us." She took off down the path, gravel flying up from her heels. Eva hiked up her skirts in her fists. A revolutionary picked up a lantern from behind a sculpture of a slender young man and passed it to Cevette. She lifted it high, and then all of them were running.

The Nautileum had been built atop a seaside hill. A small, well-concealed harbor sat beneath its eastern slope. After two minutes of hurried running, they reached the wall of the estate. A narrow iron gate had been opened for them. Eva's breath caught as she stepped through. Dozens of lanterns glowed at the foot of the hill, on the docks and on the water. A small crowd had gathered. Pale faces turned up to stare at them.

It can't be, she thought, following the revolutionaries down the twists and turns of a switchback trail, Cevette, Cornellia, and Andreas close behind her. A cool wind whistled through the night. The scent of wild honeysuckle wafted up through the hillside bracken, and the sound of familiar voices rose with it. *So many of them. Here. How?* But it was true. She could see them clearer and clearer as she drew closer. Almost forty echoes, young and old, some alone, some with wives and some with children beside them, clad in the common dress of cityfolk, all laden down with satchels and chests. Black-clad echo pirates and tattooed revolutionaries ushered them onto dinghies.

Korinne stood at the foot of the trail. Her face was set, the picture of grim focus, her arms folded across her chest. Shimmering sequins formed a pattern of tentacles across the violet shoulders of her jacket. The necklace of silver skulls shone at her throat. An abomination, a mass of tentacles that rose eight feet high, three shark heads jutting out of it at odd angles, stood behind her. Eva flinched at the sight of it. Here was her older sister. Here was the woman whose abomination had killed Lovett. And the two truths pulled in opposite directions with enough force to split her heart in two.

"How did you know about the archive under Assembly Hall?" Eva demanded. As Cornellia and the revolutionaries rushed to the boats, she strode up to the Demon, Cevette at her side, Andreas behind her.

"From Lord Merris." Korinne smiled. A fleck of blood shone on her pale cheek. "You went too soft on him, sister. The man sold children. Well, I put an end to that. But not before he told me where the commander hid the memories he most wanted to hide."

So Merris was dead, and he had died painfully. Eva shuddered. But she would not mourn him. "You're working with the True Ink Movement?"

"I've known Thimmely and his crew for years."

"And you get along well with them? I thought you and your crew only fought for echoes."

"They also fight for echoes."

One tattooed woman stepped forward. "The echoes of Soladis reached out for us when Commander Gavon had those first posters nailed up. They've been harassed for weeks. Many have lost their employment or been turned out of their lodging. We've been helping them get along. Then the Demon came and offered them a way to evacuate. She feared the commander might move against the echoes to secure his own position. We've been smuggling echoes into the Nautileum for days, knowing it had its own harbor, so that we might move them quickly if need be."

Shouts rang out atop the hill. Korinne cursed. "Get in a boat, Captain Zarcanzi, sisters—"

"Brother," Andreas said.

"Brother," Korinne corrected herself. "Hurry. It's the fastest way back to *Shadow Queen*. Unless you can to open a portal, Evazina, but I assume you would have already done so if you could."

"I can't," Eva said. This had always been a peaceful little harbor, until tonight. Until Korinne came. "I . . . I can't go with you. You killed twenty soldiers today."

Korinne frowned. "How many did you kill when you raided *Pleasant Mary?* Don't be a fool. None of us are unbloodied here."

Eva shivered at the memory of the raid. At how it had felt, to have Death wrap around her like a warm blanket. "What I did, I did as a pirate. What you did, you did as an echo." Eva folded her arms across her chest. "Andreas and I have tried to show the citizens of the Republic what the commander has done to them. But you have shown them just how much cruelty we are capable of when we stand together. If it hadn't been for you, the vote would have passed and the echoes of Soladis would have slept easily in their own beds tonight."

"They've lived in fear for months. You don't see me blaming you for that." Korinne lifted her chin high and cracked her remaining knuckles in the crook of her elbow. "If it hadn't been for us, he would have found another story about echoes to scare the Assembly with. The vote was never going to pass. This is how he keeps his grip on power. One way or another, he finds a way to sacrifice us."

Andreas stepped forward. He had removed his pale pink mask, and he was shivering in the night wind. "That is our role in the world the commander built," he said, quietly. "The only place we can have."

Korinne nodded. "And this is what I must do: summon an army of abominations and burn his Golden Republic to the ground."

"What?" Eva stared at her. She must have misheard. *Destroy the Republic.* Not the man who broke and tormented them. The world he had built. It was most certainly flawed, yes, she knew that well. But if Korinne unleashed her abominations upon the Republic at large, thousands would die. "But *why?*"

"You two had the right idea, trying to remove him from power. That's how he controls us. The Ministry of Childhood Welfare. The army and the courts. The lies and the censorship. We may not know how to kill him, but we can kill what he's built. And once the tools of the state lie in ashes, he will only be one more oddity in a world filled with them. Easily forgotten."

"I wanted to remove him peacefully," Eva said. "Not kill innocent people. They will die, Korinne. Especially if you use abominations against them."

"The abominations are the weapons I have. This is what it will take to free us. Do you believe we deserve to be free?"

"Yes, of course, but—"

"Eva." Korinne's nostrils flared. Her face was flushed in the lantern-light. Her hand curled into a fist. "Are you ready to fight for us?"

Eva froze. "I . . ." She didn't know what to say. *Not like this,* perhaps, but she knew that meant *no.*

"I'm ready." Andreas stepped forward. "Sister. I'm coming with you."

As shouts rose from atop the dark hill, as the last of the fleeing echoes crammed into the dinghies, Andreas stared at Korinne and thought, *I must learn what she knows.* This was what an echo with true power looked like. An echo with an army of echoes behind her.

"I have little to offer your movement," he said, "save for my skills as a philosopher and a writer. They may not be—"

"You're my brother." Korinne's face softened. "You don't have to earn a place with me. It's yours."

"Oh," Andreas said. He did not think he'd ever been welcomed anywhere that easily. Not like that. "Thank you."

Korinne nodded. "We'll be quite glad to have you. Climb aboard."

He stepped forward. Eva caught his arm. "Don't do this," she said. "Andreas. Please."

Andreas looked back at her. Strands of his white-dyed hair fluttered on the evening wind. His diamond cufflinks sparkled on his sleeves. He shook his head. "What other choices do we have, Eva? Arrest? Surrender? We're echoes. That will always define us. We must make it our strength. Or the world will make it our weakness."

"No," Eva said. "You can't. I need you. You've always done the right thing." She had always looked to him for what she should do. "There must be another way. We cannot unleash these horrors on the world. Not even to save ourselves."

The shouting atop the hill was growing closer. With it came the sound of a gunshot. "Enough," Korinne said. "We have the abominations. We can do this without her. Eva, keep your distance from *Shadow Queen* and the Gray Isle. I still have one more archive to claim."

"No," Cevette said. "The Gray Isle—some of the memories stored there are mine."

"So be it." Korinne shrugged. "I'm not doing this to hurt you. Either of you. But I will not let you stop me."

Eva and Cevette shared a look. An unspoken question hovered between them. *Can we kill her?* Eva had daggers up her sleeves, and Cevette had a pistol inside her coat, but they would be two against dozens, and if either of them missed, they could hit her brother. Cevette shook her head. Eva nodded.

"I intend to find my own way forward out of this mess," Eva said. Then she met her brother's eyes. "I love you. I'm sorry."

She took Cevette by the hand and turned back toward the hill.

What am I doing? she thought as they ran back up the gravel path. Behind her came the sound of oars scraping against the dock as Korinne's dinghy pulled away. Was part of her still trying to be what the Republic thought of as a good echo? She had long since failed at that. But she could be better than Korinne. She could cling to that.

"At the top of the hill," Eva told Cevette, "we go left, along the wall, through the dark. When we reach the gatehouse, I can open a portal and take us back to *Sea Wolf.*"

Cevette nodded, and doused her lantern. "We go by moonlight."

When they reached the crest of the hill, a dozen soldiers in orange coats awaited them.

Zeke stood at their head. His drawn saber shone in the moonlight. "Arrest them."

Eva cursed. She reached for the knives in her sleeves. White light bloomed in Zeke's hand. A pulse of magic flew across the night and slammed into Eva's chest, washing through her like a wave. Stunned, she stumbled into Cevette's side. Her power felt as loose as a floppy fish in her chest. She wouldn't be able to enter Death until it wore away.

"Hands up," Zeke said. A dozen guns were trained on them. They had no choice. Eva and Cevette lifted their hands. "Bind the pirates. Take them to the ballroom. Commander Gavon wants a word with the Skullrunner."

The Remembered Revolution

In the City of Soladis, in the unceded territory of the Ketil Yata Nation, on the Island of Soladis. 22nd Morghasmonth, Year Twenty-Two of the Golden Republic.

No one cares more for the history of the Golden Republic than I. To protect it is my most solemn duty. It requires a vast investment of resources, and, even so, there are subversive little stories that slip through the net. This is why I value the loyalty of my citizens so dearly. I must trust them to trust me at my word. –Letter from Commander Jonathan Gavon to Lord Mykil Merris, Minister for Childhood Welfare

THE SOLDIERS BOUND THEIR wrists behind their backs; stripped off their shimmering masks and threw them to the ground. Zeke asked if they had any weapons, to spare them the indecency of a search; Cevette volunteered the pistol in her coat, and he took it from her. Eva told him to go fuck himself, so he sighed, lifted the outermost layer of her skirts, found the sheathed knives in her hoopskirt, and removed the whole whalebone apparatus. The skirts drooped. He took the knives from her ankles, wrists, and even the one hidden at the back of her neck. Then he said, "Your father will meet you in the ballroom."

"I will not speak with him."

"I'll be there. Watching him." His fingers curled around the hilt of his sword. "I promised you once that I would not let him split you. I keep my promises."

"Go fuck yourself." Was this how he planned to soothe his conscience? To convince himself he was not complicit in the horrors Commander Gavon had unleashed upon the echoes? She would not let him rest easy. He was no friend to her if he would only take half-measures in her defense.

She supposed Korinne might say the same about her.

Eva looked up and met Zeke's eyes. They were wide with worry. The night wind stirred the curls that had escaped his violet cap. The stars glittered behind him. "Tell me this. Did the Assembly learn of what had happened beneath the Hall before or after the vote?"

Zeke hesitated. "It was after the vote," he said, at last. "But before they ordered the arrest of the echoes."

Eva frowned. There was nothing in that to make anything better.

The soldiers escorted them back into the ballroom. The guests had fled. The servants were nowhere to be seen. Soldiers in golden uniforms, perhaps a dozen of them, strolled about the white marble floors. Some had stolen a barrel of wine and were drinking from crystalline glasses. Some were prying the gilded flowers off the ballroom's plaster wall panels. Tomis Beachamp, his face red with sweat, lay atop his own dining table. His stockings were rolled down; his right shin had swollen in an ugly manner.

"Bring me some rags and some wood for a splint," called a familiar voice. Eva's breath caught. She had never seen an echo that old. Or an echo with the tattoos of a True Ink Movement revolutionary. *All I have seen in a few months of the Republic and its horrors—she has endured this for decades.* The old woman wore a loose homespun dress. Her silver hair was tied up in a knot at the back of her neck. A rainbow of tattoos covered her bare skin. Her hands were wrinkled, but they were steady as they prodded Tomis' leg. "Well. Looks like you might just keep your foot."

"Good. It would look ridiculous if I had to hop my way up the gallows."

Footsteps sounded on the grand staircase. Eva turned and shuddered. Commander Gavon descended into the ballroom, clad in his worn and faded orange uniform jacket, his sky-blue sash of office hanging limp over his shoulder. The polished silver buckles on his shoes shone in the light from the chandeliers. "Hello, Skullrunner," he said, his voice low with threat. He nodded to Cevette. "Captain Zarcanzi." He strode past both of them to lean over the table where Tomis lay. "Lord Beauchamp. I have no intention to hang you. The people of this city are fond of you, which speaks poorly of them, and at present I lack the resources to both control Soladis and address larger concerns. Just take this as a warning to keep your mouth shut."

"You will not hear a word of criticism from my lips," Tomis said. "On my honor as a gentleman."

"Good." Commander Gavon pivoted on his heel. "Now. As for the rest of you lot."

"What do you want from us?" Cevette demanded.

"Korinne has murdered Lord Merris. The servants who hid away from her when she began her . . . interrogation . . . of him told me what she forced him to reveal. She will be racing toward the Gray Isle now, to seize the memories of the gods. If she can claim them, she'll hold the power to summon thousands of abominations. A force large enough to devastate the Golden Republic." He frowned. "She already has a small army of the monsters. The ships of the navy are scattered and cannot be recalled in time to stop her. But my scouts have spotted *Sea Wolf* within sailing distance of the Gray Isle. So, Captain Zarcanzi, it would seem your godreapers are the one force that can protect the Seaward Isles from slaughter."

"If you want us to fight for you," Cevette said, "you should treat us with more respect."

"I am not telling you what I want. I am telling you what you will do. You will sail at once to the Gray Isle, rendezvous with *Kembrielle,* and assist me in dispatching Korinne's abominations so that she may be arrested and tried for treason. If you defy me, I will split apart Madam Bly—" He paused, and nodded toward the old woman. "—and see to it your entire crew remembers nothing but a lifetime of loyal service as soldiers of the Godreaper Corps."

Cevette glared at him. Her hands tightened into trembling fists. Zeke shuddered, but said nothing. Eva went very still. She knew who he was.

She looked to Cevette. "We have no choice."

"Were this only a matter between you and I, *sir*," Cevette said, "I would duel you to the death on the spot. But I will not countenance such a violation of the crew I have sworn to protect. We will meet you off the coast of the Gray Isle."

"Good," he said. "You will wait here for the Skullrunner's magic to return, then you will depart for your ship. We rendezvous at the Gray Isle in two days; if you find yourself running behind, use the Stormbraider to make up time. Should you think of betraying me, you should know my power has no geographic limit. I can and I will purge your memories whenever I choose. You cannot evade me. Not in any way that matters." He nodded to Zeke. "Lieutenant Dare. With me." With his chin held high, he marched back up the grand white marble staircase. Zeke followed, his face as set as the bark of a tree, giving nothing away.

Eva and Cevette rushed to Tomis' side. A pair of servants had ducked out of the kitchen; they had brought Madam Bly a pair of sturdy wooden serving spoons and a set of linen napkins. They were knotting the napkins together by their corners. Cevette went to speak with them in a low voice.

Eva sat on a chair near Tomis. He looked up to her, his eyes wide with pain. Quietly, he said, "Did your sisters get away?"

Eva nodded.

"Good." Hoots and cheers filled the ballroom as a soldier ripped a gilded fleur-de-lis off the wall. The plaster beneath it cracked and crumbled. The man's fellows slapped him on the back; then pulled out their belt-knives and began slashing away at the gilded leaves and blossoms beside it. Chips of plaster tumbled to the floor. Brightly-colored paint shone beneath it. "I didn't even know there were paintings under there," Tomis said. "My family always kept those walls plastered over."

"Everything looks better with a splash of color," said Madam Bly. She smiled at Eva. "My name is Dorothea Bly. I know who you are, Skullrunner. All the echoes of the Seaward Isles know your name."

Once, to hear such a thing would have frightened her. Now, she did not know what to feel. "Do you know of the Demon of Dogshead? Korinne?"

"Oh, yes," she said, warmly. "I've heard of her. She does us proud."

Quickly, in hushed tones, Eva explained what had passed between her and Korinne as the echoes had slipped out of the Nautileum. "She says war is the only way to free us. But a war . . . it would be so cruel. So unfair. I want to fight for a better world. For us. For everyone. But I can't stand beside her. Not for this."

The servants passed Dorothea a cord of napkins, all braided together. "Hold those serving spoons steady on each side of his leg," she said. Cevette, her hands tied, watched with worrying eyes. Dorothea took the cord, tied it to one spoon, and set about twisting it into a makeshift splint. "You have a good deal in common with Korinne," she told Eva as she worked. "Both of you are echoes who fled the commander's household, killed gods, and turned pirate."

"I am *nothing* like her."

"Ah, sister. My heart aches for you. It twists the soul in knots, to hate and deny that which you are. An echo with a talent for violence and a love for the open sea. An echo with a passion for justice. Fairness. Equality. I have known many echoes like you. I was honored to call them my sisters in the True Ink Movement. Their names and stories are written on my skin. For decades, echoes like you have fought bravely to free us. It's true that none of them have killed the commander. But you and Korinne are part of an important tradition, one that I still believe in. Especially now that, for the first time I know of, the power of the Skullrunner has at last found its way back to an echo's control."

"What do you mean?" Eva frowned. "It chose me?"

"No." Dorothea tied a final knot, locking the splint in place around Tomis' shin. "You chose each other."

Eva flinched. She thought back to the moment she had thrown her knife through the Skullrunner's throat. She had tried to forget the longing she had felt for its power. She did not understand where that desire had come from. But it had been very real, and very strong.

Eva lowered her voice to a whisper, so not even Tomis or Cevette could hear her. "I wish I wasn't an echo."

"Once, I wished for that, too." Dorothea wrapped one wizened arm around Eva's shoulders and pulled her into a hug. She was stronger than she looked, and, though she smelled of hard travel, Eva was very glad to have a sister close. "But now I only wish that we might love each other as we are."

Eva drew a deep breath and steadied herself. *There is so much more than evil inside us.* As Dorothea stepped back, Eva noticed the tattoo on her collarbone: the arch with the star inside. *I've seen that before,* she thought. The True Ink Movement revolutionaries all had it. Sebastian Thimmely had told her it had once been the symbol of the revolution, before Commander Gavon had chosen the two linked loops.

But she had seen it recently. Only moments ago.

Eva turned toward the wall with the cracked and shattered plaster. Soldiers sat beneath it, drinking wine and showing off the gold ornaments they'd pried from the walls. The painting they had exposed depicted a tall woman who wore a gown of black and red, stepping out from an archway of bone and billowing smoke. An archway that was the same shape as the arch-and-star on the banner she carried.

Why is Morghaia carrying the battle standard of the revolution?

Eva frowned. She would have rubbed her eyes if her hands weren't bound. *It can't be true.* But there it was: Morghaia, accompanied by soldiers both living and dead, waving them forward. And the man by her side was unmistakable: the black hair frosted white at his temples, the blue sash worn over his shoulder. *Commander Gavon. They were allies. They fought the revolution together.*

That was how he had won. Not through genius tactics, or common courage. The man who'd freed the Seaward Isles from the gods had fought beside a divine ally all the while. *Why would she help him?* That, she didn't yet know. But only the power of Morghaia could have made Commander Gavon immortal. *He calls her a tyrant. A monster. But there would still be a Theocracy without her. And he knows that. And he kept that from us.*

Her nostrils flared. Her nails bit into her palms. Her heart hammered. A bead of sweat ran down her cheek. *How dare he tell us what we are? What our tie to Morghaia and Death means?*

Wherever she ran, the scars of what her father had taught her would bind her to him. Until she healed from them, she could not be free. She could not stop him.

She had to love her sisters. Or he would break them all.

I need to speak to Korinne.

ZEKE FOLLOWED THE COMMANDER out onto the colonnade. The cold night wind blew about them. Dead leaves and dust spiraled along the flagstones, weaving their way in and out of the pillars. A terrible hush had fallen over the estate. It reminded him of the silence had heard after his village had burned, as he'd crouched in a root-cellar, afraid to speak lest an abomination find him.

And I helped bring this about. He was glad that the Demon had managed to smuggle many of the echoes outside the city. But he knew what would come next. Zeke could tell himself that Commander Gavon was pursuing Korinne to avenge the soldiers she had killed, or to stop her from unleashing abominations on the innocent, but he could no longer deny the truth. *He hates the echoes. It's the only way he can do what he does.*

Commander Gavon took a pipe from his pocket. A lantern hung from a nearby pillar, its light a wavering flame that cast the hollows of his cheeks in shadows. He lit the smokeweed off it and pressed it to his lips. As he took a deep breath, he smiled. "What a great nation we've build."

"A great nation?" Zeke said. He frowned and shook his head. "Surely a great nation could treat the echoes with courtesy."

"We must treat all people with courtesy. They are not people. I've known hundreds of echoes. Many of them, I've fostered in my own house. It's unnerving just how similar they are. The same face, yes, but also the same sullen moods, the same anger, the same disrespect . . . I keep them close, out of charity, yes, and because they have . . . uses. But I've never known them to be anything other than agents of discord and violence. This is not the first time they've risen against me. But I can restrain them."

"By threatening an old woman."

The commander turned to face Zeke fully. His gray eyes widened. The wind blew threads of pipe smoke between them.

"Are you angry with me?" Commander Gavon said. "By the gods, Ezekiel. She's only an echo."

"Did you ever intend to give Madam Bly a trial for the crimes you have accused her of? Or did you only arrest her for use as a sacrifice?"

"She is a traitor. She has the same tattoos as the man who shot you with an arrow. And she will meet a traitor's end." The commander reached up and ran his free hand along the side of Zeke's face. His skin was weathered and cold. "If all goes well, I will split her for you."

No, Zeke thought. A wave of dizziness swept through him. He closed his eyes. "What do you mean?"

"There is a vast swathe of frontier land on New Soladis I plan to claim for the Republic. Three hundred thousand acres. I will deed it all to you. Damn the foster bond—you're close enough to twenty-five, no one will notice or care if I dissolve it. Of course, I'll need to convince the Sea People that we amended our treaty, and convince the local frontier militias to serve you loyally, but splitting Dorothea will account for that. You'll be rich. Honored." Commander Gavon smiled. "A fitting husband for the leader of the Republic."

How could this be the man I love? Zeke's guts twisted. *How did I never see him for what he truly was?* He didn't know what to say. At last, he managed to ask, "Do you . . . do you truly believe I could follow in your footsteps?"

"Of course you could. That's why I love you."

Zeke turned away from the commander and pressed his fist to his mouth. His throat burned. His stomach heaved. *I wanted this. I fought for this. I killed for this.* And all the while, he had turned his gaze from the truth, not only because he loved the man he had imagined the commander to be, but because he had loved the place in the world that love promised him. Here was his prize: the minds of his countryfolk and the soul of an echo, to be shattered and abused for his gain.

"Ezekiel?"

Zeke drew a deep, shuddering breath and turned back to face the commander. The older man gave him a look of concern and offered him the pipe. Zeke shook his head. *No.* "You honor me, sir. I . . . I hope I can put what you have taught me of leadership to good use."

"I know that you will." Commander Gavon lifted his pipe to his lips once more. He smiled. Smoke rose up to frame his face. "Go with Eva and her captain back to their ship. We will need your power on the frontlines against Korinne's abominations."

"Yes, sir." Zeke saluted, then turned on his heel. His heart hammered hard against his ribs. His head spun; he barely knew where he was until his shoes clicked on the white marble of the grand staircase. Down into the ballroom he descended, passing soldiers laden with loot—*no discipline*—and crossed the floor to where Eva was helping Tomis Beauchamp lean on a crutch.

"Zeke?" Eva looked up at the sight of him. "What's wrong?"

He quickened his stride. A pair of servants rushed in to support Tomis. When they had him secure, she rushed to the center of the floor, her disheveled skirts trailing on the marble. Zeke put a hand on her shoulder. He lowered his voice and whispered, "I'm sorry." And then, as she stared up at him, blinking as if she did not believe what she had just heard, he said, "I might know how to stop him."

THE SEA OF SPIRITS

BEGINNING ABOARD KEMBRIELLE, FIVE MILES NORTH OF THE CITY OF SO-
LADIS, AND CONTINUING ABOARD *SEA WOLF*, TWO HUNDRED AND THIRTY
MILES SOUTHWEST OF THE CITY OF SOLADIS. 22ND MORGHASMONTH, YEAR
TWENTY-TWO OF THE GOLDEN REPUBLIC.

**The ancestors should be free to travel the spirit waters; yet even there,
they face the corruption unleashed by Soladisean violence. –'Our History of the Golden Republic,' published in *The Dawn Beacon*.**

EVA DID NOT QUITE believe what was happening, even as Zeke took out
his belt knife, reached around behind her, and sliced through the ties on
her wrists. She gasped in relief and shook out her sore arms.

"What do you mean?" she whispered. "Stop him? You love him."

"I don't even know him." Zeke ran a hand along the back of his neck.
A bead of sweat ran down his cheek. His voice shook as he spoke. "He
played me for a fool—I played myself—" He bit his lip. "He said I should
go with you back to your ship. That I should add my power to yours and
fight Korinne's abominations. Please. Take me with you." His eyes darted
toward the soldiers who stood about the room. "We can talk freely there."

Eva hesitated. *Can I trust him?* She knew she was not the best judge of
character. But she looked him over, and she could not see a liar or an enemy.
Only her oldest friend, his heart in agony, reaching out to her for aid.

"Very well," she said. "I'll take you back to *Sea Wolf*."

Zeke nodded. He followed close behind her as she went to Tomis, who leaned on the crutch, servants close at hand, studying the exposed painting across the ballroom.

"So much has been hidden from us," Tomis said as she approached.

Eva nodded. "When the soldiers leave, cover it up. Don't risk more trouble with the commander." Zeke was taking in the painting with horror in his eyes. The other soldiers seemed too drunk to examine art; still, they dared not risk Commander Gavon discovering just how thoroughly Tomis and the Beauchamp family had broken the Republic's laws. Better he be thought of as a troublemaker than a revolutionary.

"I'll put some curtains over it," Tomis said. "Don't worry for me. The commander is right; he cannot punish me too harshly without alienating Soladis. Do what you must for your people. I'll do what I can for mine." Then, in a whisper, he added, "He started a war tonight. So long as I can stand, I'll stand with you."

"Thank you. Truly. I'll be back when I can." She gave him a brief hug, then turned and ran down the length of the table, to where Dorothea sat in an intricately-carved teak dining chair. Cevette stood beside her; Zeke went to cut through her bonds. The moment her hands were free, Eva reached out and took them in her own.

"Lieutenant Dare says he wants to help," Cevette said, her voice low. "Can we trust him?"

"We should give him the chance," Eva said. She met Dorothea's dark eyes. "I have to go," she whispered. "I'm sorry. I can't get you out of here." There was no practical way to carry an elderly woman to the nearest portal without the soldiers seeing them. "But we might have a plan to help."

Dorothea nodded. "I trust you, sister. Godspeed."

WHEN EVA PULLED ZEKE and Cevette out of the portal on *Sea Wolf*, it was an hour before dawn. The sails hung slack. Wisps of gray cloud floated across the fading stars. The air was frigid and damp. For all the misery of the weather, the evening watch was up and alert. When Eva and Cevette appeared, just outside the door of the captain's cabin, Lizeth and Naeri rushed up to them—and quickly recoiled when they saw who else had come.

"Who's the officer?" Lizeth demanded.

"I am Lieutenant Ezekiel Dare," Zeke said. "I don't believe we've met."

"Those godmarks—" Lizeth darted forward and jabbed a finger into Zeke's chest. "Eva, is he one of the Godreaper Corps?"

"He's come to help," Eva said. "He's an old friend. He—"

"I don't trust the fucking Godreaper Corps. They drove my family off our farm."

"I . . ." Zeke stammered. "My apologies—ah, is it *sir* or *ma'am?*—I don't believe I had any involvement with—"

"Did I say it was you? No. It wasn't. That was twelve years ago. But I don't trust you and I don't like you."

Zeke nodded. "Duly noted."

"You're Eva's friend," Naeri said. She folded her arms across her chest. The ruffled ribbons sewn in stripes down her skirt fluttered in the wind. "The one who betrayed her for the Republic. You chose the commander over her. How could you?"

Eva hesitated. It was true that Zeke had chosen the commander over her, and Naeri had a right to regard him poorly for that. But Naeri didn't know all of it. Eva had spoken to all her friends, at one point or another, how Zeke's choice had hurt her, but she had only told Cevette how the commander had taken Zeke into his bed. Zeke had loved him, or his idea of him, and the commander had used that love ruthlessly for his own gain. Her friends would show him some pity, if they knew that. But she would not reveal what he had gone through without his express permission.

"It appears that I am a slow learner, miss," Zeke said. He slid off his orange uniform coat, folded it neatly, and draped it over his arm. Then he took off his cap and ran his hand back through his curls. "But when I decide on a path, I am not easily swayed from it."

"Only a fool confuses determination with virtue."

Oh, she's quite angry, Eva thought. She had never seen Naeri this irate. Then again, after her experience with Lovett, it did not surprise her that Naeri had no patience for men who hurt feelings.

"I've come to help," Zeke said. "I was wrong to trust him for so long. I would like to make amends." Naeri scoffed and tossed her braids back over her shoulder. The tiny gold beads she had woven in them glittered. "Very well. It appears I must earn your trust. Eva, would you be so kind as to tell your friends what has happened in Soladis?"

Eva nodded. The whole tale spilled out: Korinne's attack on the archive under Assembly Hall, the vote of impeachment and its failure, the order to arrest the city's echoes. Naeri and Lizeth listened. Their faces grew more somber with each word, especially when Eva revealed his threat to steal all their memories if they didn't help him defeat Korinne.

"We need to free Madam Bly from him," Zeke said. "And we need to make certain he can never do this again. Here is what I propose. If we go along with his plan, if we chase Korinne to the Gray Isle and destroy her abominations, he'll go ashore to capture her, her crew, and every echo she helped escape Soladis. He'll keep Madam Bly close, to use her as a threat. But, right before he engages their forces, I can turn my power against him. Make it so he cannot split echoes. His leverage will be gone. You'll be able to ambush his forces, free Madam Bly, and capture him."

"Capture?" Cevette shook her head. "You're a soldier, Lieutenant Dare. You know what must be done. And I can't risk bringing you into this unless you accept that Jonathan Gavon must die."

Zeke closed his eyes. He swayed back and forth on the balls of his feet. At last, he said "I . . . I am aware. He's destroyed so many echoes. He's invaded the minds of his own people. He's admitted as much to me. I believe everyone has a right to a fair trial, captain. But he cannot be tried fairly in the Republic he built . . ."

"We will try him in the field," Cevette said. "We will have all the witnesses and victims of his crimes gathered there. We can allow him speak in his defense. And we can all vote on his fate."

Zeke lowered his head. His lips opened and closed a few moments before he finally spoke. At last, he said, "Thank you, captain. It is more mercy than he has ever shown his victims."

Lizeth folded their arms over their chest. The tails of their long violet coat snapped in the crisp night wind. "Do we even know if this soldier's magic will let us kill him? Has he tested it?"

"One can hardly test a murder," Zeke said.

"We don't know," said Eva. Zeke had claimed the magic of the Pridebreaker, the god of charity and humility. He could weaken the power of godreapers and abominations. Would it also affect a divine blessing? One that did not come from the commander himself? They could not know; they could only hope. "But this is the best chance we have."

"Well, I'm happy to murder the commander," Lizeth said. "With him dead, the Terraloro rebels would have a chance to declare their independence from the Republic. My father and his friends would leap at the chance. The echoes aren't the only people who want to free themselves."

Eva took a deep breath. It would not all be the fault of echoes if a war overtook the Isles, she reminded herself. There were countless people who had good reason to take up arms against the Republic. It was not the violence itself that bothered her; it was the knowing she would have to unleash that violence as an echo, on behalf of echoes. It was the knowing she would need to stand before the world and all its judgements and say her people deserved their freedom at any cost.

"Very well," Naeri said. "I have said my piece. I have no love for Commander Gavon, and I will not let him force me and my friends into bondage. But if you hurt Eva, Lieutenant Dare, I will make your clothing tie itself in knots and throw you overboard."

EVA SHOWED ZEKE TO her old hammock in the crew's quarters; then she and Cevette retired to the captain's cabin, too exhausted to do anything but wearily remove Eva's damaged ballgown and collapse in bed together.

The small candelabra with the crocheted octopus hanging over it swung overhead on its chain. Cold seeped in through the timbers as they held each other tightly. Cevette ran her thumb along Eva's cheek.

"Back in Soladis," she whispered, "you said you loved me."

Eva blushed. "It was too soon."

"Yes." Warmth filled Cevette's voice. "But you were honest. I quite like your honesty."

"You don't need to say it. Not until you're ready."

"I don't believe it will be long." Cevette kissed her collarbone. "You are a most fascinating woman, Evazina Gavon."

"Thank you." Eva tucked Cevette's head under her chin, and held her close. "You are the best woman I have ever met. A peerless captain, and a peerless lover. Never forget that."

"Mohyenosh ulalit." Cevette laughed. *Love fool.* "Did Donya teach you that phrase?"

"It was the first one I learned," Eva said. "But you are the wisest choice I ever made."

They clung to each other closely as they slept, but, when Eva woke, she found they had drawn apart in the darkness. Light now poured through the cabin window. It was early still, but she knew she would get no more rest. She dressed simply, in a shirt, breeches, boots, and her long coal-black coat, then left Cevette asleep as she stepped out into the overcast day.

Down the length of the upper deck she walked, and caught sight of Zeke gutting fish on the forecastle with Mr. Smoke. "And then the girl told me she was a princess, she was," said the cook, his voice booming, up to his elbows in tuna guts. They had laid the fish out flat on a bamboo mat; it was so large that its silver-blue tail flopped down on the forecastle steps. Zeke was holding the carcass open as Mr. Smoke worked. "Her mother had taught her dark magic to snare men's souls, but she said I had snared hers without trying." He flung a handful of entrails in a bucket.

"Truly?" Zeke said, an eyebrow raised.

"Really and truly." The cook slapped his chest. "Girls love the belly. You need to eat more, lad. I'll cook you up some liver."

Below the forecastle, sitting by the starboard rail, Tuk and Nukit were checking the ship's harpoons and giving Zeke wary looks. Eva paused as she reached them. "Is something wrong?"

Tuk frowned, and folded his arms across his chest. He wore the armored coat Naeri had made for him; he and Nukit had matching ones, gifts from their wedding. The cloth was a rich crimson, and the embroidery down the lapels and at the cuffs and collar was of otters frolicking in the currents, sewn in a rainbow of threads. The strings of pearl beads that tied off his braids glimmered in the sun. "Your friend said he came from New Soladis. Was he in the militia?"

Oh. Eva saw what frightened them. The village Zeke had grown up in had been one of many constructed in violation of a treaty between the Golden Republic and the Sea People who called that land home. "He left when he was fourteen," Eva said. "He never took up arms against your people, or said a bad word about them in my hearing. But I cannot blame you if you do not trust him."

"We don't choose where we're born, or the people we're born to. But we carry what they gave us wherever we go. And it can be heavy." He lifted a harpoon to the light, checking the long wooden shaft for cracks or damage. "Mr. Smoke knows that. He was born on New Soladis. I asked him to keep an eye on your friend. You should keep one on him too."

"I will," Eva said. She leaned up against the rail, gazing out over the bow, letting the crisp autumn wind play with her unbound black hair. "I brought him here." Perhaps Zeke could join Mr. Smoke in cooking Upailitian dishes he sometimes made; that had been how the chef won their respect more than anything.

From their perch in the rigging, Lizeth shouted, "Abomination off the port bow!"

Eva cursed. Shouts of alarm rose across the upper desk. *There.* Swiftly it flew against the gray of the clouds, a four-winged albatross that was five feet long from head to tail. Razor-sharp spines sprouted from its back. Fangs glistened inside its beak. Toward the foremast it flew, aiming for Lizeth like a whistling dart.

The quartermaster ducked. They grabbed tight hold of the yard they were standing on, kicked out their feet, and swung from it. The abomination's razor spines sliced through the rigging above them. Ropes snapped. The fore topgallant sail plummeted downward. The abomination made a cackling noise deep in its throat and pivoted about, positioning itself for a second strike.

Zeke lifted his arm and flung a bolt of his magic. White light streaked across the sky and struck the bird-thing in the chest. It fell. Its wings flapped and flailed awkwardly; it cawed as roughly as a dying man's cough. The abomination splashed down into the water off the starboard bow. The monster thrashed once more and dissolved into seafoam.

Zeke and Lizeth exchanged nods. Eva was glad to see that. It was not quite trust, but it was a start.

"Well struck," Cevette said, stepping out of her cabin and closing the door behind her. She wore only a loose-fitting shirt of faded white, simple homespun trousers, and worn leather boots, likely having grabbed whatever she could reach when she'd woken up to the commotion. "Are you well, Quartermaster?" Lizeth nodded at her. "Good. Fetch Miss de l'Havre and tell her to oversee the repair of the sail."

"Yes, ma'am," Lizeth said, and darted off toward the crews' quarters.

Eva strode down the length of the upper deck, stepping around barrels, coils of rope, and crates of cannonballs, and made her way to Cevette's side. The captain had a distant look in her eyes that worried her.

"What's on your mind?" Eva murmured, when she was close enough that she and Cevette might speak privately. She wrapped an arm around Cevette's waist and pulled her in close. The captain sighed, and let Eva hold her, but did not relax. She held herself as tautly as a drawn bow.

"It's the abominations," she said. "Perhaps the Tarwik shamans are willing to look the other way when Korinne summons them, but I cannot. When I see them, all I see are the monsters that have hunted my people for generations. All I feel is the haunting weight of the memory that they killed someone I loved and I couldn't save them."

Eva hugged her tightly. "We need to convince Korinne to stop using them." She sighed. "We also need to let her know what we've planned with Zeke. If we can convince her that we have a way to kill Commander Gavon, that may be enough to get her to change paths."

"You're her sister." There was a weight to the way Cevette said it. "If you speak to her as that, she may well listen. What comes from you goes to her; what comes from her goes to you. That's true for all of us, but it's especially true among one's own people. But I'll go with you. As a current woman, as well as a captain. I'll know what to say."

"Then let's go." Eva leaned down and kissed Cevette's cheek. It was such a privilege, she thought, to stand by Cevette as she carried out her duties. She loved her as a pirate, and as a current woman. Whatever memories of hers they found on the Gray Isle, whatever new facets of Cevette uncovered, Eva could only look forward to discovering her anew.

Cevette ducked into their cabin to retrieve her coat and hat. Eva briefly considered donning her armor, but that would not go well if she meant to convince Korinne that she had come with peaceful intentions. She consulted a map to verify their bearing. *Shadow Queen* had just left Soladis. *Kembrielle* would be in fast pursuit. They would approach the Gray Isle from the east; *Sea Wolf* would approach from the south. Zeke had shared what Commander Gavon had told him of the orders he planned to give the crew of *Kembrielle*: the ship would hang back from engaging with Korinne and her abominations until *Sea Wolf* was in position for her and her godreapers to lead the assault. The winds had picked up; they would likely not need a storm from Lizeth to reach the Gray Isle in two days. They had to use that time well.

Cevette re-emerged from their cabin, wearing her hat and her ornate white coat. "Tuk!" she shouted. "You have charge of the ship until we return."

"Yes, captain!" he shouted.

Cevette took Eva's right hand. "Let's go."

Eva nodded, and reached out with her left. Black smoke bloomed at her fingertips, sweeping out into a curtain of swirling shadows. An archway seven feet tall assembled itself from gray smoke that took on the shapes of femurs, ribcages, and spines. The skull capstone grinned down at her.

Eva nodded to the crew, tightened her grip on Cevette's hand, and pulled them both into Death.

Her feet struck the floor of silver smoke.

And she slipped.

Here, Death sloped *sideways*.

Her legs dropped out from underneath her. She rolled, over and over, down the tilted path. Above her, the bone walls of the Death she knew vanished from sight. Her one thought was that she could not let go of Cevette; she did not want to think what might happen if she lost her here. With her free hand, she scrabbled for a grip, but anything she touched dissolved into smoke.

Beneath them, the waves of a black sea foamed and frothed. Boats of pale white bobbed up and down in its currents, long canoes and catamarans and massive ships the likes of which Eva had never seen. Shimmering spirits crewed them, men, women, and children with webbed fingers and worried, watching eyes.

Eva took one last desperate gasp of not-quite-air and plunged down into the spirit waters.

Cevette's hand was torn from hers. She could not hold on to it. She tumbled through the black current. The water punched into her from all sides like heavy fists of a god. It was as cold as the blade of a knife, soaking through her hair and clothing. She tried to kick and paddle, as Cevette had taught her, but she did not even know which way was up. A howling noise built in her ears. The currents carried her deeper and deeper. All light dimmed into darkness.

Somewhere, deep in the shadows, she heard a cruel and quiet laugh.

Her chest burned. Her lungs ached. Instinct pressed her, heavy and demanding. *Breathe. I need to breathe.* She would drown if she opened her lips, drown or worse. She dared not give in. Too many people needed her. *Cevette. Korinne. Dorothea. Andreas—*

A hand grabbed hers. Warm and firm and alive. *Cevette.* There she was, freed of the silver threads that protected those Eva carried through Death, her skin gleaming with light. She swam up through the spirit waters with swift, efficient strokes, towing Eva along behind her. Where the raging currents touched her, they grew calm. The waters lightened and turned to a deep, midnight blue. Higher and higher they rose. Sea People spirits swam in the waters above them. With spectral hands, they reached out toward Cevette, waving her forward.

Cevette kicked once more. The world inverted around them. Eva felt her ears pop—

She and Cevette slammed down, knees first, on the deck of *Sea Wolf.* Water splashed down around them and turned to smoke as it fell. Eva gasped in air. *I'm alive,* she thought. *I'm still alive.*

Cevette wrapped her arms tight around Eva's chest. "Are you hurt?" she said. Her hat was gone. Her eyes were wide and frantic.

"I'm well," Eva said. "Those . . . those were the spirit waters?" She stood, and made to wring out her coat, but it was already dry. The whole crew had turned to stare at them, wide-eyed and open-mouthed. They had grown used to Eva coming and going through her portals. Never before had they seen her tossed out of Death on a wave.

Cevette nodded. She stood as well, and squared her shoulders. With a calm smile on her face, she nodded to the crew. Only Eva was close enough to see the pulse racing in her throat.

"Korinne has pushed too far," Cevette said, quietly. "Her abomination summoning has churned up the spirit waters. The storm will not ease until we aid them."

"So I can't enter Death without tumbling into them?" Eva asked. Cevette nodded. "How were you able to swim through that? Can all current women swim through the spirit waters?"

"No. Only the greatest priests and shamans could even . . ." Cevette fell silent. She bit at her lip. "Gods. *How* did I do that?"

Eva put a hand on her shoulder. "We'll find answers soon. When we get to the Gray Isle. When we have your memories back. That will make everything better."

When Cevette spoke next, her voice was small and quiet. "What if it makes everything worse?"

"Then at least you'll know who you are. Who your people are." Eva swallowed. "And my people are on the other side of an army of monsters."

THE STORM BREAKS

OFFSHORE OF THE GRAY ISLE, TWO HUNDRED MILES WEST-SOUTHWEST OF THE CITY OF SOLADIS. 24TH MORGHASMONTH, YEAR TWENTY-TWO OF THE GOLDEN REPUBLIC.

Abomination, death / lies in their claws and breath / the coastlines they do prowl / at night they scratch and growl / their every sound a warning. // Attention must be paid / by every lad and maid / to flee where they wander / and quickly take cover / lest their kin fall to mourning. –Entry for the letter *A* in A Children's Primer of the Golden Republic.

THE RISING SUN SLUNK reluctantly up over the Gray Island. It rose on the horizon, a lump of land that grew bigger as *Sea Wolf* approached but no less gray. Its one high hill was ringed by steep basalt cliffs. Vines tumbled down their sides; the few trees that grew from atop the cliffs were scraggly and wild. Ice and frost crept up their flanks. Even the dawn sunlight seemed to shy away from the gray lump of land.

Eva shivered as she lowered her spyglass, leaning up against the rail of the forecastle. Lizeth sat on a barrel beside her, chewing on a crust of brown bread from the crew's breakfast. Cevette was walking the upper deck, inspecting the cannons and the chains that anchored them to the decks, the pale mist that covered the morning sea billowing about her. All the sailors had gone quiet.

Only a small channel separated the Gray Isle from the mainland of Soladis. It lay tucked against the large island's western flank. Few maps even included it; nevertheless, *Shadow Queen*, with her high masts and her figurehead of a diamond-eyed echo, lay in the island's small natural harbor, her sails up and her anchor down. Beyond it, sounds of gunfire rose from within the rough-hewn wooden walls of the Republic fort that guarded the trail deeper into the island. Korinne screamed, the magic in her howls spreading out over the waves. Souls slipped into Death.

For a brief moment as they approached, Eva thought they would reach *Shadow Queen* unchallenged.

Then the tide went out, and the abominations came with it. Up they rose from the dark depths of the waves, a hundred masses of flesh, each moving as if they all shared one mind. The water between *Sea Wolf* and the shore filled with claws and teeth, fur and tentacles, slitted eyes and spider legs. The abominations floated in a loose formation, bobbing up and down with the waves, stirring fins and flippers to hold themselves steady. Every time a three-headed worm or pale kraken rose from the deeps, Cevette murmured in disgust.

I'm going to kill them for her, Eva thought, and grinned.

"Ready for a fight?" she asked Lizeth.

"Always," they said, and grinned. "You should ask if the fight is ready for me!"

A voice up in the rigging called, "*Kembrielle* to port!"

Eva and Lizeth both gazed out at the handsome ship-of-the-line. Its gilded railings were dull on that cloudy day, its ten-foot-long gold flag a flapping square of brown. But the iron mouths of its forty-eight guns were wide and hungry, and the waves painted white foam along its flanks that gave it the look of a slavering beast.

Eva lifted her spyglass again. A man stood in the bow of *Kembrielle*, waving signal flags. She read the pattern for *advance* and *ship to follow*. "That bastard still wants us to lead the attack. His ship is half again the size of ours and has twice the number of cannons."

"Probably cost twelve times as much to build." Lizeth leaned over the rail and spat. "Never realized he couldn't buy courage. I'll start calling up a storm. We may need one."

They climbed down the forecastle stairs. Eva commandeered the barrel they had been sitting on for use as a table. She laid out the map of the Gray Isle Lord Merris had drawn them, along with a series of nautical charts, all the papers covered with her scribbled plans of attack. Cevette, Zeke, and Naeri came up to the forecastle and gathered around it. Naeri was still shooting hateful glances at Zeke, who was keeping his distance from her, as much as he could on the small ship. She had consented to make him an armored coat for the battle, as they would need him alive to confront the commander, but she had made it a very plain and utilitarian brown as a mark of contempt.

Eva ran a finger along the map and pointed to the archive itself. The building, as Lord Merris had described it, was an abandoned chapel of the faith of Iunos. There were two routes to access it; one the trail that the fort guarded, the other, a partially-collapsed trail that led up from a small beach at the island's southern tip. "Korinne is raiding the fort now," she said. "But, by the time we reach the shore, she will likely be at the archive, either summoning abominations or looting memories to carry away."

"What do you know about the memories hidden on the Gray Isle?" Cevette asked Zeke.

"Nothing," he said. "It was only in recent weeks that the commander admitted the theft to me at all."

"Has he ever told you about any memories he stole from me?"

Zeke shook his head. Cevette sighed. "Very well. How much damage can you do to the abominations in the blockade, Lieutenant Dare?"

"A good deal," he said. "But I can only strike at close range. We will require some greater disruption to get both ships through their lines."

"Lizeth will be able to provide that in due time," Cevette said. "But it will take them a while to work up a storm. And the abominations will not wait patiently forever."

It was then that, from up in the rigging of the foremast, Lizeth shouted, "Look to *Kembrielle!*"

The four of them lifted their heads and saw that the line of abominations had pressed forward. A fleshy mass of them had gathered off the bow of *Kembrielle.* A kraken reached out from the currents and lashed a tentacle around the ship's rail. It *dragged.* Sailors screamed. *Kembrielle* tipped sideways. Soldiers rushed forward, hacking at the tentacle with their bayonets. It broke off in a spray of black blood.

Another three tentacles shot up from the brine.

Eva and Cevette shared a look. "We can't afford to let the commander get desperate," Eva said.

"Agreed." Cevette lifted her chin and shouted "Weapons and armor at the ready! We sail to aid *Kembrielle!*"

Eva ran for the chest bolted to the mizzenmast. She pulled off her coal-black coat with the embroidered skulls, checked her knives were in place at her wrists and ankles, tightened the belt that held her sword and pistols. She donned her crimson corset-style chestplate, pulled back on her coat, and tied on her greaves and bracers overtop it. Naeri and Donya donned their armor as well, painted and dyed in shades of indigo and teal, and Cevette donned her white and blue plate, her long white coat, and a hat with ostrich plumes as long as her arm. She strode into the center of the deck and spoke in the booming voice of a captain.

"The helm is mine! Miss Gavon, Mr. Smoke, take command of the gunning stations! Blast those monsters apart!"

Sailors clambered into the rigging, lowering sails and securing loose ropes. Cevette ran to the quarterdeck. She seized the wheel firmly in her fists and turned their heading toward port, aiming directly for *Kembrielle.* As Mr. Smoke led his gunners below deck, Eva ran to the starboard cannons. A dozen pirates followed behind her, and split into the groupings Cevette had assigned them days ago. Eva met Donya's eyes as they both reached the aftmost cannon in the line. The healer gave her a small, fierce smile. Eva squeezed her hand and shouted "Load your guns!"

Below-deck, Mr. Smoke echoed her cry. The gun crews rushed about the business of loading. As Donya forced the powder charge down the cannon barrel, Eva opened the locker chained by the rail and drew out a heavy lead ball. At a nod from Donya, she pushed it through the cannon's mouth. It rolled downward. Donya, rod in hand, pushed it home. The two of them lowered their shoulders and pushed their cannon forward. The wheels on the rickety wooden mount creaked as they pushed it into place. Sail canvas snapped and shivered over their heads. Sweat dripped down the back of their necks.

Sea Wolf flew across the sea of teeth on a quickening wind. "Hold fire!" Cevette shouted as they drew near *Kembrielle*. Abominations turned to face the oncoming *Sea Wolf*. Fins and tentacles lifted from the sea as they swam toward the small ship. "Hold!" A kraken reached up from the sea. Its gray-pink tentacles, long and covered in suckers, grasped for the deck. Its beak snapped, wide enough to devour a man whole. "Hold!"

A wild wave rushed under the ship. Eva staggered. Donya grabbed the rail for balance. The kraken twisted in the current. Its squid-like head, ten feet in length and pointed at its crown, lifted up from the brine.

"Fire!" Cevette shouted. "Fire!" Eva repeated, and brought down her fuselighter. Her cannon sparked. The ball flew. A dozen booms rang through the air. Chains rattled as the cannons slid backwards. The kraken's head dissolved into red froth. Tentacles thrashed as it sank below the waves.

"We got it!" Mr. Smoke shouted, huffing and panting as he ran back up from below deck.

"There's more on their way!" Cevette shouted. "Miss Gavon, reload your guns! Mr. Smoke, give us fire!"

The rotund sailor, his shirt off, his smile wicked, and the tattoos on his belly shining, marched up onto the forecastle. Flames, pale in the light of day, gathered in his fists. He threw them, shimmering orb after shimmering orb, and they streaked across the gray sky, falling amidst a charging horde of howling eels and shark-headed octopi. Some burned. More ducked back under the waves.

As Mr. Smoke did his work, Eva cleaned the barrel of her cannon with a sponge pole. A spark flew out and singed her thumb. Eva hissed. "Let me look at that," Donya said. She dipped a finger into one of the little pots that hung from the bandolier she wore across her chest, then smeared healing paste on Eva's burned finger and mended it with a flicker of magic.

"It was only a small thing," Eva reassured her. "You didn't need to—"

"I know. But I bet Mr. Smoke five pounds you'd take the first wound."

"Shark ahead!" Cevette shouted, hard and urgent. "Jibe to windward! Now!"

Eva cursed. Glancing out over the starboard rail, she saw it: a dorsal fin as tall as a grown man, slicing through the waters toward them. She drew a knife and flung it. A rope snapped. Every crewmember ducked as the mainsail swung across the deck with bone-breaking speed. *Sea Wolf* groaned in protest, the ship's timbers trembling as it wheeled about, the shadow of the bow arching toward the great fin. It vanished back down into the dark. Waves tainted with the rotting scent of abominations washed up across the deck. The fetid scent left Eva's stomach churning.

How dare Korinne release these monsters on the sea? She tightened her fists. *I need to get Cevette to her. I need to work out a better way. It must be possible for us to do this together.*

Back down the line of battle they flew. Cannon after cannon fired its shots. Twisted abominations corpses floated in the brine, dissolving into seafoam. *Kembrielle* followed on *Sea Wolf*'s tail, firing its barrages with a pounding, drumlike fury. *At least Commander Gavon is good for that,* Eva thought. The sea drank lead and seethed. They took a third pass at the enemy ranks. A fourth. The waters transformed into a mess of howling bloody pulp.

Eva ran up to the quarterdeck and joined Cevette at the helm. The sun had risen higher in the sky; the day was scarcely warmer than it had been at dawn, yet they were doused in sweat beneath their armor, and the damp sea air clung to their skin. Eva rested one hand on Cevette's shoulder and gave her captain a warm smile. "We're making good progress. We may not even need Lizeth to summon a storm. A few more passes, and we'll slip through their ranks like a knife through butter."

"It appears not everyone shares your patience." Cevette pointed off to port. *Kembrielle* had turned to sail into the waves, directly toward *Shadow Queen* and the small natural harbor. The mass of flesh sloshed toward it.

Eva cursed. "Is he trying to get us all killed?"

"Being unable to die must truly skew his perspectives." Cevette sighed, and raised her voice. "Follow *Kembrielle*! We strike as one! Dare—show me what you can do."

Zeke leaned against the mizzenmast, polishing one of the two sabers he wore at his belt, alongside a half-dozen pistols. A thousand feelings swam through Eva's head as she looked at him; she struggled to pick out only one. But she was glad to have her old friend there.

He nodded to Cevette. "It would be my honor, ma'am."

Cevette turned the ship's wheel. *Sea Wolf* arched. The bow of the ship swung across the waters, turning to run parallel with *Kembrielle*. Wind whistled past them as the nimble barque took the lead. Eva reached up and caught Cevette's ostrich plume hat before it could fly off her head. Zeke climbed to the forecastle. Blades shone in his hands. The first few drops of rain sluiced across his face. His jaw was set; his brown eyes were locked on his targets.

Half the abominations swimming toward *Kembrielle* peeled off and charged toward *Sea Wolf*, their fins and spikes jutting up from the storm-gray froth as they sliced through the sea. Eva's breath caught. Howling in a raucous chorus, the fleshy monsters leapt from the waters and up onto the bowsprit. Wood cracked. *Sea Wolf* lurched forward. As the deck pitched under Eva's feet, a dozen howling abominations pulled themselves onto the forecastle, ringing Zeke on all sides.

"Clear!" Zeke shouted. Eva and all the other godmarked sailors ducked low. White light gathered in his outstretched hands. Waves of magic radiated from his palms in all directions, slamming into the abominations with all the force of gunfire. They screamed in unholy fury, clacking and clicking deep in their throats, collapsing to whatever passed for their knees as the magic that fueled them was crushed by Zeke's will.

More abominations climbed atop their fallen fellows, their heavy feet grinding their kindred into meat and gore. Zeke released a second wave of power. Creatures tumbled down into a writhing mass of gelatinous tendrils and coral plate armor. Eva held her breath. *Just how many abominations did she summon from the memories from under Assembly Hall?*

Splashes sounded all about *Sea Wolf*. Claw sank into the deck from both port and starboard. Tentacles, dripping with acidic slime, coiled about the rails. A dozen abominations leapt aboard the upper deck and grinned at the crew with shining fangs.

"Damn, Zeke," Eva shouted. Descending from the quarterdeck, she drew her daggers and stepped over to the spot before the captain's cabin where she could open a portal. She dared not step through and risk falling into the spirit waters, but she found the nearness of Death comforting in a fight, not that she dared admit as much. "You'll have to use those muscles of yours after all."

He leapt down from the forecastle and walked toward her, holding his twin sabers aloft. All about the deck, pirates cursed, prayed, and drew weapons in trembling hands. Zeke's face was cool and calm. "So will you. If you've got any."

She laughed. "Echoes don't get bulky. Only lean."

Zeke rolled his eyes at that, then lifted his sabers high and banged them together. Metal rattled. The gray clouds gathering above shone, reflected, on his blades. His scars and white godmarks, the chains and tumbling coins, stood out vividly on his light brown skin. *Pridebreaker. God of charity.* A howling creature, built like a blood-red stingray, flew over *Sea Wolf*, gliding on skin wings that cast the deck in darkness. As the shadow washed over him, Zeke grinned and leapt. High. *Higher.* Both blades sliced through the beast's underbelly.

Organs and viscera rained down on the deck. The corpse of the flying monster crashed down into the sea. As its melting guts dripped down his face, Zeke rammed his shoulder into a stack of crates. They slid across the deck in a tumultuous clatter, slamming into abominations, sending the creatures sprawling. "Eva!" he shouted. She kicked one at just the right angle. It skidded into a monster with its claws mere inches from Donya and knocked the beast overboard.

A toad-like thing, armored with a turtle shell, narrowed its bloodred eyes at Zeke and lowered its head to charge. Eva drew her pistol and shot it. The beast's left forelimb exploded in a burst of seawater. Still, it leapt. Zeke stabbed at it. The monster crashed into him. The blades bounced off the heavy plastron shielding its guts. Cursing, Zeke dropped his swords and grabbed hold of the top and bottom of the shell.

He arched his back. Grunted. Twisted. The beast *ripped* down the middle.

Black abomination blood spilled like ink across Zeke's brown coat. Shards of bone flew through the air, knocking three pigeon-sized flying snakes from the sky. Zeke bashed the next abomination across the face, wielding the dead beast's shell like a shield. Then he threw it so hard it knocked a third abomination back overboard.

"I suppose pure strength has its uses!" Eva shouted.

He drew his gun and fired. She jumped as the bullet whistled past her ear, and turned to see it had hit a six-winged vulture with its talons only inches from her shoulder.

"As much use as honor," Zeke replied.

The sounds of chaos and battle rose all about them. Three abominations leapt over the ship's rail and charged at Eva. They were lizard-like things that ran on two feet, their scales deep red like clotted blood, armed with knife-sharp claws and jaws like those of a fanged seahorse. She let them come. Their scaled legs bunched beneath them. They leapt. With a wave of her hand, Eva opened her portal and ducked behind it.

The monsters screamed and howled, scattering backward before they could tumble through the portal. Eva grinned. Her heart pounded hard in her chest. She grabbed one of the long femur bones protruding from the side of the smoky archway, swung, and kicked a lizard-monster in the jaw. It reeled. Eva pulled herself up atop the bone; then reached up and hooked the fingers of her right hand through the eye sockets of the skull in the capstone arch. As the lizards leapt at her once more, she kicked out again. This time, something cracked in a monster's skull. It fell. The other two looked up at her and hissed, their long, narrow jaws opened to reveal hundreds of needle-sharp teeth. *That's it. Come at me.*

The first one leapt. Its hornlike scales turned a vivid crimson as it reached for Eva with catching claws. Her thrown knife caught it in the throat. It dropped, heavy as an anchor. The second abomination followed, not a glance at its fallen fellows, clambering up the side of the archway. Eva grinned, and waved her hand. The portal dissolved back into smoke. She fell to the deck in a neat crouch; the abomination slammed down beside her. She drew a second knife from her bracer and stabbed the monster through the chest.

"What do you think of that?" Eva shouted to Zeke.

"Impressive enough." He had climbed to the quarterdeck; now he stood with Cevette, guarding the captain as she steered the ship. Two seven-limbed starfish the size of hunting dogs lurched toward him, moving on spine-covered sucker feet. He ran one through with his saber as Cevette kicked another back into the sea. "One moment. Let me clear our flank."

Zeke sheathed his swords and wound a rope around his left forearm. Then he leapt from the quarterdeck. The rope snapped taut. He swung up the length of the starboard bow. Magic pulsed at his fingertips; he threw bolt after blazing white bolt into the sea. Abominations screamed as the power sliced through their ill-gained flesh. A winged beast with the head of a swordfish flew toward Zeke. He ducked away from it. Its steel-sharp feathers sliced through the air above him.

The rope snapped.

"Zeke!" Eva screamed as he plunged down into the sea of teeth. She leaned over the rail—then grabbed it tight as *Sea Wolf* lurched sideways. The shape of a great beast rippled below the ship. Zeke paddled through the currents, kicking to stay afloat, as a five-foot-tall dorsal fin streaked toward him.

Death lay in the shark's mouth. Eva could tell it had already killed at least three sailors that day. It picked up speed as it went. The sea poured into its throat as it opened its jaws.

She ran for the cannons. In her heart, she knew she would never get a shot off before the beast could strike. But that didn't matter. All she could think of was that the chains on the cannon mount stopped it from rolling backwards. Not forward.

She lowered her shoulder and struck the cannon with bone-jarring force. The wheels on the wooden mount squealed as it slid forward. Her muscles screamed as she took three back-breaking steps and shoved the cannon overboard. Chains rattled as it fell. The rail the cannon was anchored to cracked and tore free in a cloud of splinters.

The falling cannon struck the great shark directly between the eyes.

Water sprayed up in a white arch. The beast went still, dazed from the blow. Up on the deck, Tuk and Nukit rushed over with their harpoons. They flung the barbed spears. They whistled through the air and sank deep into the monster's flesh. The Upailitian men took tight hold of the ropes tied to the harpoons and wrenched them free. Flesh ripped. Gore streaked the sea. The shark bellowed in pain and dove back into the deeps. Tuk shouted curses at it as it fled.

Zeke bobbed in the currents, treading water, going nowhere, looking as stunned as the shark himself. Eva grabbed a coil of rope. "Zeke!" She had to call his name three times before he looked up at her. When she threw him the rope, she held her breath, and she did not let it out until he grabbed on and climbed back aboard.

"Thank you," he said, nodding to both Tuk and Nukit. "I . . . I'm truly grateful. Thank you." They nodded back at him. Then he turned to Eva, water dripping from his clothes. "I . . . gods, Eva. I'm sorry. For all of it. For everything I did, everything I said. I . . ."

"I understand," she said. "I grew up in the Republic, too. All I ever heard was how great Commander Gavon was. I denied so much of what I knew and felt to make myself believe in him. But we can free ourselves from what they taught us. We can choose who is truly worthy of our regard. And I am still your friend."

"Your friendship is the honor of a lifetime." Zeke drew the swords from his belt and grinned at her. "Let's send these monsters back to hell."

Eva grinned, and drew her knives.

Side by side, they dove back into the melee. Zeke swung about himself with the double sabers. Abomination after abomination fell before him, sliced to ribbons. Black blood and sea slime sprayed up over his coat and face. Eva darted about him, light on her feet, each slash of her knives sending another abomination squealing away in pain. On they went, the fight morphing into a heart-pounding, foul-smelling dance that brought a fierce and vicious smile to Eva's lips. The abominations fell backward, diving off the rails and dropping down into the sea. *Good,* she thought. *You face the Skullrunner. You face death.*

The wind picked up, whistling through the masts. The sails billowed out above them. The cold grew in the air, as did the dampness. The first drops of rain slid down Eva's face. Pressed close to Zeke in the ranks of battle, she could feel his warmth, as she could glimpse Cevette's smile from where her captain stood at the helm. The thrill of combat sung in her veins. Death wrapped about her shoulders like a cloak. It was very good indeed to know her friends could see a blood-streaked echo with knives in her hands and stand beside her.

"Get back!" The high, clear voice carried over the wind, as loud and as resonant as the call of a god. A charge of potential hummed in the air. The hair prickled down the back of Eva's neck. She stabbed one more abomination in the throat and looked up.

High above, Lizeth clung to the rigging of the mainmast. Wind billowed in the sails and the dark violet fabric of their armored coat. Clouds raced across the blue above them, like stallions in a cavalry charge, forming up into a thick gray shroud.

Lizeth grinned and tightened their fist.

Spears of lightning stabbed into the sea, tearing into the abominations that swam just off the ship's flanks. The world went white. Thunder crashed in a terrible crescendo. Zeke and Eva grabbed for each other's hands, scrambling for balance, blinking away the blinding light as the deck tossed beneath them.

"Forward!" Lizeth shouted. The storm wind blew. Waves raced across the dark sea, their whitecaps colliding with the ranks of enemy abominations. They lifted *Sea Wolf* and *Kembrielle* as easily as if the ships were children's toys, carrying them toward the harbor. The wind picked up.

Rain streaked through the sky in driving sheets. Eva and Zeke dropped to their knees as drops of rain pierced their coats like stinging daggers.

And Lizeth laughed. Lightning bolts pierced through the abominations as the waves tossed the mass of corrupted flesh asunder. The beasts thrashed in the current. Their skin bubbled and collapsed in on itself. Algae and seaweed and puffs of yeasty foam bloomed up from the remains of the collapsing beasts, mixing them back into the sea. Outward and outward, the white-hot spears of lightning flew. Terrible pops and crunching noises filled the howling sea as the abominations melted away.

Eva staggered to her feet, her arm around Zeke's waist. The two of them made their way toward the helm as the wind caught at their coats, tugging them backward. When they made it to the quarterdeck, Cevette took one hand from the helm and placed it on Eva's shoulder.

"Go belowdecks and get some dry pistols, Dare," Cevette said. "You'll need them."

Zeke nodded, and ducked back down the stairs. Cevette and Eva exchanged a brief look of relief. Then the captain lifted her chin and smiled out at her rain-drenched, shivering, bleeding—but still alive—crew. Many clung to the rails or rigging for support. They gazed up at their captain with wide and frightened eyes.

"Well fought, all of you," Cevette said. "The worst of it lies behind us now. To the shore we go. This ends today!"

It was true, Eva realized, with a sense of dizzying relief. Soon this would all be over. The commander would be dead. Cevette would get her memories back. And she would make things right with Korinne and Andreas. All they had to do was deceive Commander Gavon long enough to lead him into their trap.

"Listen to me, Eva." Cevette lowered her voice. "I need you to do something very important for me."

"Anything."

"If we take back control of the memories, we must not burn them. Not until we've sorted through them first. I want to make certain that mine won't be on the pyre."

"What?" Eva didn't understand. "Those memories . . . without them, you'll never find your kinfolk, your home, *yourself*—"

"I'm happy as I am." Cevette lowered her brow and looked away from Eva's gaze. "I can be a current woman without them. I understand enough of who I am. The rest can stay in the past where it belongs."

"You're afraid of what you might find." Eva said it softly, with no condemnation in her voice. Cevette squeezed her eyes shut and gave a short, brisk nod. "I know what it is, to be defined by that which you cannot control. I will not blame you if you choose to forget." She hesitated. "So long as you do not choose to forget me."

"Never," Cevette said. Eva smiled, and they both looked to the shore.

COMMANDER-IN-CHIEF

THE GRAY ISLE, IN THE UNCEDED TERRITORY OF THE KETIL YATA NATION, TWO HUNDRED MILES WEST-SOUTHWEST OF THE CITY OF SOLADIS. 24TH MORGHASMONTH, YEAR TWENTY-TWO OF THE GOLDEN REPUBLIC.

Ariella showed me an illegal newspaper she had found, a fragment rescued from a fire. It was badly burned, and yet from what we could read, it appeared to be the account of an echo who had narrowly escaped being split at Father's hands. "It reads like lurid fiction," she told me, "and clearly this author is not too bright." I reassured her that Father would never do something like that. He created the echoes as an accident of magic when he first unleashed the power of Iunos. He would not make more of us purposefully. He should know better than to make his own enemies. –from the diary of Korinne Gavon.

THE DECK OF THE *Shadow Queen* was nearly deserted.

As Zeke rowed his dinghy through the shadow of the Demon's ship, only a handful of coral-headed abomination guards gazed down at him, clutching heavy axes in their gelatinous fists. It appeared that not a single echo remained aboard. The Demon of Dogshead must have brought them ashore with her. Perhaps she had needed all of them to attack the fort, but many of the echo refugees from Soladis had been servants and laborers, not soldiers. *She took them with her because she knew Commander Gavon was chasing her. They're her family.*

Zeke understood family. He would do anything to see his parents and sister alive once more. He was glad the echoes had escaped the city; guilt twisted his stomach up in knots when he remembered the part he had played in Commander Gavon unleashing this onslaught against them. And yet the guilt only eased slightly when he told himself he was doing what he could to make this right. He had been friends with many of his fellow soldiers, though those bonds had lessened as he had devoted himself fully to the commander's service. Korinne had killed dozens of soldiers, folk who had taken up arms in service of a man they thought they could trust. Eva had killed soldiers. If he continued down this path, the blood of soldiers like him would stain his hands crimson.

But if he faltered now, Commander Gavon would plunder those same soldiers' minds until the end of days. If he faltered now, he would allow echoes to be split for his own peace of mind.

Commander Gavon had built this world. Today, Ezekiel Dare would change it.

The winds of the storm had died away, but a steady rain still fell over the hilly lump of the Gray Isle and its small natural harbor. *Kembrielle* had dropped anchor five hundred feet to port from *Shadow Queen,* and *Sea Wolf* waited two hundred off its starboard bow. Zeke rowed with his head down. His violet beret (for he had re-donned his uniform) shielded his eyes as the dinghy bumped up and down over the waves. The sea slapped up across his chest and face. At one point, he paused and bailed out water with a bucket. Stroke by stroke, he made his way to shore.

The beach was brown-gray sand, sodden by waves and rain. High gray cliffs towered above it. Zeke leapt out of the dinghy and marched through the muddy sand, water sloshing about his boots as he dragged the boat up onto the sand and toward the knot of Republic soldiers that waited for him. Thirty of them had come ashore with Commander Gavon. They stood around their leader, a tight cluster of orange coats, shooting horrified glances at the fort.

The attack had been merciless. Smoke rose from within the palisade walls, which had once stood ten feet tall. They had crumbled in numerous places, brought low by the fists of abominations or knocked flat by the power of the Demon's unearthly screams. Fallen soldiers in orange coats could be seen through the gaps, lying face down in the sand, their blood washed away in the rain. *They seem as if they could be sleeping,* thought Zeke. His nails dug into his palms. He felt the cool air of a root-cellar brush his cheek.

The commander, wearing his gold uniform jacket, a half-dozen medals, and a scowl, showed no expression as he took in the numbers of the dead. The firm lines of his jaw reminded Zeke of that old painting he had glimpsed at the Nautileum. *Everything we've been told about his courage and valor is a lie. He won the revolution because he had a god on his side.*

"Could we not take a moment and search for survivors, sir?" said a soldier as Zeke approached.

"There is no time. We must honor their sacrifice by defending the Republic they gave their lives for. The echoes must be stopped."

He may very well plan to split them all the moment he has them in sight. Zeke's stomach churned once more. His heart hammered in his ribs. *I loved him. I loved everything he stood for.* His skin prickled. His lips curled. He tightened his fists and told himself not to give the ruse away.

The soldiers murmured amongst themselves. As they shifted back and forth, a familiar face became visible among their ranks. *Dorothea.* They had carried her ashore on a chair. Her wrists were bound in fetters. A ragged gag had been forced into her mouth; her eyes burned with defiant light even as her hands trembled. He saw Eva in her, and his own grandmother, too. He promised himself that he would do whatever he could to free her.

The commander lifted his chin and nodded to Zeke as he approached. "Glad to see you well, Lieutenant Dare." The relief in his voice was genuine. Zeke made himself smile. "Will the pirates be joining us?"

"Captain Zarcanzi said she did what you asked of her. She doesn't fight for free."

"A shrewd woman," Commander Gavon said. "It takes a good deal of leadership to bring so many godreapers to her cause. The Republic could use someone like her."

Zeke frowned. Was there a threat lurking in those words?

"Come along," Commander Gavon said. "We have echoes to catch."

THROUGH HER TELESCOPE, EVA watched as Zeke, the commander, and his soldiers set off up the trail that led to the archive. The moment they were out of sight, Eva and Cevette led a small party of pirates into the ship's dinghies and set off rowing. They pushed their way through the choppy, storm-tossed currents, working the oars hard as their backs ached and their palms bled. They could outpace the soldiers if they pushed; carrying along Dorothea would slow them down. But it would take every moment they had to convince Korinne to trust them.

They rowed around the backside of the southern cliffs. A narrow trail rose up the side of the rocks. They tied their dinghies to a boulder; then Eva and Cevette led the crew up the trail. They advanced single-file; in places, they had to climb up rocks on their hands and knees. At the top of the cliffs, they found a trail that was overgrown; their sabers flashed as they cut through the vines and scrub trees that had grown over the thin dirt path. Brush and flecks of green flew up at each cut. The wind blew cold. A gentle rain began to fall once more.

"This place is familiar," Cevette murmured, climbing over the trunk of a fallen pine. "I . . . I've been here before."

"For what purpose?" Eva said, taking Cevette's offered hand and letting Cevette help her over (though she could manage quite well herself.)

"There's only one thing of value here." Cevette squeezed her hand. "Please. Don't burn them."

"I won't. Don't be afraid."

"I *am* afraid," Cevette said quietly. "And you?"

Eva shook her head. "I can face this." Death hung in the air, wrapping about her like a warm, invisible cloak. It brought her a queer and quiet comfort. She dared not say it out loud. She was dearly grateful for all the members of the crew who stood beside her and the captain—Donya, Naeri, Lizeth, Mr. Smoke, Tuk, and Nukit had all come to aid her and

Cevette—but even their loyalty might have its limits if they knew how closely connected she was to Death.

At last, the trail opened onto the south end of a muddy field, a wide expanse that ended in a cliff on the eastern side plunging down to the sea. No tree or bracken grew within five hundred feet of what lay at its heart—a chapel built in the style of the dark age of the Theocracy. It was a rectangular building, with walls of weathered gray stone, no more than seventy feet long and thirty across. A short belltower rose at the northern end. The narrow, arched windows had once been set with stained glass, but that was now all smashed into glimmering fragments. The door had been ripped off its hinges. A dozen Republic soldiers, who must have fallen back there when the fort fell, lay dead in the mud around the foot of the stairs.

The echoes stood gathered about the ancient church. Eva's breath caught. She had never seen so many of her sisters in one place. Nearly a hundred of them turned to face her and her crew as they approached. Some were old, some were young. Some wore breeches, some wore gowns. But nearly every one of them held a rifle or a sword, and all of them turned to gaze upon her with terror in their eyes.

"Sister!" Korinne shouted, as the crew of *Sea Wolf* fanned out to stand around Eva and Cevette. "What are you doing here?" She strode forward, placing herself between her people and Cevette's crew. The Demon of Dogshead wore a suit of solid black, with onyx buttons on her coat and breeches, and her necklace of shining silver skulls. Andreas, clad in the simple dark clothing of her crew, hurried up to stand at her side. "You think I'd welcome you in? You destroyed my army."

"I had to," Eva said. "Listen, Korinne—"

"You're too late," she said. "The archive is mine."

As she spoke, the abominations rose.

They had been behind the chapel, no doubt feasting on the memories Korinne had fed them. There were three of them, each one nearly twenty feet tall, great black spiders with long legs and dripping mandibles, armed with the heavy claws of crabs. A shiver of fear ran through the pirates gathered at her side. Even Cevette whispered a curse. A dozen other abominations, of all shapes and sizes, fanned out along the edge of the cliff. With hungry eyes, their jaws dropping with slobber, they watched the pirates, the echoes, and, most of all, the open crate Korinne carried under her arm.

Eva's breath caught as she glimpsed the memories, so many of them that they nearly spilled out to the ground. They were nothing like the ones she had seen before; like crumpled paper, yes, but paper gleaming with inner light, printed with vivid rainbow ink. *The memories of a god.* How many had Korinne captured? How great an army could she build with them?

"Listen to me," Eva said. "Commander Gavon forced us to attack your army. He's captured an elderly echo, Dorothea Bly, and he's threatening to split her so that he can force me and my crew to serve him. He's landed on this island and he's leading a troop of soldiers to attack you—"

"You're the reason he's here," Korinne said. "How do I know you're not in league with him."

"I'm a terrible liar," Eva said. "Andreas, you know that."

"She is a terrible liar," he said.

Eva took one step forward. Korinne put her hand on the hilt of her sword. Eva lifted her hands, to show her sister she held no weapons. A cool wind washed across the clifftop as they met each other's night-dark eyes.

"I should have gone with you back in Soladis," Eva said. "But I let everything the Republic told me about us cloud my vision. You . . . you understand. I know you do. I read what you wrote in your diary. *I hate the part of me that is the goddess of death, for she is the worst part, most unworthy.* It is so hard for us to think well of one another. But our hate for ourselves is the greatest weapon the Republic has to use against us. I want to put it aside. I'm not here to condemn you. I'm saying I have a plan that may let us kill Commander Gavon. Today."

Korinne closed her eyes. Her face fell. Her lips pressed together in a tight line. They moved, once, twice, but no words came forth. At last, she said, "You sound so much like Ariella."

"Korinne . . ." Eva took a few more steps toward her.

The Demon of Dogshead looked up at her. A tear slid down her cheek. "What do you propose?"

Eva's heart leapt. *This is it. She's going to listen. We're going to do this together.* "Lieutenant Ezekiel Dare, the commander's bodyguard—he's a member of the Godreaper Corps, and he's secretly on our side. When the commander reaches our position, right before he can strike, Lieutenant Dare will use his magic to disable the commander's powers. We'll be able to defeat his soldiers and capture him. Then we'll hold him to account. All of us. Everyone he's hurt. We believe the effect of Dare's magic might even be strong enough for us to kill him."

She held her breath. Hoping.

Korinne shook her head. "You would have me trust my life and the lives of my people to an officer of the Republic? Absolutely not. Go, Eva. You've already wasted my time. Do not provoke me to rage."

ZEKE AND THE REPUBLIC soldiers had followed closely behind as Commander Gavon had set off toward the trail, the muddy sand of the brown beach grinding under their boots. The commander had stepped into the gap between two tall black boulders and urged his soldiers to follow. Zeke had clambered through behind him and found himself at the foot of a narrow, shadowy trail that stretched through a gorge, sloping steeply upward. Another soldier had passed him a lantern; now, he held it up high to light the way as they went along.

The rain had shifted from heavy to light to heavy once more. The sky remained dark, and the gorge was blanketed in eternal shadow. Rotting fish and empty snail shells littered in the dry brown undergrowth. Dead leaves and bracken crackled as the soldiers climbed the slope. They kept their voices down to hushed whispers, no louder than the whistling of the wind. Even the commander held his tongue. Zeke was left alone, his questions swirling like a maelstrom in his head.

Can I truly kill him? He didn't know. He wasn't a philosopher; what he knew of his power was how to aim and fire it like a gun. He'd spoken a bit with the other godreapers on *Sea Wolf,* most of which had left him rather confused; the way they thought about the gods they had slain was like nothing he had even realized he *could* think about. *He promised me a place in his world. But taking it made my world so much smaller.*

The trail led up into a small field atop the cliffs. Bracken and heather grew from the thin soil, the sprigs damp and drooping, easily crushed underfoot. Waves crashed against the rock below. The damp wind carried the scent of salt and rotting things. There should have been birdsong, but the birds had fallen silent, as beasts often did when abominations were near. Pale sunshine crept through the heavy clouds, but there was not nearly enough of it to bring color into the gray afternoon.

At the head of the column, Commander Gavon halted, and turned to face his soldiers. "Take a rest," he ordered them. "Have a drink, eat some food. I want you fit to face what lies ahead."

Zeke wanted to see that as compassion. Even now. But he could see the commander was breathing heavily, with sweat building up on his brow. Whatever magic sustained his life, it did not give him the vigor of a younger man. *He's tired.* Zeke was tired, too.

The soldiers carrying Dorothea knelt and set down her chair. The old woman's fingers trembled where they rested on her lap. Zeke walked over to her, drew the canteen from his belt, and began untying her gag. "Here. Let me give you some water."

"No," Commander Gavon said, putting a hand on his arm. "Don't. She's dangerous."

"She cannot walk more than a hundred yards," Zeke said. Then he frowned, and bit the inside of his cheek. He had spoken too sharply.

"Is aught amiss, Ezekiel?"

"I . . . my apologies, sir." Zeke took a step back from the old woman and from the commander's touch. Loose shale shifted under his feet. He looked to the other soldiers, but they had already gone to gather about a mossy boulder and share hardtack bread. And what help could he expect from them?

The commander narrowed his eyes. "Even the oldest and youngest echoes can be dangerous. You'll need to know these things as you advance."

"Thank you, sir. I am always grateful for your mentorship." Zeke made himself smile. "It's just all a great deal to learn."

"It's a good deal to come to terms with," the commander said. "Our world is hard, and knowledge of its true nature is not always a comfort. But I am here to guide you. If you have any questions . . ."

Zeke chose the safest one. Better for him to question the commander than for the commander to question him. "Why did you conceal the history of your alliance with Morghaia?"

The commander blinked. His brows knit tight together. "What?"

"She was your ally, back in the revolution. Wasn't she? I understand that, at some point, you decided to break away from her. Why? Did you know, even then, you would need echoes to secure the world you were building? Or did you decide it was politically unfeasible to have a god on your side when you were fighting against them?"

"Where did you learn of this?"

Zeke would not give away where he had seen the painting. Beauchamp had conducted himself honorably in defense of the echoes, and he had no wish to cause him trouble. "It was . . . a rumor passed about in the barracks. But I found it credible. It does explain how you won so many of your early victories. I always wondered how you were able to defeat Iunos in single combat, and why he came to the defense of Morghaia, when she had been a rival of his for centuries. But he knew you were working together. So, when you offered to betray her, he must have rushed to meet with you. Then you betrayed them both. It was cunning—"

"I won because I bested my enemies in the field." The commander's famously stoic face flushed pink. He ran a hand along the back of his neck. He took a step backward. "The revolution was my victory. I will not stand for anyone to say elsewise."

Zeke held his tongue. *Why is he so unsettled?* If the truth was known, some might judge him a hypocrite, but there were a thousand darker secrets he had concealed, one for each echo. "Of course, sir. You won because the people of the Seaward Isles fought beside you. Because they believed in your cause. They rose up and claimed their freedom, and, regardless of what the gods did, you played a great part—"

"It was my victory, Dare." His voice had gone cold as ice. "I will have this filthy lie erased."

He turned back toward Dorothea and stripped off his gloves. Golden godmarks flashed on his skin. *What is he doing?* Zeke thought. *He needs her.* But he needed nothing more than the myth of his own greatness. He had broken into the minds of innocent people and plundered their pasts for power. He had sacrificed countless souls. And yet, Zeke saw now that there was nothing truly extraordinary about him. His greatest talent was a knack for picking out the lies folk wanted to hear, and by chance he had found an opportunity to wield this talent on a grand scale. But that was all Jonathan Gavon truly was.

Threads of power wove themselves about the commander's fingertips, gleaming with a terrible, inevitable light. Zeke found his own magic, calling it up from inside him as swiftly as he might draw his pistol, and flung a bolt of shining light into the commander's chest.

Commander Gavon stumbled backward. He stared at his hands, where no power bloomed, and pressed them to his chest. His medals shone in the thin sunlight.

"Soldiers!" he shouted. "Arrest Lieutenant Dare!"

EVA STARED OUT ACROSS the rocky field: at Korinne, with fire in her eyes, at Andreas, who studied them both intently, at the ragtag band of echoes that surrounded the ruined chapel, at the towering spider abominations and the memories glistening under Korinne's arms. *Go,* Korinne had told her. But where did she have to go?

"I'm not turning my back on this," Eva said. "Not when we're so close."

"For what it's worth," Andreas said, "Lieutenant Dare is one of the few Republic soldiers I've met who truly does believe in the concept of honor.

Cornellia, you told me of how he saved you from that loose abomination, didn't you?" He glanced back over his shoulder and nodded to her.

Cornellia, who clutched tight to a rifle with a long bayonet, said, "It might be worth it, trusting him. Many of the echoes on our side once fought for the Republic."

"But they're echoes," Korinne said. She shook her head and folded her arms over her chest. "Sisters, we have a plan. We have the abominations."

"You must abandon the abominations," Cevette strode forward. She had removed her hat; the wind stirred her short hair. "The pain you feed them is leaking back into the realms of the dead and strengthening the Hell's Eye that lurks there. It stirs the spirit waters travelled by the ancestors of my people into a tumult."

Korinne frowned, and studied her. "You're a current woman, Zarcanzi? I thought you remembered nothing of your past. Who are your people?"

"We are," Donya said, stepping up behind the captain.

Cevette gave her a grateful smile, and continued. "What you have done here compounds the pain of souls who, for centuries, have only sought to find calm waters." An undercurrent of anger hung in her voice, though she held herself as steady and as self-controlled as if she was made of stone. "Even the largest of our soul ships cannot find stability. Even the souls of our children must work all hours to keep them afloat."

Korinne's eyes widened. "I . . . I didn't know."

"It has been too hard for too long for us to see the spirit currents clearly," Cevette said. "But now you know. Your people are not the first in the Seaward Isles to experience great suffering. I ask you not to inflict it upon us. If you persist, I will do more than ask you."

A hush fell over the field.

From deep in the undergrowth came the rumble of marching feet. The gathered echoes shouted to one another; a child screamed as they pressed back against the chapel walls. Soldiers clad in orange coats and carrying long rifles stepped out from around a bend in the trail. Commander Gavon marched at their head. They fanned out into a semi-circle along the western side of the field.

Eva's breath caught as she scanned their ranks. Where was Dorothea? Where was Zeke?

"Lay down your weapons and surrender!" Commander Gavon bellowed. "Submit peacefully to arrest, destroy these abominations you have unleashed, and you will be allowed to leave this island with your miserable lives. If you resist, I will rip apart your rebellious souls where you stand!"

"Evazina," Korinne said, quietly. "Where is Lieutenant Dare?"

"I . . . I don't know."

Korinne shook her head. "You never could have helped us," she said quietly. Then she turned to face the commander. A vein pulsed in her neck. Her fist tightened around the hilt of her sword. She drew it and held it aloft. "Sisters and monsters, attack!"

Liberty and Death

The Gray Isle, in the unceded territory of the Ketil Yata Nation, two hundred miles west-southwest of the city of Soladis. 24th Morghasmonth, Year Twenty-Two of the Golden Republic.

You ask me if I have any regrets. I shall tell you, as we are both gentlemen of the Assembly, that I have a fair number. But I do not regret the decision to split Morghaia. It is both sentimentally and strategically rewarding to watch the pieces of her fight against each other. They will never unite against me. –Letter from Commander Jonathan Gavon to Lord Mykil Merris, Minister for Childhood Welfare.

At the sound of Korinne's command, the black-clad echoes of her crew rushed together. They formed a tight line, standing shoulder to shoulder, and drew their swords and lowered their rifles. The abominations began to stalk forward. Meanwhile, Andreas ran back toward the chapel. The children in the field, the young echoes and the echo-blooded, followed him inside. Two old women leaning on canes brought up the rear. Andreas picked up a rifle and stood on-guard in the doorway, He gave Eva a firm nod, his face pale.

"Soldiers of the Republic!" shouted Commander Gavon, "Form ranks!" The soldiers, in their line of golden coats, lifted their guns.

"Defensive positions!" Cevette called. The crew of *Sea Wolf* lifted their rifles as well. Nukit waved Donya back behind their line; they could not risk their healer in the open. The pirates took a step back toward the trail they had come on, ready to vanish into the trees if Cevette gave the word.

But Eva could not flee. She cursed and drew her sword, not yet knowing what she wanted to do with it, only knowing she wanted it close to hand. Thunder boomed above. Bayonets rattled behind her.

"Fire!" Korinne called, and "Fire!" said Commander Gavon.

The first shots filled the air with a popping sound. Two soldiers dropped, and three echoes. Blood stained the dirt. "Reload!" Commander Gavon shouted, and half the soldiers lowered their bayonets into a defensive formation while the other half pushed charges down their barrels. A pair of abominations with panther-like bodies and the jaws of snapping turtles charged across the sand. "Bayonets up! Shoot it!" The nearest soldiers lifted their weapons. The creatures darted around the blades and leapt into the ranks of orange coats. Korinne opened her mouth and *screamed*.

The sound cut through the air like a stinging hailstorm. Republic soldiers flew backward under the force of her magic. They slammed into the dirt. Ribs cracked. Skulls broke. Soldiers died. Even Commander Gavon had been knocked to the ground.

Korinne locked her eyes on him and charged.

There's my opening. Eva ran after her sister, her armored coat flapping in the wind. Mud flew up under her heels. A bullet whistled past her ear. "Korinne! I'm with you!"

Commander Gavon rose to his feet. He drew the saber at his waist and lowered it at the onrushing echoes. His soldiers cheered. "Gavon! Gavon!" The rain picked up. Silver droplets slid down his face. He glanced wildly about him as both echoes and soldiers reloaded their guns, readying to let bullets fly once more.

Eva braced herself. Commander Gavon was of average skill with a blade, but he could not die. She supposed that might give him an advantage. *Unless Zeke used his magic on him. Unless that magic works as we hope.* The commander set his jaw and dropped into a fencer's stance, his frame twisted sideways, his weight on his back foot. If he felt vulnerable, he did not show it.

Korinne lunged. The tip of her blade shot toward the commander. He dodged nimbly to the side, and pivoted. The air whistled as he cut at her chest. She parried. Metal clanged. "Ungrateful brat," the commander said. He pressed his advance, his sword buzzing like a hornet, and Korinne took three steps backwards. Lighting forked across the sky above. Loose rock shifted under Korinne's feet. Her arms stretched outward, reflexively, to keep her balance. Commander Gavon stabbed at her unguarded chest.

Eva cursed and pushed herself forward a few desperate steps. With a flicker of silver, she knocked the commander's blade aside with her own. Then she rammed her shoulder into his chest. Her bruise from hitting the cannon ached. Commander Gavon stumbled backward.

Korinne met her Eva's eyes. "What are you doing?"

"Fighting for my family," Eva said.

Korinne only stared at her. Eva thought she might be somewhat over-whelmed. It was a feeling she knew well.

Two soldiers rushed toward Korinne, one from the left and one from the right. She twisted away from the nearer man's blow and took a quick step to his side. Her sword jabbed toward his kidneys. He pivoted and blocked her blow. The second soldier grabbed for Korinne's right arm; Korinne elbowed her in the gut, and kicked her in the shin for good mea-sure. But then the soldiers locked eyes and nodded; then stood together, advancing on Korinne as one. It was all the Demon of Dogshead could do to parry their blows as their swords wove a silver web before her. Backwards she danced, step after frantic step.

"Sister!" Eva gasped. She was about to run and then her eyes caught a flicker of motion.

Commander Gavon swung at her with his blade. Eva darted backward. Their swords clashed, low, high, a ringing blow. *He's taller than me.* She glanced about her. *I should get to higher ground.*

An ancient stone altar had been dragged out from the chapel and now lay nearby: a great stone slab, its sides covered in a fresco of vines and marching soldiers, eroded from rain and covered in moss. As the comman-der sliced at her twice more, she dodged, turned, and ran for it. In one great jump, she leapt atop the altar and stood tall, balancing on the balls of her feet. The commander pressed forward. She struck down at his shoulders. The air whistled around her sword. He blocked three times, the flickers of his blade outlining a triangle over his head. Sweat ran down his brow. With each successive block, the furrows in his forehead grew deeper.

"Where's Zeke?" she shouted. "What did you do to him?"

"What did *I* do? Wretched girl. It's what you did. You turned him against me."

Commander Gavon sliced at her knees. She jumped over the blade. It hummed beneath her. He frowned, set his jaw, and leapt atop the altar. His boots nearly slipped on the moss. He caught his balance and stalked toward her. Lines of lightning blazed across the sky. Thunder crashed in the clouds.

"I will have him back," he said. "I will rip you and Korinne apart, and purge all memory of you from his mind."

"That won't work. He is a man of honor—of virtue—and you can take his memory, but you cannot change who he is. You took Cevette's memory, and she never stopped caring about the Sea People."

He frowned. "I never took a single memory from Captain Zarcanzi."

"Liar."

"I don't care enough to lie to you. And I don't care enough about Zarcanzi that I would have targeted her in any way—at least, not before she started robbing archives—"

"No. I remember your conversation with Lord Merris. Cevette organized a raid on an illegal fort on Upailit. You said you would take away everything but the knowledge you had stolen her identity. You wanted to distract her from helping her people and force her to devote herself to stealing her memories back. And you implied that you'd done it before."

His lips parted. His eyebrows arched upward. A few moments passed; then, he said, "And you think I was speaking about *Cevette Zarcanzi*?"

He would tell her nothing of use. Eva lunged. Their swords clashed, once, twice, three times. Eva darted across the top of the altar, trying to get at his left side; he moved to counter her. A jab at his chest. A swipe at her neck. Eva advanced two steps. He pushed her back three. *No time for honor.* She pivoted and drove her foot into his stomach. He doubled over, coughing and hacking.

Eva lowered her blade at his neck.

He pulled a dagger from his boot and slashed a wild cut across her thigh.

Red pain shot up her leg. She staggered, cursing, and stumbled backward. The commander advanced, striking with textbook precision, the flashing tip of his sword seeking any hole in her defense. Eva blocked and parried, stumbling down the length of the altar. She slipped in her own blood. Her legs shot forward; her arms reeled in the open air and found nothing to grab hold of. Gravity seized her. She slammed down, back-first, on the shale. The jolt knocked all the air from her lungs.

Commander Gavon leapt off the altar and landed beside her, light on his feet. He lowered his chin to look down on her. His lips pinched tight together. He said nothing; perhaps he had nothing more to say to the girl he had raised as a daughter. He drew back his sword to strike. Eva rolled sideways—

Clang!

Korinne's hook hand locked around the blade. The Demon of Dogshead was covered in blood—some of it from her enemies and some from an open cut that dripped along her collarbone—but her dark eyes shone with triumph. She pressed a pistol to the commander's head and pulled the trigger. There was a bang and a flash of smoke—black smoke, the smoke of Death. The commander cursed and grabbed at his ear. He stumbled sideways, wrenching his blade free of the hook. Korinne turned to Eva.

"Find Lieutenant Dare," she said. "We need to end this."

A stunned Eva pulled her feet back underneath her. She stood, nearly tripping on loose shale, and ran. Gunfire rang out behind her. "Fire!" shouted sergeants, and "Fire!" shouted echoes in reply. Cries of pain filled the dark afternoon. At the edge of her awareness, souls slipped into Death. The line of the Republic's defense had broken into several separate clusters of soldiers. Not one of them stopped Eva as she made her way back down the trail of muddy bootprints they had left on their advance, limping slightly from the pain of her wounded leg.

She found Zeke and Dorothea a hundred yards back past the bend in the trail, tied to a pine tree. Their eyes lit up at the sight of her. She sheathed her sword, drew a knife, and sawed through the rope that bound them to the trunk. As the thick, damp hemp fell to the ground, Dorothea wavered, and nearly fell. Zeke darted around the tree and caught her, helping her to stand.

"All's well," he said, and pulled the gag from her mouth. "I've got you, ma'am. I won't let him—"

"You fool," Dorothea said when the gag was free. "Why did you ask him if he had an alliance with Morghaia? All you did was make him angry."

Eva stared at him. "Is that why he tied you to a tree?"

Zeke winced. A bruise was blooming around his eye, and his uniform jacket had torn at the shoulder, but he seemed otherwise unhurt. "I . . . I didn't realize it would anger him so. I was only trying to distract him."

"Well, we need you in the field now," Eva said. "Once you turn your power against him—"

"I already did. To save Madam Bly. That's why he had me tied to a tree."

Oh. Her stomach sank. *That would be why he hasn't split any of us yet.* "But . . . Korinne . . . she shot him. In the head. And it didn't . . ."

They had no way to kill him.

For a moment, all three of them fell silent.

Then, through the trees, there came an unmistakable cry. "*Eva!*"

"Andreas!" Eva knew it. "He's guarding the echo children. If he's in trouble—"

"Go," Dorothea said. "Leave me here. Go."

Quickly, they helped her to sit at the bottom of the tree. Zeke wrapped his uniform jacket around her to keep her warm. Then they ran back down the trail, their hearts in their throats. Pain shot through Eva's wounded leg. She had to stop and stagger once or twice; it took only heartbeats for her to recover, but each one felt like a full hour. She and Zeke turned the corner and found the battle transformed.

The abominations had turned against the field. The smaller wolf- and cat-like creatures, for the most part, retained their positions menacing the Republic soldiers, though some bit and snapped at the echoes trying to urge them on. But the great spiders had shed their restraints. They stalked across the rocky field, their claws and mandibles clicking, hunting for pain. One had two bodies in orange coats impaled on its sharp, spine-covered legs. One, only yards away from the chapel door, had sunk its mandibles into the belly of a screaming echo while Andreas looked on in horror. On the edge of the field, Mr. Smoke was hurling fireballs at a third, and Naeri was tossing balls of thread at its legs to trip it.

"Where's Commander Gavon?" Zeke shouted. "I should use my power on him again. It's been too long. It's about to wear off. We can't let him split more echoes."

Eva scanned the battlefield, looking for Korinne or her father. She could not see them in the tumult. Only Andreas, his jaw set and his eyes narrowed, rain pouring down his face, raising his bayonet as the abomination looked up from the dead echo to face him.

She gritted her teeth and stagger-limped forward. As the spider took a step toward her brother, she waved her hand. This field had known much death today; had known it since ancient times. A portal opened by the foot of the chapel steps; one, then another, then another. The three archways of swirling smoke formed a makeshift wall around the chapel door. The spider brushed a spiny leg against the bone archway and recoiled. Eva and Zeke stepped through a narrow gap between portals and bent double, panting, on the chapel stairs.

"Lieutenant Dare!" Andreas said. "I've never been so pleased to see you in all my life."

"What about me?" Eva gasped.

"You're my sister. You have to come when I need you. It's expected."

She sighed. "Let's get them all out of here before the abominations can feed off the memories."

Andreas nodded, and waved them into the chapel.

Inside, the air was thick with dust, and long shadows stretched from wall to wall. The pews and candle holders had been long since carried away, smashed to splinters, or burned as kindling. Memories filled the chapel in their place, hundreds of them, white, shining memories. They covered the flagstone floor, fallen from chests and boxes overturned by plundering echoes, and hundreds more must have rested inside the many crates stacked up along the walls. The ink that covered them was as bright as godmarks.

At the end of the central aisle, on the stone dais where the great altar had once rested, sat a cluster of children and two old women. Many of the youngest were crying. A few small echoes held up kitchen knives as weapons. "It's the Skullrunner!" gasped an old woman. The children looked up. Their eyes found Eva's godmarks. Part of her mind was occupied by keeping the ring of portals shielding the chapel door open; but she could not miss the hope blooming in the children's dark eyes.

"We're here to help," Eva said. "There's a side trail to get you out of here. The crew of *Sea Wolf* can take you to our boats—"

A massive crab-like claw punched a hole in the roof.

Beams, bricks, and shingles tumbled down in an avalanche of debris. Eva, Zeke, and Andreas reached up to shield the backs of their heads. The echo children huddled in a tight mass and screamed. Spider legs, each one tipped with a sharp black spike, slid through the gap in the ceiling. A claw reached through a broken stained-glass window and ripped down half a wall. Stones fell. Rain pelted downward. Dust filled the air as the chapel shook around them.

They want the memories, Eva realized.

"Hurry!" she said. She took one more step toward the children. Pain shot through her leg. She stumbled. Andreas cursed and ran to her side. "Take them all to my crew," she said, through gritted teeth. "Now."

He nodded. "With me!" he shouted, and waved the children forward. They ran to his side, grabbing at his hands and the hem of his untucked shirt. "Stay close," he told them. "Go to the pirates on the edge of the field."

He gave Eva one last nod, and ducked through the door. As the last child followed him out, another spider leg stabbed through the broken roof.

Zeke looked to the older echoes. "Can you walk, ma'am? Will you need me to carry you?"

"We can walk, if you help us," said one of them. "But if echoes fancied men, we'd take you up on that carry."

He wrapped his arms around their chests and helped them stand. Together, they stumbled up the aisle. The floor shook beneath them. Shingles fell from above and shattered near their feet. Through the broken windows and the holes in the walls, spider abominations watched them with glittering black eyes. Smaller abominations leapt through the gaps. Cat-like creatures and lizard-like creatures, snake-fanged deer and rats with scorpion tails, all crawled across the chapel floor, over the broken and dusty pews, sinking their teeth into divine memories. Their bodies shimmered with light as they grew, larger and larger, and the more they grew, the more they feasted.

"Go!" Eva urged them. Zeke nodded as he pushed past her. There was fear in his eyes, but none of it was for himself. She positioned herself behind Zeke and the old women and drew her pistols. Abominations looked up from the shining memories and stalked toward her. She fired. One lizard-like abomination collapsed, black blood spilling from the hole in its chest, and began to dissolve back into sea-foam. A creature like a fanged squirrel with two heads tried to dart around her. Eva took another shot. It fell. *No time to reload.* She dropped her pistols and drew the knives from her bracers. A well-practiced throw sent them both into the throats of advancing monsters. She drew more daggers from the straps beneath her armpits. Each streak of silver through the chapel brought one more down.

There's too many, she thought, her heart sinking. On the edge of her awareness, she felt the portals she had opened to guard the doorway melt back into smoke. A scorpion-rat the size of a feral dog advanced on her, sniffing at her bleeding leg with its long nose. Venom dripped from its tail as it readied to sting—

A gunshot cracked. The abomination collapsed. Black blood spilled from the hole in its side.

Eva turned and met the brown eyes of Cevette Zarcanzi.

"I've got you." Cevette stepped out in front of Eva and held her bayonet at the ready. Abominations hissed at her. She jabbed at them. The steel blade shone. "Back up with me." Eva took a step backward, wincing as she did. An abomination leapt. Cevette drove her bayonet through its guts. Black blood spilled onto the flagstone floor. The abomination howled as it fell. Eva took another few steps. The abominations hissed and clacked deep in their throats, growling with jaws that held three rows of teeth. Cevette skewered one more and kicked another away with her boot. The pain in Eva's leg was red-hot fire, but the sight of Cevette strengthened her. She limped up the aisle and staggered back out through the door.

The spider Mr. Smoke and Naeri had been fighting was dead. It lay sprawled out on the south end of the field, slowly dissolving. Andreas and the children had made it back behind the pirates' line; Zeke and the elders were halfway there. The pirates were now advancing across the field; their guns cracked, and a Republic soldier fell with every shot. On the western edge of the field, Commander Gavon stood with a handful of soldiers, his fist clenched tight on the saber at his hip. Rain dripped down his cheeks. His dark eyes were cool as midnight.

His line of battle had already broken in several places. Still, some soldiers lifted their rifles and took aim. Naeri, in her long indigo coat, threw tangled balls of rags and thread that arced through the air and coiled about their limbs, knocking the soldiers flat on the ground and binding them hand and foot. Lizeth lifted their arms and the wind rushed past them, howling like a wicked ghost. Waves of fire flew from the fists of Mr. Smoke, catching soldiers in orange coats and lighting them aflame. The scent of burning flesh filled the air.

"Run!" screamed a soldier. "It's the gods! The gods have come for us!" Shouts of *gods! gods!* filled the dark afternoon. Soldiers turned on their heels and ran, sprinting back down the trail to the west. A small few fell back around Commander Gavon, clumping into a tight circle around their leader. "Sir!" one shouted. "What do we do?"

The commander did not look at him. He did not even seem to notice how many of his soldiers had fled, or how many were whimpering and dying in the dirt. His eyes were locked on the ranks of the echo pirates.

The rain-soaked crew of *Shadow Queen* fell back into a tight knot around the chapel doors. They reloaded and shot at the Republic soldiers as quickly as they could, though their powder was damp, and every other trigger-pull only brough forth a shower of sparks. Korinne cursed, threw her useless pistol aside, and climbed up the chapel stairs.

"Eva," she gasped, her voice hoarse. "You're alive!"

Korinne pulled Eva into her arms. The rain was cold, but her embrace was warm. Eva hugged her back. She pressed her face into Korinne's shoulder and breathed in the faint scent of vanilla. Tears flooded her eyes.

"Did they all make it out of the chapel?" Korinne asked.

"Yes. They're back with the crew of *Sea Wolf*."

"Thank you. Gods, Eva." She lowered her head. Her shoulders drooped. "You may well be right about the abominations. But I don't know if there's another way."

"*We* are the other way. I'll fight with you. We'll win this war together. As sisters."

"As sisters." When Korinne stepped back from the hug, there were tears on her cheeks, along with the rain. "We do this as sisters."

Cevette, in the doorway of the chapel, drove her bayonet through the chest of a two-headed toad. "Korinne, I will stand beside you, and I will ask my crew to stand beside you, so long as you pledge not to use these creatures as your weapons. For far too long, I have sailed only to right the wrongs done to me. It is time for me to sail for the ones I love best. And the crew of *Sea Wolf* deserve to live free of the commander's rule."

"We stand together, then," Korinne said, and smiled.

Warmth filled Eva's chest. Korinne was no saint, no savior, but neither was she some monster. It was time they stood together. It was time they cared so much for each other that they knew themselves to be worth the pain of the fight.

"Here." Korinne slung the satchel of memories down from her shoulder and offered them to Cevette. "You can burn these. I know you wanted them to go free."

Cevette pulled a gleaming memory from the satchel. She frowned as she studied them. Printed on its shining surface, in ink of bright purple and blue, was the name *Heraline.*

"Did you find any mortal memories in the archive?" Cevette said.

"I didn't see any. There were a good number of Heraline's memories, though. It seems Commander Gavon has stolen her past more than once."

Cevette made a strange and choked noise in her throat.

Eva looked out across the field. Her leg still hurt, but there was no time to go to Donya. They only had a small length of time. "We have to strike now," she said, pointing at Commander Gavon. "Before . . ."

Her voice trailed off.

Commander Gavon was smiling.

Across the field of corpses and abominations, within the tight knot of his soldiers, the commander stared out at Eva and Korinne, the corners of his lips curling upward. His gray eyes danced with light and glee.

We're too late, Eva realized. *He has his power back.*

The commander lifted his hands. White light pulsed in his palms. His eyes locked on Korinne.

Korinne, who could free them all.

Korinne, her sister.

The light streaked across the field, cutting through the gray afternoon. Eva leapt, her injured leg screaming, and threw herself into its path.

His magic struck her in the chest. It felt like a punch to her soul. Eva fell to her knees. Light blossomed from the point of impact, bubbling out of her chest, wrapping around her. "No!" Cevette screamed, and Korinne was screaming, too, but their voices were distant, muted. She could barely hear them. She could not move her arms or legs. Her body was no longer quite flesh and blood. She was energy, poured into human shape like water in a jar. And she was a soul—*no*—

She was *two* souls. They orbited one another, deep in her chest. The soul fragment that had become *her* when Ariella Gavon had been split apart, and the fragment that had come from the god-echo she'd killed. *The Skullrunner.* Her smoke-gray sister.

On the day Eva had killed her, she'd told herself that the god-echo was little more than an object, a fraction of a person, a dark memory best destroyed. But their souls hummed the same soundless notes, flashed the same lightless patterns, so alike that she could barely tell one from the other. They were home to each other, her and the magic of death. And the tears that ran down her cheeks as she felt those two dancing souls pull apart from each other were in mourning of a great number of things, but greatest among them was the loss of her selves.

I'm sorry, she told that part of herself. *I killed you.*

I chose you, whispered the magic of the goddess of death. *And now, at last, I can show you the truth.*

A memory swept her up. It was as vivid as the one she had tasted in a pear on the Isle of Kites. She saw Commander Gavon standing before her. She towered over him. He was only half her height. Dark pines rose high around them. The night was cold and still.

"More assassins came after me in the night," he said. "One day, they will succeed. Or perhaps time will. Already, the war demands a great deal of me. I need your protection, holy one."

"It is not a simple thing you ask for," Eva—Morghaia—answered. "I cannot prevent aging or death. Such things are intrinsic to the nature of life. I can only shift those burdens onto others, and I cannot place them upon your enemies—only those with a bond to you. If your soldiers are willing to accept it—"

"I cannot risk my soldiers," he said. "But . . . but there are a number of orphaned children in the camp who I have taken up the guardianship of. They're too young to fight, but they all wish to serve."

"You would have me make it so your foster children will age and die in your place?"

"There are dozens of them. They will not miss the lost time." He took a step closer to her. "This will secure the victory of the revolution."

"Very well," Morghaia said. She knew what he was asking for, and she could do it. Every weapon that would strike him down, every poison or sickness that would fell him, could be pulled away through Death to strike his fosterlings. She would make it so the fosterlings who escaped his grasp would be not be harmed; it felt a bit more fair, to give them a way out, and so long as he did not mistreat them, he would have naught to fear. (She meant to look into this more thoroughly. She did not know she did not have the time.) "But when the war ends, I will remove my blessing. No leader should hold power forever. Do you understand?"

Commander Gavon smiled at her. "I understand."

Free them. Kill him. The voice of that splintered soul grew dim. Commander Gavon was pulling it away from her. *Save us, Eva. Save us.*

"Mr. Smoke!" Cevette screamed. "Burn these memories! Burn them all now!"

There came a distant rush of heat.

Then her souls slammed back together. The white light disappeared. Eva collapsed down on the chapel steps, blinking away spots. Commander Gavon stared in horror at something behind her. His remaining soldiers lifted their guns. "Heraline!" he screamed.

And a ten-foot-tall goddess slithered out onto the field.

Heraline, the goddess of the sea and the great Three Currents, had a heart-shaped face and short golden hair that was shaved flat on both sides of her head. Her well-muscled torso was bare from the waist up; her shoulders were broad and her arms mighty. In her right hand, she held a fishing trident, in her left was net of silver thread. Instead of legs, she had three white, snakelike tails that ended in spade-shaped fins pierced with shining gold hoops. Her eyes were as brown as the hull of *Sea Wolf* and Eva knew them like she knew her own name.

Cevette lifted her hands. Her pink-webbed fingers flexed purposefully. She tilted back her head and smiled.

There came a roar. Then the smell of salt.

The sea came over the cliffs. Gray waters, billowing with foam, poured across the battlefield and swept through the broken chapel. The building collapsed, stone walls and wooden beams twisting inward with a great splintering sound. The water swept shining memories and scrambling abominations out on a tide of debris. Dancing around the crew of *Sea Wolf* and the echoes in the field, it washed up over the remaining abominations and pulled them down into the flood.

Then the waters raced toward the soldiers. They slammed into the commander's last defenders, knocking them down into the current. Their screams died, strangled, in the rush and roar of the waves. Gray water swept up over Commander Gavon's head; he and his golden uniform vanished into the froth. Cevette waved her hand. The waters retreated, carrying abominations and drowning soldiers over the edge of the cliff. Eva thought she caught one more glimpse of the commander's furious eyes. Then he was gone.

Eva's heart leapt. *She's marvelous.* How could she not have noticed? Of course, she had only ever heard the tales of Heraline. But none of those came anywhere close to describing the woman she loved. This was the truth of Cevette Zarcanzi, and she was beautiful.

In the stillness that followed, Eva pushed herself up onto her feet. Pain shot through her wounded leg. She limped forward into the field and put her hand on the small of Cevette's back.

"I'm sorry," she whispered. "You didn't want to remember. And I . . . I made you do this for me."

"I love you, Evazina Gavon." A new depth filled Cevette's voice, a resonance that seemed to rise from the bottom of the sea. She leaned down and cupped Eva's cheeks in her hands. "I cannot keep running from the truth. I owe you nothing less than all of me."

Godspeed, Sister

The Gray Isle, in the unceded territory of the Ketil Yata Nation, two hundred miles west-southwest of the city of Soladis. 24th Morghasmonth, Year Twenty-Two of the Golden Republic.

What will it take to bring peace between the Sea People and the Soladiseans? This I know: they will need to honor the agreements they have made with us. I do not know what will it take to teach the Soladiseans the value of honor. But I and many of the Wichil have lost patience with the way of Heraline. She sought peace with the Soladiseans at any cost. What we must now seek is victory. –'Our History of the Golden Republic,' published in ***The Dawn Beacon.***

Eva refused to let Donya treat her leg until she had seen to the wounded echoes. There were a good number of them. Six of her sisters had died in that muddy field, and three more had died in the battle to take the fort. Korinne gave the order to have their bodies lain out along the top of the cliff. "We burn our dead," she told Eva in a low voice. The pair of them stood at the leftmost end of the row of makeshift pyres being carefully assembled by the crew of *Shadow Queen.* "Their smoke and ash will travel into Death and forever preserve the place from whence we came."

"Is that how it works?" Eva asked her.

"That's how I say it works." Korinne shrugged. "The books say that Death is shaped differently for different peoples. That it grows and changes based off what they believe in. We're our own people, and we need our own beliefs. They have to start somewhere."

"I have a tie to Death," Eva said quietly. "It's not only a place I have the power to travel through. When I fight, when I kill, I feel it close to me. And it is . . . comforting."

"I feel it, too. We all do. So do children with echo blood. Part of us will always be bound to it. The Republic says we're all linked to Morghaia. Well, that much is true. But the nature of that link—well, that's for us to decide. Not them."

"She wasn't what we've been taught she was." Eva sighed. "She wasn't *better,* but . . . when the commander nearly split me, I . . . I remembered a moment. Buried deep within the fragment of Morghaia's soul that held the power of the Skullrunner. The two of them were working together to bring down the Theocracy. He convinced her that his life was in danger and he needed her magic to protect him. She placed a blessing on him. It ensures that his foster children will age and die in his place."

Korinne nodded. "Ah. Gods, we can all be too trusting. It seems she had that flaw as well." She winced. "Every time I tried to kill him, I killed a child somewhere. That's a hard thing to carry."

"I know," Eva said. "But you're hard enough to carry it." Korinne nodded at that. "I'm sharing this with you. No one else. If he discovers we know this, he'll do anything to make us forget. He holds hundreds of children in foster bondage, especially down in the Sapphire Isles, serving as farm labor. But if we can free them, we can kill him."

Korinne frowned. "If we start freeing his fosterlings, he'll catch on fast."

The fall of rain had slowed, though a bitter wind still whipped through the air, and on it blew the scent of blood. The clouds had cleared. The orange of sunset gleamed on the western horizon. Slowly, the echoes gathered about their fallen sisters. They stood in a tight semicircle, heads lowered, voices hushed. Andreas stood with them, lips moving in a silent prayer. Mr. Smoke walked down the line of pyres and set each one aflame. Smoke billowed up into the sunset sky. A harsh warmth washed over the mourners. Eva leaned on Korinne's arm. Pain shot through her leg whenever she tried to move.

Korinne played with the silver skull beads of her necklace. Eva simply drew a deep breath. Then another. Death felt very near to her. Korinne bowed her head, slipped the necklace of silver skulls off her neck, and draped it over Eva's head. The metal was as cold and heavy as the pact forming between them.

Quietly, Eva said, "Is it my fault these echoes died?"

Korinne shook her head. "This is the war Jonathan Gavon made. Remember that. Always. It's how we'll face what's to come."

Eva stood there, and watched her sisters, the living echoes with their bowed heads and the dead ones vanishing into the flames. Her fingers fiddled with the lacing on her bracer. The marks on her hands seemed to dance in the light of the flames. She thought of the moment she had killed the Skullrunner. She still did not fully understand the desire that had swept through her. But she did know she had taken up a power that had once belonged to all of them. And with it came a duty to them all.

CEVETTE HAD FORGOTTEN WHAT divinity asked of her.

Her head spun. Part of that was simple disorientation; she stood twice the height of her human body in this form. Part of it was from prayer; Tuk and Nukit, who were searching the bodies of the dead soldiers for coin and information, were quietly murmuring protective incantations. Their faith pulled on her like the tide.

She set off toward the men. Her three serpentine tails traced parallel waves behind her as she slithered over to the collapsed chapel, holding her torso upright in the fashion of a cobra about to strike. Her silver net and her trident, her sacred symbols, vanished into the aether as she reached out and put one hand on each man's shoulder.

"Don't be afraid," she said, in Kossket. "Their spirits will not harm you. I am with you now."

They were both clad in their armored coats and wore shirts and breeches in the Soladisean fashion; neither one wanted to damage the clothing they had brought from Upailit in battle. One of Tuk's braid ties had broken and lost its pearl beads. Nukit had a scrape down his cheek. He gazed up at her, his eyes wide and full of tears. "Why did you abandon us, Parha?"

"He stole my memory. I didn't know who I was."

Tuk set aside the orange coat he was searching through and put a hand on Nukit's shoulder. His fingers shook. His breath came fast and angry. "You abandoned us long before the Republic rose. Look at you. This form you wear is the Heraline the Soladiseans know. Not our Parha."

Cevette closed her eyes. Memories swirled through her mind, centuries of them. She knew why Tuk was angry and why Nukit was so torn. She knew why she herself had hated Heraline for so long. *She left us. She became one of them.* It was true. She had done her best to assimilate into Soladisean culture. But she also knew now *why* she had done what she did.

How could I ever explain myself to them? At last, her search had come to an end. Tuk and Nukit *were* her people. So many of the Sea People were hers. She belonged to dozens of nations, in dozens of ways. She had many names and faces. The whole wide breadth of the world was her home.

And she had failed it.

"If I explain myself," Cevette said, "will you listen?"

Nukit lowered his head. Tuk placed his forehead to the other man's brow. There was a moment of silence. Then, Tuk said, "You have been a good captain to us. We will hear you. But—in the morning."

Cevette nodded. "In the morning. We have time."

She went to Donya next. The healer knelt in the mud beside an echo girl, who was holding back her skirts to expose a ragged gash in her leg. Donya's fingertips glowed as she smeared paste across the wound. Blood splatters covered the apron she wore over her dress. Broken and empty potion bottles hung from the bandolier slung across her shoulder. Shards of broken glass had torn the webbing on one of her hands; it bled sluggishly. She gave Cevette a brief glance, then looked back to her patient. The girl, no more than twelve, was trembling at the sight of the god.

"I'm here to help," Cevette told her, in Soladisean. She made herself smile, for the child's sake. Switching to Kossket, she addressed Donya. "Is there anything I can do?"

Donya drew a needle from the pouch at her waist and threaded it. "Just stand there and look frighting. It'll take her mind off the pain." She slid the needle into the flesh of the wound. The girl flinched. "Listen. I'm not my grandmother. I don't know how to speak to gods. If you're going to turn me into a fish, wait until I've finished up here."

"I wouldn't turn you into a fish," Cevette said. "Why would I do that?"

"I killed my clan's god and ran off with her power. In the elders' stories, doing that gets you punished real badly."

Cevette's heart twisted. "I'm not here to punish you. Donya, I . . . I also ran away."

For countless years, she had sailed in search of the truth of herself. And she had come close to it many times. She had learned of the secret archive of divine memories. She had traveled to the Gray Isle. She had stood before the Soladisean chapel. And she had turned away. Sometimes, she had sought out Sea People villages where a current woman was needed. Sometimes, she had sought out isolation and shame. But she had never once let Heraline's memories burn. Because Commander Gavon had also stolen from her a great deal of pain.

But she had always come to this place alone.

"You're still my cousin," she said. "You'll always be my family."

Donya put the last stitch in the girl's leg. "Go on," she said, in Soladisean, and the girl limped away. Donya stood and wiped her hands on her apron. She looked up at Cevette. "Right, cousin. Put yourself back in a shorter body so I can hug you."

A slow smile crept across Cevette's face. Tears prickled at the corners of her eyes. With a flick of her thoughts, she shunted the flow of energy through her body onto a different course, imagining herself as water shifting to fit the shape of a new pot. Her head and torso shrank; her tails collapsed inward like folding spyglasses. The scent of salt filled the air. Her white leather coat billowed out around her; and then she was only a current woman, only a pirate.

Donya reached out to her. Cevette threw her arms around her cousin and held her close. Their hearts beat loudly together. Tears slid down their cheeks and necks. They held one another like the sea cradled a ship.

For the first time in centuries, she felt hope.

As Eva watched the pyres die down to ashes, Donya bustled over to her, a pot of healing salve in her fist. "Stand still. I need to treat your leg before it drops off."

Eva nodded, and let Donya tend to her wound. There was a small scar left when she was done, but Eva could once again walk without pain. *If only all the wounds left by Commander Gavon could heal so easily.*

She threw what was left of the gods' memories on the flame. Some had been carried away in the flood that purged the field of abominations, but others still remained. She briefly considered keeping them—the gods were dangerous, though many of them had gone into hiding since the Theocracy fell, and she didn't know what they might do with the memories returned to them. But whatever else they were, they were people. They deserved to know the truth of everything they had done. Everything that they were.

There were only a handful of memories she kept back from the blaze. Printed on them, in red ink, was the word *Morghaia*. She felt some lingering responsibility to keep them safe.

There were a good number more of Heraline's memories. Cevette gathered up each one she could find and threw them in the fire. Tears slid down her cheeks as she worked. Her hands trembled. Eva, with a small chest of Morghaia's memories tucked under her arm, went and put a hand on Cevette's shoulder.

"We don't have to burn them all now," she said.

Cevette shook her head. "I want him out of my head. It's only—gods, Eva, it's so much."

"He'll pay for everything," Eva said, and squeezed Cevette's shoulder. "This is only the start."

As the sun sank below the horizon, they gathered in the center of the field. Lit torches sent shadows dancing across battle-worn faces. Korinne, Chaz, and Patience stood side-by-side; Andreas sat on an upturned crate before them. Zeke carried Dorothea up on a chair; he had gone to find the old woman after the battle and found she had successfully covered herself with leaves to disguise herself as fleeing soldiers ran past her. He set her down beside the crew of *Shadow Queen,* then stood behind her chair, hands tucked behind his back in the practiced stance of a bodyguard. Donya stood to Cevette's right, with Eva at her left, and Lizeth stood before them all. Threads of lightning still danced in their brown curls.

"We're here because we share a common enemy," Korinne said. "Commander Gavon lost a battle today, but he's still alive somewhere out there. We need to decide on a course to stop him."

All about the circle, pirates and rebels nodded. Eva frowned. *Aren't we going to free the fosterlings?*

"For far too many years," said Dorothea, her voice cracking, "the True Ink Movement has fought to overthrow Commander Gavon. We have allies across the Five Sisters. But his army is strong, and the people of those lands love him fiercely. We never achieved the support necessary to overthrow him. It was all we could do to survive."

"Did anything you attempted succeed?" Eva asked.

Dorothea frowned. "Sometimes, we'd weaken him. We disrupted shipping routes, burned government buildings, and released counterfeit currency. It is hard to disrupt the myth of Commander Gavon; but the Republic he built is easily disrupted."

Korinne nodded. "You do good work. I won't ever forget the role you played in helping me escape my foster father. But Eva, Andreas, and I are not the only foster children he holds in bondage. He holds the contracts of hundreds. If we free them, we can hurt him where it counts. We can burn his forts and raid his ship, too. If we make war against the keys to his wealth and power, we can bring him low before us."

Oh. Eva saw it now. Commander Gavon might not suspect they knew his secret if, for every fosterling freed, a fort was raided or a ship was sunk. It would look like a tactic of war. He would fight against them to the bitter end, but he might not suspect they knew his weakness. *Many people will die for what we have begun.* But this was what it would take to free the echoes. So she would judge it well worth the cost.

"The Terraloro will fight beside you," Lizeth said. "Give me a year or two. We can light the Sapphire Isles ablaze."

"The military is funded by the Assembly," Andreas said. "And the Assembly is easily divided. I can turn them against each other. Lord Beauchamp will help me. He lives for such chaos."

"He'll come for our memories," Zeke said, his low voice wavering as he spoke. "Whenever he gets his hands on some unlucky echo, he'll target us."

Nervous glances were exchanged all about the circle. Korinne cracked her remaining knuckles on her elbow. "So we do our damned best to keep echoes away from him. We have two ships here; there's a half-dozen pirate captains on Dogshead who have sworn their loyalty to me. We build an armada. We get every echo we can find, and put them behind a wall of cannons that can blow any Republic ship to kindling. Then we go on the offensive."

"A fine plan," Dorothea murmured. "Perhaps, this time, it will be different. Perhaps we'll win."

It was settled. A war lay ahead. They would face it together. By the light of flickering torches and the green fire that danced over the face of the rising moon, they marched down the twisted trail to the beach, the wounded limping along behind them or being carried on the cloth stretchers Naeri had quickly assembled. It was a quiet, exhausted journey. When they reached the harbor, *Kembrielle* was already gone. *Sea Wolf* and *Shadow Queen* bobbed at anchor, battered but whole. Cevette waved an arm, and a wave washed over the deck of *Shadow Queen,* sweeping Korinne's remaining abominations away. The Demon of Dogshead grunted in quiet acceptance.

A number of dinghies already waited at the shore. A few pirates from *Sea Wolf* stood guard aboard them. Korinne's crew had hidden their boats in the undergrowth and in the ruins of the fort they'd burned. As they rushed to haul them out, Korinne turned to Cevette. "Let's set a course for Dogshead. We can gather the other captains and choose the first target to strike."

"Very well," Cevette said. She looked to Eva, who stood beside her. "I have other duties that might call me away. I'm naming you the first mate. I'll need you prepared to lead *Sea Wolf* in my absence."

"Me?" Eva said. "Why not Donya? Or Naeri? Or Tuk, or Nukit—"

"You're all good sailors. But Donya isn't a warrior, and Naeri doesn't plan to live out her days at sea. Tuk and Nukit will want to bring their Upailitian brothers into the war, so they'll have ships of their own to captain soon. If you're to stand by Korinne in this war, you need to learn leadership. And I need to know my ship is looked after by someone who loves it."

"Then it would be my honor," Eva said. She reached out and squeezed Korinne's hand. "Godspeed, sister."

"Godspeed, sister." Korinne squeezed her hand back, then turned and walked to Dorothea's side. Three echoes helped the old woman into a dinghy bound for *Shadow Queen*. Eva smiled to watch them go. *At the very least, she'll live out the rest of her days among her own people.* She climbed into one of the dinghies bound for *Sea Wolf,* sat down on the back bench, and reached for an oar. To her surprise, Andreas sat down beside her.

"Sister," he murmured, his head lowered. "I . . . I'm sorry for the way we parted, back in Soladis. Believe me when I say that I had no wish to leave you behind."

"It's not your fault. You were smarter than me, as usual."

"If I were truly intelligent, I could have persuaded you to come along."

"True enough. How did you find *Shadow Queen*? Did Chaz and Patience let you help mend that large basket of stockings?"

"I'm hopeless with a needle," he said. "But I learned a few lessons about what ties us together. Do you remember my thesis? The one that got me into the guild?"

She had read it, because her brother had written it. The pages had been a bit over-stuffed with blather, but she thought she understood the general point. "Great changes in society create new ways for us to understand who we are, and the ways we understand ourselves drive further change."

"We echoes have a chance to see ourselves as a people, a nation unto ourselves. We have our own values—brevity, solidarity, justice—and our own culture, which currently seems to resolve around wrestling matches, but it shall grow. A people can become a power. All we need is to find the right path."

"Let me know when you find this path to power of yours," Cevette said as she climbed in the dinghy. It rocked from side to side as she walked down the length of the little boat and stood before the two of them, arms folded across her chest. "Give me your oar, Eva. You earned some rest, and I need a distraction."

"Holy one," Andreas said, "I must confess, I'm not skilled at this sort of hard labor—"

"Mr. Gavon, start rowing."

Andreas picked up the oar.

A few minutes passed before the two of them coordinated their strokes, in which time Andreas tried to make suggestions for how they might do it better and Cevette had to remind him she held dominion over all the waters of the world. Out across the dark sea they went. When the dinghy bumped against the side of *Sea Wolf*, Eva reached out and put her hand on the hull. A smile tugged at the corners of her lips at the familiar feel of the weathered, sea-damp boards. Whatever else came next, she was home.

Her crewmates tossed down ropes. She and Cevette tied them to the hooks mounted on the dinghy, then climbed up the side of *Sea Wolf* hand over hand. Andreas needed a rope ladder tossed down to get up.

Whispers spread across the upper deck as the landing party climbed back aboard. Eva overheard several as she worked the winch to lift the boats. Someone murmured, "Our captain is a goddess?" Lizeth, grinning, replied, "Our captain is a goddess." Cevette simply went about her business. She ordered Mr. Smoke to prepare a late supper, then set to inspecting the damage caused by the abomination attack. They would need to say something to the crew soon, something clear and definitive about who Cevette was and the promises they had both made Korinne, but Eva could not blame her captain for struggling to find words.

Mr. Smoke cracked open their stores and cooked a victory banquet: spiced red crabs, fresh oysters, potato mash with rosemary and salt, boiled cranberry sauce, all served with cup after cup of rum. Eva ate two servings, and drank until a pleasant hum filled her head. As they finished their meal, pirates lounged across the upper deck. Mr. Smoke began a dice game by throwing three sixes. Lizeth and Donya painted smiling crimson skulls on the ship's cannonballs; Tuk and Nukit made a game of throwing spears at a stolen Golden Republic flag, their matched crimson coats with the rainbow otters billowing out on the wind. Pipes were passed from hand to hand, a pungent aroma filling the air. Zeke found a carved wooden flute and began to play an old Five Sisters tune, a leaping, jumping jig. Sailors gathered in the center of the upper deck to dance.

Eva went to Andreas, who sat atop an old crate on the forecastle, reading an old, leather-bound book. "What's that?"

"I found it in the chapel when Korinne and I first got there. There was a loose flagstone where the altar had sat. When I lifted it, I found this book in the compartment beneath. It's full of secret knowledge—"

"If it's sat there for centuries, it can wait one more night." Eva took his hands. "Come on. Dance with me."

He sighed, but let her tug him to his feet and lead him down to join the dancers before the mainmast. Neither could quite remember the intricate steps of a Five Sisters jig. They whirled together in a dizzy spiral, both of them trying to lead and tripping over the other's feet. After one such stumble, Eva began to laugh so hard she couldn't stand. Andreas helped her to her feet, and both of them leaned against the mainmast.

"What's this?" Naeri strode across the deck and put a hand on Eva's shoulder. She wore a gown the color of buttercream, with a robe of solid-colored satin and skirts patterned in floral brocade. Embroidery of shooting stars ran from her elbows to her wrists. "Are you well, Eva?"

"Quite well," she said. "My brother's here with me."

"I saw. He's an awful dancer."

"I am awful, aren't I?" Andreas said. "Far be it from me to argue with a beautiful woman. Andreas Gavon, ma'am. At your service. And you are?"

Naeri giggled. "Naeri de l'Havre. I'm the ship's seamstress."

"You made this gown?" He met her eyes, asking permission. When she nodded, he ran a hand along the length of her arm. "The embroidery is so fine. Your dedication to your craft does you credit."

Her fingers fluttered as she touched her cheek. "Oh, it's all magic."

"No. This is passion, and care, and profound intelligence. You must show me how you work. In the morning, perhaps." He offered Naeri his arm. "I'm certain you must dance as gracefully as you sew."

Naeri looked to Eva. There was a question in her eyes.

Eva lowered her voice. "I should warn you," she told Naeri, "he's never been with a woman longer than two weeks."

"But," Andreas said, "I also haven't had the honor to be with Miss de l'Havre."

Naeri smiled, and threaded her arm through his. "You're a most forthright young man."

"Life is too short to leave our desires unspoken."

Naeri laughed as Andreas swept her into the dance. A small smile crept across Eva's face. It was good to hear Naeri laugh again.

There came a quiet scoffing sound. Off by the starboard rail, Zeke sat atop an old barrel, sharpening his belt knife with a whetstone. The blade was already worn down to a sliver. He watched Naeri and Andreas with one eyebrow arched. Eva went, and put a hand on his shoulder.

"Jealous?" she said, her voice teasing and light.

"Hardly. Those two deserve each other. And I have no desire to fall in love again. Ever."

Her heart twisted. "What do you mean?"

"I cannot trust myself. Love brings out the worst in me."

"It isn't your fault what happened. The commander . . . he lied to you."

Zeke shook his head. Dark circles had worn themselves under his eyes. "He said what I wanted to hear."

Up by the foremast, Cevette climbed atop a stack of crates and lifted her cup high. "A toast! To Evazina Gavon!" Cheers erupted all along the deck.

"Go to her," Zeke said. A hint of light flickered in his eyes once more. "Go on, Eva. This will all still be here tomorrow."

She nodded at him, and darted off across the deck, wobbling a bit as she dodged the dancers and a ring of sailors playing cards. Cevette continued her toast. "Evazina is bold, magnificent, and fearless—and now, she will serve as the first mate of the *Sea Wolf!* It has been the honor of a lifetime to sail beside her. I cannot wait to watch her grow into the role."

Eva clambered up atop the crates, took the cup from Cevette's hands, and lifted it high. Wine sloshed out onto her fingers and ran down her godmarks. "To Cevette Zarcanzi! In every way I can measure a captain, she's the best of them. To sail with her is my second-greatest joy—my greatest is loving her—"

The crew hoots, hollers, and *aws* as Cevette grabbed her by the waist and pressed their lips together. The kiss sparkled like bubbles in wine.

"To freedom!" Zeke shouted. There was not quite joy in his voice, but there was pride, and Eva was glad to hear it. "To the downfall of Commander Gavon and the freedom of the Isles from his power."

"To victory!" Lizeth shouted. "To freedom!"

"To gold!" Donya added, and Tuk elbowed her in the side.

Cevette pressed her forehead to Eva's. A cold wind blew. All the stars of the night seemed to swirl around them. The captain lowered her voice and whispered, "Gods. I wish this moment could last forever. I hate wars."

Eva squeezed her hand. "Let's go back to our cabin."

Together, they clambered down off the stack of crates. Cheers and laughter followed them as they crossed the deck. *I wish I could bottle up this night and keep it forever.* Cevette had one hand on her lower back; Eva's was wrapped around her neck. They stumbled through her cabin door and collapsed back on the bed together.

Removing their armor was a complex matter; tired drunk fingers were no good for fumbling with ties and straps, and there was a knot in the lace of Eva's bracer. Cevette laughed as she undid it, and kissed the pale, godmarked skin of Eva's wrist once the armor was free. As the bracers and greaves fell to the floor, they pulled off each other's coats and went to work on the chest plates. Eva unhooked Cevette's, dropped it to the floor, and pulled her shirt up over her head, laying bare the hot, scarred, firm skin of her shoulders. Then she stripped off the reinforced stays that secured Cevette's breasts for combat. Cevette grinned, working at Eva's armor with unceasing determination. When her crimson chest plate was off, her shirt and stays followed in the blink of an eye.

Cevette rolled atop her. Their tongues danced together, hot, pressing, flavored by rum. Cevette slid her lips down Eva's neck, planting kisses down the length of it, then bent to explore her collarbone. She pressed her lips to every inch of bare flesh, though she avoided the bandages wrapping Eva's wounds. At last, she kissed Eva's belt buckle, and said "Let's get you out of those breeches."

Eva kicked off her boots. She wiggled her hips, and fumbled with her fingers. The breeches made it halfway down her legs; then Cevette slid between her thighs, kissing the tender flesh inside them. Her mouth found the slick core, between her lower lips; her tongue swirled in it, tasting it, and Eva gasped in delight. Cevette moved upward. Her hands held tight to Eva's thighs. She found the heart of Eva's pleasure and began to flick it about with her tongue.

Eva arched her back against the quilts. Shocks of pleasure swam through her belly. The world narrowed to a single point, and Cevette steered her over the edge. She gasped as liquid ecstasy rushed through her, surging like the tide. Her fists curled about the quilts and let go.

"There you go," Cevette whispered, satisfied. "I've got you."

Cevette sat up, grabbed Eva's hand, and kissed her fingertips. She ground herself against Eva's thigh. Eva, belatedly, kicked her breeches off completely, then pulled down her lover's. "I want to feel inside you. I want to know every inch of you."

"Touch me," Cevette whispered. Eva slid her hand through the thick blonde hair. Her fingertips—gods, she was glad for her trimmed nails—entered the wet hollow. She slipped one inside, feeling the heat and the pressure. Her free hand worked the nub of Cevette's pleasure. Round and round it went, and she was rewarded by the light shining in Cevette's eyes, the gap in her lips that grew with every beat of her heart. At last, she came with a cry like the earth cracking open. The sound still filled the air as she lay down beside Eva on the bed.

Eva exhaled against the warmth of Cevette's bare chest, breathing in her salty scent. "How are you?" Eva whispered. "With—everything."

"Overwhelmed. The rum helps."

"Can goddesses get drunk?"

"What's the point of godhood if you can't get drunk?"

Eva laughed, stroking Cevette's cheek with her thumb. "Cevette—do you prefer that name, or Heraline?"

"Just Cevette. I don't quite remember why I picked *Cevette Zarcanzi*, but I like it better than the name the Empire of Soladis gave me."

Eva kissed her collarbone. "I like it as well. I like a great deal about you."

"Mmm." Cevette ran her fingers through Eva's hair. "You know, if you love a goddess, your life will become a good deal more complicated. And that's without a war coming. You can still back away."

"Why would I do that?"

She said nothing.

"Cevette," Eva said. "All's well. We made it. After all we've been through, we're here. Alive. Together. We have a chance to be *us*."

"I was the wife of the goddess you once were. Do you not find that strange?"

"It is strange." Eva took a deep breath. "I have . . . a connection . . . to her. One deeper than the face we share, or the history that binds us. One I do not yet understand. But I am not afraid to face that. I would face anything for you." She turned her head. "I imagine it must be quite a shock, to know her fate for certain. That she's . . . broken. How do you feel?"

"Like a fool. We were both aware of the flaws of the Theocracy. Trying to fix it was the last thing we shared in common, at the end. When she told me to go back to my people, I told her to go to Commander Gavon and see if the rebels could bring change. I . . ." Cevette shuddered. "I sent her to her doom. I put the Isles in the hands of a tyrant."

"You had no way to know his true character. You cannot let the guilt weigh on you."

"I can carry a good deal of guilt. I am quite skilled at that." She gave a small, bitter laugh. "I must confess, I cannot fathom why you hold no bias against Heraline. I am despised by my own people."

"Have you seen those posters with my face on them? All the Republic hates me. But I don't care for their opinions. The only people who matter are the ones who know me best. They know my true character."

Cevette sighed. With the pad of her thumb, she stroked Eva's cheek. Candles shone high above them. The ship bobbed, and a drop of wax fell down onto the bedsheets. "My true character, I'm afraid, is that of the goddess who failed to protect her world. All the deepest-rooted troubles in the Seaward Isles can be traced back to me. I would give anything to help build a better world, Eva, but I have tried a number of times, with all the might of a pantheon and an empire behind me, and here we find ourselves still, sinking in injustice."

"You've never tried with me," Eva said. "We can do this together. If you'll still have me."

"If?" Cevette drew a deep breath. "I have spent centuries chasing shadows. All that time, I dared not love. You gave me what I thought I had lost forever. And you gave it so effortlessly. You are a miracle, Evazina Gavon. I will have no one else."

It was as if the sun had risen inside her heart. The warmth was like nothing Eva had ever known. Andreas could debate philosophers and Korinne could summon abominations, but Eva could love this woman with all her heart, and that would define her place in history.

Eva squeezed Cevette's shoulder. "I may only be a fraction of a goddess, but I have a whole tongue. With the tails . . . where do I . . ."

"It's been so long, I've forgotten myself." Cevette laughed. "You want to give it a try?"

Eva grinned. "Do it."

In the hours that followed, Eva learned the body of her goddess. How solid were her shoulders, when the strength of them pressed down against Eva's nipples and neck. How soft were her cheeks, her breasts, the hollow of her naval. Eva learned the sacred hollow between the sea goddess' tails, the taste of the heart of the sea, a sweet honey. Waves tossed the ship as Cevette strained against her.

Then her tails, smooth, scaled, and warm, pulled Eva's legs apart and they started anew.

The pulses of pleasure continued long into the night, and, when Eva fell asleep, she dreamed they were still tangled in one another. She knew nothing but bliss until the early hours before dawn, when Cevette sat up in bed and woke her. "What's wrong, love?" Eva said. Cevette's eyes were as wide as coins.

"I need to make sure that the Crownbearer is still in his prison."

Kasperos. The Crownbearer. In some tales, he was a tragic prince. In others, he was a butcher of his own people. To Heraline, he would first and foremost be . . . "Your son."

Cevette nodded. Her eyes squeezed shut, as if she was holding in tears.

"I can take you there," Eva said.

"I have my own ways to travel. I need to do this alone. "

Eva drew a deep, shuddering breath. "Travel safely, then. I love you."

Cevette smiled, leaned down, and kissed her forehead. "Go back to sleep. I'll return soon. I love you."

Eva rolled over on her side. Cevette ducked out from the cabin.

She was fast asleep when the unthinkable happened.

Andreas sat on the bowsprit with Naeri, gazing out as the moon set into the sea. Their view was blocked by *Shadow Queen*, which bobbed at anchor nearly two hundred feet away, but they'd had an interesting time watching the goddess of the sea dive overboard and vanish into the waves. Now Naeri leaned on his shoulder, a bit awkwardly, as she was three inches taller than him. His fingers were tangled in her braids. She was smiling. He was thinking.

She had just taught him the chalk rule.

Naeri was beautiful, powerful, intelligent, and profoundly vulnerable. She had told him a little of her love affair with Selig Lovett, how it had ended, how he had died. There was an awful jagged wound in her, a good number of them. She needed someone to treat her kindly. That, Andreas would be most happy to do. They would all need as much kindness as they could get in the days to come.

But he could not help thinking of how she'd said she wanted to go back to Soladis, to open a dress shop. His road led to Soladis, too. He could not fight like his sisters, but his mind was his weapon, and he knew enough about people to know Naeri could open doors for him. *I will always be just an echo to them. But an echo can have friends, family, even a wife. An echo can have power.*

He gazed across the waves at *Shadow Queen*. This late, only a handful of echoes still moved about the deck. At this distance, he could not tell most of them apart. He had only sailed with them for a few days, and the chatter had grown awkward when he'd asked about books and learned that only half of them could read. But he recognized old Dorothea, sitting on a high-backed chair near the forecastle, the wind blowing back through her white hair. She had a pipe in her hand, and a dozen blankets piled atop her. He could not read her face, but he hoped her expression was a peaceful one. She deserved as much.

"What's that?" Naeri pointed at the hull of the ship. Andreas squinted.

A man was climbing up the side of *Shadow Queen*. Sheltered from view by the bowsprit, he pulled himself up along the side of the carved echo figurehead. His movements were ungraceful but determined. The light of the setting moon shone on his waterlogged orange coat.

"How did he get out there?" Andreas said. "The currents Heraline summoned must have dragged him out. I assumed every soldier she threw in the sea would have drowned by—oh, gods. It's him."

Commander Gavon pulled himself onto the forecastle of *Shadow Queen.* Dorothea sat up in her chair. Light flashed. And then—

Andreas blinked, rubbing his eyes. His head had gone foggy. *What am I looking at?* There had been something strange on *Shadow Queen.* There it was. Two echoes stood in the forecastle, both nude, scrambling with the blankets on the ground to cover each other. *What are they doing?* Rings spread through the water beneath them. Had someone dived off the bow? He gazed at the dark sea. No one surfaced.

On his shoulder, Naeri began to cry.

EPILOGUE: JETSAM

ABOARD *SEA WOLF*, OFFSHORE OF THE GRAY ISLE, TWO HUNDRED MILES WEST-SOUTHWEST OF THE CITY OF SOLADIS. 25TH MORGHASMONTH, YEAR TWENTY-TWO OF THE GOLDEN REPUBLIC.

It does not escape my attention that the blame for recent upheaval in the Republic has fallen on Miss Evazina Gavon. Indeed, it is by her hand that your captive memories have been released. All she has done (to the great majority of us) is give back what is ours. That we have been so uncharitable toward her shows that perhaps we want the truth of the Republic to be concealed from us. We sense that it is so distasteful and repulsive that we expect, as a function of our government, to be shielded from our own history. I cannot say if the Assembly is truly democratically elected; I believe they have ways to shift the electoral numbers, though fraud is difficult to prove. But I do know that they hold power because we citizens have willingly offered up our agency in exchange for our comfort. The price of our ignorance is the lives of the echoes, who cannot vote and whose votes would be too few in number to effect change if they could. Democracy, if indeed we have a democracy, has its limits. But our courage, love, and imagination can be boundless, and these are all we need to step into a new and fearful day. –'Citizens Beware,' published in *The Silver Sentinel*.

WHEN EVA WOKE, SHE was weeping.

This is a nightmare, she thought, as her fingers scrabbled at her chest, feeling for the great bloody hole she was near certain she'd find there. She felt as if a cannonball had gone through her chest. Tears rolled down her cheeks, hot with rage. A wild, inhuman howl escaped her lips. *Her face.*

Think of her face. Try to hold on, to resist—but the face of the woman she loved slipped through her fingers as if she was trying to catch the whole sea.

"Eva!" Donya pounded on the cabin door. "Eva, are you hurt?"

Eva pushed back the quilts and slid out of bed. She grabbed a nightshirt off the floor, pulled it on, and rushed to the door, flinging it open to find Donya gazing up at her with lost and tear-reddened eyes.

"What happened?" Eva said.

"Thank the gods, you're still here. I . . . I forgot. We've all forgotten." Her voice cracked with pain. "All I know is that the captain . . . she's *gone.*"

It was the early hour before dawn, yet all of *Sea Wolf* was awake to face it. Naeri sat on the stairs to the forecastle, weeping, as Andreas held her close. Lizeth was pacing the upper deck, their traditional tarkalma robe flapping out behind them, murmuring curses. Tuk and Nukit stood together, sharpening harpoons and murmuring in low, enraged voices. Some sailors were weeping; some sailors were praying. As the cabin door opened, they all turned to gaze at Eva. Their eyes were wide with fear and shocked mourning.

This is no nightmare. The emptiness in her heart. The emptiness in her bed. Her body knew something was wrong, even if her mind could not tell her what. Commander Gavon had stolen the captain of *Sea Wolf*, her lover, from their memories, and both the ship and her body were calling out in pain. "We can resist him. We have to try."

She turned to look around her cabin, at the blue velvet rugs, the swinging candelabra, the stuffed octopus that hung from it. *Yim-yim, she called him.* Nautical charts covered one entire wall, scribbled on by a frantic hand. Paintings and sculptures from all over the Seaward Isles had been shoved up against another wall. *I was trying to convince her to let me tidy it all up.* The clothes of the missing woman still lay scattered on the floor. Eva picked up a shirt and breathed in the scent of salt and ceder.

"Come back to me," she whispered. Tears rolled down her cheeks. She felt the brush of phantom hands all over her skin. Heard a woman weeping in the night. Tasted the sweetness of an orange. "Come back to me." She tightened her fists. Bit her lip. Willed herself to remember. But nothing came. *Nothing.*

"Can you read this?" Donya picked up the sketchbook on the captain's desk. She had drawn a shoreline overgrown with reeds, pied ducks foraging amidst the roots. Pine trees grew on a distant hill. Up in the clouds was a messy signature. "It looks like . . . Cielle? Cevette? I think I've heard that name before."

"So have I." A spark of hope gleamed in her chest—then went out. "Oh. Cevette Zarcanzi—it's the name of the commander's new general."

"Gods, you're right." Donya frowned. "Maybe it's . . . Coretta? There must a thousand women in the Seaward Isles with that name. But we could find the right one. If we searched for her."

Eva looked over the captain's desk. A number of items lay scattered across it, one of them being the chest she had brought back from the Gray Isle, packed with Morghaia's memories. Then she found what she was looking for: a comb. Short strands of golden hair were still entangled in it. She wound them around her godmarked fingers. *That old bastard.* He'd done this before. She'd recovered a memory once of him talking with Lord Merris. He'd planned to steal someone's memories—*who?*—to distract her from fighting against him. Now he'd done the same to her.

Zeke knocked on the frame of the open cabin door. Both Eva and Donya turned to face him. "There's a boat coming over from *Shadow Queen.* They'll want to know what we plan to do next." He looked to Eva. "I don't remember all of what happened yesterday. But I know we fought Korinne's abominations. We tried and failed to kill the commander. You intercepted the magic that would have split her. And then . . ."

Free the fosterlings. She did not remember how she had escaped being split. But she remembered what the other soul she carried in her chest had shared with her. She remembered the alliance she had made with Korinne.

She remembered that her captain had trusted her with her ship.

"Eva!" Lizeth ran up beside Zeke and leaned through the cabin door. Their head was level with his ribcage. Their voice wavered with fear. "What are we going to do?"

Eva closed her eyes. With all her heart, and will, and love, she tried to make herself remember.

Nothing came.

"Gather the crew," she told Lizeth. "I'm going to get dressed."

HUMMING A LOW TUNE, Eva washed her face in a porcelain basin, brushed out her hair, changed into a fresh shirt, and donned her breeches and boots. With her pistols re-loaded and her hidden knives heavy at her wrists, clad in her long dark gray coat and a tricorn of crimson velvet, Korinne's necklace of silver skulls at her throat, she felt some eagerness trickle back into her. She was not free of Commander Gavon yet. But she knew how to make herself so.

As the sun crept up over the horizon, Eva strode out of her cabin and climbed the stairs to the quarterdeck. Standing tall before the helm, she fired one pistol aloft. "Listen up, sailors!" The crew stilled. All eyes fell on her. "We've lost one of our own. A sailor. A leader. We don't know who she is or where she's gone. But we know Commander Gavon took her from us. And we know we can stop him. When his regime falls, we'll get our memories back. But we can't let him distract us from what we must do." She drew a deep breath. "I'll be your captain, if you'll have me. I'll sail us to Dogshead, to build up our numbers. I'll lead us to raid the riches of the Republic. And I will keep us united with the Demon and her crew because together, we will crush our enemies like the tide!"

She drew her sword and held it aloft. In that moment, she knew what they would see in her: that she was an echo, asking them to follow her, asking them to fight and die joyfully alongside yet more echoes.

Cheers spread across the upper deck. Zeke clapped. Donya hollered. Mr. Smoke threw back his head and shouted, "Skullrunner! Skullrunner!" Lizeth grinned, lightning sparkling in the corners of their eyes. "Skullrunner!" shouted Naeri, and even Andreas gave her an approving nod.

Eva took hold of the helm. The smooth wooden knobs fit neatly in her hands, as much part of her as the black godmarks of tumbling bone that stretched from her palms to her elbows. Her hair whipped back in the wind. A smile tugged at the corners of her lips.

She gazed out across the morning. The sea was a thousand shades of blue, painted with wisps of white foam and the silver flickers of leaping fish. Above, the gray and purple clouds shifted with every flicker of the wind. *The old disappears. The new becomes the old.* She took a deep breath, taking in the world as it changed into something else, perhaps something better. She was ready to see everything it could become.

TO BE CONTINUED...

Acknowledgements

Thank you for reading *Skullrunner*. If you would like to receive updates on Book Two, you may sign up for my newsletter via my website: vyvr eargent.com. If you enjoyed the book and would like to recommend it to others, you may leave a review on Amazon and Goodreads, or simply share it with your friends.

This book was born out of years of writing, re-writing, and research. Fantasy has the power to bring times of myth to life, and the mythology of the American Revolution is a ripe place to draw inspiration. A key resource in crafting this story were the letters of George Washington, nearly all of which are available to read for free online through the National Archives, and which in their entirety present a more well-rounded and complete picture of the Founding Fathers than is often taught in schools. I would encourage readers to acquaint themselves with his letters to Major General John Sullivan from May to October of 1779 as they concern the Clinton-Sullivan Campaign against the Haudenosaunee, which, while described as military action against British allies, primary sources depict as an undiscriminating campaign to destroy the homes and food supplies of Haudenosaunee families, and which Washington himself provided the goal to make "the destruction of their settlements so final and complete, as to put it out of their power to derive the smallest succour from them."

I would also encourage readers to learn about the Indigenous nations of the lands they call home. Ten percent of the proceeds from this book will be donated to the Tongva Taraxat Paxaavxa Conservancy to support their mission to rematriate land in Los Angeles County to California native plants and to Tongva people. More information is available online at tongva.land.

Thanks are due as well to my beta readers, sensitivity readers, and the friends who have supported me through the process of writing this book. I am deeply, profoundly grateful for you all.